DRAGON REBEL

IMMORTAL DRAGONS BOOK FOUR

OPHELIA BELL

Blood is thicker than water.

My color had always acted as a lure to me, and the blood that emerged from the cut I'd made in the tender part of my wrist was no different. I couldn't take my eyes off it.

Red. The color of my scales in my true form, the color of my breath, my fire. The color of my lovers' auras when my nearness promised passion beyond the scope of their imagining. The thick liquid emerged like a subterranean beast, slowly at first. The pain was a red fire behind my eyes, beneath my skin.

Red. All red.

My color infused all these things—passion, pain, rage. Beneath their skin my brothers were no different from me; their blood ran just as red, their pain flared just as brightly. Their own auras were tinged with the same mixture of love for our sister, anger at our enemy, passion to do whatever it took to ensure the survival of our race, our children.

Red.

I owned this color and all the things it branded. The color was as sacred to me as the night was sacred to my Black brother, Ked, or the winter snows were sacred to my White brother, Aodh. I owned it and rejected the thought of sacrificing what belonged to me—not to the beast of a man who stood before us with his strangely shifting gaze that reminded me of shuttered windows with a secret resident hiding somewhere beyond.

With that thought—that reversal of intent—my blood changed course, the flow running backward, retreating into the vein I'd opened.

"No. This is not the way. There must be something else we can bargain for. Take my seed … take my entire body. I will give myself to you in exchange for Belah's blood. Just don't take our blood."

My brothers stared at me in wide-eyed alarm. Their own sliced wrists flowed red, their life's blood draining into the open basins our enemy had provided. My basin remained dry and I backed away, raising my voice so my objections could be heard.

"This is not the way. We must keep our blood—every drop. We cannot let … *it* … have that much power."

Ked gave me a pained look but didn't cease his own bloodflow. "Our power is nothing compared to what he has with Belah's blood. We agreed, brother. Please."

Our enemy turned his empty eyes on me. With one blink, his eyes were occupied by that thing that he'd become. Nikhil was no longer Nikhil. The thing that he'd become I only knew as unworthy.

His lips twisted in a sneer. "If you dare break our bargain, you will never see your sister draw breath again," he said, though his voice had a strangely high-pitched lilt that sounded nothing like the fearless warrior I'd faced countless times across the battlefield.

"We must do this," Ked said.

"Come back, brother," Aodh said.

Both my brothers moved away from their vessels, their blood-covered wrists still dripping as they advanced on me, but this would not stand. I couldn't let this happen.

"It's the wrong way! Not our fucking *blood*. It gives them too much power over us!"

"This exchange takes away more power than it gives," Ked said, his human shape expanding as he came nearer. Ebony scales emerged and massive black horns erupted from his head. His eyes flooded with darkness that was all at once empty and dense—a void that sucked in all feeling, all light. My brother may be no match for me in passion, but I was always impotent in the face of Ked's cold determination.

Red was the color of my terror when the darkness surrounded me and showed me how empty my life had become. I sent a silent plea to Aodh, who answered with a useless platitude: *"It's all right, Gavra. We agreed. Belah needs us to be united in this."*

What did a few measures of my blood matter when I was empty inside already? I sagged and my brothers propped me up between them, dragged me back to the vessel that awaited its offering. Aodh held me still while Ked raised the blade— the one tempered by all three of our immortal dragon fires— and reopened the vein in my wrist.

I watched in a detached haze as my blood flowed freely. Within moments, the bowl was filled but I didn't have the presence of mind to command my body to heal and staunch the tide.

"It's for family," Aodh said in my ear. "If there's any cause worth shedding our blood for, it's family. Nothing else matters … we sure as shit don't have anything else worth bleeding for, do we?"

I knew he was right, but despite the exchange that day, our enemy's relentless onslaught never ceased. In the end we retreated, hiding like thieves, forsaking all we had built and leaving it for our descendants to divide amongst themselves.

Mother forgive me, I did love my sister, and her resurrection gave me hope, but I would always wonder if there'd been a better way to save her. One that didn't require me sacrificing my truth.

Red was the color of sacrifice, but what good is sacrifice when true love was not at stake?

I vowed that day that I would find the love to make that ancient sacrifice worthwhile. Never again would I shed my blood for anything less.

CHAPTER 1

ASSANA

Assana clung to her sanity the way a shipwreck survivor clings to the last scraps of flotsam on the water. Her shaky hold on her own mind made it difficult to convince an insane immortal like her mother to do something rational, like not start a war with their allies.

"Mother, don't do this, please!" Assana's repeated arguments fell on deaf ears. Her mother hadn't ceased ranting about betrayals for the last two days, and that morning had raged her way through the Haven in full primal shift all the way to the deep pools of the Source, claiming she would make the entire Sanctuary pay for their mistake.

Assana could do nothing but stand by and plead with her mother. The ursa's sacred home would wither and die if her mother cut off their connection to the life-giving power the waters of the Source offered. The other higher realms belonging to the dragons and the turul wouldn't be far behind.

Nyx stood over the pools of the Source, her statuesque body clad in gauzy mist and green moss, with vines twined around her towering antlers. Her voice echoed through the entire Haven as she cast her spell to draw the barrier closed between their realm and the outside world.

"Daughter, I will give you one chance to warn them. Stay here and let them rot outside, or go and remind them how they failed our alliance. If they wish to set things right, they must make the dragons pay."

"But Uncle Neph is still out there! Calder and Father will be stranded too. This is crazy!"

Assana realized how ridiculous that word sounded when it came to her mother. In her true form, any nymph walked a tightrope on the edge of sanity—it was a side-effect of their deep connection to the River and its capricious nature. Its true power lay in its disregard for the effects it had on the world. It moved forward, a constant, inexorable flow toward the future.

Her mother was every bit as mindlessly set on her goal now, which seemed to be finally and completely shutting down all access to the Haven, including the life-giving power the Source bestowed upon the entire outside world.

"And when they do it? How will I get back in to tell you?"

"You are of my blood, Assana. You know how."

Blood … Assana winced at the reminder of what her mother had done. Seeing her brother, Calder, mated to a dragon and an ursa had driven Nyx mad. That was when they'd learned that Nyx had done the unspeakable—she'd blood melded her Thiasoi soldiers and was mind controlling them to attack. Assana's uncle Neph had stepped in at the last second, shifting into his powerful primal form and carrying the endangered trio away from the madness.

To where, Assana didn't know. All she knew was that he was likely in the drift, or would be soon if he attempted to return. But what would happen to him if her mother cast this spell while he was somewhere inside the River's current?

Eleven primal shifted nymphs stood guard around the

Source now, stiff and mute. They were still under her mother's thrall, and Assana had no idea how to break the spell.

"How could you do this, Mother? They're still out there! You're condemning them to exile at the very least. Don't you see what you've done?"

"I have seen what is to come and must protect the Haven at all costs, daughter. When you find your mate and become a mother, you will understand—you will do *anything* to protect your home and children. The nymphs are all that's left now. We must protect them."

"What of the ursa males who trusted us?"

"They will do their duty and give us satyr children soon enough. We have enough ursa males here now for that."

"Many of them have chosen a mate already—they've committed and aren't going to stray. They won't allow themselves to be shared."

"Then go to the Sanctuary and find me a damn solution! The dragons for the Source—that is the deal. If they comply, then we can renegotiate our breeding exchange. This is your last chance, Assana."

Nyx waved her hands over the pools, thick mist flowing from her fingertips and settling thickly over the surface of the water. They may have appeared as placid tide pools scattered across the water-worn rocks beneath the waterfall, but they were in fact the source of the water's power. Many of the pools were already locked beneath a layer of mist, but the largest—the one that fed the Sanctuary—was still exposed, Nyx's magical barrier gradually coalescing in a swirling cloud above it.

Assana had no choice but to go if she wanted to do anything to keep her mother from completely destroying the nymphaea's alliance with the other races. She only hoped that the ursa would understand the ultimatum.

Holding back a final, futile plea, she stepped to the edge

of the pool, and in one fluid motion dove into the inky depths. Above her fog quickly blotted out the sky, and all she could do was dive down until the power of the River caught her and carried her to her destination.

The River spat her out into a still pool. She swam to the surface, looking up at the dripping clifftop above her, and her heart broke. She was in the Sanctuary now, she knew by the clear blue sky and the wind rustling through the dense forests. But the unrelenting power of Gaia's Falls should have been crashing down in a churning froth around her, and there was nothing. Only trickles of water filtered over the rocky ledge above.

The water slowly receded as she swam to the shore. By the time she stepped onto the nearby path, the pool had completely dried up, leaving only a rocky bed.

Sickened by the news she carried, Assana closed her eyes and drifted, finding no comfort in the constant thrum of the River's connection to her mind. That power only gave her knowledge, and right now it told her there was nothing to do but move forward—just like the River did, and just like her mother's madness.

When she arrived in the gardens of the Stonetree lodge, she stood in the middle and stared up at the intricate face of the huge clock she'd first seen on her last visit.

The still waning power of the Source filled the construct, which was clearly counting down to some future event. A series of brightly glowing stones at the apex of its face portended some significant occurrence all the races were on alert for—the thing that had put them all on guard when their enemy's behavior had suddenly changed this past year.

Frowning, she realized that the change had occurred shortly after the current brood of young dragons had awakened from their hibernation. Mentally casting about again, she found the past threads and tugged. Putting the pieces together made her skin prickle with understanding.

The dragons were at the core of it, as well as a single human man who possessed powers beyond any that a human should possess. She'd heard his name—Nikhil—but he was only a legend to her, his stature increasing every time her mother's frequent River-induced trances had caused her to mention his name. Only recently had Nyx's strange recitations shifted from referring to Nikhil as "the Lamia's favored pet" to "the dragons' cursed champion"—neither of which were said with any reverence. Assana knew him by reputation alone, and he was every bit as terrifying as the Lamia herself—the corrupted nymph who stole the offspring of the higher races and conducted abhorrent experiments on them for some unknown purpose.

Nikhil mattered less to her than the dragons did, even if he truly was on their side and was no longer the monster her mother's visions made him out to be. Only one dragon had the power to affect the balance of her sanity. He wasn't just any dragon, either, but the oldest, most powerful red dragon in existence.

Gavra. He was somewhere in the Sanctuary now. Ever since she'd set eyes on that glorious red-maned dragon male, she'd had a coiling ache in her womb that grew stronger every day. She'd managed to stay strong for the first week after meeting him, her goal of following through with the breeding pact she'd negotiated with the ursa driving her forward and keeping her focused. But in the last few days, she'd found it increasingly difficult to focus on the things her mother had done long enough to try to fix them.

Her mother's ill deeds were far too similar to an ancient betrayal of one of their own kind. Dragons were at the core of that event as well.

Assana recognized it all now, with the clarity of hindsight, and it made her mother's actions all the more atrocious. Blood melding was not the answer—how could her mother resort to the very thing their old enemy had done and risk getting herself banished from the Haven? The very thing she'd done to wield her power over the higher races, and even any unwitting human who fell into her trap?

The six members of the Dragon Council were right to return to the world and seek out their mates. They may have been tied to those ancient betrayals, but they were also the core of the power that Assana hoped would ultimately prevail when the war this magical clock predicted began.

"I don't quite know how it works, either," a deep male voice said, startling Assana out of her contemplation.

She turned to see a burly man with a closely trimmed gray beard standing on the path leading from the lodge. He frowned up at the clock.

"Why would you?" she asked him.

"Because I built it. My wife … or mate, as you all say … asked for it. Had I known she'd spend her last breath giving it the power to run, I never would have built the damn thing. I'll be damned if I let Emma put anything into it."

Assana gave the man a soft smile. "You're the Queen's father … a human man. You must be very proud."

His frown faded and his weary eyes brightened slightly. "That I am, and her mother was too, before she died." He shot another defeated glance at the clock.

"I know how it works," Assana said. "Though I don't know exactly what it predicts. That event …" She pointed up to the glowing stones. "… isn't supposed to happen for a couple more decades. Twenty-five years in the future, there will be a war with our enemy. We have plenty of time to prepare … but what worries me is this." She tapped her finger beneath a lower stone. "This is much sooner, and I can't fix my power on what it means."

"How soon?"

Assana clenched her fists and turned to him, steeling herself for the conversation she would need to have.

"Too soon to waste any time. I need to talk to your daughter. I believe events are in motion already and we need to prepare." Though she hoped like hell that the timing marked by the glowing stone on the clock didn't mean it was going to take that long to appease her mother and set things right with the ursa. By her calculations, that particular event would occur within days of the coming Spring Equinox. That was still more than two months away, but a far cry from the event that would be more than two decades in the making.

If it was her mother who was the threat, Assana believed she could still fix this. Nyx was driven by fear and love, her heart broken by the loss of the three most important men in her life. Assana wasn't immune to the same grief of that loss, and she wasn't oblivious to her mother's despair. So she knew she had to tread carefully to fix this, but ultimately felt confident that she could.

However, if that ominous glowing stone suggested what Assana dreaded, there would be no good way to prepare for what came. Meri and the Ultiori she led were wildcards, but Meri was as good as invisible to Assana when she looked for her, as were her father and the other missing Thiasoi soldiers now. She had no way of knowing whether the Ultiori were in hiding as the rumors had suggested, or if they were merely biding their time for an opportunity to attack.

All she knew now was that if Meri were the true threat the clock predicted, she needed to make sure all their alliances were intact. She only hoped that the ursa and dragons understood the lengths she had to go to in order to ensure they remained at peace.

CHAPTER 2

ASSANA

Assana stood at the edge of the dry lake bed, trying her best to weather the stares of the four clan leaders in front of her. Emma Stonetree, the youngest of the four, thankfully looked more worried than hostile, though the other three glared at Assana with arms crossed in various states of anger, disbelief, and full-on rage. She briefly felt blessed to have grown up with a mother who was generally tolerant and understanding, even if she had completely gone over the edge now.

In a brittle voice, Solina Windchaser said, "This had better be good."

"I'm afraid it's not," Assana said. She took a deep breath, rehearsing the words again to make sure she remained as diplomatic as possible before she spoke. "The Haven, as you know, is the core of earthbound power for the higher races. We must protect the Source at all costs. If we lose control of it to our enemy ..."

"Don't beat around the bush, lay it on us straight," Solina said, her pale hair and red-eyed gaze disconcerting.

"My mother's been diligent about ensuring the security of

the Haven. Ever since my father and his squadron of Thiasoi soldiers were captured by the Ultiori, we've restricted access. You all know this already."

"That was when we originally erected the barrier around the Sanctuary," Emma said. "It's been thousands of years … I know things have changed recently, but what could have made her do *this*? Especially without any warning. The Sanctuary needs the Source's power to survive. Nyx knows this."

"Our males are gone," Assana said. "I think my uncle Neph may have been the only thing keeping my mother from losing her hold on her sanity. Our breeding pact was only the start of efforts to try to rectify the imbalance in the Haven, but it's too soon yet to know whether it will work—whether any satyrs will be born from this arrangement. Recent occurrences …"

Solina huffed and dropped her hands to her sides in exasperation.

Assana winced. "I'm sorry. The dragons' breach is the issue. Mother sees it as a betrayal of trust… that the ursa haven't kept the Haven's security at heart. When one of the dragons made it into the Haven …"

"Girl, you'd best not whitewash the true events, not in front of me," Solina said.

"No," she said, shaking her head. "I know. I let Aurum and Nicholas in. I believe we need to foster these alliances … these *bonds* between our races, but Mother isn't so flexible. Not when the Haven is at risk. That the dragons even made it past your barrier is a threat, as far as she's concerned. It adds insult to injury that one of them has disappeared with my brother …" She took a deep breath to steady herself for the last part. "And my uncle helped them escape."

The three older clan leaders all glanced at each other. In a rich, low voice, the mahogany-skinned Sathmika said, "Why would they need to escape?"

At the same time, Emma said, "Is my brother all right?"

"They're all fine, as far as I know. Neph left the Haven with them two days ago. Mother …" She took a deep breath again, struggling with the thought of divulging the full extent of her mother's insanity. For the sake of this alliance she should be completely honest, but she hated the idea of allowing the strong, beautiful, woman who'd borne her seem weak in any way. Voice trembling, she finally let it out. "Mother isn't well. She's taken an extreme measure none of us could have predicted, and I fear it's put everything we've worked for at risk."

"That's clear," Solina said. "The Sanctuary is *dying* without its water source. If it weren't for the dragons, the barrier would have failed completely by now—thanks to their magic, it still holds. If we had known it would take air and fire magic to truly fortify the thing, we'd have done it long ago. But that doesn't help what's happening to the Sanctuary itself. What has your mother done?"

"She has blood melded the Thiasoi maidens… the entire squadron, except for me. Their minds are compromised. I have to get back inside to fix this, but I'm stuck until I can prove to her that the ursa have met her demands."

All four clan leaders cursed. The Autumn shaman, Brigit, bowed her head.

In a smooth, warm voice, Brigit said, "As unthinkable as it is that Nyx has resorted to blood melding to accomplish her goals, I understand your mother's pain. I nearly lost my son due to my inability to see past my own desires to what he truly needed. He is happy now, as I must believe your brother is. The dragons are not our enemies—their methods may be risky, but what they do is in the best interest of the wellbeing of all the higher races. What are Nyx's demands?"

Assana met Brigit's golden-eyed gaze. The Autumn clan leader's jaw was set and her expression cautiously expectant.

"You are right. Mother won't restore the Source's power unless the dragons are taken into custody. You have to lock them up."

"No!" Emma said. "They're our friends. Our allies, and they came here in good faith to find their mates. They brought my brother home. They fixed the damage they caused to our barrier, and even improved the Sanctuary's security by doing so. I won't betray their trust. There has to be another way."

Assana closed her eyes, struggling to keep her emotions in check. She'd feared this reaction from the ursa queen, but Emma wasn't a sovereign power here. She may have the final say as queen, but the other three together could override her decision.

"There is no other way," Solina said. "But we will not lie to them about the dilemma we face. The dragons may be impulsive and emotionally driven, but they aren't stupid."

"They also hate being locked up. Can we even hold the likes of the Council themselves?" Sathmika asked.

"If we pool our power and call the Guardians home to help, we can contain them long enough to find another solution. At least long enough to keep Nyx happy and convince her to turn the damn water back on," Solina said.

Emma nodded, worry clearly etched on her face. "As long as we agree that this is a temporary solution. I don't want to hold them any longer than absolutely necessary. They're family now, at least to me. My brother is mated to their sister."

"You're sure they went through with it?" Sathmika asked.

Solina laughed. "There was no way that cub was going to give that dragon up. If they've caused this much trouble, you can bet it's because they followed through and found the satyr they both loved, to boot."

Emma's comment about family hit Assana with a jolt. The

dragons were family to her too, now that her brother shared Aurum with Emma's brother. And when she finally found a way to be with Aurum's intense red brother, her ties to them would be even closer.

She couldn't let her desire for the red dragon distract her from her responsibilities, though. The Haven came first. Her mother and her fellow Thiasoi came first. She understood her brother's need to put his brothers-in-arms ahead of love. Now the soldier-nymphs who had taken the place of her father's lost squadron were in danger, and Assana was the only one who could help them.

She met Emma's gaze and saw the desperate worry deep in the ursa queen's heart. They were sisters now, through the bond their brothers shared. And they had to tread carefully. Her own family might be falling apart, but Assana would be damned if she let their troubles drag everyone else down with them.

Emma took a deep breath and gave Assana a comforting smile. "We will do what we must, sister," Emma said. "But it would be good if you were there to help the dragons understand."

"Unless she can be in three places at once, I don't think that's a wise idea," Sathmika said. "We need to coordinate the dragons' capture. While we can hope for a reasonable response from them, we need to be prepared if they aren't receptive to being locked up, even if it's temporary. When the Guardians return from their duties outside the Sanctuary, we close down all the portals and have the Guardians prepared to detain each dragon at the same time. The lives of all the ursa in the Sanctuary are at stake here … we're not fucking around."

Brigit looked at Assana. "That means you should choose which of them you want to witness first. Your mother will have you make a blood link to see them each trapped, will she not? She'll want proof that we're complying with her demands."

Assana swallowed, realizing that this was the moment she had to decide whether to stand by and watch the man she desired get trapped, or first see one of his siblings locked up. She owed Gavra that respect … to be present when it happened, since she was in part to blame. But she couldn't be there in the thick of it. The idea of seeing the wildness he embodied bound by whatever magic the ursa used to control a dragon as powerful as he and his siblings destroyed her.

"Mother will want to see them all locked up, but as to which I witness first, I will stay with the Queen," she said. "The white one is at Stonetree, if I recall … Aodh … Of all of them, I think he's the best option for me to speak to. He strikes me as the most reasonable. Then he can communicate to the others the wisdom in submitting, and hopefully they will agree to remain your prisoners for the time being without a fight."

Emma nodded. "Good. We will call the Guardians home immediately. If we time the dragons' capture right, we may not need a confrontation at all. We will cast barriers around all three dragons just before dawn while they rest."

CHAPTER 3

GAVRA

"I still don't get why you won't fuck them."

"They aren't mine to fuck," Gavra said, gamely fielding the same round of commentary he'd been repeatedly forced to endure from the pair of ursa males he'd been spending his days with.

"But they want you. Every single female we've serviced together has begged for your cock. And you actually *can* fuck them without consequence. Yours or not, you can be damn sure if Theron and I were in your shoes, we wouldn't say no."

Gavra didn't want to burst Bekim's bubble by explaining why he had no real desire to fuck any of the ursa females he'd helped the two ursa males service through her estrous.

"It's more complicated than mere desire, Bekim. If fucking was what I wanted, I'd be doing it. I don't need to fuck them when I can fill my well just by tagging along with the pair of you."

"That's just fine by me," Theron said. "Because we don't need any competition. It's better if the females are aware that you're just a bystander. Do us a favor, though … if you ever *do* get the urge to mate one of them, let us know, all right?"

"Fate has already chosen my mates for me. Until I can be with them, I'm happy to do what I can to help the fertile Rainsong females through their estrous. Who are we visiting today?"

"The clan leader's niece, Revna," Theron said.

"The closest we'll get to Sathmika's daughter," Bekim added with a sigh. "I keep hoping Vrishti will hit her estrous and ask for us."

Theron laughed. "In your dreams, brother. She barely gives us the time of day, even *with* a red dragon in tow."

Gavra smiled to himself. Vrishti was not only fated to mate his brother, but she also knew Gavra a little too well to care whether he came or went.

"Let's just focus our attention on Revna today. Every female deserves to be the center of your world when you service her."

"Any other words of wisdom, oh dragon master?" Theron asked with a smirk.

Gavra shook his head, chastened by Theron's remark. After seeing the pair in action for the last few weeks, he knew how capable they were at pleasing women. They sometimes put him to shame. Today would be no different.

"I will follow your lead, as always," he said with a nod.

Theron paused outside a heavy wooden door on the upper floor of the Rainsong clan lodge and knocked. From the other side, Gavra heard plaintive moans before the door opened and an anxious young woman peeked out. Her expression relaxed and she opened the door wider.

"Thank Gaia you're finally here," she said. "Revna's in the bedroom." She stood back to let them in, her curious gaze drifting over all three men, then lingering on Gavra's face for several seconds.

Gavra glanced around the room, aware of the young woman's curious stare. He would let her look her fill. His presence at the Rainsong clan lodge was well-known, but he tended to keep to himself. He'd only started accompanying Bekim and Theron to help fulfill their duties out of necessity. The two males alone weren't quite enough to fill his well, especially since he wasn't interested in fucking them—or anyone, for that matter. But a female ursa in the throes of her estrous was an incredibly potent source of sexual energy that more than made up for it.

This young female wasn't old enough yet, though she was certainly old enough to wonder, and Gavra could feel the curiosity flowing off her in waves as she regarded him.

Had he met her a couple months ago, he would not have hesitated to introduce her to the pleasures of coupling with a dragon. But ever since meeting the mates Fate had sent him visions of, he had very little desire for anyone else.

Still, he needed to maintain his energy, and what awaited them through the next door would more than satisfy that need.

"We will tend to Revna, love," Gavra said, finally gracing the young woman with a direct look and the full power of his gaze.

She breathed in sharply, her aura flaring with her sudden arousal. It only took a look? This one was primed for sampling and Gavra almost wished he were interested. His cock stirred at the idea anyway—too bad this pretty thing likely wouldn't hit her estrous before he had to leave the Sanctuary. He had no idea exactly when that would be, but it had to be soon. Events were converging already, and quickly, now that his sister Aurum had found her mates. There were only three of them left … He, Aodh, and Numa still had to find and mate their fated partners. He hated that knowing the identities and locations of his own didn't make it easier to complete the task.

He would be ready for them when the time came, and

that meant ensuring he had a full well for whatever eventuality occurred. It hadn't been an easy task to get Aurum to her mates, so he had to be prepared for anything.

The fact that one of his mates was the daughter of a Dionarch worried him. Assana had only hinted at the potential instability of her mother. He had known Nyx a long time, but hadn't seen her for thousands of years. In that time she had lost both a son and a mate, neither of which were likely to have helped the ancient, immortal demi-goddess's already shaky hold on sanity. Now that her son had returned, Gavra hoped she'd recover somewhat, but Assana's lack of contact since her trip back to the Haven didn't bode well.

She should have returned to the Sanctuary by now to gather additional ursa males willing to mate any of the hundreds of nymphs hoping to produce male offspring. That description matched roughly every unmated male in the Sanctuary—eligible ursa females weren't exactly plentiful, and even though almost all of them required a pair of bonded bachelor males like Theron and Bekim, the prospect of being sent to the Haven where they would have females tripping over themselves just for a taste of virile male had all the single males itching to be chosen to go.

Assana had departed less than a week ago with the first collection of around a hundred males, and had smuggled Gavra's sister and her ursa lover into the Haven as well. Gavra hoped Aurum and Nicholas had found their third and were happy.

Not knowing the outcome of their particular quest was yet another thing that made him itch. The lack of communication left him with a distinct sense of foreboding. His last contact with Numa and Aodh confirmed what he felt—they needed to be on high alert, because they already knew too well how much damage a mentally unbalanced nymph could do.

He had a task to focus on for the present, though. After closing the door behind the ursa maiden with a regretful sigh, he turned back to the one who actually needed him and his friends today.

Theron moved to the inner door and pushed it open. Potent pheromones washed through like a wave of fertile energy, making Gavra's hair stand on end and his cock stiffen in his pants. His nostrils flared and he chuckled.

"Sweet Mother, I do love that scent," he said.

Theron and Bekim smiled back. "Nothing better than a female in estrous, right?" Bekim said.

"Except your own female in estrous, I would imagine," Theron said.

"If you two do well today, maybe this one will choose you." Gavra eyed the voluptuous, naked body on the bed.

Revna's black hair was splayed across her pillows, her head tilted back. She panted quickly as though in labor, but he knew from weeks of witnessing the same sight in other female ursa that her body was far from in pain. The ache of need was one he knew well enough, however, and it was often as agonizing as true pain.

Her aura blazed bright red with that need, her dark skin coated in a sheen of sweat. Both hands were pressed between her spread thighs, the fingers of one buried to the last knuckle in her slick pussy, desperately seeking a release that wouldn't come. This was where he and his pair of ursa friends came in. A female ursa in estrous suffered through wave after wave of desperate sexual need that could only be relieved through the aid of a male. And as powerful as most ursa females were, a single male was rarely enough.

When in this state, her body was flooded with overwhelming levels of fertile energy. She had to either be fucked until the energy coalesced into new life inside her, or she had to be serviced without intercourse and the energy allowed to flow through a conduit and given back to Gaia.

Unmated females weren't allowed to be fucked by unmated ursa males. The race took new life far too seriously to allow any accidental pregnancies. An unmated pregnant female was a danger to their home—without a male to balance the constant flood of energy the new child attracted, the female was in danger of self-destructing and taking the child along with her.

So until females like Revna chose their mates, males like Bekim and Theron existed to service them through their ordeal.

Gavra could think of worse arrangements. The two males had each other to turn to for sexual release, and they had the honor of assisting a multitude of ursa females just like Revna on an almost weekly basis. He only hoped that Gaia didn't mind him "borrowing" some of the energy the females produced in the process.

This particular female was ripe for fucking, but he wasn't here for that. Even though as a dragon he was in no danger of impregnating her without marking her first, there was another female his cock belonged to, and Assana wasn't here. Nor was Silas, the male ursa he'd only had a single, too-brief encounter with before venturing into the Sanctuary three weeks ago. The pair of them were who his body truly craved, and until he was with them again, he'd survive on second-hand pleasure.

He stripped with the other males and followed them to the bed. Theron climbed on first and gently touched Revna's shoulder. At the contact, the writhing female relaxed, and the bright pulsing of her aura surged into Theron's fingertips as though magnetically drawn to him. Theron's own aura swelled, and not just from his obvious arousal. All it took was a touch to begin to ease the female's lust, but it would take much more to fully sate her.

"We're here, Rev," he said. "Tell us what you need."

Bekim knelt between her feet, wrapped his hands around each of her ankles, and slid them up her lower legs. Gavra moved to lie beside her, squeezed her hand, and waited for her command. He could feel the static tickle of her aura against his skin, but unlike with the ursa males, the power couldn't be transferred to him until she orgasmed.

Her fevered eyes opened to slits and she licked her lips. "Please, touch me. Make me come. I need to …"

Attending a female in estrous was an exercise in willpower that always made Gavra marvel at the restraint the males had. She was desperate for release, and he could have given it to her in a heartbeat with a few flicks of his tongue between her thighs, but the ursa had very strict rules when it came to servicing females, aside from the "no fucking" rule— and one of them was to do nothing unless explicitly asked.

"Like this?" Bekim asked, caressing her lower legs and squeezing her calves. "What else, Revna?"

She relaxed slightly and nodded. Removing her hands from between her thighs, she spread her legs wider.

"Touch me … touch my pussy. Put your fingers in me."

Gavra suppressed a moan at the idea of being invited to feel the clench of this female's muscles around any part of him. Bekim's gaze heated and he slid his hands up higher, palms pressed against her inner thighs. He rested one hand on the top of Revna's dark mound, pressing his thumb to her engorged clit. She tipped her hips up toward his touch and sighed. With his other hand, he spread her slick folds open and pushed two fingers into her.

Revna reached up, clasped both hands at the backs of Gavra and Theron's necks, and pulled them closer.

"Mouths on my nipples now," she commanded. "Suck me.

Hard." Glancing down between her thighs, she said, "You too, Bek. Suck my clit while you finger-fuck me."

Gavra chuckled at her insistent tone as he bent to take her nipple in his mouth. He tongued her slowly, then did as she asked and sucked hard, squeezing her breast in one hand. Revna dug her into the back of his neck and her chest arched up into his and Theron's mouths.

Bekim dipped his head between her thighs, and within moments she was crying out in ecstasy, her climax flooding through her body in a rippling wave of raw, fertile power. Gavra reveled in the potency of it when it sank into him, but the best part was that he knew this was only the first taste of many. It was early morning, and they would likely need to service her until dusk.

She came down from the orgasm with a sigh and the pair of them pulled back. Gavra had a moment to take in her features, noting the family resemblance to Vrishti, with her jet-black hair and deep caramel skin. Revna was older than her cousin, and clearly had been through an estrous or two considering how she didn't hesitate to tell them what she wanted.

"You like the taste of my power, do you, dragon?" she said, smiling up at him seductively.

"You are delicious," Gavra said.

"Too bad I hear you're just here to touch, not actually taste. Would you at least honor me with a kiss when I come again?"

"That I can manage," he said.

Revna rose and shifted to face him, pushing him back against the pillows and sliding her arms around his shoulders. Her full breasts pressed pleasingly against his chest as she pulled her knees beneath her and tilted her ass in the air. Glancing behind her, she said, "Does this work for you two?" She wiggled her backside in front of the two ursa males.

Theron grinned. "Just tell us where you want us."

She looked at Gavra with a pretty frown. "What do you think, dragon? How can they best please me today?"

Gavra slid a hand between them and thumbed her nipple, gratified by the way her lips parted and her breath left her in a gasp.

"I think you need a mouth on that sweet pussy of yours. Theron looks like he needs to have his face fucked by your snatch."

A slow smile spread across her lips and she nodded. "I like the way you think." Turning back to Theron, she added, "Let me ride that tongue."

"As you wish," Theron said. He eagerly moved to lay between her thighs with his face aimed right at her pussy. He gripped her ass and spread her cheeks as she lowered herself down to his waiting tongue.

Her eyelids fluttered closed and she sighed as she undulated her hips against Theron's mouth. "Oh, yes. What a marvelous idea." Opening her eyes again, she asked, "And what about Bekim? He needs a task too."

Gavra cupped her cheek and smiled. "How hungry is that pussy of yours, Rev? Can you take his entire fist?"

Revna's body shuddered and she licked her lips. "Ohh, that *would* be nice." Looking over her shoulder again, she tilted her ass up slightly. Theron slid his hands down to grip lower on her ass and spread her open for his friend, while at the same time lifting his head to keep his tongue in contact with her clit. "Fill me up with your fist, Bek," she said.

Bekim straddled Theron's hips to get closer. "My pleasure."

Revna let out a moan when he slid three fingers into her, slowly working his way up to four. "Are you ready?" he asked.

"Mmm, not until I see you ride that hard cock underneath you. Theron needs to come too, don't you?"

Gavra loved how forceful this female was. There was something about a woman who knew what she wanted that turned him on more than anything. As much as he enjoyed topping other males who were every bit as alpha as he was, his most vivid fantasies involved a particular dark-haired nymph holding him down and fucking him into a stupor. He would gladly submit to Assana, if she asked him to. Though he had to admit, in the dreams Fate had sent him, she never asked—she just took, and he loved every second of it.

"Fuck yes," Bekim said. He withdrew his hand from Revna's pussy and reached down to grip Theron's cock, his fingers slick with the female's copious juices. He stroked his hand up and down Theron's shaft, coating him with Revna's lubricating fluids. Then he shifted his hips, positioning himself. With lips parted and eyelids barely open he sank slowly down onto Theron's thick length.

A low growl sounded from between Revna's thighs and Theron pivoted his hips up to meet Bekim's downward thrusts. Bekim diligently held onto Revna's hip with one hand while he returned the other to her pussy and worked his fingers deep into her again, somehow managing to stay focused despite the ecstasy pulsing through his aura now that his ass was filled with Theron's cock.

Revna's aura thrummed just as intensely when Bekim fit his thumb into her, hand disappearing to the wrist inside her channel. She opened her mouth in a soundless cry of bliss, her dark gaze meeting Gavra's, wild with pleasure.

"Kiss me," she commanded, and Gavra hungrily complied.

Their tongues tangled and another moan vibrated through her mouth. He wrapped his arms around her, threaded his fingers into her hair, and yanked her head back to look into her eyes.

"You love his fat fist fucking you, don't you? Come for me, Rev. Let me taste that magic again."

Revna moaned louder, her entire body rocking with the rhythm of the two males who were fucking each other at the same fierce tempo. There was even more power to be had from the pair of them, and Gavra slid a hand down her back to grip over top of Theron's on her ass. Sensing Gavra's goal, Bekim clasped his hand on top of Gavra's.

Within seconds the room echoed with feral cries and smacking flesh. Revna bent her head and sank her teeth into Gavra's chest, her bite hard enough to rend flesh, if his could be pierced by normal means.

When the three of them came, the torrent of power that filled him was like a summer storm, wild and unchecked and over almost as soon as it began, leaving all three wet and sticky and gasping for breath.

Gavra let out a rumble of approval when Revna collapsed onto his chest. Theron rolled out from under her, resting his head on Gavra's thigh, while Bekim curled up on Revna's other side.

"You want us to take care of this for you?" Revna murmured, reaching for Gavra's throbbing erection.

Gavra grabbed her hand before she could touch him.

"Not today," he said.

Revna shrugged. "You dragons are odd ones."

Gavra snorted. "Not odd, just cautious. No sense starting a bond with someone I don't intend to mate."

"You say that as if it's a bad thing," Theron said. "It's only humans who are in danger of going mad if you fuck one too many times without marking them. Ursa can handle your magic thanks to our link to Gaia, the turul just sing their way sane, and nymphs start out mad already, so there's no danger there, either."

Revna snuggled closer and traced her fingertips in a

pattern over the hard muscles of his stomach. His skin tingled and the illusion of a green infinity symbol glowed around his navel.

"It's a bad thing for one with this much power to do," she said. "Can't be too careful with the immortals."

Gavra knew only too well how true that was, but his immortal siblings were the last of his concerns.

AFTER HOURS of seeing to Revna's needs, Gavra returned to his own rooms in the Rainsong lodge at midnight, flush with power and too hard to think straight. Theron and Bekim knew better than to offer him a casual fuck after a week of being turned down. They would probably be returning to their own quarters now and going another round with each other while fantasizing about taking Gavra's cock—he'd seen the hungry looks they both gave him when they said their farewells.

But his mind was filled with thoughts of a nymph and another ursa male. His body ached for the touch of his fated mates—one who he'd had only a brief taste of, and another whose soft curves he had only imagined.

He had a vivid memory of the first time he'd laid eyes on Assana in the ursa queen's meeting chamber their second day in the Sanctuary. They had been discussing the dragons' breach of the Sanctuary's barrier and the damage they had accidentally caused. The Queen had introduced Assana as an honored guest, and though the dragons knew access to the Haven had been highly restricted for some time, they were comforted by the nymph's presence. Assana's attendance meant progress, where Gavra and his siblings were concerned. If the nymphaea and the ursa were agreeing to interbreed, it was a good sign.

He'd been aware of the importance of her presence only superficially. It had only been by sheer force of will that he hadn't grabbed her and run for the nearest bed … or hell, fucked her in the middle of the meeting. When their eyes had met the first time, her gaze had been a seductive caress that drilled down to his soul. With only that first look, he'd felt her silent promise … and he'd needed no words from her to know she understood their connection as well as he did.

It was the memory of that deep connection that drove him now. He quickly shed his clothes once inside his room, then lay on his bed naked with his cock held tightly in his fist. In his mind he felt Silas's hard body against his, the other man's ass parting and ready to take him, but it was Assana's hypnotic gaze that drove him to the brink. Just the idea of her watching while he fucked Silas was enough to send him over, and the energy that had been building in his cock and balls all afternoon and evening surged forth in a blast of sensation. Gavra let out a long, harsh grunt as he orgasmed, the hot flood of his semen coating his entire hand.

He reached for a cloth beside the bed and cleaned off just as the lethargic aftermath of his pleasure hit. Within another minute he was sound asleep.

CHAPTER 4

SILAS

Bright light burned at Silas's closed eyelids. He groaned, roused from sleep and ready to lash out at his roommate for the inconsiderate awakening. But his other senses told him something was off. The cabin was too quiet, the light too warm on his face.

He opened his eyes and was blinded by a ray of sunlight filtering in through a rare gap in the jungle canopy that sheltered his home outside the ursa Sanctuary.

Silas frowned. Sunlight itself wasn't alarming, but it was definitely unexpected, considering where he lived. The densely forested mountains in eastern India tended to be socked in with fog at this time of morning. If the sun chose to shine it wouldn't be until late afternoon, and it definitely wouldn't make it down to his private patch of the jungle. He'd gone to sleep the night before to the sound of a heavy rain falling, and had dreamed all night of making love to a powerful red-haired man and a voracious nymph with jet-black hair and eyes that swirled with lust and madness.

It had been a wet dream in more ways than one. He'd woken up sticky in the middle of the night and had cleaned himself up before falling back into a dark, dreamless slumber.

He rose, blinking and looking around the cabin for Raj. A pot of coffee steamed on the little potbelly stove in the corner. A fresh loaf of bread was on the table. At least Raj wasn't completely heartless, even after the fight they'd had. Silas had finally grown weary of the silent treatment and lashed out, confessing that he was done with their bachelor bond; it wasn't working out. Raj had argued that there was no way Silas would find a female of any worth without him.

Silas didn't bother sharing that he already had a female waiting for him, whether she knew it or not, plus an immortal red dragon who had decided Silas belonged to him. He almost wished he'd allowed Gavra to mark him that night just so he could throw it in Raj's face. The man could be such an asshole when it came to his desire for status.

Their growing animosity was no excuse not to do his job, however. Silas poured himself a cup of coffee and gulped it down, then ripped off a huge chunk of bread before heading out into the forest, naked as always. Raj should've been finishing his patrol around the portal stones right about then, so it would be Silas's turn to shift and begin his route.

Spring equinox couldn't come soon enough—he couldn't wait to get back home and request a reassignment from the monotony of his job as a Portal Guardian for the ursa Sanctuary.

Now that he knew Gavra was somewhere inside, he itched to get there even more.

The jungle was hot and muggy, the air so thick with moisture it was suffocating. This heat was all wrong. The blazing sun was all wrong…

"Hey, Silas!"

Raj's worried tone was also all wrong…

He turned halfway up the path toward the circle of

stones that demarcated the Rainsong Portal entrance to his home. Raj was running toward him, his dark eyes wide with panic. An unfamiliar male ran beside him, easily keeping pace.

"We need to pack our things now," Raj said. "Come on."

"What? Why?" Silas asked, squinting at Raj and eyeing the other man.

The man, a tall, bearded male ursa with powerfully muscled legs that betrayed his Windchaser heritage, stepped forward. "The Sanctuary's in trouble. All the Guardians are being called home today."

A sickening rush of alarm flooded Silas's chest as he stepped closer to the man. "What happened?" He tried to quash the dread that somehow he'd been responsible by allowing Nicholas Stonetree in with his dragon friends ... with Silas's future mate. Gavra wouldn't betray him. He couldn't.

"I don't know the details. You'll be briefed when we're inside. I just know we had some unexpected visitors, so ... put two and two together and you get dragons."

Silas's blood chilled and he tried to swallow, but his mouth had gone bone dry.

"Get your shit together," Raj sneered and brushed past him to head toward the cabin. "You've wanted this long enough. Now you get your wish—you can be rid of me *and* get back home all at once."

"Is it really dragons?" he asked. "That can't be that bad, can it? I mean, we're allies ..."

The Windchaser shrugged. "Your guess is as good as mine. All I know is they came, the weather went to shit for a couple weeks, and now things are worse. The Source has been cut off. The clan leaders have called all the Guardians home to help. All the waterfalls are dry as a fucking bone, and with the summer sun it won't be long before things start to die from the lack of water. The portal's only open temporarily—just long enough to get all of you inside."

Silas stared up at the patches of blue sky visible through the trees above. The sun blazed in the East, the heat a reminder of the way Gavra's hot breath had felt on the back of his neck while they'd fucked. The sun was a force of nature, though, its power too dangerous to take lightly.

When he turned to head back to the cabin, he couldn't help but wonder whether it had been complete folly to fall for a creature born of fire. That heat had felt good at the time, but now he was reminded of how easily it could burn.

CHAPTER 5

GAVRA

The silent morning woke Gavra, and a disorienting sense of wrongness settled into him. Living for the past few weeks at the Rainsong clan lodge meant waking to the pleasant rush of morning rain hitting the windows of his quarters and the din of clan life going on around him.

It was quiet. Too quiet. When he opened his eyes, bright sunlight was streaming in, but the beams refracted, casting tiny rainbows over the foot of his bed.

Muffled noises carried from outside his door. Voices, smothered in a way that made them reverberate in a disjointed drone.

He inhaled and could only smell the familiar scents of this room—pine and old ash from the fireplace's recent use—and his own belongings. Morning should mean scents of breakfast and the accompanying din of the Rainsong clan itself converging on the lodge for the morning meal many of them shared.

"Brother, are you awake?" Aodh's somber tone filled his mind.

Gavra rolled out of bed and went to the window. *"Yes.*

What's happening? Are you experiencing anything unusual like I am?"

He stared out through the glass, looking for the land-marks of the mountain peak and waterfall near the portal where they'd arrived. The view was often the first thing he observed upon waking. The placidity of it calmed him, reminded him why he was here, and kept his itch to seek out his mates in check. All in good time.

Except the view wasn't there … or rather, it was all wrong. There was a strange haze over the glass and he rubbed at it, but it didn't change. Everything beyond was a cloudy blur.

"Have they spoken to you yet?" Aodh asked.

"No. I just woke up."

"We're in trouble," Aodh said. *"Nyx has demanded our capture. Payment for Aurum's breach of the Haven."*

"She got in," Gavra said. He smiled, rejoicing at his sister's victory. *"Wait … is she all right?"*

"She is fine. She's no longer in the Haven … which is probably the real reason Nyx has it out for us now. Calder left the Haven with her, as did Neph. Now Nyx is after blood one way or the other and has forced the clan leaders' hands. They've imprisoned us."

"The ursa wouldn't …" Gavra shook his head in disbelief, even though his predicament was obvious. He opened the window and stuck his hand out, only to have it meet a solid barrier of energy barely a foot beyond the sill.

"They had no choice."

"Numa …?"

"I am here," his sister's rich, feminine voice intoned.

"Neither of you are harmed?"

"I am comfortable … in my quarters at the Sundance lodge, but unable to leave," Numa said. *"The barrier is Earth magic. Impervious to us without a portal built in … which they didn't provide."*

Gavra pressed his palm against the field of magic,

summoning his power and forcing it out through his skin. The barrier hummed slightly but didn't weaken.

He inhaled and focused, pursing his lips and pushing out a narrow column of flame funneled into a single spot. With a sizzle, the flame cut through, leaving a glowing, charred border around a hole the size of Gavra's fist. When the flame ceased, he had a clear view past the barrier to the forested mountains beyond. The view looked off, however. The lush greenery was the same as he recalled, but there was something missing.

With a pop, the hole closed, the barrier reforming as though he'd never damaged it. It wasn't until his view was obscured that he realized what was missing; the waterfall in the distance wasn't the gleaming white he remembered, but a dull gray of solid, sun-dried rock.

"We can burn through it with enough firepower," Gavra said.

"Don't," Aodh replied. *"We won't garner any sympathy by going on the offensive."*

"I don't need fucking sympathy," Gavra argued. *"I need to get out and find out what the fuck is going on."*

"Wait until you speak to Assana. She's coming to you soon. You need to let her explain."

"Assana." He let out a breath. *"She's here? You saw her?"*

"Yes, brother. She is coming to you. Don't do anything stupid."

"I'm not the impulsive one," Gavra reminded him.

"No, but when you decide you want something, the world may as well burn, and Belah isn't here to keep you in check. Our situation requires cooler heads. Promise you'll consider the rest of us before you do anything."

Gavra turned away from the window, irritated by his brother's words. He grabbed his clothes and began to dress in abrupt, jerky motions. What he wanted was to see her, but not from the inside of a fucking prison.

"Fine, I promise not to get us in deeper shit, but you can be damn sure I'm finding a way out of this."

"Your breath won't breach the barrier without serious destruction," Numa said. *"Don't bother trying. Just do as they ask."*

"They've fucking trapped us against our will, sister. I'm not going to do shit unless they can prove they're justified."

He turned toward the door, prepared to pound at the barrier until he got the attention of whatever ursa might be around to hear him.

When he opened the door, the sight on the other side completely stole his momentum.

"Silas … How …?"

The dark-haired ursa male stared at him, his face a mask of impassivity, his arms crossed over his broad chest. But the pain in his gaze shoved a blade straight through Gavra's heart.

"I should have known better," Silas said. "The fucking seduction was all about you, wasn't it? How many lies did you tell me that night? Begging me to let you mark me … to come with you … it was all bullshit."

Gavra closed his eyes. "No, Silas. I never lied."

"Then how the *fuck* did this happen? My home is being destroyed because of you. Because of what I …" His voice caught and he clenched his teeth. His eyes were wild and glassy and wet. He tilted his head back, his Adam's apple bobbing as he struggled to hold back whatever rage or hurt had grabbed hold of him.

Gavra ached to reach out to him, to touch him and prove that everything they'd shared their first night together had meant something to him. He lifted a hand and pressed it to the shimmering barrier between them.

"This wasn't us, Silas. It wasn't me. Please believe me."

"This isn't how I wanted to come home," Silas said.

"But you're here," Gavra said, finding hope in Silas's presence despite the animosity. "And she is here, too. We can fix this if you just let me out. You have to trust me, Silas. There's more to this fucking issue than you're seeing."

"She? The imaginary female you promised would be waiting for us, who would complete our triad? You're as full of shit as Raj ever was, you know that? At least his intentions were always clear."

"My intentions were always to be with you. Things are just complicated now, for fuck's sake. You know the threat we're under."

Silas shook his head. "*You're* the fucking threat. To my goddamn home!" He took a step closer, his eyes blazing. His gaze darted wildly around Gavra's face, down his body, and back up. His aura was a crackling cloud of rage and hurt, and an underlying rising glow of pure lust.

Gavra pushed at the barrier, letting out a frustrated growl at how impotent he felt just then.

"Just let me fucking *out* and we can talk."

"What the fuck could you say, you son of a bitch?" Silas leaned even closer, his face inches from Gavra's. "You've destroyed my trust. You used me."

"You loved it," Gavra shot back. "You loved it because it was fucking meant to be. I'd prove it to you again, if you'd just let me."

Silas's aura flashed bright red, betraying his sudden arousal at the suggestion.

He gritted his teeth and said, "Oh yeah? Do it. Prove it, you fuck. Prove you're not a filthy fucking liar."

Within a split second, Gavra's senses were filled with hot, angry ursa. The barrier stretched with a whining keen, like a high string had been plucked and continued to vibrate. Then Silas's hand was at the back of his neck, his other at his shoulder, fingers digging in and pulling him tight. His kiss was hard, hungry, and hot. Gavra moaned as he took it in, not caring *how* the other man had breached his prison, just so long as he did.

He was here now. Talking could wait.

Silas pushed him back across the room, his hands scrabbling at Gavra's clothes, fingers hooking into fabric, ripping with an angry growl. Gavra's thin shirt fell in tatters to the floor as the backs of his knees hit his bed.

His ursa mate loomed above him as he stumbled back and sat, gazing up defiantly. There was no apology to be had. He had none to share, though he sensed that was what Silas wanted when he paused to look at him.

"You fucker. Why?" Silas asked.

"Because you're mine," Gavra said.

"That goes both ways." Silas shoved him back and climbed on top, straddling him and grinding his hips into Gavra's. Their erections rubbed against each other through their clothes and Gavra arched his back with a groan that was quickly muffled when Silas captured his mouth again in a brutal kiss.

"You're mine," Silas said when he broke away for breath. "If you meant it, then this is what it'll take to prove it." He reached between them and shoved Gavra's drawstring waistband down, freeing his cock. Silas gripped him, stroking his hand up along Gavra's length in a distracting caress that contradicted the otherwise rough treatment.

Then he stood back and yanked Gavra's pants down, pulled them off his feet, and tossed them aside. He stripped from his own sole garment—a pair of brown cargo pants—and was on Gavra again, one strong thigh nudged between his legs. Silas's skin was hot and smooth as he pinned him down to the bed and pressed hard against him.

Gavra itched to flip them both, to take Silas the way he had that first night, first with his magic, then with his cock. But Silas's sense of betrayal still flickered through his aura and Gavra knew better than to discount that. As much as he hated being the passive recipient of this level of passion, he feared spooking Silas too much to become the aggressor. Not only did he desperately want a way out of his current situation, he knew Silas was the way to get it, but he wouldn't risk the other man's tenuous trust.

He was suddenly very unsure of the submissive role he'd chosen when Silas gripped him behind one knee and pushed his leg up, then knelt with one knee between Gavra's thighs and his balls brushing the juncture of Gavra's hip in a distracting caress.

Silas's gaze roamed down his body and lingered on where his cock lay against his stomach. He dropped his hand to the length and gripped it, then slid his hand down, over Gavra's balls. With his thumb, he traced a line beneath the center of his sack.

Gavra let out a sharp gasp, his ass flexing when Silas gently probed at his puckered opening.

"Don't tell me you're shy," Silas said. "Not used to being on the bottom?"

"I'm a giver," Gavra said, giving Silas a pleading look.

"Thought as much. This'll mean even more when I'm finished, then."

"Fuck, Silas. Please …" He hated the way his voice caught, the way he was helpless under this man's touch. Never had he been at so much of a disadvantage as he was in this moment, and in the moment he'd first laid eyes on Assana.

"Is she even real?" Silas asked.

"You haven't seen her?" Gavra asked. "She should be here."

"What's her name if she's so real?" Silas asked, leaning back on his heels and gripping his cock in one hand as he toyed with Gavra's balls with the other. "Describe her. Tell me what she looks like, tastes like. Tell me what kinds of sounds she made when you made her come."

"Assana …" Gavra said. "But I haven't yet. I haven't touched her."

"Tell me," Silas said, beginning to slowly pump his cock from root to tip. "I want details." He pressed his thumb harder at Gavra's ass, the blunt tip breaching the barrier and making him groan at the sudden intrusion.

"Fuck, all right! She's fucking beautiful … black hair, olive skin, and these big eyes that are hypnotic just to look into. It's like she can see all your filthiest secrets, like she knows you fall asleep at night imagining having her lips wrapped around your cock. Then she smiles and licks those lips and leaves them wet and glistening. Your cock gets hard at the thought of what she'd do with that tongue. Because she knows you want her, even though you probably wouldn't know how the fuck to handle a woman like her if you had her."

Silas's attention focused intently on Gavra's face as he spoke, describing exactly how he imagined Assana, how he remembered her. He forced himself to focus, despite the distracting caress of Silas's hands on his balls and occasional probe of his ass again.

"She's wild, primal, and unpredictable. The first time you see her, you can't do a damn thing about it because you're in a room full of people, and all you can think about the entire time is whether she's really as naked as you think she is under that useless scrap of a dress she wears. Somehow it covers everything but reveals everything at the same time. Like you can just about catch a glimpse of her sweet pussy if she'd shift her hips a little to the left, but when she does, the dress shifts too and you can't see shit. And it leaves you itching to just reach out and rip the fucking thing off so you can just *look* at those ripe tits, suck on those nipples that you're sure have to taste like cherries, the way the pink tips look dark red through the half-invisible fabric of that damn dress."

He paused to catch his breath, his cock aching for more contact, but Silas was too distracted manhandling himself and staring raptly while Gavra continued the description.

"And you itch to bend her over and spread her ass and slide your tongue all the way down between those cheeks until you taste her dripping honey. Then when you meet her eyes again it's like she caught you jerking off to dirty pictures of her, and she moves in just the right way … For a split-second, you actually see heaven between her thighs. She's bare except for the softest-looking patch of black fur right above a clit that peeks out from between her pussy's pink petals. It's shining and slick, and you just *know* she's wet for you and that she wants your mouth on her as much as you want to take that bud between your lips and suck it until she's screaming your name.

"You can picture it all within that split-second … you can picture her underneath you, that stupid fucking dress crumbling away like it was made of sea foam, dissolving under your heat. You can feel the way her hot cunt sucks your cock in deep and her long legs wrap around you and hold on like she never wants to let you go, and you hover over her, mesmerized by the swirling eternity in her eyes. And then she says your name for real and it's like a fucking orgasm exploding inside your eardrums just to hear her speak it …"

Silas's gaze was fixed on Gavra's face, hanging on every word while he stroked his cock. He groaned and pushed his thumb deeper into Gavra's ass, shifting his hips until their balls brushed against each other.

"Tell me more," he said, his voice rough as his hand picked up tempo along his shaft.

Gavra closed his eyes, recalling the dreams he'd had every night for nearly the last century while trapped inside the

Glade. He'd never been under Silas in the dreams, yet knew better than to take control before his mate worked out his anger over the perceived betrayal.

"She's hungry and hot and flips you over to ride you, her cunt squeezing and tightening on your cock over and over. She's so fucking wet her juices flood over your belly and thighs, coating you. She smells like rain and you wonder if she tastes as good, and the second you even think it, she's off your cock and spun around, that sweet pussy of hers spread above your face, just beckoning to have you bury your tongue in it. Then her sweet, heavenly lips are around your cock, her cunt against your mouth, and she does taste as good as she smells … better, even, with her clit against your tongue as she fucks your face and sucks your cock and it's all you can fucking do to hold on, to stay in control long enough to make her come. And then you're fucking *there*, flying over the fucking edge into her sweet mouth, and she swallows every drop while she's coming all over your face. She lets go of your cock, her cunt spread over your lips, her juices flooding your mouth and she says your name …"

He opened his eyes at the rolling growl Silas made, his balls tightening against Gavra's own aching shaft. Silas's aura crackled hot against his skin, flooded with lust and potent power, tinged with the telltale green of a full-blooded ursa well-connected to Gaia's magic. He was at the razor's edge of climax, his jaw clenched and his eyes blazing, his hand madly working his cock.

A shadow filled the doorway and Silas flinched, but he was too far gone to stop now. The single word uttered from that figure sent him over like a shot.

"Silas."

Gavra's own cock pulsed in response to her voice, but it was Silas she'd called to. They both turned their heads to the doorway where Assana stood as though conjured from his very words. She was just how he remembered her, just how he'd described, her lips shining as though she'd just licked them, her nipples hard and showing almost blood-red through the useless scrap of fabric she called a garment. And he could scent her need from there, through the shimmering barrier.

CHAPTER 6

ASSANA

Assana had requested she go alone to speak with Gavra, self-conscious enough that she might have to endure the scrutiny of his guard. She didn't want the added onlookers of the clan leader and her daughter when she faced the dragon meant to be her mate and told him it was her own mother who had demanded his imprisonment.

The sounds that flooded from the open door to the room piqued her curiosity. Male voices, moans of obvious pleasure, and then she'd distinctly heard her name spoken and her body responded instinctively. The rush of awareness of Gavra's proximity awakened every cell, put her on alert. Her primal being was aroused, too close to the surface. Her control wavered as she approached, the buzz of sudden arousal flushing her with heat, and she struggled to keep it in check. She needed to remain rational to speak when she saw him.

There was no guard outside his room as she'd been told, but there were two distinct voices coming from inside.

"Tell me more," the new voice said as she came to stand outside the doorway. That gruff, lust-filled voice sent a tremor of raw need down her spine and deep into her core. The primal power inside her reacted instinctively when she saw the pair of them. It had been one thing to face Gavra in the flesh so recently. She'd controlled her urge to be with him in favor of her larger goal, but had seen his own struggle. He was only one half of the pair she knew together would complete her.

A magic barrier stood between her and the pair. She forced herself to stand and watch. She had appreciated the multitudes of ursa males she'd met so far. All of them had behaved in a respectful and deferential manner, more than thrilled to be offered the chance to become the solo mates of nymphs as cock-starved as her sisters.

She hadn't admitted to herself that she was every bit as hungry for a taste of male sexual power—there were only two males in existence who would truly fulfill that need, but she couldn't indulge so soon, not when the Sanctuary was in danger and her own Thiasoi sisters mind-controlled by her mother's blood meld.

Her self-control wavered at the sight before her. The fierce and cocky red dragon she'd met a week ago was on his back in a position she'd never imagined she'd see him in. Above him hovered a beautiful, dark-skinned male ursa with black hair falling across his face. He gripped his cock in his fist and pumped it while he stared down at Gavra, who continued to speak, describing the most explicitly dirty scene featuring none other than Assana herself.

She almost didn't want to give herself away. She'd happily stay here and watch them, enjoying the sight of the two males pleasing each other. She wasn't quite sure what to do with a male anyway, not in detail, though her body had plenty of ideas.

But her empirical reasoning crumbled at the sound of Gavra's words and the way the other male responded as though he were experiencing exactly what Gavra described. She pictured the scene as vividly as if she were experiencing it too. Her core ached and flooded with wet heat and her nipples pricked, pushing at the gauzy wisp of her dress. The males' scents managed to reach her through the barrier—a spicy heat mixed with a rich, earthy aroma, bear and dragon together.

When the ursa growled, rich and throaty, she could stand it no longer.

"Silas," Assana said, hearing the name whispered in her ear as the River's power flooded her with visions of the dark-haired ursa Gavra so easily submitted to. This was the other male—the one meant to complete their triad, to combine his seed with the dragon's in her womb and create the child who would finally give her the control she needed over the unpredictable power that plagued her.

She reached out a hand and placed it in the field of the barrier to Gavra's room. She could go inside, could be with them now, and knew neither male would object. The words on Gavra's lips told her as much—his dreams vividly wrought for Silas to see, the power of his breath potent enough to conjure images in her own mind that set her juices flowing. She could make that dream come true with only a few steps through that door.

Silas and Gavra both turned their heads at the disturbance … and she realized she'd said Silas's name aloud. At the sight of her, the ursa let out a rough groan and his head flew back. His body tightened and arched as he gripped his cock tighter and a white stream of semen erupted from his tip.

Assana gasped and her core clenched in a sympathetic spasm. By Dion's blood, she wished she could feel the pulse of him inside her now, or taste the salty seed he'd just coated Gavra's own cock with.

As she watched, Gavra's red gaze heated. He kept talking,

describing the continuation of the scene of her mouth on his cock and her pussy hovering over his tongue while he fucked her with it. He reached down between himself and Silas and coated his cock with the other man's fluid, pumping his fist along the length.

She held her hand up to the barrier, her palm grazing the transparent sheen of it until she felt it nearly give. It was crafted of Gaia's magic, which a nymph like her could manipulate to pass through if she chose, but it would not allow a fire creature like Gavra to escape. She could go inside … She swallowed harshly, imagining how he'd taste, how that glorious cock would feel between her lips all coated in the spend of the other man, how she would suck him until …

"Assana …" Gavra groaned. His eyes remained fixed on her and her upper thighs drenched with arousal. His nostrils flared and he let out a rough yell.

She turned away, but not before she saw Gavra's hand shoot up and tangle in Silas's thick hair, yanking his head down. The other man didn't resist, letting himself be pushed to Gavra's groin and opening his mouth to take the shining cock between his lips.

Her mouth watered and she licked her lips. Her entire body ached for release, but she didn't dare let herself indulge for fear that her primal nature might come to the surface. She didn't trust herself when she was pure nymph and not bound by the tenuous magic of her human shape. She could be rational within the confines of this illusion. And she had to be, if she were going to set things right.

It only took a moment of Silas's mouth on Gavra's cock before the dragon cried out and bucked his hips. He clutched hard at the ursa's head with both hands, forcing him to take his entire length until Assana winced, wondering how Silas could keep from choking. But the ursa's gaze flashed up once to look at her and his eyes were filled with triumph as he swallowed what Gavra gave him. Somehow that look seemed to challenge her, to say, "See what I have and you don't?"

Then it was over, and Silas slipped his mouth slowly off Gavra's cock and sat back with a smug smile. He licked his lips, then moved off the bed, grabbed a garment off the floor, and approached the door.

Assana stumbled back when he passed through the barrier. The field of magic made a little hissing pop as it reformed behind him and he bent to put on his pants. Her head swam at the potent mix of scents that surrounded him. He was awash in Gavra's essence as well as his own, and the addition of a fresh surge of immortal dragon magic made his skin glow with a faintly ruddy sheen, as though he'd just been sunburned.

Once dressed, he regarded her with only the barest flash of desire that he quickly hid.

"You didn't see that," he said.

Assana frowned, confused for a moment until she regained her bearings and realized what he meant.

"You're his guard. Why would they send you to be his guard?"

Silas swallowed and looked back into the room where Gavra was now sitting up, naked on his bed and glaring at them both.

"No one else knows about us," Silas said. "And it needs to stay that way, all right? At least until I know what the fuck is going on here. If he's a traitor to our alliance, there's no fucking way I'm letting him mark me."

Gavra stood and stalked to the door, fists clenched. With a frustrated yell, he pulled one fist back and punched the barrier. It flashed with light and thrummed in a discordant rhythm. Assana jumped back, startled.

"Let me fucking *out*, you sonofabitch!"

"No!" Silas yelled back.

Gavra tilted his head back and let out an incoherent, frustrated yell. Panting to catch his breath, he stared at them again, sneering at them both.

"Thanks for the fucking blowjob, asshole," he said, then slammed his door shut.

Assana was as rattled by the display as she was aroused, and the presence of huge, virile ursa male in the corridor with her didn't help. She moved to walk away, to give herself some space, but Silas reached out and grabbed her arm.

"Wait. I need to know if it's really you. Was he telling the truth?"

Assana kept her eyes fixed on the window at the end of the hallway, her arm twisted uncomfortably in his grasp. It was bad enough that her head was filled with the scent of them both; to try looking at him now as close as he was would be too much.

She swallowed and nodded. "If you mean the lovely little picture he painted for you to get off to, yes. I have seen the dreams he has of me, and he was very true to the details of them."

Silas squeezed harder, pulling back on her arm. "So it's really you?"

She closed her eyes and pulled away. "Yes, it is. Please don't come any closer to me."

"But if it's you … he wasn't lying. Why won't you look at me?"

She winced at the hurt in his voice and held up a hand, palm out. "Just … stay over there, all right? It's too much. The two of you, your scents are too much."

"All right," he said, his footsteps retreating.

Slowly she opened her eyes and took a hesitant breath. The overwhelming aura of both men had dissipated and Silas stood at the far end of the hallway now, leaning against a windowsill.

"Thank you," she said.

Silas crossed his arms and nodded. "I need to know."

"And I'll tell you everything, but I need a blade first, and a witness."

From a pocket in his cargo pants he produced a bone-handled knife and withdrew it from a sheath.

"Will this do?"

She stared at it, then at him. "Ah … can you throw it?"

"I can come hand it to you."

"Any chance you can bathe and come back?"

He raised an eyebrow. "Last time I checked, there was no water to bathe in. What's remaining in our cisterns needs to be saved for drinking."

She let out an exasperated sigh. "Just toss it. I can catch it."

He slid the knife back into its leather scabbard and lobbed it at her. She snatched it out of the air and moved back to Gavra's door. She gripped the latch and was relieved to discover he hadn't locked it from the inside.

The barrier tingled against her skin, feeling as though she'd pushed her hand through the surface of a pool when she pushed the door open slightly.

She let out a little yelp when a huge hand gripped the edge of the door and pushed it open the rest of the way. Gavra stood there, completely nude, with his long, red hair wild and tangled around his shoulders. He stared down at her with a deep frown.

"Couldn't get enough of an eyeful of your captive dragon, eh? You planning to break in and molest me too? I promise the next fucker who tries that, I'm not going to lie down for." His face relaxed slightly after he eyed her for a second. Then he smiled. "Although, I might make an exception for you,

Assana. If you come in, I'll lie down for you. I'll do whatever you ask me to."

Voice shaking, she said, "I just need you to stand there like that." She took a step back from the barrier, grateful for the shield it gave her from the full power of his scent. She was already familiar with his ancient spice, but the combination of his and the ursa's scents could send her over the edge … and then he would get his wish.

Taking a deep breath, she unsheathed the knife and drew the blade across the pad of her thumb. When the blood welled, she closed her eyes and dabbed a drop on each eyelid. Under her breath, she whispered the incantation to the flow of her life's blood, the only fluid current that linked her to her mother now that the Source was blocked by her mother's magic.

Within a moment, her mind was invaded by the maelstrom of her mother's psyche and she felt the other woman's gaze peering out through her own eyes.

"See, Mother? The dragon is captured. I've shown you all three now … please restore the Source to the ursa like you promised."

She felt her mother's gaze move over Gavra's naked body. Within her mind, Assana sensed an idea taking shape that wasn't her own, one that made her ill to even ponder.

"*Bring the males to me, daughter. Both of them. I will restore the Source if the ursa repay me by sending the dragons to us as breeding stock. They are far more worthy as mates to my Thiasoi than those filthy ursa males who aren't even allowed to fuck their females.*"

"Mother, no! That wasn't the arrangement. They can stay here, locked up. You don't need to do that!"

Before her, Gavra's brow creased, the taunting sneer disappearing the second she voiced her objection.

"What is she asking for?"

Assana shook her head. "She can't do this. I won't let her."

"If you want their precious Sanctuary to survive, you'll do this. I want those dragons. I'll even allow the ursa to release the female dragon and do whatever they wish with her. The males are mine. You have one chance. I will open the way at midnight for one hour. If you do not bring them, I am closing it again for good and you are no longer my daughter."

A wave of nausea hit Assana and her skin grew clammy as her mother's presence slipped away. She wanted Gavra and his brother … to give to the nymphs for their seed. Or worse yet, to use as toys for her mindless drones of Thiasoi.

"Assana, dammit, tell me what's wrong!" Gavra smacked a palm against the barrier, making it reverberate like a huge drum.

She bent over, shaking her head and struggling to breathe. His and Silas's nearness wasn't helping. She was too overwhelmed by sensory input and her own distress.

"Please, no …"

Their scents washed over her again and a warm hand pressed against her back, another at her elbow, as Silas reached her.

"Assana, come, sit," Silas said, and she let him pull her to the bench across from Gavra's door. He was gentle as he tugged her into his lap, the comforting warmth of his arms easing her anxiety even while his scent caused her need to spike.

"Oh, Gaia, why is she doing this to me?"

"What is Gaia doing?" Silas asked.

"Not Gaia… my mother. She … ohhh …" Before she could get the words out, a fresh wave of primal need flooded her and she pressed her hands to her belly.

"Assana, you aren't coherent. What's wrong?"

"You …" She shook her head, the world tilting like a seesaw around her. On the other side of the hall, Gavra loomed in the doorway, still naked and glorious. "I need you, Silas … Gavra … the madness, the lust, it won't stop. It's too much. I need my mind clear, but I can't … can't let it out …"

"Do something!" Gavra yelled.

Her skin prickled with the sensation of her primal essence as though it dug at her human shape from the inside, seeking freedom. With clawed fingers she gripped at Silas's bare shoulders and peered into his eyes, hoping he understood the desperation … She couldn't let the beast she really was out. If she did, she would never recover in time to fix what her mother had done.

"Please don't let me hurt you," she whined.

His dark brows furrowed and a smile quirked at the corner of his mouth. "I highly doubt you could damage me even if you tried. If I can deal with a female ursa in estrous, I can deal with you. What is it?"

She burrowed into his arms, pressed her nose against his throat, and inhaled.

"Hungry," she said, then licked the sheen of sweat from his collarbone and moaned.

"If I didn't know better, I'd think you were in estrous, too," Silas said, almost to himself. He moved his hand down her arm and she sighed at the cool, tingling sensation that followed. The swell of madness in her mind abated a tiny bit, but her physical need remained.

When his hand came to rest at her midsection, she let out a moan against his skin.

"Is this where the trouble is?" he asked, pressing a little harder at her belly, just beneath her navel.

"She's on the verge of madness," Gavra said. "Her aura's going wild with it. You have to do something."

The rich sound of Gavra's voice made her turn to look at him. The world wobbled and tilted, the light blurring around the big man, making him look softer than she knew he was.

"So pretty …" she said, and reached out a hand as though to pet the outline of him in her vision.

Gavra chuckled. "You're already mad, love, if you think that."

Her gaze shifted down his body, taking in the contours of his strong muscles, the ridges of his stomach, and the prominent vee of corded muscles that defined his hips, pointing to the pinnacle of his virility that hung long and thick between his thighs. She licked her lips and lurched toward him.

"I need …" she groaned, frustrated by the strong grip that held her back. "Nnn …"

"What you need is to release some of that magic in you. How long has it been since a male saw to your needs, Assana?" Gavra asked.

"N-never …" she said. Though she had a vivid memory of a naked satyr she once threw herself at when filled with the same uncontrollable urge to … what? To taste, to lick, to suck, to fuck. But no, that was wrong, that image … that satyr was her brother, and she knew how wrong it was of her to have wanted him, but the powerful ache in her belly had been too strong then, and it grew stronger now, even though she wasn't in her primal form.

She needed a cock.

No … she needed to regain control of herself.

"Silas, help me," she whimpered. "Don't let me hurt you."

Even as she begged for it, her body rebelled, her hips twisting on his lap where the unmistakable bulge of his erection strained at his pants.

Silas grunted when she pressed her ass back against him. His hands went to her hips, squeezing to immobilize her.

"I'll help, but you have to hold still."

"Need you," she whined, spreading her legs and pressing her slick core to the ridge of him.

"She's at the edge, man," Gavra said. "Don't let her have your cock or she'll lose herself. Nymphs are funny that way."

"But she needs to get rid of that energy. I can feel it pushing at her limits."

"She doesn't want to fuck … you heard her. She's never had a man before. She isn't ready."

Silas chuckled. "You think I can't take care of her without fucking her? This is what I'm made for, even more than you."

"You know me, Silas. I *was* made for fucking. I was made for fucking the two of you, and you can be damn sure if I wasn't trapped in this room that's exactly what we'd all be doing now. It's what she *needs*, but I know it is not what she wants."

Beneath the writhing tangle of pure lust, Assana's conscious mind rejoiced at how well he understood her.

"Don't want … madness," she said, shaking her head, though she kept shifting in Silas's lap, reveling in the sensation of his arms around her body and his clothed cock against her ass.

"I'm going to take some of it from you," Silas said. His hands shifted from her hips, one arm sliding up her body to wrap beneath her breasts. He pressed his lips against the side of her face from behind as he pulled her back against his chest. "You'll feel better soon, baby."

She sighed and gave into his light touch, tilting her head back to rest on his shoulder as the hand at her hip moved down to her upper thigh. Silas groaned at the slick wetness that coated the inside of her thigh, and his cock twitched beneath her.

"By Gaia's essence, I'd love to be inside you now," he murmured. His fingers found her core, slippery with her need, and he probed gently, his touch tantalizing enough to make her cry out.

The madness loomed closer as he dipped his fingers in

between her folds and stroked. She reached back and clung to his neck, her nails digging in as she struggled to hang onto her mind in the face of the pleasure he inflicted on her. He promised he could help relieve the press of insanity. She trusted him because he belonged to her … because they shared a need for the same man. And that man was watching them now.

Assana opened her eyes and Gavra was still there, standing on the other side of the barrier that blocked his doorway. His arms stretched out, hands gripping either side of the doorframe so hard his knuckles were white.

"Don't draw it out, Silas," Gavra said. "She needs relief before the primal power takes over."

"Don't fucking tell me how to make a woman come," Silas shot back.

His fingers swept up through the channel of wetness between her thighs and found the hard apex of her desire. Assana cried out at the first touch of his fingers on her clit, arching her back and spreading her thighs wider.

"Yes," she moaned, forcing herself to hold still while he rubbed her clit in swift little circles. Silas slid his other hand higher, cupping her breast and gently sweeping his thumb back and forth across her nipple. His touch aroused her, but also calmed her with a cool, tingling magic.

"Feel me, Assana," Silas murmured. "Focus on where I touch you, where the pleasure is. You need do nothing—only feel. Be in my arms, let your body belong to me. Your mind is yours, your body is mine. I'm the one who controls your body, not the primal magic."

"Yes," she said, sighing and quivering as his steady tempo continued in a hypnotic cycle. His fingers at her breast swirled in tiny spirals, the pattern shifting directions every few circuits. Between her thighs he did the same thing until she was completely lost to the rhythm and the rising swell of pleasure that was his to control.

"Give me that need, Assana. Let it go. I've got you."

"Silas … Oh, Gaia." She opened her eyes and met Gavra's hungry stare. His gaze was filled with a combination of raw need and worry. What did he see when he looked at her?

"Come for him, baby," Gavra said. He licked his lips, the strange flick of his forked tongue sending a shiver through her as she imagined how it would feel between her thighs. She had the sense that Gavra was imagining the very same thing when his mouth spread in a wicked smile.

"When I'm out of here, you can bet I'm having a taste of you, and as soon as you're ready for it, I'm burying my cock deep in that sweet, juicy cunt."

The promise sent her spiraling. She cried out as the rush of sensation flooded her core, seeping into her limbs. Silas murmured more words of encouragement into her ears as Gavra urged her on. She bucked her hips, writhing and riding Silas's fingers as they continued to work her, pulling her climax from her body with quick, deft strokes until finally he plunged his fingers deep into her clenching core and fucked her with them.

"That's right, baby, fuck my fingers. Squeeze me until you're done. Gaia, you were so flooded with power I think I've grown roots."

Her body continued to shudder and convulse in his arms, but he held her, seeming to know exactly how long to keep massaging the inside of her pussy. Gradually the spasms subsided and she fell limp in his arms.

Both men let out relieved breaths and Silas gently removed his fingers from between her thighs. He repositioned her on his lap, cradling her against his chest. She let herself be held, the safety of his arms a welcome change from the worries she'd come here with, though she knew she would have to deal with those soon enough.

The most wonderful part was that her mind was clear now—clearer than it had been in a very long time. Not even after her visit to the Diviner had an orgasm left her feeling so free and unburdened.

She let out a long sigh and straightened, looking into Silas's eyes. They were a rich, woody brown with greenish flecks that reminded her of mossy logs. There was an odd ring around his iris that glowed blue, however, bringing to mind the blue stone in the clock at the Stonetree lodge. Nymphaea magic … it was the power he had taken from her.

"Are you all right?" she said.

"I'd be lying if I said yeah," Silas said, his voice strained. "It probably should've been two of us, off-loading that power from you. Holy fuck, how long have you been walking around with that?"

She glanced at the ceiling, thinking back, but couldn't recall a time without that dull throb, an incessant presence in her mind like the buzz of a beehive had taken up residence not long after she came of age.

"Only a couple thousand years. Since I grew these …" She cupped her breasts, remembering the first time she learned how much she enjoyed having them touched when she and the other Thiasoi maidens would play together in the Haven.

Silas groaned at the sight of her breasts pushed together and closed his eyes. "Sweet fucking earth mother fuck …" When he opened his eyes again, he seemed to struggle to focus on her. "But you're feeling better now, right?"

She smiled at him. "Better than I've felt in forever. Thank you." Leaning in, she pressed a kiss to his lips. She'd meant it only as a quick thank-you peck, but his arms were suddenly around her, his tongue sliding between her lips. His embrace was hot and urgent, and she allowed herself a moment to indulge in the closeness and the delicious hunger evident in the way he tasted her. After a few seconds, she pushed back.

"I will make it up to you, I promise," she said, then moved to stand. "I must speak with the clan leaders now about my mother's new demands."

When she stepped away from him, she looked back and gasped. "Silas, what happened?"

His feet had been bare before, but now where they met the floorboards, they seemed to merge into the wood, his skin covered in rough brown bark that flowed into roots. The woody tendrils twisted through the floor around the bench, burrowing as though seeking the earth beneath.

"Gaia is drawing your power from me," he said. "I've had this happen before … an ursa female was pregnant and her mates were away. I stepped in to help. She was so flooded with fertile energy I nearly couldn't take it, but it's what male ursa are meant for—helping give the excess magic back to Gaia. I usually have a partner so this doesn't happen. It'll pass … don't worry. I just might not be going anywhere for a little while. The good news is that it's definitely power from your Source. I think the Sanctuary's sucking it up pretty quickly."

"You could say you gave him wood," Gavra said, and Assana shot him glare.

"I'll stay and wait," she said.

"No, you should go. I'm supposed to be here anyway," Silas said. "Just … can you tell us what your mother said first?"

Assana winced. Glancing between the two men, she took a deep breath. Finally, she met Gavra's eyes. "She wants you and your brother. Says she won't restore the Source's power until the two of you are in the Haven." She swallowed the bile that rose at the idea of what her mother had planned for the pair. "I have to bring you both tonight at midnight or she's cutting off the Source completely."

"Why the hell would she want them?" Silas asked. "The breeding pact was for ursa males."

Gavra was the one to answer. "Because we're more powerful. She likely wants to breed me to her nymphs, but I don't trust her intentions for Aodh. Fate only knows what she'll do to him if she gets her hands on him."

"I don't have a choice," Assana said. "Mother won't accept anything less than what she demanded. At least he's not …"

"What?" Gavra asked. "Not fated for another female who would miss him? Put him and Vrishti in a room together and see if you still feel that way, and you know the reason your mother wants him has nothing to do with his bloodline or his virility. She's hated him since he fell in love with your uncle."

"Forgive me if I'm less concerned about your brother. It's *you* I can't stomach being in her clutches. Seeing her force you to breed with … with anyone else."

Gavra had the audacity to laugh then, and she stared at him with wide horror. "Why do you think that's so funny? You're *mine*! I love my mother, and my Thiasoi sisters, but they can't fucking have you!"

"Assana, baby. Who do you think you're looking at? You have to know that it's *impossible* to force a dragon like me to do anything he doesn't want to do." Glancing at Silas, he raised an eyebrow. "You know better, don't you, Silas? When you had me on my back, you were about to try to fuck me. I'd have allowed it, not because you overpowered me, but because I fucking needed you to know I would give anything for you to trust me, and that includes taking your cock."

She glanced at Silas, who was smiling back and shaking his head. "I figured as much," he said. "So, I realize I missed something here … are you saying that it's your mother who's caused all this, out of some vendetta she has against the drag-ons … that she's carried around practically forever? Why are we having this issue now and not before?"

Gavra answered for her again. "Because my sister has somehow managed to disappear with both of Nyx's remaining men, and if there's anything I've learned about nymphs over the years, it's that you don't fuck with a nymph's men or you risk driving her insane."

Silas frowned and gave Assana a confused look. She sighed. "He's talking about my brother and my uncle Neph. Ever since my father was captured by the Ultiori, Mother's been hard to deal with."

"I'm not just talking about her," Gavra said. "Meri's the real threat. Something happened between her, Aodh and your uncle. I doubt it was a simple love triangle, but she sure as shit wanted what they could give her. When that was taken away from her, she lost it. I'll gladly go with you if it means I can help get Nyx to back down from this insanity. We need Nyx back on our side if we're going to be strong enough to beat Meri when she comes."

Assana swallowed, taking in Gavra's words. She wished like hell she could see some way to take these two and just drift out into the human world and hide from her troubles with them in some island grotto. But her family was falling apart, and she was the only one who could fix it.

"I wish Calder were here," she grumbled, though she was happy that her brother had made it clear of their mother's madness. Her uncle's continued absence worried her, though.

"You have me," Silas said, standing up and taking an unsteady step toward her.

"You're free," she said, smiling up at him.

"My feet still feel like they're made of wood, but it's fading. That was some potent water magic you flooded me with. I always knew there was a woman out there who'd make me want to put down roots."

"Oh, for fuck's sake," Gavra said. "Go do what you need to do. I will warn Aodh to brace himself for a face-to-face with one of the two women who hate him most in the world. He'll be ready."

CHAPTER 7

SILAS

Silas hobbled along beside Assana, wincing as the blood flow returned to his legs and feet. The sensation of being so tightly bound to Gaia was never a bad thing, but the moments of immobility caused panic to well inside him to the point he was prepared to rip himself from the floorboards, regardless of how badly he was sure it would hurt.

None of that mattered in the presence of the woman who walked beside him. Assana was real; he still couldn't quite believe it. He hadn't been sure what to believe when he'd returned to the Sanctuary to learn that all that had gone wrong within the past week was a direct result of the dragons' presence in his home. But if Assana existed, then perhaps Gavra had told him the truth about his own significance.

Not only did the beautiful nymph exist, but she'd just allowed him to service her through an ordeal that rivaled any female ursa's estrous. His body still buzzed as much from the energy he'd channeled as from his awareness of her. His cock was still uncomfortably stiff in his pants, but gradually relaxed as they made their way to the grand hall of the Rain-song clan lodge to speak with Sathmika. The idea of facing the imposing woman was enough to dampen any lust he might have felt. Until his arm brushed against Assana's and the charged sensation of her skin on his woke up every cell in his body again.

"You reek of dragon," she said under her breath as they descended the staircase to the first floor. "Is your clan leader going to find that suspect?"

"Fuck." Silas stopped in his tracks on the bottom step and looked at her, fresh panic rising up in him. He swiped a hand over his mouth and groaned. "She's going to know what I did. Fuck, fuck, fuck."

"You reek of me, too, but I think that's excusable. If you don't mind smelling even more of me, I think I can help."

Silas inhaled deeply, taking in Gavra's aroma along with hers. Both mixed in a tantalizing combination of different spices—one intensely masculine and the other delicately feminine.

"I like the way you're both all over me," he rumbled. "But my clan leader is not going to be as thrilled if she finds out I was messing around with the captive I was sent to guard. What can you do?"

"Come," she said, stepping into a shadowy alcove beneath the staircase and leaning against the wall. Silas's cock perked up at the sight of her barely clad curves and the coquettish tilt to her mouth. He stepped into her arms and bent his head when she tilted hers up to gaze into his eyes.

Those dark, swirling orbs were hypnotic, and he lost himself to the feel of her when she pulled him close and kissed him.

Assana cupped his face in her hands, and he had the oddest sense of plunging into deep, cool water as she slid her palms over his bare shoulders, down his chest, and dipped beneath the waistband of his cargo pants.

She drifted her lips across his, caressing his cheek with the barest brush of silken skin. She inhaled as she went, and he realized she was scenting him, her nose brushing the edge of his jaw, the side of his neck, and her mouth leaving cool, wet kisses as she went.

"He's all over you," she murmured in an almost hungry tone. "Seeping from your pores." Her tongue darted out and licked at his pulse point, which only made his heart pound and his cock rouse to painful stiffness again.

She gripped his hips just beneath his waistband and turned him, sliding around his body as she pushed him against the wall. Her gaze heated with avid interest and she continued her deliberate exploration of his body, like every inch she touched was more fascinating than the last.

"He kind of was all over me for a few minutes before you got there," Silas said, his breath quickening when she brushed her palm down the ridge of his erection through his pants.

"You swallowed his Nirvana. You're filled with his energy. His power will be tricky to mask, but I think I can manage it."

Assana's mouth moved back to his and she plunged her tongue between his lips, the power of the kiss enough to make him weak. He drank her in as she continued to touch, her hands still roaming. She unfastened his pants and pushed them down until they slid past his thighs and pooled at his ankles.

How she could feel so deliciously cool and smooth, yet make him so hot made no sense. Her touch seemed to leave a sheen of icy wetness on his skin that soothed and aroused at the same time, like she was skimming ice cubes over his body. She released his mouth and slowly slid down, trailing her tongue along the center of his chest, down over his stomach to his navel. His abs tightened in anticipation and his cock kicked against her chest when the tips of her breasts grazed his thighs. The hard peaks of her nipples pressed against his flesh through the gauzy wisp of her dress.

"Please, yes …" he moaned, tangling his fingers in her hair.

Assana's cheek brushed along the length of his aching cock, her eyes wide and almost fearful. She hesitated as he stared down at her.

"Are you afraid of something?" he asked. "It's just my stupid dick."

She swallowed and shook her head. "I've never been this close before … allowed to touch, to taste."

He raised an eyebrow. "Was his scent just an excuse for you to touch me? Not that I'm complaining … You just had to ask."

"No, I … well, maybe." She lowered her gaze and her cheeks flushed.

He touched her chin, urging her to look up at him and struggling to keep from groaning in outright lust at the sight of such a beautiful creature on her knees with her lips mere inches from the tip of his cock.

"You've really never been with a man … and you're how old?"

She swallowed again and licked her lips, leaving a sheen of moisture that made his mouth water.

"I was twelve when my brother and his squadron of Thiasoi soldiers were captured by the Ultiori. That was more than two thousand years ago. Mother didn't let me leave the Haven after that. By the time I was old enough to learn about sex, the only male left in the Haven was my uncle. I've never melded with a man before. Never touched one like this."

The significance of the moment made him pull back. "Assana … we shouldn't be doing this here. Not in a fucking hallway. I thought you just needed to—I don't know—magic his scent off me somehow with your watery essence."

She smiled. "That's one way to put it, but I need to meld with you to do that. We don't have time to make a big production of it. I need *your* essence first."

"Won't it seem suspect if you go in there smelling like *me*, though?"

"Not if I tell them I've chosen you for my mate. They already know I'm looking. May I …?"

He stared at her, confused until he realized she was asking fucking *permission* to suck his cock. It was such a contrast to the way he envisioned nymphs, not to mention to his recent experience with the dragon he loved and Gavra's rough, wordless insistence only a little while ago. He could still feel the dragon's fingertips digging into the back of his neck as Gavra forced him to take his huge cock into his mouth—could still taste the spice of the other man and the hot pulse of his semen as it shot into the back of his throat.

"Fuck, Assana, you don't fucking need to ask. I'm yours."

Her cool hand cupped his balls and he threw his head back against the wall with a groan. The first tentative lick around the head of his cock had him struggling with all his might to maintain control.

"Gaia, I can't wait to fuck you," he said. "When we get Gavra out of this bullshit, and we get to share each other … the three of us … I want to taste him on you. Can you taste him on me? Does it taste good?"

She held his cock with one hand and slowly slid her tongue along his length. "You taste good," she said.

Then her mouth was on him completely, her lips wrapping around his tip and sliding down his length. If she hadn't so earnestly just confessed to her inexperience, he never would have believed her. She expertly stroked and sucked, and within seconds had him at the edge and flying beyond, his entire body in ecstasy as she drew his essence from him in long, deep swallows.

He was so dazed he mindlessly obeyed her command when she stood and shoved him down to his knees.

"You'll taste me now," she said without a glimmer of hesitance, as though she were accustomed to being in command. "Hurry." She lifted one foot onto his shoulder and grabbed him by the head. Her glistening folds parted before him, beckoning. The sweet, swollen bud of her clit was poised inches from his lips. He didn't need to be told twice what she wanted.

With a hungry groan, he grabbed her ass and tilted forward, relishing her cry of pleasure when his tongue parted her flesh and her tangy essence washed over his taste buds. He remembered how responsive she'd been to his touch, how her clit had hardened with just the slightest caress of his fingers, and he did the same with his tongue. As much as he would have loved to take his time, to bring her off slowly and repeatedly, her urgency drove him to speed things up.

"Ohh, Silas!" she cried, and her flesh quivered and pulsed against his mouth. Again he drank her in, this time the gush of liquid over his tongue more plentiful than the energy he'd absorbed before—and he was grateful that his extremities didn't grow roots again.

Before he could stand, she dug her fingers into his temples and jaw, and he stared up at her, enraptured while the surge of her power flooded not only his body, but his mind as well.

In that moment, his entire being awoke with a strange awareness of his world, as though he'd had another set of senses he'd long forgotten and they'd just been revived.

"It is me you sense," Assana said, her voice clear and strong, though her lips didn't move. *"My awareness is yours, now that*

you've tasted my essence. And yours is mine. I can feel Gavra's power inside you. It's been there for some time ... I didn't know you bonded with him before today."

Something in her tone sounded hurt and she seemed to falter, to withdraw. Silas reached out with his consciousness as he rose to his feet and met her gaze directly.

"Yes, we were together one time before ... that was when he told me about you and made the promise that the three of us would be together. I intend to hold him to that promise."

He opened his mind to her more, marveling at the intimacy of this sharing of consciousness, but more than that, he was overwhelmed by the awareness of how significant a step this was. Within that simplest of connections, he sensed all her fears and desires, and above all, her determination to keep her family together at all costs. It left him feeling small, meaningless, and insignificant.

"Oh, Silas, you are everything," she said, her eyes widening as she absorbed the unchecked emotions that flooded from him.

He gave her a sad smile and shook his head. "No, I'm nothing, but that's okay. I have no idea what I did to have Fate smile on me ... I don't deserve the love of the two of you, but I'll be damned if I'm going to let it go."

She nodded and he knew she understood. What they offered was everything he'd always wanted and more, yet his connection to her now afforded him the first peek into the trials they might face in order to keep what they had only just found.

"You smell like me now," Assana said with a smile. This time her voice reached his ears instead of echoing inside his head. "At least enough that the clan leader is unlikely to notice the dragon on you. Shall we go?"

She took his hand and they approached the great hall with its warm teak arches and carved wood columns. The roof above sported lantern windows that let in the sunlight, and his heart skipped with joy at being home again in spite of the circumstances surrounding his return.

Upon a dais at the end of the hall sat the clan leader, Sathmika, her long black waves cascading over a deep turquoise gown shot through with golden strands. Upon her head rested a crown of flowering vines, and the room was awash in the fragrant summery scents of jasmine and wildflowers. Not even her intent, watchful gaze could destroy Silas's happiness. The world might have gone mad within the span of a few weeks, but he had found his mates, so he knew he could deal with whatever the woman threw at him.

"Assana, have you contacted your mother yet and let her know we've seen to her demands? When will she restore the Source?" Sathmika's question sent a cold reminder of their plight through him. He mentally kicked himself for his internal celebration.

"I'm afraid she's added to the demands. I must return to the Haven at midnight tonight and bring the two male dragons with me."

"To what end?" Sathmika asked. "We've already imprisoned them in bonds they can't break free of without expending all their power. If she wishes us to send more males, she only needs to ask."

"She does want more males … two of them," Assana said.

Sathmika gave Silas an appraising look. "And what of Silas?"

The question made him blink. The fact that she even knew his name astounded him. He was one of dozens of Guardians and had spent the better part of the past decade outside the Sanctuary.

"What of me, mistress?" he asked.

Sathmika shook her head in exasperation. "You're covered in Assana's essence. It's clear she's chosen you, but it takes more than a few hours with a nymph for her claim to be complete. Do you plan to claim him fully, Assana?"

Silas frowned at Assana, confused. "What does she mean? I thought what we did … the melding …"

"It was just the first of three," Assana said. "Sathmika is right …" She turned to face his clan leader. "Mother does not want more ursa males for the Haven yet, but it is still my right to choose a mate from among the males here. I have chosen Silas to return with me as well."

"What, pray tell, will change your mother's mind, then? Two dragons … immortal ones at that … may make good mates for her nymphs, but she's effectively allowing all the living females of her race to become the treasures of another higher race. If she intended to give the dragons that much power over the Haven, she didn't need to cut off the Source to do it."

Sathmika rose from her carved wooden throne and descended the dais to stand at eye level before Assana. "We don't need this breeding pact. Our males are more than content with each other. They're satisfied with the intervals they're allowed to venture on their pilgrimages to mate with human females, if they choose. We make those allowances for their happiness when ursa females are as scarce as they have been of late. What is it Nyx hopes to gain?"

Silas watched Assana closely, and though her face remained still, her eyes merely reflecting the room around her, his connection to her was still strong. She was as still as a placid pool on the surface, but beneath her calm appearance churned a desperate need to maintain her mother's reputation while still keeping the peace.

"They are not for the nymphs," Assana finally said, and Silas caught the hint of a careful lie forming inside her mind. A small part of her awareness focused on him, and he sensed an apology in that mental touch as she completed the lie to his clan leader.

"Mother and my uncle have quarreled and she knows he loves the white dragon. She wants to form a stronger alliance with the dragons—to appease my uncle in the hopes that he will return to the Haven once she shows that she can co-exist with the man he loves. She wants to do this by offering herself to … to his brother. Her methods were regrettable, but she was struck by grief when my uncle left. These aren't fresh demands, but a compromise. You know my mother was never very good at asking for help."

Sathmika regarded Assana silently, though her expression was far more transparent. She didn't believe a word of what Assana said, and Assana's panicked mind scrambled for more excuses. Using his presence in her mind, Silas silently urged her to stop, a break to her rising flood that diverted the emotion, controlled it, and let her gather herself.

It wasn't much, but it gave Sathmika time to draw her own conclusion. He met the ancient elemental's gaze and felt it drilling into him, plotting something he wasn't sure he would like. Finally Sathmika returned her gaze to Assana.

"The nymphaea are still our allies, and while I cannot speak for the ursa as a whole, I know what our reigning queen's wishes are. We will comply with your mother's demands under one condition, which is for *you* to agree to, Assana. Something we ask that you keep from Nyx unless Neph is by her side when you return."

"Whatever must be done, I will hear it."

Sathmika's steady gaze fell on Silas again, raked over him slowly. An uneasy sensation filled his gut, replacing the earlier elation at having a female like Assana choose him.

"This male you have chosen … he is ripe for the blessing of Gaia. A boon we have the option to bestow on only a few males in each generation. We don't often grant this blessing.

It's rarely necessary. But we will grant it to this one before you return to the Haven."

Silas's jaw fell open. Gaia's blessing was a myth, or so he'd thought.

Sathmika chuckled. "Don't look so surprised, Silas. The fact that you're a single male who is fully capable of channeling the power of a female as strong as Assana is what makes you perfect. You're the lucky one who gets to take advantage of the gift."

"I don't understand. I'm nobody."

"When I'm done with you, you'll be the only male in the Sanctuary who can use the divine magic you channel, rather than simply giving it back to Gaia. You'll be a Miteradoro."

CHAPTER 8

SILAS

ssana gasped beside him. "The roots … it isn't something other males can do, is it?"

Sathmika shook her head. "Very few show the signs of ripeness for Gaia's gift. Silas is one of those few."

Confused, he glanced between the two females. "I never realized it was such a big deal. It first happened on my pilgrimage. I met a dragon …" He gave Assana an apologetic look. "It was just for fun, and she was much older than I was at the time."

Assana didn't seem fazed by his confession. If anything, she looked amused. "I am much older than you, Silas," she said. "So you lost your virginity to a dragon … I could be so lucky." She gave him a secretive smile.

Silas cleared his throat. "Yes … well, it didn't exactly happen like that. We didn't fuck. Like I said, she was much older. She'd outlived her mate and was lonely and simply wanted company."

He frowned, recalling the lovely female with sea-blue eyes who had asked if he minded her horns and tail being visible while she pleasured him—said she needed them for balance, which hadn't made sense to him at first until he'd experienced her very particular desire to have him caress her horns while she penetrated him with her tail. The sex had been so good, he almost hadn't noticed when it was over that his lower limbs were rooted to the floor, thick woody tendrils wrapping around her bed frame and sinking into the floor beneath the bed.

The dragon herself had been excited by it, exclaiming how lucky she was, that after bedding him she needed to find a new mate because this meant she would get pregnant easily —that it was a good omen to the other races if they shared their Nirvana with an ursa male who rooted while they coupled.

"How do the dragons know about it if I don't? It never happened when I serviced females with Raj ... only when I was alone with one."

"Only when you were alone with a female of particularly strong power," Sathmika said. "It manifested with Assana today, didn't it? I felt a surge in Gaia's power not long ago. Multiple times, in fact ... shortly after Assana went up to speak with the captive."

Silas stilled, hoping she hadn't noticed Gavra's energy lingering on him somehow, but she'd focused her attention on Assana again.

"You wish to mate this male, Assana, daughter of Nyx, granddaughter of Dionysus?"

Assana took a shaky breath and gave Silas a bright-eyed glance that was filled with the truth of her feelings.

"I do," she said. "What is it you ask of me?"

"That you allow your new mate to carry out a task for me. One that must remain secret, even to your ears."

Silas felt a chill settle into his gut, replacing the warm glow of elation at Sathmika's acknowledgment of his new status.

"No secrets," he said, his voice catching. "Not from her."

Assana's face had turned stony, his link to her mind making clear the shame she felt over everything that was happening.

"No, Silas. Her request is fair." To Sathmika, she said, "Please assure me that what you're asking him to do doesn't compromise my home or my mother in any way. Or Silas himself."

Sathmika gave her a slight nod. "You have my word. Our goal is merely to restore balance between our homes. Please leave us … You may go and make preparations to take the dragons at midnight."

Unease settled in Silas's chest as he watched Assana turn and leave. When he turned back to Sathmika, she regarded him thoughtfully.

"Did you know what I was before?" he demanded.

"There were other potential males we watched, and we knew the power likely resided in one of the portal guardians. It's often strongest in Rainsong males—it presented in the Queen's mates as well, but we hoped to find a single male to avoid asking her to sacrifice one of them for the task, if a need arose."

"Why can't Assana know what you plan for me? All she wants is to fix this."

"Fix this?" Sathmika said, her voice like thunder. "The dragons said the same thing after breaking through our barrier and triggering a nearly catastrophic collapse. They didn't *mean* to cause the problem. And now the nymphaea are claiming the same from the other side. We are finished tolerating these so-called *accidents* from our allies. It's time for us to regain some control. The safety of the Sanctuary is our priority, don't you agree?"

Silas firmed his lips and nodded. His home meant everything to him. "I will do what I can."

"You will do *exactly* as you are commanded." She lifted a hand and pressed her palm to the center of his forehead. A warm tingling sensation seemed to burrow into his head, his mind filling with a vision of Assana's supple flesh and her sweet cries of pleasure echoing in his ears. Within a moment, those images dimmed and faded and his mind went blank, empty, and he grasped at the lost thread of Assana's consciousness.

"No …"

Before he could continue his objection, his mind filled with a blast of bright light that seemed to flood through his entire body, leaving him gasping for air and every cell in his being vibrating with power. His eyes flew open and he stared at Sathmika, awed by the immense power and a growing understanding of what it meant.

Sathmika dropped her hand. "Don't worry, you'll get to meld with her again soon enough. Activating your power required a cleansing of your mind. And I needed to make sure your connection to her was severed before we continue with your instructions. It isn't that I don't trust her intentions, but her love for her home is every bit as fierce as yours."

Silas swallowed thickly. "I would do anything for the Sanctuary."

"I know. You are now uniquely equipped to hold the divine power given to you in the moment of your partner's blossoming. When you are with partners who boast links to the divine, their climax pulls divine power to them. The roots you descended today were your instinctive reaction to give your own goddess the power you'd received from Assana's blossoming. If you become her mate, you will have many more opportunities to receive this power. You must hold this power you collect and keep it until the time is right. When you are in the Haven, you must find the Source and release the power. Give it to Gaia, and let Gaia do the rest."

Silas frowned. "I'm not sure what that means."

Sathmika slid her hand down his chest and cupped him between the legs through his cargo pants. His eyes widened at the light squeeze she gave his balls.

"Your power reservoir is quite capable of holding more than you have now. Go as Assana's mate. When you channel her magic, gradually you will begin to feel your reservoir fill. You will need to practice manifesting the roots on command, and not just when your partner's orgasm triggers them."

"What will it feel like when I have enough power for this purpose?" Silas asked.

"Like your pheronesis is on the verge of beginning. Find a way to get to the Source. Once there, you can use the roots to create a permanent link between the Sanctuary and the Source. One that bypasses Gaia's Falls."

"How will I know it worked?" Silas asked, relaxing now that he understood what was being asked of him. It didn't sound so bad.

"It will be clear."

"All right," he said, nodding at her decisively.

"Glad to see you being so agreeable." Sathmika's already secretive smile turned downright suggestive, and Silas wished he knew what she was thinking.

"Is there something else you want to share, Mistress?" he asked.

"You're a young ursa yet. Sex with a nymph or satyr in their primal state is an experience no one forgets … don't pass it up if you get the chance, Silas."

CHAPTER 9

VRISHTI

Vrishti jogged toward the grand hall, her palms clammy and her stomach in tangles. Terrible things were happening, events she was powerless to affect, but she had to know more. So far, all she knew was that their nymphaea neighbors had cut them off from their sacred Source and were holding it hostage if the ursa didn't imprison her friends.

Rumor had trickled back to her that the nymph Assana had returned to the Rainsong clan lodge, and she hoped that meant she could find answers. She hated how ineffectual she was, even though her status as Sathmaki's long-lost daughter had all the residents of the lodge and the surrounding ursa camps in awe. She'd only been here a few weeks, and as such her latent magical abilities were still green, though she was a fast learner. She didn't have even half the skill of her cousin Revna, nor the experience of the older ursa female. Worse yet, as much as she'd hunted through the vast libraries at her disposal, she had found nothing that even hinted at how she could help Aodh with his request.

Why couldn't he have given her more details that day he'd

81

confessed his love to her? All she knew was that he needed her help to somehow find a way to get into the Haven from outside the Sanctuary. She had to admit this had been her primary focus in her studies so far, but her efforts had yet to bear fruit. Now that Aodh was locked up, however, she had to find a way to get him out so he could follow through. Out of his prison, and out of the damn Sanctuary—even if she had to halt her studies and leave again herself. She had made him a promise, and she intended to keep it.

She slowed to an easy pace outside the great hall and forced herself to breathe. She was sure she'd look flushed when she walked in, and her mother would notice and ask. Her mother always noticed, which she'd found comforting at first, but after a week under the woman's scrutiny had become grating. She couldn't do anything without the powerful ursa shaman somehow knowing, and a lesson often followed. What lesson would Sathmika have for her today?

She hadn't even made it around the edge of the open doorway when Assana's clear voice hit her ears. "I must return to the Haven at midnight tonight and bring the two male dragons with me," the nymph was saying.

Vrishti's entire body stilled, a sudden chill washing over her, prickling the hairs at her nape. No. She didn't know why Aodh wanted to go to the Haven, but she did know he wanted to get there his own way … that it was imperative he return with the human man who waited for him out in the world she'd so recently left behind.

She abruptly turned and ran full speed in the other direction, tearing up the staircase to the third floor of the lodge and down the hallway to Gavra's quarters where he'd been imprisoned. She heaved a sigh of relief that his guard wasn't there, though she'd discovered during the past week that the male ursa were particularly deferential to her, to the point she felt self-conscious around them. They always looked at her like they wanted something … like they wanted *her* …

Gavra's door was open, the magical barrier of his prison shimmering in the sunlight that poured in through the windows and high skylights of his room. When she moved to stand opposite the opening, she saw him on the far side, leaning against the window frame with his head bowed and shaking slowly. His hands moved and his eyes flitted oddly. He looked like he was deep in conversation with some invisible visitor.

He stopped moving abruptly when his eyes found her. She gave him a little wave and a hesitant smile.

"Vrishti! Do you have any news?" Gavra asked, rushing toward the door. He stopped mere inches inside the translucent barrier.

"Only that Assana means to take you both to the Haven tonight," she said.

Gavra's shoulders fell and he nodded. "I know that much already. Assana got the command from her mother after she confirmed to Nyx that I was locked up. I've spoken to Aodh … he isn't happy about going. We may need your help to convince him."

She frowned at him. "You … spoke to him?" she asked, her stomach fluttering with both confusion and excitement to hear news of the big white dragon who'd recently filled her thoughts and dreams.

Gavra tapped his temple with a fingertip. "Dragon telepathy. For other dragons there's a distance limit, but for me and my siblings there isn't. Though we need to be in the same world, it seems … I can't contact my siblings who are outside the Sanctuary, but I have spoken to both Numa and Aodh since this happened." He swept a hand around, indicating the prison his quarters had become.

"Wh-what did he say?" she asked, struggling to suppress her eagerness.

"'The fuck that bitch Nyx is dictating where we go. I have better things to do than kowtow to her demands,' were his exact words, which is extremely out of character for him, I might add." He paused and studied her, his red eyes narrowed. "He didn't ask if I'd spoken to you, for once. I think he's too angry."

"I wasn't … I didn't…" she stammered, then swallowed and averted her eyes from his piercing stare.

"You came here to ask about him. No need to hide it, Vrishti."

"He can't go tonight. There has to be a way to stop this."

Gavra sighed. "I'm afraid there's no way around it. You've never met Nyx. Without her brother to temper her madness, the Haven's in trouble, and the Sanctuary by extension. Aodh and I can help if we go, though I'm having a hell of a time convincing *him* of that. I promise he'll come back to you when we've tackled this little problem."

Vrishti groaned at his condescending tone. As though all she cared about was being with the man. "No! It's more complicated than just … missing him. He has to get out of the Sanctuary by the equinox. Do you think Nyx plans to let him go?"

Gavra's brows creased and he crossed his arms. "No … we're likely both going to be there for the foreseeable future, at least until her brother returns. Someone needs to help lend balance to the place … keep things under control. Any strong male presence can help, but the ursa there now aren't strong enough even as a group to counterbalance Nyx's power."

Vrishti turned and paced to the bench across the hall, struggling with the details Aodh had shared with her in confidence. He'd sworn that he wouldn't leave the Sanctuary until he found out how to get into the Haven from Outside … how to help a man named Nikhil get in with him, to help them learn how to beat their enemy. If Aodh wound up in the Haven, likely trapped by a mad nymph, based on rumors she'd heard today, how was this other man supposed to get in?

Then she recalled the last thing Aodh had said to her: that he was hers, if she'd have him, and that she would understand what that meant once she understood what it meant to be an ursa female. Well, she knew enough now. She knew that as the daughter of Summer, she could choose her mate.

She turned back to face Gavra. With steel in her voice she said, "Aodh is mine. She can't have him."

Gavra's brows shot up. His eyes glazed a moment before he focused on her again.

"He says he's happy you feel that way, but it doesn't do him much good if you haven't marked him. Can you even shift yet, Vrishti? Most female ursa don't even achieve that ability until after their first estrous, and I would have heard if you'd hit yours. Every bachelor pair in the Rainsong territory is waiting for it. I'm sorry, but even if you were capable of rending Aodh's flesh, you don't have the claws to do it."

Vrishti's eyes pricked with angry tears. "What am I supposed to do? He has to wait until I've had time to learn how to help him. I need more time."

"Help him with what?" Gavra said, his voice taking on a hard edge, his gaze wary.

"I … I can't tell you. He asked me not to."

Gavra swore and turned away, his deep voice carrying a warning when he said, "Brother mine, you have something you want to share?"

Then he was silent for some time. Vrishti stared at his naked back, marveling at the rippling muscles and the way the intricate design of a huge red dragon glimmered as though shining beneath the surface of his skin. She wondered if Aodh had a similar mark on his body.

Gavra clenched his fists and swore again, then turned back to face her. "Do you think you can help him do what he seeks?"

Vrishti hesitated, her gaze darting to the window down the hall. She twisted her hands in her skirt. "I … I can't say …"

"For fuck's sake, girl, he told me what he planned. We're not exactly in the position where secrets are helping us now. He hoped you could learn how to access the Haven from the Outside without the aid of a Dionarch. Nikhil made the request so he could gather more intel on our enemy and find a way to beat them, or to at least *find* the bloody Ultiori bitch who leads them. Do you think you can help?"

Vrishti closed her eyes, hating that she had no good answer. "I have heard of magic that might work, but I don't have command of it yet. I won't be strong enough until the equinox when my mother and I perform the ceremony to grant me Summer's essence … or until I hit my estrous, but I have no idea when that will happen."

"The equinox is months away yet," Gavra sighed. "We need that magic more than we need to avoid Nyx's clutches. Trust me, Aodh and I will be fine, but promise you will go find Nikhil as soon as you learn the secret. Take my sister, if she is allowed to leave the Sanctuary by then—with luck we'll have dealt with Nyx and Aodh can come back and go with you, but if he can't, it will be up to you."

Vrishti nodded solemnly. "But won't you come back, too?"

"I will go where she goes," Gavra said, his gaze softening as it shifted down the hall past Vrishti's shoulder.

Vrishti turned to see the nymph Assana coming toward

them with a grim expression. She took some comfort in the fact that Assana didn't look pleased to have to carry out her mother's demands. Besides, if Aodh's brother looked at Assana that way, she must have *some* redeeming qualities. Though the way the nymph's statuesque body swayed as she walked, Vrishti couldn't help but feel wholly inadequate with her own full hips and voluptuous breasts. Assana had striking features that would have put the most beautiful human supermodel to shame, and grace and kindness to top it off.

"Vrishti," Assana said softly. She smiled in spite of the worry that clearly etched her features and rested a gentle hand on Vrishti's shoulder. "Oh, sister, I am so sorry." Assana pulled her into a hug that was every bit as sensuous as it was comforting, her hands sliding down her back in a light, almost seductive caress.

"Why are you sorry?" Vrishti asked. She barely knew this woman and had never shared any of her connection to the dragons with her. And why the hell would she call her "sister"? Was it a nymph thing?

Assana pulled back and cupped her face, her blue eyes swirling dizzily, hypnotically. "For taking your mate. I would offer you comfort to make up for it."

Vrishti's senses filled with crisp scents reminding her of the cooler nights in the jungle near her home, and Assana's lips brushing her own were gentle and inviting. So much so that she nearly succumbed to the pull of the nymph's seduction. Her touch was so soft, so comforting, so innocent … until it wasn't. Vrishti caught the scent of sex and her own arousal spiked. The sudden rise in heat startled her enough to pull away.

She glanced at Gavra, who stood inside his doorway, watching avidly.

"Don't stop on my account," he growled.

"We're not doing anything," Vrishti said, feeling the heat of her arousal turn to pure shame at even feeling it.

"You don't accept my apology?" Assana said, and Vrishti was surprised to see the woman looked genuinely upset at the rejection.

"I … please, it's all right. I don't blame you."

"Assana," Gavra said, "not all races use sex to say they're sorry, or to say hello, for that matter. We say we're sorry via other means, usually … like words."

"Oh," Assana said, frowning.

"For the record, when I'm out of here, you are more than welcome to tell *me* you're sorry however you wish," he added. "But Vrishti might like something different, seeing as how she's not accustomed to how most things are done in our world yet."

Vrishti's cheeks heated to molten levels. "I know about sex," she said. "Just because I'm inexperienced doesn't mean I don't know how things work. We can't all be ancient nymphs who've had a bajillion men before. Not that there's anything wrong with that." She hurriedly darted an apologetic glance to Assana, who appeared worried again.

"I have never had a man before," Assana said. "So in that we are definitely sisters."

Vrishti's eyes widened. "Oh! I … I thought … everyone says the nymphs are the most experienced. That's why all the males are so excited to be chosen to mate one."

"Many of my sister nymphs are more experienced than I am. I've only had the pleasure of females, so I would happily give you comfort if you wished … it is within my realm of expertise."

Of course she'd only had females, yet somehow that managed to make Vrishti feel just as inadequate and inexperienced. There wasn't a damn thing she had over this woman.

"On the contrary, sister," Assana said. "You have an advantage no other female has."

Vrishti blanched. "Did you read my mind?" She wasn't sure whether to be offended or just surprised.

"Just a glimmer after the taste you gave me. Your bodily fluids carry bits of your essence, letting me connect to your mind. If you had let me comfort you, I could have seen more. You are the daughter of Summer. At the equinox, you will *become* Summer. This is something I can never achieve—taking my mother's place as leader of the Haven. She is immortal and eternal, but the ursa leaders are ever changing with the seasons. Please remember me when you ascend. I promise you now that I owe you a great debt for your forgiveness today. If there is anything I can do now to ease your mind, I will do it. What other comfort can I offer?"

Vrishti relaxed, accepting that Assana really was much older and experienced, and had just as complicated a relationship with her own mother to boot.

"Can I see him before you take him away?"

"Yes! In fact, I was planning to bring him here..." Turning to Gavra and ignoring his disappointed glance between the two women, Assana said, "Speak to your brother. I will go to him and release his barrier, if he promises to let me drift him directly to your room. He mustn't run. Hopefully if he knows his mate is waiting for him, he will come easily. It will be simpler if we are all in one place when we leave later."

"He is willing," Gavra said. "Where is Silas?"

"Concluding business with Sathmika. I will go get your brother now."

Vrishti wasn't sure, but she got the distinct impression Assana was looking for an excuse to escape. While Vrishti at times dreaded assuming the mantle of Summer, she was mostly excited to take on the important role. She would still have her mother beside her, guiding her as she stepped into the role of clan leader—something that would become easier once she had the power of Summer at her disposal. Her mother had never given her the impression that she was lying about anything, or that she had any hidden agenda. Her chief concern was that the cycles of the Sanctuary were not interrupted so that her home remained safe and thriving as it had for millennia. Becoming a part of that cycle made Vrishti proud.

Yet she was surprised to note Assana didn't seem to feel the same amount of pride for her own home. In fact, the other woman seemed ashamed—perhaps it was only because of the insane demands Nyx was making.

"Do you promise the two of you can fix what's going on in the Haven?" Vrishti asked, interrupting another silent conversation Gavra seemed to be having.

"The four of us," Gavra said. "Assana and Silas will be coming with me. Somehow we will set things right. It all depends on how mad Nyx has become, but one way or the other, we *will* fix this. I promise to bring him back to you."

Vrishti nodded and sighed. "Thank you."

CHAPTER 10

GAVRA

"*D*on't make promises you can't keep, brother."

Gavra turned away from the women standing in his doorway out of reach. *"Who says I can't keep it? If anyone can gain control of Nyx, it's us. Assana needs us both. We got lucky with this demand—now we can actually be there to fix this."*

He could sense his brother's worry through their mental link, but it made no sense. The pair of them together were more than a match for one crazy Dionarch.

"You don't understand how dangerous an imbalanced nymph can be," Aodh said. *"If she's truly gone mad, she'll be unpredictable. And with the power she wields, she could be even worse than the Lamia. Our priority should be getting the ursa out first, then breaking her hold on the Thiasoi maidens."*

Gavra glanced over his shoulder and his heart skipped a beat as Silas returned to the scene outside his room. The ursa draped an arm possessively around Assana's waist and whispered in her ear something that caused her to inhale sharply and her aura to flare. Sweet Mother, he needed to get the pair of them alone and mark them both.

"We can speak more when you get here, brother," he shot back. *"We have a few hours yet before midnight."*

He was suddenly itching to get moving now that he knew what was in store for them, though he had to admit Aodh was right. They really had no way to predict what Nyx might do once they got there. He didn't like the way Assana's aura had taken on a sickened cast when she'd spoken to her mother, but if the ancient Dionarch wanted to breed a dragon, she'd soon learn what kind of power she was messing with.

A moment later Assana was gone, her form shimmering and dissolving like she'd washed away in an ethereal flow. He redirected his gaze to Silas, who was having a polite conversation with Vrishti. She looked uncomfortable in his presence—there was no good excuse for her to be here, and Silas was still technically Gavra's guardian, but as they talked, Vrishti gradually relaxed.

Her aura was stronger than it had been the day they'd met, the fertile power of a female ursa gradually ripening within her, though she was still far from ready. But Gavra could see from what she possessed so far that she would become quite powerful on her own, even without the spirit of Summer's full power filling her. She may be their only hope to achieve what Aodh had told him about. It was a crazy plan to get Nikhil into the Haven, but it had to work—especially if the ancient warlord believed it would.

Gavra had met the man on the battlefield many times before their insidious enemy existed—Nikhil himself was the reason the Ultiori had been so feared by all the higher races. He'd been Meri's perfect pawn for so long, but he was on their side now and by all accounts more than ready to wreak vengeance on the woman who had turned him into her pet monster. That he was the long-lost love of Gavra's Blue sister, Belah, only strengthened Nikhil's bond to them and to their cause.

The last time he'd seen Nikhil, he'd witnessed the most sexually charged scene between the once human man and Belah's two turul mates. He had no doubt that the four of them would find their way together somehow, and Nikhil would be even stronger for that bond once he found it. He would be their perfect champion once he reclaimed that power … the power that Belah's love granted him.

But if the Haven was in pieces, the Dionarchs lost or insane, there wouldn't be much for Nikhil to discover once he made it in. Gavra had to fix that. At the very least, the Haven needed to be secured, its power controlled by someone sane enough not to destroy the place in the name of protecting it.

"Well, that was fun."

Gavra spun around at the sound of the deep, familiar voice that had so recently been speaking inside his head. His brother stood in the center of his room, his arms crossed and a grim smile on his face.

"Aodh," he said, unable to mask the utter relief he felt at seeing his white-haired brother whole and in the flesh. He pulled the other man into a fierce embrace that his brother returned in kind, releasing Aodh when he stiffened.

Gavra looked back in the direction of his brother's gaze and saw Vrishti standing with an excited look, about to breach the barrier into his room.

"No!" Aodh said. "Please stay where you are, love."

"She wants to see you," Gavra said. "Surely you won't deny her a proper greeting."

Aodh shook his head. "A proper greeting? She's not ready, brother. Perhaps it's fine for you and Silas to tangle before you've marked him, but we can't risk her reputation while she's still learning about her kind."

Turning to Vrishti, he said, "After we've settled these issues with the Haven. I promise you no prison can keep me from you then."

Vrishti dropped the hand she had been about to push past the barrier with and nodded. Her eyes glassed over and she took a shaky breath. "I'll be ready for you, I promise. I can't stand to see you trapped like this … I'm sorry. Be safe. Keep him safe …" She directed the last comment to Gavra and Assana, who both nodded.

Gavra gave Assana a perplexed look. "Why didn't you drift into the room with him?"

Assana carefully avoided his gaze as she hugged Vrishti farewell and watched the other female go, then she glanced at Silas, a look of pure gratitude on her face. The big ursa male moved closer to her, wrapped an arm around her, and held her. Gavra's chest felt leaden at the way the pair looked at each other—like they belonged in each other's arms. They were kindred elements, both Gaia's children, and made sense together more than Gavra himself made sense with either of them. The way he and Silas crashed together with such fiery, explosive force felt right to him, but it was not easy or pretty —it was passionate, volatile, and destructive.

"He calms my primal spirit," Assana said softly. "I'm afraid to come closer to you because you only make the madness claw at my mind more. I allowed Aodh to take control of his own drift once he promised to go where I asked. I couldn't be in the same room with you for fear of losing control. I'm sorry, Gavra … I can't let myself surrender, not when my entire home and my family's wellbeing are at stake. Please understand."

He wanted to roar in protest, to breathe flames at the barrier and pull her inside, show her how right it would be to let go and be her true self—to be the wild nymph he sensed glimmers of beneath the surface whenever their eyes met.

The insatiable creature who haunted his dreams, responding to his heat so perfectly.

Aodh's hand rested on his shoulder and gave him a comforting squeeze.

The gesture did nothing to calm the blaze of need inside him. Gavra's voice was low and heated when he said, "I want you wild, Assana. The first time I'm inside you, you can be damn sure control will be the last thing on anyone's minds."

Silas tightened his hold on Assana protectively, though his aura flared bright red in response to Gavra's promise. She closed her eyes and took a long, slow breath as though fortifying herself before opening her eyes.

Her hypnotic, whirlpool gaze met his through the barrier. "I want that too. To share my primal essence with you both, to taste yours when we're thrice melded and feel your heat deep inside my mind. To feel you etch your mark on my skin. Gaia save me, I would take that now, but I can't risk losing myself to that need. There is too much at stake. Please understand … I need Silas to keep my own nymphaea madness in check, but I promise you the first time you're inside me will be the first time I'm ever filled by a male's seed."

Gavra groaned, forcing himself to pull his gaze away from her or else risk burning down the entire Sanctuary to get to her.

"It looks like Silas is going to have his hands full sating us both separately then," he said, staring heatedly at the big ursa male. "Can you handle that?"

Silas gave him a lazy smile. "I welcome it."

CHAPTER 11

AURUM

Black Mountain, North Carolina

Aurum stared out the frosted windowpane with an uneasy feeling twisting in her belly. She'd lost contact with her siblings after diving into Gaia's falls, but hadn't cared at the time. Being with Calder and Nicholas had been her only thought, and one for which she would never apologize. But now that the three of them were together and her mates were safely out of the Haven and away from Nyx's madness, she missed the easy contact she'd had with all her brothers and sisters.

The last few days since they'd arrived in the wintery forests of Appalachia had given her time to breathe, to simply enjoy being with her lovers. They'd barely spent a moment out of bed, but the heavy snow the night before had enticed Nicholas too strongly and now the young ursa was outside, fully shifted and diving into snowdrifts like a huge, rambunctious dog.

The sight made her smile, as did the irritated look on Calder's face when a naked Nicholas burst from the snow and nailed the satyr in the face with a snowball. Calder was not a fan of cold weather, it seemed, as evidenced by the layer upon layer of borrowed gear he'd donned before agreeing to accompany Nicholas out into the snow.

Aurum had spent much of the morning out with them, letting Nicholas's exuberance infect her. There was so much he had yet to experience in life after being held captive by the Ultiori since his infancy—she wasn't about to force him to come inside before he was ready. But she was hungry and knew that the two men would be starving and chilled once they came in, so she'd perused the pantry in the Stonetree family's cabin and found it stocked with enough food to last all winter long. She'd found a big electric chest freezer filled with meat, and the shelves of the canning room lined with jars upon jars of preserved fruits and vegetables. Now the entire huge kitchen was filled with the scent of roasting venison and baking pies.

She would go stir-crazy if she stayed too long, but she was willing to wait until she at least got word from her siblings in the Sanctuary about their own plans. Even if it took until spring for news to arrive.

The lack of contact was disconcerting, though. With the Sanctuary's barrier blocking Numa, Aodh, and Gavra from her mind, she reached out for Belah and Ked instead, but they were also out of reach within the turul Enclave. She hoped Nikhil had made it to her sister's side. Never in her life had she witnessed a more enduring love than theirs. Even after the atrocities the man had committed, her sister still held onto hope, and she hadn't been disappointed. Nikhil had been a victim of their true enemy—forced by a mad, vindictive, and brutally calculating nymph to do the unspeakable things he'd done during all those centuries while the other races hid.

Now that Nikhil was free of the Lamia's mind control,

he'd still taken some convincing that he was wanted and should go be with the woman he loved, even though she was now ensconced in the turul Enclave with a pair of mates who would do anything to make her happy.

But that was the key to it all, wasn't it? Aurum's chest warmed as she caught Calder's glance back toward the window where she stood. His smile was filled with love that didn't falter even when a capering Nicholas nailed the side of his face with another snowball. Calder let out roar that broke with his laughter. He lunged at the other man, barreling into him and throwing him back into the deep snow.

Aurum laughed as she watched them tumble. Despite Calder's displeasure at being out in the cold, his aura flared a joyful gold that told her he wouldn't be anywhere else in the world right now.

Her own laughter almost drowned out the sound of knocking at the front door. When she heard it, a chill prickled down her spine. Nikhil had mentioned interacting with a few of the locals, who were wary but polite, and who had rarely bothered him during the weeks he'd been here waiting for her brother to return.

She gave her cavorting mates another glance and turned to walk across the living room to find out who was calling at a perfect stranger's house in the middle of a bright winter day.

Glancing through the window, she saw a huge, bearded man who stood buck naked and completely unaffected by the cold. That level of imperviousness to the elements only meant one thing.

Aurum hurriedly opened the door, her heart pounding. The man had his attention focused on the laughter coming from the side of the house, but turned abruptly, fixing a pair of dark eyes on her.

"Mistress," he said, bowing his head deferentially. He

didn't smile, which caused a cold dread to settle in Aurum's stomach.

She pushed partway through the door and called to Calder and Nicholas. The shrill tone of her voice brought them running immediately. Nicholas bounded onto the long porch in a single stride, his dark-bearded face coated in chunks of snow and his body hair beaded with it as though he'd grown pearls. He let out a roar and sped up, aiming right at their visitor who backed up a step and held up his hands.

"I'm not here to harm you!" the man said. "My name's Arcadius Windchaser. You can call me Cade. I was sent by the Queen … your sister, I mean." He glanced around warily, his eyes meeting Calder's through the layers of knit scarves and hats the satyr was bundled in.

Calder yanked his scarf off, revealing his smooth cheeks and giving the man a clearer view of his swirling eyes. "There are no humans here, friend. You may speak freely. Come inside."

Aurum handed blankets to the two naked ursa and installed the ice-encrusted Nicholas on a towel in front of the fireplace while Calder added fresh logs to the fire. He didn't shed his layers until the fire was huge and roaring, casting a bright orange glow on Nicholas's bare, dripping legs.

"You said you have news? I'm guessing it isn't good news, is it?" Aurum asked, sitting on a comfortable, overstuffed armchair and leaning toward Cade expectantly.

He frowned and shook his head. "Regrettably, no. I've been sent to tell you that the dragons inside have been imprisoned at the demands of the Dionarch Nyx." He glanced at Calder, who had shed all but jeans and his cotton thermal shirt stretched across his well-defined muscles.

"My mother's demands?" Calder asked. "What the fuck

would she want with Aurum's siblings? They've done nothing to her."

"No, but I did," Aurum said. She sighed and stood. "Your mother wasn't exactly in a great frame of mind when your uncle took us out of there. What of Neph? Has there been news of him?" she asked Cade.

"Nothing specific. The only thing we know is that Nyx has lost both males and that she's gone mad. We fear for the safety of our brothers who joined the breeding pact and are trapped inside the Haven now. No doubt they aren't complaining … I can think of worse places to be myself, at least as long as Nyx is mad at the dragons and not at them."

Calder dropped his arms to his sides and stepped away from the fire. "You're telling me my uncle hasn't returned to the Haven? This isn't good."

"Where else would he go?" Nicholas asked.

"Nowhere. He knows how delicate a balance there is there now with no satyrs in residence. He's the only thing that's kept my mother from going off the deep end all this time. He dove back in the river after delivering us outside the Haven. He should have returned by now—this absolutely shouldn't be happening. He'd never let Mother go this far. Have you seen my sister, Assana? She was the nymph sent as ambassador to arrange the breeding pact with the ursa."

"She is in the Sanctuary now," Cade said with a nod. "Or she was when I was sent to bring the news to you. They have only made the one allowance to let me leave the Sanctuary to carry the message to you. All the guardians were ordered to return … I do not have a way back in. Not until the conflict with the Haven is settled, or until the spring equinox, whichever comes first. The barrier is locked to preserve its power."

"Power my siblings and I gave it," Aurum snapped. "Does that count for nothing?"

"I'm sorry," Cade said. "The clan leaders take threats to

the Sanctuary seriously. They didn't make the decision lightly. Your brothers and your sister are aware of the details, though. They have agreed to comply with Nyx's demands—they just asked that you and your brother and sister be notified. As of tonight, both your brothers are being taken to the Haven. That was Nyx's final demand—exchange them for the Source being restored to our home. I've got to head to the turul Enclave next to tell your brother and sister the same news."

"No," Aurum said with resignation, "we will go. I'd prefer to tell them myself. Please stay here if you have nowhere else to be. Someone needs to be here in case they return. You said it was just my brothers who were being taken to the Haven, right? So maybe there is still a chance for Numa to leave the Sanctuary."

"I expect the Sundance clan leader will release her tomorrow. She won't be allowed to leave the Sanctuary until spring, but I will stay and wait. And thank you for the offer. It's very much appreciated."

He glanced around the comfortable, high-ceilinged great room of the cabin. "That Eamon Stonetree and his brother certainly know their way around their tools," he marveled. "It's clear who built this place. For human men, they've done all right. I'll take care of the place as if it were my own."

Aurum thanked him and went to the kitchen to begin serving supper. She was anxious to get moving now, but knew better than to start a trip like the one ahead on an empty stomach. Nicholas and Calder might swear they could live on sex—it could certainly sustain all three of them for days at a time, and had since they'd arrived here—but a good, hearty meal could do every bit as much to sustain their morale.

Calder came up behind her and rested a hand at her waist. "Your brothers don't know what they're getting into," he said. "You saw what my mother did—she was dead set on killing Nicholas and would have imprisoned you for mating me."

Aurum set the roasting pan on top of the stove with a heavy thunk. "And what exactly are we supposed to do? We can't fix this from out here. I hate that we're so helpless. We should have stayed—"

"I know," Calder said. "I also know Assana will do everything she can to fix this."

Aurum chewed on her lip, recalling Calder's fierce and beautiful sister and all she'd done to help them be together. It also hadn't been lost on her that Gavra had come face to face with one of his fated mates, yet resisted the urge to be with her in favor of making sure Aurum and Calder reunited.

"She's the one escorting my brothers to the Haven, isn't she?" Aurum asked.

"If she still has Mother's trust, she's the only one who'd be allowed to."

"Then I think they'll be okay. If there's one thing I've learned recently, it's that my siblings and I are stronger when we're with our mates. As long as Gavra and your sister are together, I have to believe they'll win."

"Your brother's got both his mates now," Nicholas said, ambling over to the kitchen island and snagging a hot dinner roll from the basket that rested there.

"What do you mean?" Aurum asked.

"He said the guardians were called home. That means Silas is back in the Sanctuary."

"Who's Silas?" Calder asked.

"He's nobody," Aurum said, confused by Nicholas's mention of the handsome ursa who'd nearly blocked their way into the Sanctuary when they were on their quest to get to Calder.

Nicholas chuckled. "You thought he was *your* mate when

we met him. Just because he had black hair." He tugged at one of the black curls that jutted out on top of his messy head. "My hair hadn't turned yet," he said to Calder. "She was so desperate to find *me* she wasn't even looking past the color of his hair. Well, it turns out Silas actually belonged to her brother."

"How do you know?" Aurum asked, a stubborn blaze of defensiveness rising in her.

"Because I was paying attention." He shrugged. "And because he told me, otherwise I'd have ripped that fucker's head off for capturing your attention. Silas, I mean."

"Silas Rainsong?" Cade said, joining them at the edge of the kitchen. "He's going with them. Does he mean something to the dragons? Because I hear he's been chosen as Assana's mate and she refuses to leave the Sanctuary without him. Lucky bastard—there isn't a single male in the Sanctuary who hasn't hoped to catch her eye. As for me, I'd rather have an ursa female, if I can ever find a partner to help me entice one. I've always fancied dragons too, but nymphs are too crazy for my blood. I guess now that we're allowed to cross-breed I have more options … huh." His bearded face took on a dreamy look that continued as he happily sat down to supper with them.

Aurum didn't push the issue of Silas. As close as she was to her siblings, they all carried secrets from each other to some degree. It didn't surprise her that Gavra might have kept that detail from her—she hadn't exactly been in the most receptive frame of mind while they were in the Sanctuary.

She should be happy that he'd found them, though. And it did give her some comfort to know that he would be entering the Haven and the mad Nyx's clutches with both Assana and Silas by his side. With Aodh there to help, there may yet be hope for the Haven itself.

"All the more reason for us to find my father," Calder said. "If anyone can talk Mother off a ledge, it's him. As much as I've loved these days pretending the world outside doesn't exist, it's time we got back on track. The turul Enclave isn't my choice of places to start, but Nikhil still owes me. If Mother's getting worse, we need to not waste time finding my Thiasoi brothers and restoring balance in the Haven."

Aurum nodded. As loath as she was to barge in on her sister's reunion with Nikhil, she missed her siblings ferociously, and Calder was right. The Ultiori had been underground for months since Nikhil's defection. Calder and Nicholas were the last to come face to face with their leader herself, and none of the intelligence Nikhil had gathered gave them any clue where to find her again.

"Let's hope Nikhil is ready to go when we get there," Aurum said.

CHAPTER 12

NIKHIL

Turul Enclave, Southeastern United States

Nikhil was ready. Tight knots secured the ropes in expert coils around wrists and ankles. He glanced up at his bindings, marveling at the artistry that bound him to the heavy steel bar bolted to the beam above his head. After this initiation, he looked forward to spending time with Iszak and learning the turul prince's clever tricks to get the ropes to respond so beautifully.

Belah moved with graceful steps to stand in front of him, her beautiful smile making his heart stop. She'd changed out of her utilitarian winter clothes, the blue jeans and thick knit sweater replaced by a sheer gown of blue silk that clung to her curves.

Her smile widened at his open admiration, her long, dark lashes lowering as she raked her gaze down his body where it hung spread wide between the heavy log posts of the rustic apartment she shared with her mates in the turul Enclave.

"That should do it," a deep voice said behind him. "What next?"

Iszak rounded the post and came to stand before Belah, rubbing his hands together eagerly.

"A little candle wax, maybe?" Lukas said, moving into view with a thick candle held in one hand that he placed on a nearby table and lit. The entire apartment was lit entirely with candles now, the warm glow flickering over his lover's cheeks. She was flushed with excitement, and he recognized the familiar need in her eyes—it wasn't a need to dominate, but to be dominated, yet this was his day of atonement and she knew that.

"You'll bind her first, like this," Nikhil said, continuing the lesson that had begun not long after his arrival. "And when that's finished, you tease, with hands and teeth, then tools … a whip, a cane, a flail."

Belah's lips parted and he could tell she pictured herself where he was hanging, experiencing all the things he was teaching her mates to do while using himself as the test subject. But she was scheming too, and he suddenly didn't trust the mischievous glimmer in her eyes.

"But this is also about my pleasure, right?" she said. "I remember the first night I let you into my bed. The things I did to you, the things you endured so you would know that I am your mistress."

"You are my goddess," Nikhil corrected. "You proved it that day, and now I must prove to you again that I am your servant. That even when you are the one bound here in my place, what I do to you is to serve you."

"Ready him the way we discussed," Belah said. The two shirtless men beside her looked at him. Lukas's cock was hard beneath his jeans, his gaze filled with lust and longing Nikhil didn't quite understand. Iszak seemed more reticent. Despite the care he'd taken to bind Nikhil so perfectly, he wasn't aroused like his brother, and avoided looking directly at the naked man he'd just spent the last hour trussing up in the middle of his living room.

One thing Iszak couldn't hide was that, just like Lukas, he saw in Nikhil a piece of his mate, through his blood tie to Belah. The turul were strange creatures who knew their mates on sight, and apparently the fact that Nikhil had been on a steady, though minuscule, diet of Belah's blood for almost three thousand years made him irresistible to these two men.

It would be tricky to get used to, but they were a part of her now as much as he was, so he would adapt.

Lukas moved first, more eager than his brother. He produced a small object and held it up in front of Nikhil's face. Nikhil grimaced at the sight of the familiar circle of leather. Likely not the exact same cock ring she'd used on him so long ago, but it was definitely a well-known contraption.

"Better get this on before you get excited," Lukas said. Nikhil felt a hand drift to his dick, cup his balls, and caress in a not unpleasant stroke. He kept his eyes on Belah, though, still absorbing the crazy idea that to prove his loyalty and love to her, he would have to submit to her new pets.

Not pets. They're her mates. They bear her mark and you do not, and they are both adept at dominance, even if they're not as skilled as you are at inflicting pain.

"Lukas, stop," Belah said softly, seeming to read the lack of readiness in Nikhil's eyes.

The longer-haired brother released him. Iszak hadn't yet begun his part of the preparations, for which Nikhil was grateful, because he'd caught a glimpse of the shining, oblong shape Iszak had taken from Belah's treasure chest of toys.

"The man has the most spectacular cock," Lukas murmured, stepping back. "I definitely see the allure in being topped by him."

"Our bond was deeper than physical—our relationship more complex than who dominated and who submitted," Belah said. "I needed something then that only Nikhil could give me. He's here to teach you two to give me those things too, but I need to set some boundaries first. Nikhil, are you sure you don't want a safe word?"

He chuckled and raised a brow at the two men. "With these two? I doubt they can do anything I can't handle. I am at your mercy, *'Iilahatan*, remember? It would take your fire to hurt me, but even that I would accept with relish because I know you do it with love. The only hard limit I have is that you promise I am yours always after this. That you mark me to make it so."

"Remember my vow," she said softly.

Nikhil nodded. "I know you can't take pleasure from me until they allow you to, but once they see what pleasure I can give without even touching you, surely they would release you from that promise."

"That's the idea," Iszak said. "We're doing this for her, and for our child. She needs you, but we still need to make things square. You were our enemy. You were *her* enemy, until very recently. Even though my heart says otherwise now, you must make amends."

Nikhil met the man's gaze and saw an even deeper struggle than he had inside himself. He was mercenary enough to enjoy what they did to him for Belah's sake, because he knew it would only happen once. Iszak, however, could not fight his nature. Nikhil pitied him for that. In Iszak's eyes he saw the same deep, driving need he felt himself when he looked at Belah, but Iszak wasn't accustomed to feeling that way for another man.

They were kindred spirits, he and Iszak—they craved dominance and harbored a darkness in them that would frighten the weak-minded who discovered it.

Lukas, on the other hand, was beside himself with eagerness to move things along. He was like Nikhil in the way he enjoyed the spectacle of an undertaking like Nikhil enjoyed giving commands on the battlefield, witnessing the glorious destruction that ensued when a carefully crafted plan was carried out.

Lukas was the one who loved to watch his partner's reactions to little tortures he inflicted on them, both pain and pleasure combined in one delicious mixture. He would be the one to tease Belah with the surface tortures, things that never went beneath the skin. These were the things that primed her for deeper hurt—the things Nikhil was best at, and things he suspected Iszak was too.

Iszak was the sadist of the pair, the one who got off on simply inflicting pain. He needed to express his dark cravings the way Belah needed to find oblivion.

Nikhil both needed and enjoyed it all in equal measure. The trick today was to get Iszak to enjoy it more than he needed it.

Nikhil ignored Lukas and focused on Iszak. "What does your heart tell you?"

"That I must make you mine. That my domination of her is incomplete until you cry in both pain and pleasure beneath my hand, and until you take my breath and give me yours."

"I am Belah, Iszak. We are one flesh. Belah and I were wed more than three thousand years ago. We were bound together by magic in all but one way. I don't bear her mark on my skin the way you do. You are also one with her … that mark makes it so, and if I were the one in command of the ropes and whips today, I would own your body the way I have owned hers so many times."

Iszak licked his lips and stared down at the floor, then looked at the oblong shape in his hand. He tossed the shining dildo aside and it clattered into the open chest nearby.

Nikhil's ass relaxed until Iszak unfastened his jeans and slipped them down his thighs, bending to step out of them. When he stood again, his cock hung thick, but flaccid.

"I don't need toys to own you," Iszak said.

The look in Iszak's eyes made Nikhil feel like he was looking in the mirror the day of a battle. Nikhil would have kept his sword sheathed too, not brandishing it the way Lukas casually flaunted his own hard-on by occasionally stroking it through his jeans. That cocky display didn't scare Nikhil nearly as much as the utter disinterest Iszak seemed to show by standing naked in front of him with a potentially lethal weapon that was nowhere close to ready to fight with —as though he knew he'd be ready the very second he needed to.

Nikhil pulled at his bindings, pulse racing. Then he realized his mistake, but it was too late. Iszak's gaze shot to his struggling limbs and he smiled.

The one thing you didn't do when faced with an opponent as sadistic as a man like Nikhil was show fear. Iszak's honest response to Nikhil's question had abolished whatever hesitance the man had left in him, and Nikhil hadn't been prepared for how quickly Iszak would recover.

The heady scent of virile male hit his nostrils when Iszak moved close. Heat radiated off his naked body, Nikhil's own limp cock a sure sign of how little he was looking forward to what must happen next. He squeezed his eyes shut, aware that somehow he had failed Belah in this weakness.

There was a time when he could only become aroused if he were able to arouse another. A curse that had lasted for ages, but had only mattered recently when he'd been reunited with Belah. Now the curse was gone, but he'd yet to test his body's functions in earnest. Seeing Belah would normally be enough, but being bound and manhandled hadn't done him any favors in the hard-on department.

Iszak's skin was flushed when he stepped close enough for Nikhil to see the smoky magic emanating from the glowing blue dragon mark on his neck. The other man gripped his hips and brushed his mouth at Nikhil's ear.

"If you are her flesh, then what would turn you on the most right now?"

Nikhil's hair stood on end when Iszak's breath tickled his neck. He looked over Iszak's shoulder, his eyes meeting Belah's. She had her hand on Lukas's arm, holding him back while his brother broke the ice.

"Tell him, Nikhil," she said softly. "You know what you would do to me if I were in your place and you had no toys at your disposal."

This wasn't working.

The act of being tied would turn her on enough to start with, and Nikhil definitely wasn't responding to the ropes. But he had once. The first time they'd been together, she'd had him bound and left to hang for an hour in her room before coming to him, tormenting him with her toys, then fucking him.

She'd been so perfect that night—proving to him how easily she could overpower him if she chose, yet she was willing to submit to him in the end. The perfect woman was the one who offered him that challenge, who was a beast worth taming. Would Iszak offer him a challenge too? Would Lukas? Could he see the pair of them as extensions of her, worth subduing the way they viewed him?

"Show me your worst, *boy*," Nikhil taunted.

Iszak's head snapped back as though he'd been punched, his eyes flashing with rage at the word ... the epithet ... Nikhil had used.

CHAPTER 13

NIKHIL

Iszak's hand shot to the back of Nikhil's head, fingers twisting in his hair and yanking his head back savagely.

"I am not your *boy*," Iszak snarled. Outside the room, lightning bolts shattered through the night and thunder rolled. Nikhil's skin prickled, every hair standing on end with the crackle of static electricity.

Iszak's breath was a hot gust against his neck, filled with fiery heat just before his teeth sank hard into Nikhil's flesh. Nails as sharp as talons clawed down Nikhil's chest.

His head immobilized, he couldn't look, but his belly tightened with apprehension when the sharp points of Iszak's fingers paused at the top of his groin.

Nikhil's skin was as impervious as a dragon's, but he still felt pain, and the line Iszak made around his cock and down his thigh seared him with hot agony. He held his breath, struggling to hold back a reaction, but to no avail. When the pointed talon jabbed hard into the sensitive area at the juncture of his hip and groin, his entire body bucked and he gritted his teeth to suppress the cry welling inside him.

Blinding lightning split the sky outside and torrential rain battered the windows, wind howling and forcing the drops in sheets so hard the frames rattled.

A low groan rumbled up from Iszak's chest. The teeth still gripping Nikhil's flesh relaxed a touch, his hot, wet tongue darting out to taste. The contact was intimate and almost tender, though the talons continued to claw at Nikhil's skin, continued their relentless burn into his nerves.

Iszak released Nikhil's head, raking the talons of that hand over his shoulder. He raised his head and met Nikhil's gaze.

"You do feel pain now, don't you? Isn't it a beautiful thing? I can give you more …"

The wild look in his eyes made Nikhil realize that Iszak had abandoned the idea of giving pleasure and was completely lost in his own world now. This was a man who could truly and completely please his *Tilahatan*, so why was she still unsatisfied?

He glanced past his torturer at Belah, who watched with rapt interest, her own breathing rushed. She looked just as surprised as he was that this creature existed inside her mate. What else could he draw from her men with just his words?

Nikhil swallowed another cry as a fresh slice of pain shattered his focus, bringing it back to a point in front of him. Iszak' raked his hand up his belly and Nikhil stared down at the sharp, gleaming curves of his talons, so like a dragon's, yet so different. Those talons were meant for capturing and holding prey while their owner ripped its throat out.

Nikhil was suddenly positive that if Iszak could draw blood, he would. But something else was happening. The previous repulsion he'd seen in Iszak's eyes had changed, and when he felt the hot, silken rod of flesh brush against his inner thigh, the jolt of understanding left him reeling.

Iszak may enjoy tying Belah up, but for some reason, had

never inflicted this kind of pain on her before. And this was what he truly loved, down to the core of his being. Nikhil's awareness spiked, his body responding to the arousal of the other man. His taunt had forced Iszak's beast to show itself, to find its pleasure in Nikhil's pain, and that power drove Nikhil wild. His arousal surged, the unwanted flood of lust filling him.

He yanked at the bindings again, desperation coursing through his limbs. The storm battering outside the windows mirrored his need to escape, to regain the upper hand somehow—over Iszak or over his own traitorous body, he wasn't sure.

Iszak let out a rumbling laugh that halted Nikhil's struggles. "You won't break free of these ropes. Belah couldn't either when I used them on her. Now it looks like we found some common ground, finally. What should we do, hmm?"

He kept his gaze fixed on Nikhil's, but his pointed fingertips dug into Nikhil's hips and pulled him tight. Their erections pressed together and Nikhil grunted in unexpected pleasure.

"I'm beginning to realize that just getting you into this state is torture enough, which is the hottest goddamn thing I've ever seen. Almost makes it feel *right* for me to do this. Who knew I'd enjoy turning on another man, but only if I knew he hated the idea of it. What changed?"

Iszak's rough touch shifted, his hands moving down between them until they brushed Nikhil's inner thighs. The poking talons grazed Nikhil's balls, making him flinch, but the ensuing caress made his erection pulse with pleasure. With his other hand, Iszak raked the tip of a talon along the underside of Nikhil's hard length. He tensed with hyper-awareness of the sharp point against his delicate flesh. It didn't help to remind himself that Iszak couldn't pierce his skin—he still wasn't the least bit interested in feeling pain *there*.

"Please, no," Nikhil said, hating the sound of his own plaintive voice. He was not a man who begged.

"Tell me what changed, Nikhil. What did I do to be blessed with *this*?" He wrapped a hand around Nikhil's hard cock and stroked. Nikhil's eyelids fluttered closed, his body rocking into the other man's touch. What he saw now in Iszak's eyes was the thing he so often felt when torturing a prisoner … he was nothing but a piece of meat to this man. A thing to provoke a reaction from, and Nikhil was most certainly reacting.

"You took my bait," Nikhil croaked. He forced himself to remember that this was all for Belah, that Iszak had needed a push, and what he endured now was exactly the reaction he'd been going for.

"I think you hate how good this feels more than I do," Iszak murmured. His stroking sped up and Nikhil groaned, for the first time grateful for the ropes holding him up because he might have collapsed from the pleasure. "This is what gets my blood hottest, you know. Not the way my talons dug into you and made you hurt, but the fact that getting you worked up like this causes you so much pain. Did you know Belah's submission happened like this? Not exactly, of course, but we didn't need to lay a finger on her to break her."

He took a step back, releasing Nikhil from the torturous, unwanted pleasure. Nikhil opened his eyes to see Iszak clutching his own cock and slowly stroking it. The distance was just far enough for him to feel the other man's heat, yet not the touch of his skin as his knuckles pistoned over his length.

"You withheld your Nirvana from her," Nikhil said, finally understanding the complexity of Iszak's sadism. It was about more than just physical pain for the man. He felt a surge of respect that was accompanied by curiosity. How far would he go? And was Nikhil willing to endure seeing this to the end?

Not that he had a choice, so he may as well enjoy it. His cock agreed, involuntarily twitching.

The reflex wasn't lost on Iszak, who smiled at him, then turned to his brother. "Bring that candle over, Luke," he said. "Then you're on his six."

On my six. Nikhil blinked at the phrase and glanced between the pair, scrutinizing them more closely. He'd spent almost no time with these two, but he should have noticed by their bearing that they had military training. That knowledge suddenly made all the pieces click into place and he cursed himself for not choosing a safe word. Not because he couldn't endure their torture, but knowing more of who these men were reminded him of his mission, and he couldn't discount the significance of their training to his larger goal. If there was one thing he'd learned over the centuries, it was that Fate had some twisted schemes when it came to showing people their destinies, and to throwing them together with exactly the partners they were best suited for.

If anyone could break him, they could.

He couldn't stop now, though, and the presence of the lit candle now hovering over his hard cock wasn't going to stop him from following through on this promise. Iszak held the thick column of wax with one hand and gripped the head of Nikhil's cock with his fingertips, angling him parallel to the floor.

Lukas slipped behind him and he heard the subtle zip and rustle as the other man slipped out of his jeans before sidling up to Nikhil's back. His skin prickled with an odd tickle, and he heard a distinct crackling sound and jumped when the sharp sting of electricity hit his spine between his shoulder blades.

Lukas chuckled and slid his hands around Nikhil's chest, splaying his fingers before circling his nipples with little caresses. Except they weren't caresses so much as a means to torture him more. He tensed as another charge of electricity hit his nipples and glanced down to see bright, silvery arcs jumping from Lukas's fingertips into his skin.

"It's not that bad, is it?" Lukas purred behind him, shifting closer until Nikhil could feel the other man's erect cock resting full length against the cleft between his cheeks. "I *could* make it hurt, but I'm pretty sure what you feel now is just surprise. Close your eyes and let it happen, Nik."

Close his eyes and let it *happen*? Fuck. Where was Belah? He hoped she was enjoying this. He glanced away from the flickering candle that Iszak threatened him with and found her lounging opposite him in a huge armchair beside the roaring fire. This was all just a show to her, but the look in her eyes reminded him how much she wanted what he was receiving. Oh, the things he would do to her once he was allowed to give her pleasure again.

Lukas's electrified touch trailed up and down his torso, tickling over his hips, up his spine. The first few times the energy zapped him, he reacted with surprise, but soon had to agree that it didn't hurt. What would hurt was what Iszak seemed intent on doing to him. He was apparently waiting for enough wax to pool in the bowl around the wick, but while he did, his hand trailed a maddening caress up and down the length of Nikhil's cock.

"Just fucking do it," Nikhil growled.

"Waiting for Lukas to tell me you're ready," Iszak said, his gaze flashing.

What the hell did Lukas have to do with it? The sudden

invasion of cool liquid seeping between his clenched ass cheeks made him curse.

"Fuck!" he yelled, then bit his tongue. No weakness, for fuck's sake. Don't show them weakness. Lukas laughed, his face close to Nikhil's ear. Then he brushed his lips down Nikhil's neck and lightly bit his shoulder while spreading Nikhil's ass apart and probing with his fingers.

"How humiliating would it be to get fucked by another man in front of her? Do you think the enjoyment will be worth the humiliation? If it makes you feel better, I'll be happy to give you a chance with my ass later." Lukas's slippery fingers pressed against his hole and Nikhil forced himself to relax.

He'd been down this road before, but only once in his life. Belah was the only other person he'd allowed to become so intimately acquainted with his body. He fixed his gaze on her, ignoring everything else but the rise and fall of her beautiful, creamy bosom and the way her nipples strained against the silk of her gown. She was leaning back in the chair, her arms resting on the sides, her fingers clutching at the armrests, every bit the poised queen he remembered. He wondered if she had silices wrapped around her thighs beneath that gown, digging into her flesh to keep her in that constant state of pain and pleasure she loved so much. He couldn't tell from here. Her knees were demurely pressed together and her feet on the floor, but she shifted ever so slightly as though either uncomfortable or highly aroused.

He wouldn't engage her more than that look—he didn't want to encourage the men to torture him any more than necessary, but he begged with his eyes for something more from her to help temper what was happening.

'Lukas pushed his fingers into Nikhil and he let out a soft grunt of surprise. Belah's gaze darkened and she licked her lips.

You wish you were the one torturing me, don't you, my love? Or that I was torturing you, he thought to himself, but thoughts soon abandoned him in favor of sensation when Lukas twisted his slick fingers and pushed against the core of Nikhil's pleasure. His entire body tensed and an involuntary groan escaped his lips. His cock pulsed hotly in Iszak's grip.

"Now," Lukas said.

Nikhil's mind was clouded with pleasure, his entire body tingling from the delicious pressure of those fingers on that perfect spot inside his ass. The fingers disappeared from both front and back for a split-second, and Nikhil had the strangest sense he'd entirely lost touch. Then something hot and thick pressed against his tender opening, Lukas's fingers dug into his hips, and his lips brushed at his ear.

"I think you're hot enough for it now," Lukas said as he held him tight and pushed his cock in deep.

At the same moment, Iszak's rough grip tightened around the head of his cock and molten heat charged up the length. Nikhil bucked and cried out, though he was confused where the pain ended and the pleasure began. The heat that coated his cock tightened the skin, flooding him with fresh sensation. Lukas's cock stretched his ass, the burning sensation just as painful as the wax on his cock, but as he thrust in, he hit that unbearably glorious pleasure spot with just enough pressure to make Nikhil's entire body sing.

Nikhil grasped at the ropes above him. Even though he was bound, he felt like he was losing himself, falling, or flying—he couldn't be sure which. His pleasure intensified when Iszak tipped the candle a second time, trickling a fresh trail of pale molten wax up along his throbbing length.

He threw his head back with a groan. His mind reeled and he tried to cling to his identity, but lost even his small connection to that.

"That's right, give it up. You're ours now," Iszak said,

coating his cock in yet another layer of wax, but the previous layers protected him and all he felt was tight heat as the coating hardened and clung to his sensitive skin. His cock was hotter and harder than he'd ever imagined, pleasure straining under the surface.

Iszak disappeared for a second to set the candle down and pick up a small bottle. With Lukas still fucking Nikhil with slow, deliberate strokes, he didn't have the presence of mind to put a thought together. He wasn't coherent enough to ask or even wonder what Iszak was going to do next, but none of the previous maliciousness was present in the man's eyes. All Nikhil could see was pure, raw lust and that constant need both men had when they looked at either him or Belah.

Iszak bent over and blew along the length of Nikhil's cock and he felt the wax harden further until his entire cock felt encased in ice. The heat dissipated quickly, the pain he'd expected to linger nonexistent. Then Iszak wrapped his hand around it and squeezed. The wax crackled and fell away in crumbles, leaving his skin fully exposed to Iszak's continued breath.

Iszak held Nikhil's cock cradled in one hand while he tipped the bottle above it. Nikhil braced himself for more discomfort, but only felt warm liquid as the scent of jasmine hit his nostrils, making him groan. Belah's favorite oil to use during sex—he'd recognize that smell anywhere.

One long, slow stroke of Iszak's hand and Nikhil lost all sense of gravity. His mind spun with the room around him. Soft lips found his and he latched on, grateful for the kiss to ground him. Iszak's strong body pressed against his, his hand moving and pressing Nikhil's cock against his own, wrapping his hand around them both together.

The sensation made him balk and try to twist, but there was nowhere to go. Iszak let out an admonishing rumble and squeezed their dicks tighter together, threaded his other hand into Nikhil's hair again, and gripped tightly. He pulled Nikhil into his kiss. Teeth grazed his lips once then bit down hard.

"Fuck!" Nikhil yelled, pain lancing through him as brightly as the pleasure that invaded his entire body from front to back. He glared at Iszak, who merely gave him a sardonic smile before leaning in and taking his mouth again, just as fiercely, but less violent now while his hand continued to pump their cocks together.

Nikhil kissed him back, the rising pleasure overtaking him with need for a deeper connection. At his back, Lukas's breath gusted over his neck and sharp, tickling shocks skittered over his sides where Lukas clutched at his hips and waist while he fucked him.

He was lost. Completely and utterly lost, but regretted nothing because this was all for her. And when the pleasure inundated him completely to the point that he no longer knew where he ended and these other men began, she was there.

His body shuddered as he surrendered to the pounding invasion and the rough stroking from both Belah's mates. The sensations flooded his body until he burst from them, and she was there, her soft lips against his cheek, her gentle hands sliding up his arm and her fingers twining with his as the power of the climax charged through him.

Iszak released his mouth out of reflex as his orgasm took hold. Both men groaned and bucked against him, their semen flooding his ass and coating his belly in turn, but all Nikhil cared about was the pair of blue eyes that met his.

"I am your beast to tame, my love, my master," Belah whispered, then kissed him softly on his bruised lips.

CHAPTER 14

GAVRA

Gavra would've bent over and invited Silas to fuck him if it meant being able to touch Assana. Her distance was pure torture, but her erratic aura was enough to remind him how tenuous her control over her sanity was. They stood at the edge of the dry lake bed, waiting for midnight to arrive. Assana's scent filled his mind, though there was the cushion of Silas and Aodh separating them.

He tried to focus on their task, pulling his brother away to discuss the details. Aodh followed, his expression dark, his jaw tense.

"This isn't what you planned, brother, but we have to make the most of it. Nikhil can't help us yet."

"I don't trust Nyx," Aodh said. "Especially without Neph in the Haven to temper her wild moods and Nereus gone as well. If she's as mad as Assana says, this won't be easy."

Gavra feigned a good-natured smile. "Try to look on the bright side. She wants us to service hundreds of nymphs. In our prime, we would have jumped at the chance."

Aodh's expression darkened further, his pale brows

drawing together. "She wants us to *impregnate* them, brother. You know that means we must mate them. And we have no idea whether any of these females are even willing. Assana is convinced that her mother has mind-controlled the Thiasoi maidens. How do we know she hasn't done the same to all the nymphs? She's had time."

Gavra's false cheer fell away. He sighed and glanced at the depressing, muddy pit beside them.

"She's had thousands of years to get over hating you. You'd think she would have forgiven you by now."

"I think it stopped being about Neph and Meri a long time ago. If she's willing to trust me to come to the Haven now, even under duress, perhaps she doesn't hate me as much as she used to. I have to believe that the friend she once was still exists. The woman who once encouraged me and Neph to be together—to choose a female for our third so we could. I just wish we'd chosen more wisely."

"You couldn't have known that Meri would become the Lamia. If we fix this, at least you'll get another chance. But I don't want to waste time once we're in the Haven." Gavra's gaze shifted to Assana, who had been facing him, but swiftly turned away and into Silas's embrace. "I can't let this go on any longer than it has to."

Aodh followed his gaze and nodded. "She's her mother's daughter. They were always powerful nymphs and determined to protect what's theirs, but that level of power comes with a price. It's good that you have Silas as a buffer. I'm fortunate that Vrishti is my fated mate—I think Neph and I would implode if it were just the two of us … though maybe he's changed after all this time."

Aodh quieted, his gaze growing distant, wistful.

"He'll return," Gavra said. "He cares for the Haven and his family as strongly as his sister does. He wouldn't leave it vulnerable by choice."

"He did it for us," Aodh said, his voice catching. "For our sister."

"And his nephew."

"He did it for Nicholas," Assana said. Gavra's body heated at the sound of her voice, closer now and with no barrier between them.

He looked at her, closing his hands into fists lest he reach out to touch her. All he needed to do was lift a hand and he could reach her skin, as close as she stood. He swallowed and his brows twitched as he forced himself to focus on what she'd said.

"Nicholas?"

Assana gave him a half-shrug. "Your sister and my brother weren't the ones in danger. Mother would never hurt Calder. Aurum could've survived anything Mother threw at her. She knew who was the most vulnerable of the three … Nicholas was her target when she sent the Thiasoi after them. She would have had him killed if it hadn't been for my uncle drifting them all away at the last second."

"And she would have started a war with the ursa had she done so," Gavra said.

"I don't think she understood how important he is to everyone. All she knew was that he was instrumental in taking Calder away from his duty to the Haven … at least as Mother perceived it."

Gavra snorted. "So now Aurum's brothers get to take his place. I suppose it's a fair trade, if you look at it that way."

Assana's sharp intake of breath sobered him. This was no laughing matter.

"I'm sorry," he said, impulsively reaching out to her before dropping his hand by his side again and gritting his teeth. Sweet Mother, he wanted to touch her, to comfort her.

Assana shook her head, her whirlpool eyes glassy with emotion. She took a small step closer to him and Silas shifted with her, as though guarding her safety with his body.

She reached out and took Gavra's hand, her touch sending a spark of profound longing through him. Her skin was cool and silken, but when she drew his hand to her lips and kissed his knuckles, he met warm, soft flesh. Then she turned his hand palm-up to press it to her cheek and let out a shaky moan as she leaned into his touch. He shivered with the pleasure of that simple touch, barely containing the need to pull her against him. She contained her madness well, proving how strong she was, but her aura didn't lie. She was hanging on by a thread.

"The idea of you with anyone else makes me ill," she said in a brittle tone. "But if this is something you want … something it would please you to do, I understand. You can't deny your own needs for my sake."

"Assana, I don't *need* to fuck another woman. I haven't since the day I found you. And if I'm being completely honest, the last person I fucked was Silas. I hope you don't have any issue with that, because he's all we have."

Silas gave him a withering glare. "Are you regretting the moment we shared earlier?"

Assana shook her head, cutting off any response Gavra might have had. "I'm not talking about Silas. He's the only way I can stay sane around you, Gavra. Without him, I couldn't go through with this."

"But you'd be my wild nymph without him," Gavra said.

"You know it's more complicated than that," she said. "And *I* know how much you want him, too. I just need to know what else you want … if it's a female you crave, I can't be yours yet, but the others will be happy to bed you and I can't stop that."

With a growl, he slipped his hand away from her cheek to the back of her neck and pulled her close, wrapping his arms around her. She shivered against him, her aura flaring as she looked up into his eyes.

"You're the only female in the fucking universe I want, Assana," he said. She pressed her hands to his shoulders and tilted her head back. Her eyes were feral and fearful and on the verge of panic. Despite that, her body melted to his and her pelvis pressed hard against his growing arousal.

"Gavra ..." Silas warned. The large ursa stepped closer and rested both hands on Assana's upper arms, ready to pull her away.

Gavra was playing with fire. Despite the fierce control he kept on his powers, his desire for her was innate and something he couldn't fully deny. Assana responded to that pull as surely as iron filings to a magnet, but her entire body was charged with a desire even stronger than his and her restraint was wavering with every second he held her.

Still, he bent his head, reflexively needing a taste, just one small kiss. She let out a soft moan when his lips brushed hers and her fingertips dug hard into his muscles—partly clawing to get closer and partly pushing to get away. The way her body twisted in his arms was a maddening contradiction, as though she were split, but he couldn't get enough, even after that soft kiss.

He groaned and held her tighter, brushing his mouth down her neck and shifting his hands lower, seeking to cup her ass and pull her even tighter against his erection.

"The fuck, man, let go of her!" Silas said. He clasped Gavra's shoulder with one large hand and pushed. "She can't deal with you, all right?"

Something in the ursa's touch snapped his control back into place. Abruptly, Gavra let go of Assana and she twisted back into Silas's arms, burying her face against his neck and wrapping her hands around his shoulders, gasping for breath as though she'd nearly drowned.

Gavra stumbled back, shaking his head, and his brother was there with a strong arm to steady him.

"Give it time," Aodh said. "I'm here to help. We'll get her mother under control and then you can be together. I promise."

Shaking himself, Gavra turned away. He didn't know how he would manage this trip. The only female he wanted, he couldn't have until this was fixed. He stared up at the sky, impatient for midnight to arrive. They couldn't fucking get there soon enough for his taste.

Only a few moments later, the air grew thick with damp mist that seemed to coalesce from nowhere. The dark pit of the empty lake seemed to shimmer with rippling liquid and was suddenly filled with water once more, the sound of it first a tinkling trickle, then a rush, then a roaring flood again as Gaia's falls resumed flowing.

"It's time," Assana said, but Gavra was already running toward the edge and leaping over. The chilly water of the falls did nothing to cool his burning need for her.

CHAPTER 15

AURUM

The moment Aurum flew past the shimmering barrier protecting the turul Enclave, she reached out with her mind, broadcasting her arrival to her siblings. Nicholas clung to her back like his life depended on it, though he hadn't gotten airsick, which was some consolation. He wasn't possessed by the same crippling fear of flying he had been when they met, but he still didn't love being in mid-air if he could help it.

Calder flew beside her, having taken the shape of a huge, graceful water bird with long legs and pristine white feathers. He was completely unsuited for the gusting winds of the blizzard they'd flown through to reach this mountainside hideaway where the North American turul had retreated.

The fierce winds and snow had broken abruptly and the air was still chilly but calm, though eddies of cold wind tickled beneath Aurum's wings, reminding her how flirtatious the North Wind could be. He whispered in her ear as she flew toward the Enclave, speaking of ancient dalliances they'd had when she was young, but it had always been her sisters the Winds loved the most.

"Welcome, sister." Her brother Ked's deep voice reverberated in her mind, filled with more happiness than she'd ever heard. She banked abruptly, causing Calder to squawk in annoyance and Nicholas to curse from her back, his legs tightening around her flanks.

She craned her head around, looking for the source of the voice.

"West entrance," Ked said. *"Look for the three of us."*

She turned, flying around the massive mountain peak covered in platforms and scaffolding and huge stone buttresses that had been haphazardly built on over the centuries. It all looked like some strange, misshapen beast that had grown organically out of the mountainside, half the posts of the buildings having rooted and grown branches covered with deep green needles.

Finally she saw them, standing at the edge of a sturdy wooden deck. The two big men waved, and the petite woman between them beamed and bounced excitedly.

She shifted as she landed, conjuring warm clothing for Calder first, who was far more sensitive to the elements than she was. Nicholas had dressed before they left and carried an overstuffed pack filled with necessities that Aurum wouldn't be able to conjure on the fly.

Once dressed, she rushed into her brother's arms, hugging him fiercely.

"What the hell happened to you?" she demanded, pulling back and staring up into his mirthful gaze. "Who are you, and what have you done with my brother?"

Ked laughed. "I could say the same to you, sister. Had I known these two were yours, I'd have brought them out kicking and screaming that night I saved Evie."

Calder and Nicholas flanked her, each man reaching to accept one of Ked's proffered arms and grasping firmly in greeting.

"You know we wouldn't have gone," Calder said. "Evie needed you more than we did. Besides, you did come back, and for that we're grateful."

Evie squealed and rushed into Aurum's embrace. "I'm so happy for you!" she said. "I love that your dreams came true. And didn't I tell you? There were two! I knew it!"

Russet-haired Marcus stood back from the group, smiling, though wary. Aurum had only known him from the point of Ked's rescue more than a month ago, but was aware that he had a much longer, more complicated history with her two mates.

"Marcus," Calder said, breaking the silence that lingered between them once Ked and Evie had completed their greetings. "You look well."

Marcus's green eyes studied the satyr for a moment before he nodded. "Now that I'm clear of him, I am."

Aurum frowned, sensing a deeper, lingering hurt in the man that didn't seem to exist in either of his mates. Evie gripped Marcus's hand and looked up at him, her gaze filled with love and concern.

"You know Nikhil's at the Enclave now, don't you?" she asked.

Marcus nodded and pressed his lips together. "I know."

"My sister's forgiven him," Aurum said gently. Marcus only responded with a pained look.

"You don't understand. The man was in control of my mind for fifty years. Even knowing he was as much a victim as I was doesn't make it any easier to face him. Evie's forgiven him too. Ked's seen all his secrets and has no issues anymore. I didn't have the luxury of a one-on-one with him to help me get over it. He was the man who forced me to be a monster for five decades."

Nicholas finally moved, stepping toward Marcus and holding out his hands. "You and the other Elites were always good men," he said. "It wasn't lost on us that you were forced into the role."

Marcus stared at Nicholas for a moment, blinking in confusion as he took in the big ursa's black, shoulder-length waves and dark beard. The last time Nicholas was in the Ultiori compound, his coloring had been drastically different. Finally Marcus's eyes widened, and he let out a loud laugh.

"Nick? Holy shit, is it really you? Oh my god, man. This is …" He paused, dumbstruck, then reached out and pulled Nicholas into a tight hug. "You made it out. How's the real world treating you?"

"Ah, aside from the lingering fear of falling into the sky, pretty damn great. Except I almost got skewered by nymphs a few days ago … and Nikhil's our best hope to fix things. We need his help, and yours, if you can."

"I'll think about it," Marcus said, glancing back at Evie and Ked. "It's not really a good time to leave."

"You can still drift," Calder said. "That ability in itself is valuable enough to give us an advantage. With you and the other Elites and Nikhil, we can go places the Ultiori will least expect. We can find where they're keeping my father and the rest of our Thiasoi squadron. Please think about it."

"Come inside and rest," Ked said. "We can talk more by the fire while we eat. Perhaps my sister will even honor us with one of her famous meals."

"Where is Belah? She didn't respond to my call when we passed the barrier," Aurum said to her brother as he led them into an expansive apartment that reminded her of her home in the Glade. Her eyes drifted around the comfortable interior, lingering on the polished stone floors and counters of a kitchen that even had modern appliances installed. The turul had always been more immersed in human culture than the other higher races. She took a step toward it, itching to get her hands on the goods as she turned back with an expectant look at her brother.

Ked's mouth twitched. "She's a bit tied up at the moment," he said.

Aurum rolled her eyes and sent her sister a mental message. *"Any time you'd like to come and say hello ..."*

"I just got the love of my life back, sister. Don't rush me," came the impatient reply.

"Fine. When you are done working up an appetite, come to Ked's apartment. I'm making dinner."

There was a pause, and then Belah answered eagerly, *"We'll be there."*

CHAPTER 16

NIKHIL

Nikhil's wrists ached despite the fact that the skin hadn't been broken. When Iszak unbound him, he managed to support himself and was grateful that the two men stood back and let him stand on his own. He struggled to stay upright, though, and Belah slid in and wrapped her arm around his waist, her warm curves a welcome presence after her mates' rough treatment.

She led him past the fireplace and through a doorway back into the mountainside. Despite the wood paneling and hanging tapestries, he saw dark granite through the gaps, betraying that this entire Enclave was built right into the rock.

After a few steps they reached a cozy room lit with candles and filled with a moist heat that smelled just like her.

He let out a low groan of gratitude when she led him down into a wide, recessed tub filled with hot water.

"Do you need my breath?" she asked in a worried tone. The truth was Nikhil felt a profound sense of wellbeing now as he sank deeper into the water. Belah descended beside him, her silk gown dissolving as she went, and urged him to immerse himself to the shoulders.

"No, little beast. My conscience is the clearest it's been in a very, *very* long time." Glancing at the doorway, he saw her two mates standing just beyond in the shadows. "Thank you," he said to them.

Lukas smiled, but Iszak averted his gaze. The sadistic brother's dark brows twitched with some inner conflict before he looked up again, meeting Nikhil's eyes directly.

"I think I need to thank you," Iszak said. "I know what was missing now. What was holding me back. I forget sometimes how strong she is … it always felt wrong to take things that far. She's the mother of our child …"

He trailed off as Belah slid onto the bench behind Nikhil and poured fragrant soap onto his shoulders.

"I'm also immortal," she said, looking over at her mates while skillfully working the soap across Nikhil's shoulders, digging into his abused muscles in a way that provided both pain and the best kind of pleasure.

Nikhil let out a long groan and tilted his head back against her bare shoulder.

"She's always been the one in command," he said, watching the other two men through low-lidded eyes. "The moment I understood her desires fully, it freed me to be what she needed. You both need to trust that she needs you as you are, and I mean as you *truly* are. Don't hide from your darkness. Give it to her."

The pair of them came farther into the room, but Nikhil was too drunk from Belah's expert touch to object to their nearness again. He wasn't bound by ropes this time; now he was held prisoner by the hypnotic working of her thumbs into his muscles and the slide of her thighs at his sides under the water.

He'd missed this, though in the past, their roles had been

reversed—she'd been the submissive having her recent hurts eased by his gentle touch.

The tub was barely large enough for all four of them, the water sloshing over the edge when both Iszak and Lukas slid in. Nikhil found he didn't mind the intimate quarters now—he knew he could leave if he chose, but being here meant so much more at the moment. He didn't mind when each man took one of his feet and began massaging the sore skin of his ankles where the ropes had dug in.

Lying there in the heat of the water, hearing Belah's murmur of approval in response to two pairs of hands moving up his thighs, he understood what it meant to be here, what it meant to her and to these two men she called mates. He and Belah were one flesh, and the swirling storms in her mates' eyes proved to him again that they saw him as an extension of her, sought to please him as much as they sought to please her.

He closed his eyes and let out a sigh of pure pleasure when one large hand wrapped around his cock and another cupped his balls. Their bodies bracketed him and Belah in the water, a pair of lips pressed against the corner of his mouth and he turned, accepting Lukas's kiss as they both began to stroke. Just behind him, Belah let out a soft moan, a sound she only ever made when she kissed him, and he knew without looking that Iszak was kissing her.

Lukas broke the kiss just enough to whisper words in an ancient language that Nikhil struggled to place, but the meaning came to him quickly once he did. *"Boreas breathes for us ..."*

"... We breathe for each other," Nikhil said, his instincts taking over as he recalled the mantra both men had recited in his presence so recently, after the Lamia had ruthlessly used his body in an attempt to kill his love.

Lukas chuckled softly, the laugh fading when he pressed

his lips to Nikhil's again. Cool breath that tasted of a winter wind filled his mouth, pushing its way deeper into his lungs. Nikhil inhaled, the world tilting as the power of the North Wind filled his body, awakening every cell as though he'd been deflated and was now filled, engorged with power. His cock pulsed under their touch—he thought it was Iszak's hand there, still stroking him, and the man squeezed.

Lukas pulled away and Iszak bent his head, breathing the same words of the turul mating mantra against Nikhil's mouth before giving him his own deep dose of power.

Belah's hands moved lower, her massaging fingers easing into lighter touches, trailing over his chest to tease his nipples. She moaned again, a new kiss from another lover … and Nikhil felt her hips push into his lower back, her slick folds rubbing against him.

He ached to please her, but one formality hadn't been observed yet—her mates still had to release her from her promise. She was physically unable to take pleasure from him until they allowed it.

His own reflexive moan of bliss escaped him into Iszak's kiss. The other man's hand still worked his cock slowly and Nikhil let his hands drift, his body charged with awareness of their presence on either side of him.

While bound before, he'd been forced to feel their arousal, but now that he was in control of his body again, he deliberately sought them both out, determined to master them in some way now that he could.

The breath exchange continued, with both men alternating, though their mantra came in only half-articulate, hitching syllables once he wrapped each hand around their cocks and began to stroke.

When Iszak released his mouth and Lukas took over again, Iszak let out a low growl.

"That's so fucking good," he said, his hips tilting up, meeting Nikhil's strokes.

The feel of them was both alien and familiar, and the hand on his own cock helped it feel almost commonplace that he'd be so intimate with them. The power flooding his limbs now made it even less unusual, and as he squeezed their cocks, he felt them both give in.

"By the Winds, we are made one," Iszak said, his gaze meeting Nikhil's for a second to finish the mantra before his lids fluttered shut and his lips parted in an incoherent curse. His head fell back, water droplets trickling down over his shoulders.

Belah tilted her head to Iszak's arched neck and kissed him, flicking her forked tongue across the pulse point while Nikhil watched.

"Make them come for me," she murmured, glancing at him. "Own their pleasure and give it to me."

"They must say it," Nikhil growled. "I am master here." He gripped their cocks, tugging roughly under the water, then releasing them. Both men moaned in protest. They knew the power of withholding pleasure as much as they knew the power in giving it.

"Jesus, fuck," Lukas cursed. "That was never up for debate, man. We're not stupid. You're the fucking master. You've always *been* the master, to hear her tell it."

"But he isn't just the master," Iszak said, lifting his head to look at them. "He's *our* master. We were never in control. He was. He had all the power, even though he was tied up."

Nikhil returned his hand to Iszak's cock, his own hips involuntarily tilting up into Iszak's fist as he began to stroke again.

"Yeah, I ..." Lukas moaned as Nikhil began to please him again. "I get that now."

"Good," Nikhil said. "After today, though, we are not

taking pleasure with each other unless it's giving pleasure to her to do so, got it?"

"Fine," Iszak agreed, almost absently as his hips pushed rhythmically into his stroking fist. He gently moved Iszak's fist away from his own cock, hoping to save his orgasm for her, if they'd just say the words.

"You too shy to admit you liked the way I fucked you?" Lukas asked, pulling Nikhil's hand back to his cock and wrapping his fingers around it. "You and I could have a lot of fun together. Belah would get pleasure from it no matter what."

Belah's lilting laugh hit his ears and her hands slipped down his belly to grip his erection. "My pleasure? Did you two forget I need your permission to gain any pleasure from Nikhil?"

Then both her hands moved to join Nikhil's on each man's cocks, her fingers teasing where his weren't, around their tips and down to cup their balls until they both grunted and tensed. Iszak slapped his hand down onto the flat stone edge of the tub, bucking into Nikhil's hand as he came. Lukas's orgasm soon followed.

Nikhil laughed. "I could have finished them, but I guess that just goes to show who the real master is here," he said, turning his head to look into her eyes.

Belah's irises flashed with blue light, a smile playing at her lips. "Is it my turn to be mastered yet, now that you three are finally getting along?"

"I don't know," Nikhil said, giving each man a look. "Am I allowed?"

"Maybe …" Lukas said. The brothers shared a glance.

Iszak shook his head. "You can give it to her only after you let her take her pleasure from you first. She's allowed to use you while we watch, to enjoy you right here where we sit."

Nikhil frowned. "You know what she is, and what I am … you're like me, after all."

"I do, but one thing I've always wanted to see, besides you being tied up and taking my brother's dick in your ass—which was pretty much the best thing ever—is getting to actually *see* her top you. We'll let your ass have a break, and I think she's too impatient right now to let us tie you up again for her, so for now just let her have you right here … however she wants."

"And after, I have free rein?" Nikhil asked, needing to be sure that there was no question to the allowances they were giving him.

"You are our commander, our general from here on out," Lukas said, making a fist and pressing it over his heart. Iszak confirmed, mirroring his brother's gesture with a nod.

"Good, because my orders are going to extend far beyond Belah's pleasure after tonight."

Her body shifted behind him, a little sound of displeasure escaping her lips. Iszak shifted backward out of the way as her slender body slipped around and she straddled Nikhil's hips.

"If I'm still in charge, I have one rule," she said. "No talking about 'after tonight' until after tonight. Got it? I believe I have something pretty important to take care of now."

Nikhil' slid his hands up her back and she responded with a gasp. She closed her eyes as though the simple caress was close to orgasmic. This was what he'd missed the last time they were together, when she'd been under that cursed vow that she wouldn't take pleasure from any other man but her mates. That he could still give her pleasure so easily made everything suddenly worthwhile.

He wanted to take the time to do this right, but Iszak and Lukas had made one final request, and he intended to follow through so they couldn't come back and say they weren't square. His ass couldn't handle another round of atonement.

"I am yours, little beast, as I always was. Take your pleasure however you wish."

"Do you want them to leave?" she asked, sliding her hands down over his chest as she shifted her hips distractingly on top of his. The movement only served to press her hot core more solidly against the base of his aching cock, and he dug his fingers into her hips to maintain control. He'd dreamed of this moment for three thousand years … the moment when she'd finally be his again, body and soul.

"I want whatever will please you most, *Tilahatan.*"

She smiled and glanced at both her mates. "Then they will witness so there's no doubt. We were wed once, and made love witnessed by the entire population of Egypt while we were carried through the streets after the ceremony. It was like this, if I recall," she said, slipping her hand between them to slide her palm up along his hard length. She lifted her hips, gripping one of his shoulders to raise up and gazing down into his eyes, her wet, black tendrils framing her face.

Nikhil turned his gaze up to her, as reverent as he was that day all those years ago. The day his queen—his goddess —had become his wife.

When she sank down onto him, her hot sheath squeezing his thickness and taking him to the hilt, he said a prayer to Isis, even as the goddess herself gazed raptly down into his eyes.

"Mark me so that I never forget who my mistress truly is," he said. "While I may master you for the rest of my life, and you will wear my collar, I want a mark that shows that my heart and my soul are yours to command, always."

Belah whimpered as she began to move on his cock, so he couldn't be sure if she was surprised by his request or was overcome with pleasure at the penetration. He kept his hands on her hips but didn't force her movements, letting her set the pace. He was aware of Iszak and Lukas relaxing beside them, their gazes fixed on her.

She was at the center, after all, and would always be the core of their quartet.

"Yes," she whispered, her voice shaky. "This will hurt, but it will be the last time I ever hurt you. After today, I am yours. My body and soul are yours."

She gripped his wrists and lifted his hands, twining her fingers with his. Starting at his left wrist, she flicked her tongue out, the double points lashing with stinging precision and drawing a searing line of magic in a band around his flesh. She moved to the other wrist and repeated the process, her hips moving swifter now atop his cock.

Nikhil's focus sharpened when she completed the second wrist and he realized what she'd done. Magic flared from the twin marks she'd given him … shackles that bound him to her. It flooded his mind and his head fell back against the side of the tub.

Power the likes of which he'd never felt rocketed through his body, agony taking up residence in every cell like she'd filled him with pure fire.

But still she fucked him, her tight, wet heat drawing his focus back to where they were joined, reminding him that she was his too with the way her body responded to the pleasure his cock gave her.

Just when the fire that seared his cells seemed to cool to a warm glow, she pressed her body against his, breasts sliding along his chest and hips surging atop him. She let out a long moan that signaled her impending climax, one he couldn't wait to feel. His hands went back to her hips, the shining bands of blue magic distracting him with their glow for a moment.

Her lips went to his throat, her voice rough as she murmured, "I'm not finished yet, my love."

No, but she would be soon, and it would be glorious when the magic of her climax flooded him the way it used to, and all the power of her pleasure would be for him.

Then her tongue flicked out, and a knife blade of pain sliced across his throat. He opened his mouth in a soundless cry and arched his entire body into her. His eyes flew open and he dug his fingers hard into her hips, but it was only her lips on his neck, so why had it hurt so much?

The pain came again as she moved to the other side of his throat, a hot line of fire extending across his Adam's apple. It felt like she'd slit his throat, even though he knew better. His cock only grew harder, hotter, and though he'd lost focus and the ability to move, she kept fucking him, the pleasure of her core tight around him, drawing him ever closer to climax.

A hot coil wrapped around his neck, his eyes streamed with tears. She'd said it would hurt, and this must be a part of it, a part of the warning and her worry all along—why she'd never marked him to start with. As impervious as he'd become to pain and physical damage since their wedding night, *she* could still drive agony deep into his soul if she tried.

The talon claws of her mates were nothing compared to this … this soul-rending torment her tongue gave him. A part of her body that had pleasured him so perfectly so many times. Had he only known … what? That to become hers completely he would have to endure such torture? He would have done it then, and he could stand it now too.

But the pain, oh goddess, the pain. It pierced his mind, flayed his consciousness, tore his soul into pieces. If it weren't for the sweet pleasure of her pussy to act as counterpoint, he'd have been lost completely.

"Come," she said, and he was too lost to argue. His body was hers now, all hers, and his cock responded instantly, his orgasm surging from him as though she'd simply pulled a chain and let the floodgates loose.

Nikhil's last sense of self rushed from him when his seed shot through his cock and into her. Belah bucked and shuddered and her power filled him completely, obliterating everything that was him before. Nothing was left but the bright awareness of her thrall over him, and that he lived to serve her and only her.

CHAPTER 17

NIKHIL

"Nikhil, no," Belah commanded.

"Yes, *'Iilahatan*. I'm yours," he said, and it was the truth, though he didn't understand why his mistress stared at him with such sadness.

"I have made you cry. I am sorry, mistress. You may punish me for displeasing you. Let your mates tie me up again. They enjoy giving punishment."

The pair of his mistress's mates both cursed, and he didn't understand their displeasure either, but he was willing to endure their punishment if it made his mistress happy.

His mistress kept saying "no" and crying. So he tried to comfort her. When she slid off his lap, he climbed out of the tub and got to his knees, pressed his head to the floor and begged for her forgiveness for whatever it was he had done.

"I have to take it back!" she said. "I shouldn't have marked him. Sweet Mother, what have I done? Please, Nikhil. Please be in there. Give me some sign that you remember what we really are to each other. I'm your little beast. I'm yours to command, to own, not the other way around."

I'm your little beast. The words sparked in his mind as her hands grabbed at his shoulders, urging him to sit up, to look at her. She cupped his face in both her palms, her red-rimmed eyes staring at him.

His mistress was sad because of him, but he lived at her whim. Perhaps he should kill himself.

"Should I die for you? Is that what you wish? If you wish it, I will do it."

"No! Oh, Nikhil, that's the last thing I want. I want you to *choose* what you do for me."

Her mates came to her sides and comforted her. Nikhil relaxed, glad that she had two strong males who were worthy of her. Perhaps he would learn how to be worthy of her again.

The dark-eyed one with the grim face hauled him to his feet.

"Tell me how to please her, and I will do it," Nikhil said, turning a pleading gaze to the man who led him down a hallway into another room. He remembered this room. This was where he could be made worthy. He pointed at the ropes that dangled from the ceiling. "Tie me again. Make me worthy of her."

His mistress's mate shook his head. "Brother, you already succeeded in doing that in spades. It's your turn to be the master again. That's what she needs from you. Snap the fuck out of it."

"Tie me up," his mistress said, rushing into the room behind them, naked and frantic. "Show him. Maybe that will spark his memory. Bring him back."

Her long-haired mate followed her to the center of the room and grimly wrapped her wrists and ankles in the ropes. It looked wrong to Nikhil to see her this way. She was the mistress, not the slave to be bound and whipped. She was supposed to inflict the punishment on him because he'd displeased her.

"Sit," the short-haired mate said.

Nikhil knew he should remember their names, but all he knew was hers. His mistress. His Belah. Nothing else mattered but giving himself to her, fulfilling her every wish, pleasing her through servitude.

"This had better work," the short-haired one said. He picked up a wicked-looking whip from a chest and went to the other side of his mistress, pulled his arm back, and with a fluid strike, the whip cracked.

His mistress cried out, her nipples hardened, and the mate behind her also grew erect. He struck again and Nikhil's brow twitched. Something wasn't right—he should be the one tied, being punished, shouldn't he?

The long-haired mate came to him and rested a hand on his shoulder. "You got any suggestions? You're the master here. You're supposed to know what she likes."

Nikhil shook his head. "I'm the slave. She's my mistress. I do what she says."

The man snorted. "Not until about five minutes ago you didn't. You know her better than we do. I sure fucking hope this isn't permanent. We need you to be the badass you are."

Again the whip cracked, and Nikhil flinched. Something about this scene was wrong, but seeing his mistress tied and whipped wasn't it. Something about the sight of her bound like that stirred him. She was the one with the power, so why should she be bound? He didn't know, but he decided it was good that she was … it was right … and she was pleased by her situation.

The long-haired mate went to the trunk and retrieved something, then moved to stand in front of her. She let out a soft gasp and Nikhil craned his neck to see around her mate. He was bending to affix barbed bands around her thighs, which he tightened until she yelped, though Nikhil couldn't tell whether her harsh sobs were moans of pain or pleasure.

The sounds coming from her lips made him hard, which-ever it was.

"A blade," his mistress said, fixing him with a determined gaze through her tears. "We need a blade."

The mate behind her dropped the whip to his side. "No, Belah. You said bleeding you was bad, that we shouldn't."

"Just once. Fuck, Iszak, it can be a fucking butter knife. A pen knife. A scalpel. Something to cut! He hasn't tasted my blood in weeks. It clears his mind when he does."

A blade. Nikhil's memory sparked on some distant image involving a blade. His most feared nightmare merged with his most beloved moment in his life. But that wasn't him. That was another man—a man who was not her servant as he was. This was his true purpose—to serve her, to do her bidding, to fill her womb with his seed and give her children. That was all.

The long-haired mate disappeared for a moment and returned with a hefty steel dagger. He held it up in front of his mistress's face and she exhaled brilliant blue-white flames that licked up and down along the edge. She continued until the steel glowed white and her mate averted his gaze, wincing and white-knuckled as he held onto it.

"There, now give it to him," she said.

Her mate came to Nikhil and pressed the hilt of the now blackened blade into his palm. It was almost too hot to touch, but she wanted him to hold it, so he did.

"Nikhil," she said in a commanding tone that filled the room and made him stand up straight and ready to do her bidding. "I want you to come to me."

"Yes, mistress," he said, eagerly stepping toward her.

"Make a cut on my breast, my love. Just a small one."

Seeking only to please her, he raised the blade and made the cut, a small one above her left nipple. Blood immediately welled, flooding from the wound and trickling in a crimson line around the full curve of her breast.

"Taste me, Nikhil. Taste my blood and remember what you are, who you are. I command it."

He bent his head and licked up along the side of her breast, catching the wayward droplet and tracing its path to the cut.

She tasted like life and memories. Like a piece of him that belonged, but had been removed without his consent. And she wanted back in, but was seeking the space that was now filled with his need to serve her.

This wasn't right—his mind kept telling him that he belonged within the framework of her desires, that there was no room for the opposite to be true. You couldn't exist in two places at once, after all. She didn't exist to please him; it was the other way around. That's why he did her bidding now and tasted her, sucked her.

"Nikhil, remember what you are to me. What I am to you. I am your little beast. Remember."

She took in a deep breath, her breast rising against his mouth as he continued to suckle at her nipple, reveling in the taste of her luscious essence flooding his tongue with sharp, sweet flavor. After he was finished here, he would kneel and please her with his tongue in other places, if she wished.

Fragrant smoke tickled his nostrils and he inhaled her scent, sucking it into his lungs like she had given him her life's breath.

Inside his mind her words repeated: *"I am your little beast. Wake up and collar me again. Be my master."*

But that wasn't right. *She* had marked *him*. That meant he was the beast. He was the pet, the one branded by her magic to show the world who owned him. No, if she wished him to be the master …

"I must mark you," he said, the words sounding forced,

like they came from some buried part of him clawing out of the depths beneath the magic that filled him. Her magic. "If I am your master, you must be branded like the beast you are."

He held the blade up before her face again. "Breathe your fire for me, mistress," he said, though he knew not why he made the request, only that the clawing beast he'd thought tamed by her magic wished it, and the slave meant to serve her wasn't strong enough to keep the creature contained.

Belah's flames licked out and the blade heated again. Her fire seared his knuckles and he let out a rough cry, but held steady until the steel glowed white from her fire once more.

Then, with hand burned nearly to the bone by his lover's fire, he aimed the tip of the glowing blade to her flesh above her breasts and began to write his name.

With each cut her skin split and blood welled for a second before it sizzled and blackened. His aim was true, his cuts precise. With each character he wrote, the cobwebs fell away from his mind, her magic holding less and less sway over his will.

Halfway through, he'd written "Nik" and lifted his gaze to meet hers.

Her eyes were glazed with pleasure, her lips parted, and though her body shook from the pain, she loved every cut.

"So beautiful," he said and shifted closer, needing to feel more of her body against his. He angled his hand differently for the last three letters so that he could tilt his hips against hers. He needed her to know how hot this made him, though he was still foggy as to exactly why.

He pressed his erect cock against her mound as he made the next cut and she gusted out a soft *yes* that feathered his cheek. Her core slickened against the ridge of his cock and he rubbed harder, feeling the small, hard nub of her pleasure and pushing against it.

Two more letters.

His mind sharpened with his need, his body heating as the blade cooled. Belah's burned flesh filled his senses, the taste of her blood still on his tongue. He made the last cut with a growl of triumph, observing his handiwork and knowing in that moment that this was right. This was what pleased her most, and what made him whole. The slave was the master, and that was as it must be between them, always.

He cut her breast again and her head fell back, a moan of pleasure escaping her throat when he bent to taste the blood that welled.

Her essence, her gift to him, and all he needed to master her forever.

"Please," she begged.

"You are mine, Beast. Forever now."

He dropped the knife to the floor and caught Iszak's eye where the man stood waiting behind Belah, still gripping the whip in his hand.

"Resume," he said. "I need to make sure my little lapse there is completely clear. Hearing her pain should do the rest, but I intend to fuck her while she screams."

CHAPTER 18

NIKHIL

Iszak's sure, steady strokes with the whip drove Belah into a frenzy while Nikhil fucked her. She screamed out her ecstasy, her body convulsing with the pain, each strike causing her to clench tighter around his thrusting cock. She reached her peak with a sonorous cry that was music to his ears, but he wasn't done with her yet.

He pulled out of her, his cock still aching for more, but he had to clear his mind completely of that disturbing impulse to grovel at her feet. He swiftly unfastened her bindings, secured the rope around her neck, and forced her to kneel and take him in her mouth.

She eagerly wrapped her lips around him and he tangled his hands in her wet hair, guiding her as he pushed his shaft as deep as it would go. Her tongue coiled around him, sliding along his length with each thrust, reminding him how perfect she could be when on her knees for him like this.

"You are mine, little beast. Mine to command, mine to own. Your mouth, your body, your cunt are all mine."

Tears streamed from the corners of her eyes, but the blue gaze that met his was filled with worship and utter submission that triggered an orgasm more glorious than any he'd felt in eons.

When he spilled his semen into her mouth, she begged for more, and he continued to guide her head with her hair tangled around his fist while she serviced her other two mates in turn. When all four of them were spent, they returned to the bath to lounge in the steaming heat.

Belah let out a deep, sated sigh, snuggling into Nikhil's chest with her legs draped across Iszak's and Lukas's laps.

"We're having a little family reunion tonight," she said softly.

"Oh?" Nikhil asked, idly tracing wet fingertips over the outline of his name so precisely carved into her chest above the luscious curves of her breasts.

Iszak made a rumbling noise of agreement. "The winds announced her sister's arrival some time ago, just after we untied you. No doubt they're waiting for us."

"I didn't expect them to follow me up here," Nikhil said. "The three of them seemed intent on falling into bed and staying there when I left."

"There was news from the Sanctuary," Lukas said.

Nikhil tensed. "What news? And how do you know this?"

"The wind tells us everything. If a word was ever uttered, we can hear it."

"Of course you can hear it," Nikhil grumbled, knowing what Lukas said was true. His own magical blessings gave him a similar power.

"The news isn't good," Iszak said. "Makes me want to lock all the doors and hunker down, in fact. Not that I'm one to avoid a conflict, but we went through enough bullshit to get where we are now, so I'm not exactly itching to leave again."

"What *is* the news?" Belah asked, sitting up straighter on Nikhil's lap and slipping her arm around his shoulder. Her breast pressed against the center of his chest so alluringly he found it difficult to care about anything but her curvaceous figure in his arms. But he knew there would be more work to do. The bitch who'd mind-controlled him for the last three thousand years was still a serious threat, and as much as he would love to forget all his worries and spend every day living to please his goddess, he had unfinished business.

"The Haven is in danger," Lukas said. "And when a Dionarch's son shows up and admits his mother's gone off the deep end, it's worth a listen. They don't admit to madness easily, even though everyone knows they're always flying a little higher than the moon."

Belah leaned forward with interest and Nikhil let out a soft sigh of contentment when her breast brushed against the inside of his arm.

"What did Nyx do?" she asked. "And where's Neph? Why is my sister here and not shacked up with her mates some-where?" She surged up, scrambling to climb out of the tub. Nikhil let out a grunt of surprise when the pleasant press of her breast was replaced by the pressure of her hand as she braced herself on him for balance. "Never mind. I should just go talk to her myself."

He let out a sigh of resignation. "Well, boys, I guess it's back to work."

THE REUNION WOULD BE an odd one, and Nikhil wasn't sure he was entirely prepared for it so soon after nearly losing control of his mind again. He was still a little shaky, but after having Belah on her knees and collared again, he knew that power was never something he would relinquish for the rest of his days, and it gave him a renewed sense of command that he held onto like a lifeline.

He gritted his teeth when they walked into another apartment in the Enclave that was as spacious and richly deco-rated as the one Belah shared with Lukas and Iszak. Only this one was filled with people. There were thirteen others, some dragon, some turul, one familiar ursa who smiled at him in welcome, and a few more guests who were surpris-ingly human.

All heads turned to face the door and he stopped inside, surveying the scene with a careful eye out of habit, though perched as the place was on the side of a mountain over-looking a bottomless ravine, there were few avenues of escape. Not that he should need to run—these people were his family now, whether they liked it or not, and his mission affected them as much as it affected him.

Lukas and Iszak brushed past him with comforting pats and a shoulder squeeze just as Nikhil's eyes found Marcus, who stared grimly back at him.

His oldest memories had been dissolving since his conversation with Zorion, but ever since Belah's command to remember, the memory loss had halted. The worst memory of them all was also one of the most recent, and he forced himself to face his victims now.

As he made his way down into the sunken living space, the din of conversation subdued, then completely halted when he paused to stand in front of Marcus, who held Evie tight against his side as though he feared losing her again.

He glanced behind them to Ked, who watched impas-sively, though with no evident hostility. He and Ked had made their peace with each other, but he hadn't had the chance to truly make amends with the two people he'd hurt the most.

"I don't know how to begin," he said, his words a harsh scrape against his throat. Regret nearly strangled him and he had to take a deep breath to say more. Marcus only watched, his stare darkening.

"Don't," Marcus said. "Better to just keep your distance, if it's all the same to you."

Gritting his teeth, Nikhil said, "It isn't all the same to me. I refuse to excuse what I've done. My weakness made it possible for a vicious beast to use me as her tool. That's all on me, but we are kindred whether we like it or not. Our blood makes us brothers—you, me, Naaz, and Sterlyn ... and Neela is our sister. I was an only child, then general of an army. I had some sense of brotherhood with my fellow soldiers, but that ended when I became their commander. These dragons are here to ask me to become their general again, but I cannot say yes to that without knowing you and I have made peace. Marcus, forgive the injuries I inflicted on you while I was under the Lamia's spell. Join me in the fight to beat her now that we are free."

"But are we?" Marcus asked, his face incredulous. "Are we really free of you? I can feel the tickle of our connection still. The blood cocktail you infused me with when you made me connected us all. That hasn't gone away, even after Ked marked me. I still feel it. What's to stop you from using it?"

"My honor," Nikhil said, "of which I'm sure you believe I have none, but give me a chance to prove I do still. I've promised the others never to take advantage of our mental link to control them the way I once did. You can talk to them, if you choose—I only use it now to communicate. That's it. And if it makes you feel better, I have these ..."

He reached up and traced the tingling lines of the dragon mark that circled his throat, then pulled his sleeves back to reveal the matching ones at his wrists.

Marcus's eyes widened and he idly rubbed a spot between his shoulder blades. "She marked you?"

"Yes," he tested his mental control and confirmed yet again that his connection to Belah was still there, like a shackle around his will, but one with the key left in the lock.

She was only granting him free will because she chose to. "I belong to her. No doubt the same way you belong to him." He tilted his chin to Ked.

Marcus glanced at Ked with one eyebrow raised and a soft smirk on his lips. He eyed Ked in an almost proprietary way, and the huge, dark-haired dragon's eyes narrowed. Finally Ked laughed and looked at Nikhil.

"You could say we own each other now. We're both at Evie's mercy, though," Ked said, placing a large hand on each of his mates' shoulders before him.

With the touch, Marcus relaxed and smiled at Nikhil. He shook his head, letting out a sigh and proffering his hand.

"You have always been an impressive leader. Naaz, Neela, and Sterlyn have been chattering in my head for weeks, arguing in favor of following you, but aside from that night with the dragons, I had yet to see the new you in action. I'm looking forward to it."

With a sigh of relief, Nikhil grasped Marcus's hand and squeezed. He hated the memory of what he'd done to Marcus and Evie after he thought he had lost Belah for good. If he could go back in time and change anything, he would fix that.

He suddenly found himself wrapped in Evie's embrace, her delicate frame enveloping him in a fierce hug that caught him off guard. He hesitantly reciprocated, resting his hands gently on her back.

"I forgive you, Nikhil. You were broken before, and so you broke us, but we're whole again. And so are you."

He closed his eyes, fighting back a surge of emotion as he held her tighter. "Yes, Evie, I am whole, and I probably wouldn't be if not for you." He swallowed back the emotion, but when he opened his eyes, he was met with the glassy stares of three dragons who seemed to know without asking exactly what he was feeling. In the end it had been Evie's song that finally cleared his head of the Lamia's thrall, and for that, he would be forever grateful.

Something had happened to make all these people gather, to get Aurum and her new mates to leave their comfortable cabin and search him out. Setting aside his regret for the moment, he released Evie and faced Aurum, Calder, and Nicholas where they were gathered near the kitchen.

Belah joined him, pulling her sister into a fierce hug. "What are you doing here? I hope everything's okay. Are the others in the Sanctuary still? Did they find their mates?"

Aurum's expression remained grim, as did those of her mates. "I'm not sure where they are at the moment," Aurum said. "They may be in the Haven by now." She glanced at Calder, who nodded and faced Nikhil and Belah.

"My mother's been fragile for a long time—ever since my father and I were captured by the Ultiori. It's taken all my uncle's power to keep her stable, but when he helped us escape the Haven ... well, things have gone from bad to worse."

Nikhil frowned. "Your mother ... you mean Nyx, one of the nymphaea Dionarchs?" His skin prickled with unease. The two nymphaea leaders were integral to his plan to track down the Lamia, but if there was upheaval in the Haven, that plan might be in trouble.

Calder let out a sigh. "Yeah. She's highly protective of the Haven and the remaining residents. The nymphs can't produce male children with human mates, so there are no satyrs left. When I made it home finally, she locked down the entire place, insisting that my uncle and I be the ones to service all the nymphs and repopulate the Haven with satyr babies. It was all my sister and I could do to convince her that a breeding pact with the ursa was a good idea. We need male children—and it's our hope that breeding with the other higher races, now that the dragons and turul have set the precedent that it's acceptable, will help with that. But Mother's a very single-minded woman."

Ked let out a gruff chuckle and crossed his arms. "That's an understatement. Your mother was probably not thrilled when you brought home a dragon for a mate. I never understood why she disliked us so much. Before she mated Nereus, she was more open-minded."

Nikhil filed away Ked's comment and told Calder, "Go on."

"She's taken full control of the Source since Neph helped us leave the Haven. She refuses to restore the Source's power to the Sanctuary unless they send Aurum's brothers to my mother as prisoners … or breeding stock. Probably both. She's completely lost her mind if she's gone this far. She's risking the Haven's alliance with all the higher races."

"She's destroyed it, as far as I'm concerned," Belah said icily.

Nikhil glanced at Ked, who he was surprised hadn't nodded in agreement.

"Do you have a solution in mind, Calder?" he asked. "She is your mother, after all. You would know her best."

He took a deep breath and nodded. "I believe if we can locate my father and bring him home to the Haven, his presence will restore balance to her sanity."

Calder stopped speaking and stared expectantly at Nikhil. Nikhil knew what he was hoping for, but regretted that he didn't have the answer.

In a quiet voice, he said, "I don't know where your father and the other satyrs are. I was the Lamia's puppet, not her confidant. She used me for my ruthless, brutal nature, but I was never privy to her more devious plans. I remember fighting you and your squadron. Capturing you and imprisoning you. You were the only member of the team I had any contact with afterward. The others were separated, each of you sent to a different facility. There's no way to know precisely where they are now."

Calder pressed his lips together, visibly disappointed. "There has to be a way to find them."

"Naaz and Sterlyn are still in close contact with the military arm of the Ultiori. Many of those men have been loyal to me and remain so, despite answering to a new leader. Naaz and Sterlyn can't show their faces in any of the facilities, but we have men inside. It's tricky for them to gather intel and maintain their cover, but they're working on it. I'll make sure they know what to look for. In the meantime, we should split up …"

He glanced around the room at the close-knit group. Mated trios, some he didn't recognize, but it was clear they were close and loyal. All of them looked eager to help.

"We hunt them, the way the Ultiori once hunted you all under my command. Marcus knows their tricks as well as any of my Elites. He can share with anyone who wants to help. This hiding that you all have been doing for the last several eons worked well enough to protect you, but if you want to *win*, this has to stop. We can take down their numbers from the outside easily. Still, there's no substitute for information to give us an edge."

"We can help with that," Ked said. "Our Shadows have resources to infiltrate the Ultiori's information systems, if you can provide us a reliable contact. That still won't help us learn how to beat the Lamia."

"That's why I was hoping for was a face-to-face with your mother, Calder. This development with her worries me. Aodh was planning to help me get into the Haven from outside. Is there any chance you can get me in instead? I was willing to wait until the Sanctuary's portals activated again, to let Aodh out, but if he's gone into the Haven … if he's

Nyx's prisoner … there's no telling when he's making it out again."

Calder frowned at him, but his response was drowned out by Belah's, Ked's, and Aurum's shocked exclamations about what made Aodh think he could get into the Haven any other way.

Nikhil held up his hands to stall their confusion. "It turns out your brother and I have a lot in common," he said. "Which is to say, he lost control to the creature I knew as Meri the same as me, but luckily, she was a lot less powerful at the time and he was able regain control. The residue of her spirit is what gave him the ability to drift."

"We know about that," Ked said. "But he always just passed it off as a bonus from some old affair. We assumed it was from Neph, but never asked."

"Whatever his reasons were for keeping the secret, it's in our interest now for everyone to know. Meri tricked him into a blood meld, and when she was banished for it, she sought revenge, her corruption turning her into that beast. I need to know how the blood meld works, and what we need to do to break it—not to mention what the Lamia's agenda might be now."

"If anyone would know, it would be Neph," Calder said. "My mother might have some information, but considering the state she's in, good luck getting her to be coherent. Why didn't you ask me all those times we talked?"

Nikhil gave him a sardonic smile. "You mean all those times I had control of myself enough to indulge in social interaction for pleasure? The Lamia was still in my head then, her agenda still drove most of my actions. There was no way in hell I'd have asked you any questions that might hint at our larger goals. Unfortunately, I never got into *her* head enough to know what she was really after. All she let me have was the hatred of your kind and my desire for a child. She nurtured both until I wanted nothing else but to breed or to kill."

"Now your purpose is to kill her?" Evie asked, her jaw set.

"Exactly," he said.

"But if we're going to fight them, we need all the help we can get," Calder said. "There's a hell of a lot of power in this room alone, but it isn't enough."

Nikhil nodded. "We'll find your father and the other soldiers. Securing the Haven is crucial. We need the help of both Dionarchs to beat her even if they just share her secrets."

"Mother's got more up her sleeve than secrets," Calder said. "That's what makes her so dangerous now. If uncle Neph didn't make it back to the Haven, there's no male energy to temper her insanity. She'll destroy the Haven in the interest of saving it, in the state she's in. And if the Haven goes down, the rest of our world will be vulnerable. All the Enclaves, the dragon Glade, the Sanctuary ... they all depend on the Source for power, to some degree. There's a reason the Haven is so well protected. And I'm sorry to say it, but you sent Aodh on a fool's errand if you were hoping he could get you inside. He'd have to have the kind of command of the Source that only one of Gaia's immortal children can possess. Dragons simply aren't capable of controlling it. Only one of the Dionarchs or one of the four ursa clan leaders has that ability, and I can promise you the ursa are every bit as keen on protecting their home as Mother is."

"Well, I hope those women are keeping their heads on straight," Nikhil said. "Because we're going to need their help too."

Calder glanced at Nicholas and rested a hand on his shoulder. "They've got an advantage in the power of their males," he said. "And if my sister's succeeded in her goal, the Haven will at least find some balance among the residents now that they're mating with ursa males. This is why we need to find my father so badly. Mother always insisted he was dead, yet refused to take another mate. I believe he's alive."

"Then that's where we'll start," Nikhil said.

Nicholas cleared his throat and Nikhil looked at the big, dark ursa, still marveling at how intimidating he looked now that he had color.

"What is it, son?" he asked.

"I'm all for getting out there and hunting the bitch down, but can we wait until after we eat?"

Nikhil laughed and lifted his brows at Aurum. "I hope you were prepared for this one's appetite. I remember the tons of food he used to go through when he was a boy."

Aurum smiled. "Feeding Nicholas is one of my absolute favorite things to do, and the food is ready, so we definitely shouldn't wait if you're done with the meeting."

The entire room shifted as a unit, gravitating toward the long dining table. The table was hewn from a single giant tree and extended almost the entire length of the room in front of the floor-to-ceiling windows displaying a dark, rainy night beyond.

The group seamlessly worked to set out the dishes and cutlery, followed by the food with very little instruction. They anticipated each other's needs even at the most basic level, whether through mental links or simply ages of famil-iarity, Nikhil wasn't sure, but it gave him hope that once it came time to fight, they would prevail.

He sat with the rest and enjoyed the meal, restricting his words to casual conversation until the end of the night. There would be time enough for him to shift into the role of general again and take charge, but for now, he would enjoy the sense of family before he had to turn them into an army.

CHAPTER 19

GAVRA

After an invigorating swim through the Source's waters, the current tossed Gavra onto the mossy bank of a wide river. He lay there catching his breath and staring up at the small patch of sky he could make out beyond the high, wet stone of the multitude of grottos that surrounded them. Silas panted beside him, but didn't move. He sensed footsteps and turned his head to see Assana rise, water still dripping off her body. She was turned away from him and he took the opportunity to marvel at her beauty, even though the simple act of looking made him ache.

That was when he realized she was holding up her hands as if to ward off an attack, and he jumped to his feet, immediately on guard. Aodh lurched up at the same time and they stood back-to-back, warily eyeing the circle of nymphs who all had arrows nocked and aimed at their heads.

"You guys can't damage us," Gavra said. "Might as well not bother with the weapons. We came willingly ... well, mostly. Just take us to Nyx."

"These arrows will still hurt if we loose them," one nymph said.

163

"Give me your hands, dragon," the lead nymph commanded, moving close to him and setting down her bow.

"Clio, where are you taking them?" Assana said, her voice shaky. Silas slipped his hand into hers and with a stronger pitch, she said, "What are my mother's plans?"

"She only gave us instructions," the leader said. "She requested that you join her when you arrived and that we secure the dragons in their cells."

Gavra lifted his hands, pressing his wrists together. The nymph swiftly wrapped a smooth length of green vine around his wrists and tied it with an elaborate knot. He sensed the power in the binding, but he tested it anyway, using his full strength to try to break it but having no luck.

"You must go to your mother, Assana," the lead nymph said as she steered Gavra away. "She is waiting."

The four remaining nymphs eyed Assana and Silas, and one stepped forward to grab at Assana's arm.

She yanked away from the other woman. "I'm not leaving them until I make sure they're treated well, Clio."

"You have your mate, Assana," Clio said over her shoulder. "Our mistress wishes to breed me and my sister Thiasoi to these dragons. They will be well cared for."

"Go, Assana," Gavra said. "Aodh and I can handle these females."

"They've bound you with naga vines, Gavra. You won't be able to break your bonds."

Gavra eyed the scantily clad women around him, catching his brother's similar assessing look as his eyes passed over him.

"Who said I intend to break free? Being tied down and used by a nymph is one of my deepest fantasies." He turned his gaze back to Assana and gave her a wicked grin. Her aura flared, and her lips parted with that longing look she'd given him before he'd broken down and kissed her earlier.

Silas tugged at her hand, urging her to follow him.

"If any of you hurt them, you will pay," Assana said.

Clio nodded. "Understood, sister," she said softly, then picked up her bow and pointed it at him again. Two of the nymphs grabbed his arms while the other two walked behind, keeping their arrows steadily aimed at him. The group around Aodh took up a similar formation, directing them down a wide path along the grassy riverbank into the vine-infested forest.

Clio took the lead and a pair of other nymphs followed. Eleven total, Gavra counted, glancing around. These were all the Haven's Thiasoi maidens, save Assana. As they made their way through the forest, he noted how they all seemed to walk with a strange, stilted gait, their heads turning like automatons.

"Nyx, I know you can hear me," Gavra said. "You've got your claws sunk into these poor nymphs and you're making them do this. It won't last. Do whatever you wish with me and my brother, but know we intend to help your daughter regain control of the Haven. What you're doing won't be tolerated by the higher races for long."

Something sharp suddenly jabbed him between the shoulder blades and pushed hard. "Shut up, dragon," a familiar voice said at his back. It was Nyx's, though he knew the speaker wasn't her in the flesh. "You know nothing about keeping your home safe. You abandoned yours."

"My home is the entire world, Nyx. And I haven't abandoned it. If you're talking about the dragon Glade, it's more secure than this place. Perhaps you should move there? If your nymphs really want dragon mates, I know there are hundreds of eligible males who would be happy to accommodate them."

Simultaneously, all eleven nymphs' auras flashed with identical irritation. In Nyx's voice, the nymph at his right said, "The Haven is the most sacred home of all the immortals. To abandon the Source would be to destroy the world, and you know it. We must have stronger offspring. Breeding with humans has made us weak. You and your brother will provide the seed for the army we need to destroy our enemy and ensure the Haven is secure."

They rounded a bend in the path and came to a placid pool with blooming water lilies floating on the surface. On the far side was a huge, circular structure that seemed to grow out of the roots of a monolithic tree. As they approached, he realized the roots of the tree created an intricate crisscrossing web only big enough to allow light in, like the bars of a woven cage.

"What about your pact with the ursa?" Gavra asked. "Are their males not enough?"

"Their males are not immortal. My Thiasoi deserve stronger mates." Nyx's voice came from a different nymph this time, and Gavra had the weird sense that he was conversing with a multi-headed beast. The nymphs who were guiding him directed him up a ramp into the lit interior of the cage. They lifted his arms, securing his bound wrists to a stray root that dangled from above, then retreated.

The opening they'd entered through grew over with a tangled web of thick roots until the smallest gap was just barely large enough for him to fit his fist through.

"Why not get it over with now?" Gavra said. "Send them all in. I'll mate each and every one tonight and we can get the fuck on with our lives."

He spun, twisting the root above him to meet Aodh's eyes through the mesh of his cage. They must be taking his brother to a different cage, though he'd seen no other similar structures nearby.

The nearest nymph laughed. "Do you think me a fool,

dragon? If I give you free rein, you'll mark them, and we can't have that."

Above him, the root he was tied to receded, taking the knotted bindings from his wrist. He stalked to the cage barrier.

"Nyx, you know that's the only way these females can be impregnated by a dragon."

"It isn't the only way." The nymph turned away and the group headed back down the path without another word, herding Aodh between them.

"What the fuck does she mean?" he shot to his brother.

"No idea. If she was putting herself out there for mating, I could see it—two immortals can procreate without the magic of a mating bond as long as one of them wants the offspring. It won't work with these maidens, though."

Gavra spun around and paced the circular enclosure. It offered no privacy with its latticework walls on all sides, but at least it was comfortable. There was a large bed against one side, a stone fireplace taking up the center, with a partitioned bathroom containing a steaming, sunken pool beyond the fireplace on the opposite side of the cage. Light streamed in through the gaps in the tree's roots. He went to them, testing again to see if he could break through, but the roots didn't budge, nor did they respond to his breath or his fire.

He let out a yell and punched, but it only bruised his fist. Nyx had crafted the perfect prison to hold a dragon.

"Ask her how fucking long she's going to make us wait," Gavra said.

"Already did. She's planning to starve us for a while first, so we're more pliable when she sends the first maiden in. And I don't mean we'll be starved of food, either ..."

"Fuck," he said out loud. *"We need a plan, brother."*

"Hang on, I think they're taking me to see Nyx herself."

"Why would they take you and not me? Where are you now?"

"I'm at the Source."

"I thought we were at the Source when we arrived."

"No, brother. When we traveled in here, the current chose our destination for us. Nyx probably had our arrival point set. She'd never allow us in where the true power is."

"That's where you are now?" He gripped the lattice of roots on the side where he sensed his brother and stared off into the distance. He saw nothing but mossy forest with the occasional glowing pixie flitting among the foliage. Those wild creatures were the only fauna that lived in the place.

"Yes ... I will try to find out more."

Gavra tightened his grip around the roots, his teeth gritted in impotent fury. He should have used his power to subdue the nymphs who'd met them, but he'd made a promise to Assana to go willingly.

For several more minutes he waited, his anger surging with each moment of silence.

"Brother, tell me what's happening!"

Aodh's presence was still there, a mental beacon in the distance.

Finally, he heard the familiar, deep voice. *"I guess she hated me a lot more than I thought. When you get out, tell Vrishti to find Neph. Help her, if you can. For me, brother."*

"Dammit, Aodh, what is she doing?" Icy dread trickled down his spine at the finality of his brother's words.

Then his brother was gone. No glimmer of mental power in the distance, no voice in his mind. He reached out, searching the entire Haven, but Aodh had completely disappeared.

Gavra tilted his head back and roared.

CHAPTER 20

ASSANA

$\mathcal{A}$ssana paced the empty great hall, pissed that her mother would summon her here and then not even have the courtesy to meet her. She should have stayed with Gavra, made sure they didn't abuse him, but the truth was that the distance eased that insistent urge she had to meld with him.

"Assana, I'm here if you need me," Silas said.

His steadfast presence calmed her enough to pause and look at him. "I'm sorry," she said. "You didn't have to come, but I'm glad you did."

"I'm yours, remember? Where else would I be?"

"Safe in the Sanctuary. I saw what my mother almost did to Nicholas. I'd die if I let you risk your life for me."

He took two steps and pulled her into a warm embrace. "I would do anything for the two of you, Assana. Who knows where Gavra is right now, but hopefully he's figuring out a plan. I need to stick with you. This is bigger than just the three of us. We can't forget that."

She inhaled his calming evergreen scent and let out a deep sigh, sinking against him. "I know. My instincts want me to go to him, though. They want me to take you both and find an isolated grotto and never leave. The need presses at my mind like a constant, nagging voice and makes it hard to concentrate. I can't lose focus on finding a way to talk my mother down."

Silas lifted a hand and cupped her chin, tilting her head up to look into her eyes. His brow was creased with concern.

"You know we may have to do more than just talk her down, right? What she's done goes beyond reason. I saw how the nymphs who met us behaved. They weren't in control."

Assana winced, remembering how oddly her sisters had acted, their movements jerky and strange, their eyes a mad swirl of too many colors.

"Assana," Silas said, stooping down slightly to look into her eyes. "You know we may have to subdue her, to take her out of the equation. You'll have to take control of the Haven if that happens."

"I know," she said, setting her jaw. "I just wish my uncle were here to help. Or Calder."

"You have me and Gavra and Aodh. We'll figure out a way. Any ideas where your mother's holding them? What she plans to do?"

Grateful for his urging to actually think, she nodded. "There's only one place she'd keep the two of them that they wouldn't be able to escape. As for what she plans to do ..." She shivered, unwilling to even ponder the idea of Gavra being coerced into mating anyone else.

Before she could finish the thought, the doors flew open and Nyx sailed in with swift strides, pieces of her gown billowing out behind her like trails of sea foam. Assana's eleven Thiasoi sisters followed in formation, moving more naturally now, she was grateful to see.

Silas inhaled sharply at the sight, and Assana pressed her lips together. Few males could resist ogling women as beautiful as these, and her mother was a shining star compared to the other nymphs. Her gown seemed to be made of all manner of growing things, with vines and mosses and dark leaves stitched into intricate patterns that strategically covered the more sensitive parts of her curvaceous body.

The Thiasoi maidens wore more utilitarian uniforms, though no less revealing. They had no enemies inside the Haven, but the squadron of soldiers was always at the ready.

"Daughter, you have returned," Nyx said, smiling invitingly. The shift in her demeanor gave Assana hope. Perhaps she was willing to see reason now.

When Nyx reached her, she pulled away from Silas and went gladly into her mother's outstretched arms. Relief washed through her in the other woman's embrace.

"Mother, I'm so happy you're back to normal. Where are the dragons? Did you let them go?"

"Nonsense, Assana," Nyx said, taking her place on her throne. That was when Assana finally noticed that there was only a single throne on the dais at the end of the great hall, and her mother didn't seem the least bit aware of the strangeness of that sight.

"Why not?" she asked, her gut clenching with renewed worry. This smiling woman looked like the mother she remembered from ages ago, before her father and brother's squadron had been captured by the Ultiori, but she realized that everything was wrong with her mother's behavior now.

"The red one will serve his purpose before he is released. As for the other ... I have sent him somewhere he can no longer tempt any of my nymphs or my brother to break our laws."

"What do you mean, Mother? Where did you send Aodh?"

Her mother's smile didn't budge. "Oh, he'll be quite comfortable, though when his power wanes he will likely go mad, but he'll be far away from the Lamia's clutches. He's what she wanted from the start, back when she was still a nymph named Meri. Did you know that?"

Silas uttered a soft curse beside her. "Gavra's not going to like this," he said.

"The red dragon won't have a care once my Thiasoi are ready for him. We'll keep him in such a sexual stupor he'll beg for more when we stop."

"You can't do this to him, Mother. When the dragons find out, they'll come for him, and all the work you've done to protect the Haven will be for nothing. Please, just let them both go."

"No!" Nyx yelled, her voice echoing through the hall. She stood and glared down at Assana. "They're the ones who have put the Haven in jeopardy by taking my men away. It's that white fool's fault that any of this has happened. He tempted Meri to taste his blood without a true bond of love, and it corrupted her. If I could execute them both, I would, but at least the red one has some use to me alive."

Assana raised her hands in a pleading gesture. "Mother, you are wrong. Meri was never quite sane—you said it yourself to father once, after you banished her. How she'd never been the same after you melded father."

"She was only hurt and lost. That dragon took advantage of her weakened emotional state. Tried to get her to do abominable things for the sake of pleasure. It's too late for her now, but I can make sure he doesn't hurt us again. If she comes for him, she won't find him."

"That isn't what happened, Mother, and you know it."

She'd heard the recounting of Meri's transgressions, though she was barely old enough to understand what had happened. When she was older and asked her brother why her uncle was so sad, he'd told her the full story. Whether her mother's memory of the events was tainted somehow by her own actions, Assana wasn't sure. Blood melding was outlawed for a reason. It was enough of a challenge for the nymphaea to maintain control of their sanity if they didn't carefully manage their sexual energy. Add to that the temptation of power granted through a blood meld and all bets were off.

Her father had been gone too long. And while her uncle and brother weren't ideal for balancing her mother's power, they'd been better than nothing. Their very presence had made a difference that she noticed now by virtue of their absence and her mother's increasingly irrational behavior.

She needed to get her mother in a room with a male, but rejected the idea of subjecting Gavra or Silas to the task. They were *hers,* dammit.

"Daughter, the safety of the Haven is no longer your concern. When my melding with the Thiasoi is complete, I will birth a new army of immortals to protect us. You should take your new ursa mate and go get started on a child. Your mental state is in dire straits from the looks of it. Have you even fucked him yet?"

Defeated and confused, Assana could only shake her head. "We have melded once. I—I'm not ready."

"I sometimes forget that I never let you out of the Haven to play with the human men. How have you not had your fun with a dozen ursa males by now? I'm sure even those two dragons would have happily accommodated you and helped you lose your virginity."

She clenched her eyes shut, hating her mother in that moment, though the woman had once been infinitely understanding.

"I don't know, Mother. Maybe you were just a little too careful after father was captured. I miss him too, but this is insane. Clio and the others don't deserve what you're doing to them. They're loyal soldiers, and you're abusing that loyalty."

"They understand the sacrifice. They're willing to do what needs to be done for the safety of the Haven, no matter how long it takes."

Silas stiffened beside her, his hand slipping around her waist. "Let's give her some space," he said.

Assana reluctantly let him pull her away and they left the great hall. She wasn't oblivious to the pained looks in the eyes of her sister Thiasoi and longed to speak to them, though she knew better than to do it under her mother's scrutiny. She didn't even have the presence of mind to reach out for the River to see if she could glean some detail about the course of action that might lead to her success. She'd only had the power for a short time, but even in that time had learned that she would only encounter blankness when she sought information linked too closely with her own path, as opposed to that of others.

She saw nothing of Silas or Gavra, either, which should have comforted her because it meant they remained closely linked to her, but that blind spot was a weakness.

Finally outside the great hall, she took a breath and looked up at Silas. "Thank you."

"For what?"

"For being you, I guess," she said, giving him a small smile. "Let's see if we can figure out where they took Gavra. Then get some rest."

"Are you going to be okay?" he asked, turning to lean on the stone rail of the terrace and face her.

She took a shaky breath. "I don't know. Ever since I first saw Gavra, it's like my hormones are in overdrive. I've never had to deal with this before, but I've heard of other nymphs who fell for human men who did. If a nymph waits too long to find a mate and conceive a child, even the sight of another man can drive us mad, especially if we're in our primal form."

Silas pushed his lips out thoughtfully and nodded. "I

know what you mean about Gavra. He's …" He took a long breath and then let out a chuckle. "There's no word for what he is, but you saw first-hand what he does to me. But I have to ask. I'm a male, yet you seem perfectly … ah … sane right now."

She looked into his eyes, surprised that she didn't see any confusion or hurt—only curiosity. Biting her lip, she turned her gaze to the ground and teased her bare toe over a gap in the stones beneath her feet.

"You're different," she said, struggling to find the words to describe exactly how Silas made her feel. The primal ache for a child burned in her belly, filling her with unfettered energy, an anxious need to breed and sate that hunger inside her. Her skin felt charged with that power with every passing moment, but with Silas near her … touching her … She reached out a hand to him and he instinctively took it. The swelling pressure immediately dissipated.

Letting out a long breath, Assana said, "With you, I feel grounded."

He smiled. "I get it. You guys are like ursa females on crack. Are you always like this?"

"It's been worse since Mother locked down the Haven. But yeah, as for me, I have been like this ever since I came of age, but it's gotten worse every century. I don't shift, as a rule, because I learned in my primal form I go a little crazy."

"But there are no men here. At least, there weren't until the ursa you brought in. Where are the ursa males, anyway?"

"They're spread out among the other grottos. You probably won't see any while we're here, though. It's only been a few days since they arrived, it'll be a few more before they even come up for air. They probably don't even know anything's gone wrong."

Silas frowned. "Should we warn them?"

"Not yet. It's too soon to worry, and I doubt Mother will

harm them. She's too concerned with producing male children to interfere."

He tugged her close. "All right, but if things start going south with your mother, or her soldiers, I want to give them the choice to fight. They'll want to know, and I have an obligation to them to keep them safe."

"I know. If it comes to that, we'll tell them."

She sank against his warm chest, marveling at how swiftly his simple touch could calm her wild urges. Odd that he didn't have that effect on Gavra. The red dragon seemed more likely to incite lust in a calmer person than the other way around.

The thought of Gavra made her push back and look into Silas's eyes. "Did you like what he did to you before?"

He raised his eyebrows, studying her for a second, then his tongue slipped out and licked along the curve of his lower lip before being replaced by his teeth. He made a little humming sound that became a rumble deep in his chest.

"You mean when he forced me to suck his cock?"

Her breathing grew shallow and she nodded, envisioning the scene as it had unfolded when she'd arrived. She'd scented them both through the magic barrier of Gavra's room, and it had taken all her shaky will to keep from entering and having her own taste of both men.

Now she'd tasted Silas, had melded him once, and that connection had provided a link that would help keep her grounded for a time.

"I love everything he does to me," he said. "But I especially love that you need me to balance what he does to you."

She shook her head. "He hasn't done anything to me. I never even touched him before that kiss."

"And yet you're in danger of falling to pieces just imagining his dick in my mouth. Or are you imagining his dick in your mouth? We still have a little bit of a mental link, but it wouldn't take a genius to know what's going through your head after that question. This is what he does to us both."

She let out a groan and pressed her face into his chest. "Yes. He's in my head so deep—has been since the first time I saw him."

"So …" Silas drew the word out as he rubbed both hands down her sides. "Maybe we need to get into each other's heads a little more to balance him out."

She breathed him in, tempted to say yes and take him to her quarters and stay there, fucking away all her worries. But Silas was only half of a piece that would make her whole, and she couldn't keep hiding from the other half.

"Not yet," she said. "I need to know he's okay first." She stretched up on her toes and pressed a kiss to his lips, pulling back just as he began to open up and ask for more.

"I'm sure he's fine," Silas said, looking a little irritated.

"Come on," she said, ignoring his comment and taking him by the hand. "Brace yourself. The drift is short and easy here, but still discombobulating for non-nymphaea."

Without giving him another second to prepare, she closed her eyes, reached for the River, and dove in.

There were a dozen major grottos in the Haven, and each one had a small collection of cages that would be suitable for someone like Gavra. It didn't take long to find the one where he was being held. Her mother would have wanted to keep him close.

They ended the drift in the shade of a tree near a small pond with blooming lily pads floating on its surface. Before Assana could step onto the path, the air filled with dense fog right in front of her and there was a familiar rushing sound. A second later, a figure appeared with a loud pop.

Silas jumped and let out a curse beside her when the nymph appeared out of thin air.

"Ephyra! What are you doing here?" Assana asked.

"Guarding this beast," the nymph said, casting a sidelong glance back at the structure where Gavra was being held. "He's a wild one … I don't recommend getting too close. He keeps trying to seduce me into letting him out."

"We just wanted to make sure he's all right," Assana said, cautious not to say more lest her mother be listening in.

Ephyra smiled shakily, her good humor appearing forced. "He's more than all right. It's just a shame there's only one of him for all of us. I'm only disappointed that it's going to take longer before we're ready to have a go at him. We're still debating whether we want to have him one at a time, or all at once. You're acquainted with him already. What do you think he'd enjoy?"

Assana frowned and narrowed her eyes. She didn't believe a word of the forced enthusiasm. Beside her, Silas made an odd sound that might have been a laugh. She shot a look at him and he raised a fist to his mouth, feigning a cough.

"I think it's inappropriate to speculate. You should just ask him, if he has any choice in the matter."

Ephyra's expression darkened and she seemed to shrink inward. "Sister, I don't like this," she whispered. "The fact that it's *him* we get to couple with is the only silver lining, but it's all wrong. You're lucky you landed an ursa mate, or your mother would have dragged you into this plan too. She said as much while you were gone."

Assana's eyes widened in astonishment. "Ephyra, is she not in your mind now? Can she hear you? Be careful."

The other nymph shook her head. "It comes and goes. Small blessing that we can tell when she's got hold of us, even if we can't do anything about it. She hasn't melded us deeply enough yet to control us all at once for more than an hour or two."

"Why won't you fight her? Band together to overpower her," Silas said.

Ephyra's brows shot up and she let out a rueful laugh. "You don't know Nyx. She's always got enough of us under thrall to keep the rest in line. Besides, we all agreed to do this. How do you think she got our blood to begin with? She didn't force us into it."

"But I thought … When I saw Clio earlier with the rest of you, I could swear she didn't look like she liked what she was doing."

"Assana, we hate having our minds invaded. It's the most unpleasant sensation. Like being asked to take a big mouthful of foulness and hold it without spitting or swallowing. It gets easier each time, though, and it's to protect the Haven, so it's worth it. You must understand, or you wouldn't have brought him back to us … I know you were friends with your brother's dragon. But the safety of the Haven …"

"How long until you go through with the breeding?" Assana asked, hoping she could have time to come up with a plan.

"Nyx says she needs a week for the connection to be strong enough with all of us. Like I said, it's getting easier, even though it's only been a couple days. When she's in my head, I can feel the power." She took a shaky breath, darting a glance over her shoulder at Gavra's cage. "I keep trying to remind myself that it's worth it. I mean, we want it to be … but we want to conceive with a mate, not through some weird ritual where we aren't even the true mothers of our babies."

"No one wants that," Assana said, though she wasn't sure what Ephyra meant. Who else would be the babies' mothers?

"We will bear the children for the Haven. Oh, Assana, why couldn't you have convinced your mother to try the breeding pact ages ago? There aren't enough ursa males to go around yet. The Thiasoi all agreed to be last, but now we're faced with this."

"Gavra's not that bad," Assana said, though she wondered why she'd try to comfort her friend when she hoped they'd figure out a way to divert her mother's plan before she managed to carry it out.

"He isn't the man any of us want. Having your mother in our heads … her spirit taking over our bodies, making us all extensions of her just so we can conceive without being marked … I mean, I would love to mate a dragon someday, but not this way. Not this dragon. Is there anything you can do to make her stop? Please, Assana."

"But you agreed to it …" Assana began, her mind reeling as the scope of her mother's plan became clearer.

"We didn't know it would be like this. She claimed it was our duty, so we agreed. You would do anything to protect the Haven, too. This is what we have to do!"

The nymph was shaking now, her lips trembling and tears threatening to escape her eyes.

Assana reached out to console her friend and Ephyra suddenly went completely still, her eyes glazing over for a second before they cleared again. The whirlpools of her irises swirled with a different color and her mother's eyes looked back at her. Assana gasped.

"Daughter, what has this nymph been telling you?"

"Nothing, Mother," Assana said through gritted teeth.

Ephyra turned and surveyed her surroundings. "I see you found the dragon's prison. You will see he is unharmed. I trust he will remain within that cell until I have need of him. I'd rather not be forced to demonstrate what I can do to your sisters if you misbehave." Ephyra casually unsheathed a sharp dagger at her waist and lifted it so the point was aimed at her own eye.

"I only wish to speak to him, Mother," Assana said, her voice weak with fear for Ephyra's welfare.

Silas took charge then, swiftly reaching out for the nymph's wrist and twisting the dagger out of her hand. Her focus didn't waver from Assana.

"Don't test me, daughter. You should be in your quarters completing a second melding with your new mate. You will join me for breakfast tomorrow. I trust you can prove you are going forward with the melding to give me a grandchild soon."

Assana let out a long sigh. "Fine, we will be there."

Just as suddenly as she appeared, the presence of her mother was gone from Ephyra's eyes. The nymph sagged and stumbled, but Silas caught her as she began to sob uncontrollably.

"Ephyra, I promise we will fix this. As soon as we can figure out a way to," Assana said.

Through her hitching sobs, Ephyra shook her head. "She's too strong. Unless that dragon can use his powers. Do you think he'll help? Please tell me he can help!"

Assana glanced across the expanse of lily pads toward Gavra's cage. He was an immortal, like her mother. They'd hoped that he and his brother together could find a way to subdue Nyx, but perhaps Gavra's powers alone were enough. It had to be worth a try.

They comforted Ephyra until she had calmed. When Assana was sure she would be all right, they left her sitting on the mossy ground beside the pond, catching her breath.

They'd barely reached the outside of Gavra's cage when he rushed toward them, grabbing hold of the bars.

"What the fuck did she do with Aodh!" he yelled.

Assana winced, wishing she had a better answer than the one she was about to give him about his brother's whereabouts.

"He's in a more secure prison," she said. "Which means Mother's probably sent him into a temporal bubble."

Gavra swore. "What time period?"

"I have no way of knowing. Somewhere Meri can't find him, so it's likely a time before they knew each other. We'll get him back when we figure out how to get through to Mother, I promise." She took a deep breath, ill-prepared for what she was about to suggest next. "I think if you can use your power on her it might help shake her out of this."

Gavra shook his head. "Assana, she's immortal like me. Her power as strong as mine is. I can't affect her with my power unless she already had some desire. I knew the moment she and your father got together that she would want no other male. So short of divine power, it's unlikely I can make a difference, and I doubt you'll be able to talk my mother or Gaia, or even Dionysus into stepping in."

"But you're male," Assana said, clinging to her wish for balance in the Haven, sure that somehow his sex must be enough to help.

"That in itself isn't enough. She doesn't *love* me. She loved the men who left her or were taken. If anything, my presence would do more harm than good."

"Do you think I could help?" Silas interjected, looking at her. "You said yourself that my touch calms your mind. Maybe it would calm hers too."

Gavra snorted. "She'd see right through you, man. Somehow I doubt seduction's your strong suit—the females you've been with had no other options."

"You can be a real ass, you know that?" Silas snapped.

"Gavra, please," Assana said, frustrated by the males' bickering. "As much as I hate the idea, I am at a loss right now. We have to try something. At least let me get you out of this cage."

She stepped close and placed her hands on the bars,

commanding the living roots to part. Vines sprouted from them, twining over her hands as tiny leaves and flowers unfurled and reached for the moonlight, but she failed to create even a tiny gap in the web of roots that held Gavra prisoner.

She concentrated harder, her throat constricting with frustration until she was nearly in tears over her inability to break through. Gavra wrapped his hand around hers and squeezed.

"Stop," he said softly, the heat of his hand sending a jolt of desire through her that did nothing to comfort her, and everything to make her want to drift into the cage with him instead. Reluctantly she pulled her hand away.

"Mother's probably enchanted the cage so that she's the only one who can open it. There's nothing I can do."

"It's all right," Silas said, taking Assana's hand. He took a deep breath. "I think I have an idea. Just hear me out."

CHAPTER 21

SILAS

Silas struggled for a moment with the idea of telling them more of what he'd learned from Sathmaki. Gavra knew none of what had occurred when he met with his clan leader, and though Assana had heard some details, she didn't know everything. Finally, he decided that he could tell them more without compromising his mission.

"I am what the ursa call a Miteradoro, an ursa who is uniquely capable of receiving Gaia's gift. Remember when I grew roots when I was helping Assana?"

Gavra let out a hungry growl. "As if I could forget being forced to watch her come for you and not being able to taste even a drop of that power, or the sweet honey dripping from her snatch."

Assana inhaled sharply, her scent growing strong enough to make him hard. He squeezed her hand and the aroma of her arousal subsided slightly.

"That happens whenever I absorb Gaia's divine power. Assana's filled with it because she's the daughter of a Dionarch. Gavra, you say your own power isn't enough to seduce her, that you need more to have any chance at controlling her, right? What if I give you everything I've collected from Assana?"

"Assana's still not as powerful as a goddess," Gavra said. "Even if my own power were magnified, I don't think it'd work on Nyx. She and Nereus were too close. I don't see Nyx falling for an attempted seduction, no matter who tries. Whatever energy you give to me won't be any more effective because I'm still not the man she loves."

"He's right, Silas. If my father were here, this wouldn't be happening."

Silas frowned, feeling defeated. "There's got to be a way to get through to her. Is there any way to at least break her bond to her soldiers? You're close to them, aren't you, Assana?"

"We grew up together, trained together. We found pleasure with each other when the need arose. We are as close as sisters. But a blood meld … I don't even know how it works. I just know it's always been forbidden because it strips the parties of their autonomy when the other person takes control."

"Aodh said it was like being a passenger inside his own body when Meri took over. He was so surprised by her betrayal, and then somehow she pushed his spirit out entirely and it took the Diviner's help to get his body back. I suppose the only bonus was that it left him with the power to drift."

Assana visibly blanched. "I can't ask the Diviner for help," she said.

She'd gone pale, and Silas reached out to her, pulling her close. "Why not? If this Diviner person knows a way to help, we have to try. Fuck, Assana, why didn't you try her first?"

"I don't like what I turn into when I go to her. It was enough when she granted me my connection to the River. When you go to her, you have to enter her chamber in your primal form. There's no dishonesty or lies in there … but when I take that shape, my desires control me, and it's impossible for me to regain my human shape without a fight."

Gavra made a low rumbling sound. "You let your wild thing out, don't you? How I would love to be there for that."

Silas swallowed, remembering how intense her need had been when he'd held her in his arms and fingered her to orgasm, then later when she'd pressed his face between her legs and urged him to do it again with his tongue. That she could be any more wild than that excited him, but for some reason, even letting go to that degree terrified her.

"Hey, you don't have to go. If you show me how to get to her, I'll visit her alone."

Assana's shoulders sagged, betraying her exhaustion. She nodded. "I will, but can we do it tomorrow?" She turned back to Gavra and Silas caught the look of weary longing in her eyes, as strong as if there were a chain binding the pair together.

"Come," he said, wrapping an arm around her shoulders and steering her away with a worried backward glance at Gavra. The other man nodded after them, his fists white-knuckled on the bars of his cage, making it clear that he'd have torn the place apart to be with them if he could have.

CHAPTER 22

ASSANA

"I hate leaving him like that," Assana said, making her way on autopilot down the pixie-lit breeze-ways to her quarters after drifting herself and Silas back to the Dionarch's palace.

"He knows what needs to be done, just as we do," Silas said, his warm presence beside her easing her agitation after the brief but incendiary touch of Gavra's fingers against hers through the bars of his cage.

She glanced at Silas when she reached her door and opened it. "Do you really think he'll tolerate it for long? I can't break Mother's spell on the cage. I'm not strong enough."

"We'll figure out a way to either override her spell or convince her to set him free. Maybe tomorrow after I talk to this Diviner of yours we'll have a better idea."

Once inside the sanctuary of her rooms, she felt the tension of the day ease. There was comfort in the familiarity of her home and she ached to restore the normalcy she was used to. Still, she found some peace in the quiet mist that filled the air around the windowed exterior of her home, this small extension of the palace that took up most of the central grotto of the Haven.

The lack of tension only made her ever-present craving for a mate … a child … more evident. It was a strange feeling that she'd simply grown accustomed to over the years. But being in the presence of the two men who she knew she was destined to mate increased that sensation's urgency.

She crossed the living space and exited a glass door framed by thick vines. Her balcony overlooked the palace itself and the majestic mossy stone behind it with all its white webs of waterfalls cascading down. Despite taking deep breaths of the air of this home she loved, she couldn't shake the frantic need to act, though she had no idea what she could do now.

Silas came up behind her and slipped his arms around her waist, pulling her against him. Immediately her unease melted away and she turned in his arms, returning his embrace and sighing into his broad chest.

"I wish I knew what to do *now*," she said. "I've never been so impatient before, but ever since I found the two of you, I can't shake this feeling that I need to hold you close, to get on with mating you so we can fight this dilemma together."

"Would it be better for you if we did?" Silas asked. "You and I, I mean. Your mother seemed insistent on it. And if it helps stabilize your psyche …"

She stared up at him, his lovely face shadowed, but his dark eyes visible from the pixie lights that glowed from inside her living quarters. There was only a hint of desire— mostly she sensed concern and a willingness to please her.

"We should meld a second time," she said. "That will mollify Mother for the time being. But as for breeding … I'm not ready yet. Besides, once we start, I won't want to do anything else until I'm pregnant, and I'm afraid …" She buried her face against him and shook her head.

"There's nothing to be afraid of, Assana. It's just sex."

"I'm not afraid of that. I'm afraid I'll fail. Fail my sisters, my brother, my uncle … my *father*, if he really is still alive. And my mother, because I know if she were herself right now, she'd be horrified by what she's done. She isn't really like this, Silas. I wish you could have met her when she was happy."

He lifted a hand and brushed a lock of hair from her cheek. "We'll find a way to protect the Haven, save your sisters, and fix her. The breeding part can wait, if you can stand it."

"I have no choice, but melding with you will help."

Silas's gaze slid from her eyes to her lips, lingering for a second before following the path of his fingertips over her jaw and along the top of her shoulder. Her skin tingled pleasantly from his touch, hot tension rising in her, but far more welcome than the anxious tightness she'd been bound up with all day.

"Even if all we ever do is meld, I don't think I can complain. Besides, I admit it would feel strange taking you fully without him here."

"I promised him I would wait," she said. "When we're together for the first time, with you inside me … and him inside me … I want you both to have an equal chance to give me a child, and he has to mark me for that to happen."

"Then we wait," Silas said, his voice low and distracted as he pressed her against the railing and brushed his lips over her temple. "He'll be rough with you. Right now I think you need someone willing to be gentle …"

Assana's breath caught in her throat at the way the heat of his palm sank into her, even though his skin barely grazed hers as he brushed his hand down her side. His lips were as gentle as the river's current in her favorite secluded swimming spot. She could almost imagine she was alone and floating along the surface with the lazy waves lapping over her skin, except his touch made her hot instead of cooling her off.

Silas's mouth found hers, and before she knew it, he'd lifted her in his arms as he kissed her and carried her back inside toward her bed. His light touches continued, lips sliding down her neck as his fingers tugged at the cords that held her gown closed.

"Need to see you naked," he murmured and hovered above her, slowly unlacing the closure until the front of her gown fell open. "This thing hides nothing and everything. It's maddening to see you in it, knowing you don't even wear panties or a bra, but somehow every time I think I'll catch a glimpse, the light changes and I don't see a damn thing."

Assana let out a husky laugh. "That's the beauty of nymph gowns. They're far more utilitarian than they look at first glance. But now you get to see."

His dark eyes blazed as he stared down at her, not touching, though the slow graze of his eyes made her skin tingle as they trailed over her torso down to the apex of her thighs. Silas licked his lips and seemed to force his gaze back to her face.

"You're so beautiful, Asana. Every inch of you is perfect. I never imagined I'd be so lucky."

He lay down beside her and rested his hand on her stomach, his breath sweltering against the side of her face. Slowly he resumed his stroking, up her belly to cup her breast and roll her nipple between thumb and forefinger. The touch sent a spike of pleasure through her and she turned to face him, craving the feel of him under her own hands.

"Silas, let me touch you."

"You don't have to. I'm all about making you feel good."

"But I want to … touching you makes me feel good. I didn't get to touch you enough before."

He pulled back enough to look down into her eyes. "My dick in your mouth wasn't enough?"

"You weren't naked. I want to look at you too." She tugged at the hem of his loose green shirt, then pushed it up to reveal his tight, brown stomach. She also revealed the huge bulge of his cock inside the front of his trousers and her breath caught. "You're hard again."

"It's a perpetual state around you and Gavra. Especially since you reminded me how amazing it felt to have your lips wrapped around me."

A pleased smile tugged at her lips. "You liked that? I wasn't sure if I got it right."

"I doubt you could do anything wrong when it comes to making me feel good."

"Can I undress you?" she asked, already reaching for his button to unfasten it. He seemed about to protest, but her attention fixated on the tightness in his pants and the way his zipper closure parted as she pulled the tab all the way down. His familiar scent washed over her, and she reverently brushed the backs of her fingers up along his hard length, reveling in the hot, smooth silk of him.

Silas let out a groan and rolled onto his back. "You can do whatever you want to me. *Please* do whatever you want to me. I'm all yours."

Swallowing, she gave him a grateful look and then sat up, shedding her own dress completely before straddling his thighs. She gripped the waist of his pants and tugged them down, slipping lower along his legs as she went until she yanked them off his ankles. He sat up and hurriedly pulled his shirt off over his head, tossing it aside.

He was magnificent naked, with his broad shoulders and tawny skin gleaming in the dim pixie lights that twinkled like a canopy over her bed. The little sprites liked watching and would continue to glow like that as long as there was activity to observe. His jet-black hair hung in tangled waves just brushing his shoulders and his dark eyes, slightly slanted, drank her in where she knelt at his feet.

But his cock was the thing that caught her eye the longest, its hard, throbbing length almost begging for her attention. It reminded her what that glorious tool was intended for, and she suddenly was awash in guilt.

"I'm sorry we can't make love," she said. "I mean, that I'm not ready to."

Within a breath, Silas was on his knees in front of her, sliding his hands from her shoulders to her cheeks.

"Assana, you don't need to apologize for that. I already told you I'm happy simply pleasing you."

"But I can tell how much you want it. You're a fertile ursa male, ready to share your seed with me. I'm depriving you of something you must be used to having."

He let out a soft snort of laughter that made her stare at him in confusion.

"Baby, you're not depriving me of anything. You're naked and I get to touch you. What more could any male want? And it's not like I've got any more experience fucking women than you do fucking men. Ursa males aren't allowed to stick their dicks in any ursa female who isn't his mate. Since you're my mate, you'll be my first … but not until you're ready."

She shook her head, confused. "But you lived … *outside* … before. My sisters played with human men. Surely you had human women?"

He shrugged. "Never had any interest. I had my partner at the time. Raj and I were close once, believe it or not. Though our relationship never had much depth, we were very well-matched, physically. And where we were stationed, there wasn't exactly an abundance of females to tempt us. Other ursa guardian pairs have different experiences, but we were both content waiting for our mate, until we got tired of each other. That's when Gavra came along and everything suddenly started making sense for me for the first time in my life."

She blinked up at him in astonishment, her entire perception turned on its head. "You've only made love to other males?" A little surprised laugh escaped her.

Silas raised his eyebrows. "Is that funny?"

"No … it's just … I never realized how much we had in common. I've barely been in contact with males I wasn't related to since I came of age. My sister nymphs and I would play together frequently, though. It was an enjoyable necessity."

"I can imagine," Silas said, his smile growing suggestive. "But I do have extensive knowledge of how to please a female. I've never made love to one, but I've pleasured dozens in between my guardian duties. Now my skills are all yours."

Her body warmed, her core tingling as she recalled the deftness with which he'd pleasured her before. Twice he'd taken her to orgasm, easing that unbearable ache inside her more than any other self-administered release, or even orgasms she'd had at the hands of her Thiasoi sisters.

"I'd like to pleasure you first … I need to learn how your body works, what you like. I already know my mouth pleases you …" She pressed her hands against his broad, warm chest and pushed him back. His gaze grew hooded and he eased down onto her bed again, watching her as she moved to hover over him.

"Like I said, I doubt there's a single thing you could do that I wouldn't like," he said.

"Do you like this?" She traced her fingertips along the contours of his jaw, his cheeks, his brows, touched his forehead and drew a line down along the straight bridge of his nose. She'd never had the opportunity to touch a male so freely before, and having Silas—one of her two destined mates—naked and willing was a rare treat she intended to take advantage of. She doubted she would have this much self-control if it were Gavra lying in front of her.

She grazed her fingertips over Silas's lips, warm and silken-soft. His pink tongue darted out and met her skin, wetting one fingertip. Experimentally she pushed her finger in between his lips and his mouth opened, capturing her slender digit and sucking into the warm wetness.

Assana gasped and a flood of warmth heated her core as his tongue swirled around and around the tip of her finger. One of Silas's hands brushed her thigh, sliding up the outside until it rested right on top with his thumb brushing the inside close to her aching center. He didn't move it more, but the presence of his touch made her moan.

She withdrew her finger from his mouth, drawing a wet line over his lower lip before touching lower, over the rough stubble of his chin where there was a slightly brushier patch of hair right beneath his lip. Impulsively, she bent and darted her tongue out, pressing it against the coarse bristles and enjoying the spark of sensation of the roughness of him there.

He held perfectly still, as though he were holding his breath. When she pulled back again, he watched her intently.

"I liked that," he said in a deep voice that verged on a growl. "I especially like how obvious it is that you're enjoying this. I want to touch you so bad, but I don't want you to stop what you're doing."

"You like being touched? I almost feel like I am making love to you, even though you aren't inside me."

His expression changed, grew more intense. "Assana, it will always be making love between us, whether we're fucking or not. Your touch is heaven. My body is yours to do with as you wish."

"How can you say that so soon? It isn't always Fate's choice for all of us, I know this. The turul are different, but we can choose. How can you be so sure? Maybe you and I are only meant to share him, not each other."

The sudden self-doubt made her pull back, but Silas gripped her hand and placed it back in the center of his chest. He was warm and solid, and his heart beat beneath her palm in a strong percussive rhythm that matched her own pounding pulse.

"I didn't know at first. All I knew was what he promised me. That we would have a female we would share, and I knew without meeting you that I would love you because he said it was meant to be. The dragons and turul are children of Fate. They don't get the choices our kind get, and when we are captured in their nets, there's no escaping either. I love you, Assana, because not loving you is beyond the realm of reason."

She let out a shuddering breath and flattened her hand against his breastbone. "What about him?"

He chuckled wryly. "He doesn't make it easy, but yeah, I love him too."

"I wish I could touch him like this without losing my mind." She slid her hand across Silas's chest, drawing small circles around his nipples, mesmerized by how hard and pebbled they became under her touch.

He took in a slow breath. "I have a feeling he may not be as patient with you. He's not the kind of man to lie back and let you have control."

Assana smiled as her gaze drifted down to settle on his thick shaft. "No, but that's good. I want to be wild with him, like he said, and I want no less from him. With you … this is what I want."

His stomach tightened when she slid her hand down the center, bumping over the ridges of his abdominals. She was fascinated by the shapes of his muscles, where they bulged and tapered to his groin, as though pointing toward the magnificent tower of flesh that jutted from the dark nest of curls between his legs. She deliberately avoided contact with his cock, sliding her hand down over the top of one massive thigh, then back up the other.

She shifted slightly, angling her body so she could indulge herself and take in the beauty of his virile length and the heavy sack that hung beneath. When she moved, his hand dislodged from her thigh, but returned to rest on her hip instead.

Silas let out a little hum of contentment, his fingers sliding down the curve of her ass and squeezing slightly. She felt the tightening of his fingertips into her flesh and the way her ass parted from his touch. Glancing behind her, she saw his gaze fixed on her nethers, his mouth slightly open. His hungry look made her core heat more.

"Touch me," she said. "I can tell you want to."

"Fuck yes," he breathed and his fingertips slid closer to her core, then grazed up along the outside, tracing a circle around her slick, hot opening.

Assana's attention wavered under his touch, but she refocused on the impressive specimen of fertile male in front of her, sliding her hand between his thighs and cupping his balls.

Silas spread his thighs and tilted his hips up, giving her a closer view of the pair of heavy orbs in her hand. They seemed to heat against her palm as though filled with power that made her skin tingle as she stroked them. She bent to kiss each one, pleased by the soft, low growl he made when she darted her tongue out and laved both with a long, slow lick.

She proceeded to trail her tongue up along his length to the sound of a sigh from him. At the same time, the fingers between her legs grew bolder, pushed her folds open and stroked through her channel to her aching clit.

"I want you on my tongue, Assana. Now."

He'd lain there so quietly compliant, the urgent command shot a jolt of excitement through her. She moved, eagerly placing her knees on either side of his head. She was no stranger to this position, but wasn't accustomed to the huge column of flesh in front of her. In the past she'd have faced the smooth, wet snatch of one of her fellow nymphs.

All she knew was that he enjoyed her mouth on him, and she most definitely enjoyed his mouth on her. He gripped her ass and pulled her down, then his hot tongue went at her, dipping in deep before finding her clit and teasing it in maddening little circles. She couldn't help but wriggle her hips so her pussy rubbed harder against his mouth.

Silas's hips jacked up against her absentminded stroking and she forced herself to redirect her focus to the fascinating and delicious cock in front of her. She took him between her lips and slid her mouth down as far as she could go, then farther when he pushed up into her throat. Startled by the invasion, she closed her eyes and breathed through her nose, but soon realized she'd simply have to endure not breathing while she sucked him, if she intended to do it properly. She could live for a time without air if she was prepared for it, and knew this would only take a few minutes, though with the intensity of the pleasure of his tongue teasing her clit she didn't want it to end anytime soon.

Finding a swift rhythm that matched his fingers pumping into her opening, Assana lost herself to the taste and feel of his shaft sliding between her lips. Their earlier melding had faded and she only had the barest glimmer of his pleasure from what was left, but that was enough to push her closer to the edge.

Silas's tongue continued working avidly at her clit, each stroke sending waves of fresh pleasure through her body. When he let out a long, deep snarl and pushed his hips up into her stroking fists and sucking mouth, the awareness of his pleasure made the threatening storm of her orgasm break suddenly. Her entire body convulsed, and it was all she could do to keep her mouth wrapped around the head of his cock as the exquisite sensations rocketed through her.

Silas gripped both her hips hard, holding her tight against his mouth while he consumed her orgasm, just as she held onto his cock and drank in the hot, salty-sweet jets of his.

Tremors coursed through both their bodies as their orgasms slowly subsided. His hands gradually relaxed and he reached to tug at her arm. Assana twisted around and collapsed against his chest, gazing into his eyes. She brushed a palm down the side of his enraptured face and leaned in to press her lips against his.

Silas's mouth was still tangy and slick from her juices, and her tongue still tingled from the rush of his seed across it. The flavors mingled when their tongues slid together, and they both let out mirrored sounds of contentment. As they kissed, she reached out with her mind, pressing her fingers tighter against his temples. Immediately she sensed him opening up, inviting her in, and then the meld was complete, their minds curling around each other, entwined and sated as their bodies were.

They slept, their dreams synchronized and both featuring a beautiful caged man with vivid red hair and a gaze that could incite lust. Though Assana had yet to meld the dragon, she'd tasted remnants of his power in Silas's climax and longed to taste more.

CHAPTER 23

GAVRA

Gavra gave up pacing his cage and forced himself to try to relax. After more futile attempts to burn through the bars of his cage with his fire, he accepted that there was no straightforward way out of his situation, so he decided he may as well try to enjoy himself however he could. He was as hedonistic as the next dragon, so it wasn't too far a stretch once he headed back to the luxurious bathroom of his prison, though calling it a "room" was being generous. Despite the lack of privacy, the nymphaca at least treated their captives well.

When he shed his clothes and slid into the deep, heated tub, he felt the eyes of his Thiasoi guards through the latticework walls that surrounded him. Without turning to look, he said, "Fantasizing about all the babies I'll fill you with, girls?"

The pointed silence made him turn his head. He lifted his brows at the lovely pair of nymphs leaning against the low stone wall outside his cage. Neither one was smiling.

"Not looking forward to being bedded by a dragon?" he asked.

One of the girls—the darker-skinned one he'd heard

Assana call Clio earlier—said, "They won't be ours when it's done, so no."

Gavra frowned. "Well, whose will they be? I don't intend to keep them myself, unless you want me hanging around playing daddy. Not that I wouldn't be thrilled to claim them all. I make perfect babies."

"The blood meld with Nyx means they'll be hers. We don't get to choose our own mates until we've done our duty to the Haven and our mistress."

"And you are all willing participants in this scheme?" he asked, closing his eyes and leaning his head back against the side of the tub.

When neither female answered him, he opened his eyes again.

"We are," Clio said when he raised an eyebrow at her.

He glanced at the other nymph—Ephyra—who turned haunted eyes to her Thiasoi sister before facing him again and nodding. Gavra didn't need his brother's clarifying white breath to know they weren't being entirely truthful.

"Well, I have no doubt Nyx has her reasons. She was always pragmatic, for a nymph. I haven't seen her in ages, though. Is she as beautiful as I remember? When we were young, I often wished my kind weren't restricted to mating with humans. We all had our rules to follow, though. Even we immortals aren't above the law."

"The laws have changed," Clio said. "All the ursa males living in the Haven now are testament to that. We're evolving."

He smirked at her. "Evolving and breaking old laws aren't the same thing. I'm pretty sure blood melding is still forbidden." The very thought dredged up old memories he'd just as soon leave buried in the past. Blood was far too sacred a substance to misuse this way.

Clio pressed her lips together and averted her eyes.

Ephyra's brow creased, her already anguished expression making her look like she was on the verge of erupting into tears. She bit her lip and lurched away, breaking into a run when she reached the path.

With a resolute look, Clio met his eyes again. "Wouldn't you do anything you could to protect your home, your children? This is all we are doing. It must be done, no matter how distasteful it seems, how horrifying. I ..." She paused and let out a long sigh before continuing. "I don't like the idea of breeding with an unwilling partner, though. For that, I am sorry. All the Thiasoi are sorry."

Gavra let out a low chuckle. "Who said I was unwilling? Nyx would know how very willing I can be, particularly when the promise involves making love to a beautiful nymph." Gavra chose his words carefully on the off-chance Nyx had enchanted his prison with some truth-discerning web. He had no intention of bedding any of these females, though if it came to that, he would without hesitation.

Clio seemed to relax and regarded him more thoughtfully. "Are you really all right with this?"

"Not crazy about the cage, but you don't have to try too hard to get a dragon on board with the prospect of a sex ritual. How soon do I get to have the pleasure of ... how many of you are there?"

"Eleven. It would have been twelve, if Assana hadn't returned with an ursa mate. Nyx planned to talk her into the meld as well. Gaia knows Assana's long overdue for a mate. We all are."

Gavra's skin chilled despite the heat of the water he was submerged in. Nyx was willing to blood meld her own daughter? It was all he could do to bury the rage and keep up his cheerful ruse. He was suddenly even more grateful for Silas than he'd been when he watched the ursa deftly service Assana through her near-meltdown earlier.

"I can't wait," he said, hoping his voice really conveyed at least some eagerness. "But what I'd really like to know is how Nyx thinks you all are going to get pregnant without me marking you. She knows how dragons work."

A disturbance in the air sent a genuine chill across the skin that was exposed above the water. Gavra turned again to see the imposingly stunning, statuesque figure of the Dionarch herself standing outside his cage, gazing in impassively. She turned her heavily antlered head to Clio.

"Leave us, my dear. I need to speak to the dragon alone tonight."

She returned her hypnotic gaze back to him and moved closer, her graceful movements every bit as mesmerizing as her daughter's had been the day he'd first set eyes on Assana. He didn't feel the same hot flare of need for this female, however. Only a cool wariness took hold and he was no longer able to relax in the heated tub.

He turned to brace his hands on the edge and hopped out, casting a quick glance at Nyx as he grabbed a large, soft towel from a nearby basket and wrapped it around his waist.

"Nyx," he said, forcing a smile to his lips. "It's been too long."

She only regarded him dispassionately, though her brow seemed to twitch with interest as her gaze slid down his half-naked, dripping body. Perhaps seducing her was within the realm of possibility, after all. He would have to keep that in mind if the opportunity presented itself.

"Hmm, I could have done without any dragons visiting the Haven, particularly your sister."

"You could always come visit us, you know. We haven't seen you since … when was it?"

"Your sister's wedding to that monster pet of hers. And to think we gave that man our blessings, only to have him turn into the Lamia's puppet."

"More than three thousand years is a long time to carry a grudge, Nyx. Let it go. Nikhil's no longer under the Lamia's spell. He's our weapon against her now."

"Is that supposed to console me? What's done is done. I barely got my son back after that monster's massacres, only to have your sister take him away again. Nereus is likely dead along with his Thiasoi squadron, and Neph has betrayed me. This is my last resort."

"And what would Nereus think if he returned and found out what you'd done? Blood melding the very soldiers who pledged their loyalty and protection to the Haven."

"He knew the Haven must be protected at all costs. If he died for this place, I won't let his sacrifice be for nothing."

"You don't know that he's dead. Calder believes his squadron still lives."

"In that despicable monster's clutches? If the Lamia has him, he's as good as dead and you know it. And if he weren't her prisoner, he would have returned to me already."

Her hands were clenched into fists at her side, her immortal aura flaring in a neon kaleidoscope of colors. The heart of her pain was clear enough to Gavra despite the confusion of thoughts and emotions coursing through her. All this was somehow to honor her mate's memory.

"You're right, he would have," Gavra said gently. "He loved you like no other."

"And I him," Nyx said, her voice breaking with emotion.

"But to blood meld your own daughter? Nyx, I don't think he would have been able to stand by and watch that."

She gave him a pained look and shook her head. "No. I'm glad it didn't come to that, but something needed to be done. I'm sure you have questions. I came as a courtesy to answer them so you understand."

He had dozens of questions, but knowing he'd uncovered a potential weakness, he was compelled to work at it like a loose tooth. Ignoring her offer, he let out a low chuckle and said, "Sweet Mother, Nyx, you are as beautiful as you always were. Nereus was a lucky satyr."

Nyx's intent expression softened, her eyes growing glassy. "I was the lucky one," she said, turning to pace to the stone wall where his guards had been perched earlier before facing him again.

Gavra slowly shook his head and smiled wistfully. "I still remember when he courted you. Back when we were still gods to all of humankind. None of us believed he'd win you, but we all hoped. At least I did … My brothers had their own obsessions at the time. Not that you would have given us the time of day, nor any of the Winds who craved a taste of you, for that matter."

"I'd have taken any of you as lovers if you'd been less cocky or capricious. But never mates, and you know it. Nereus was the only male for me."

Gavra chuckled again and nodded, gripping the smooth roots that made up the bars of his cage and peering out at Nyx. "I know, we all had our responsibilities to our race, but that didn't mean we didn't harbor dirty fantasies from time to time. We all played with nymphs when the opportunity struck. You were the most desirable nymph of them all, back then. That fool Nereus was the only male with the balls to chase you in earnest, though."

"He didn't chase me. I chose him simply because it was my right and I kept seeing all of you having children, so I wanted my own."

"That isn't how I remember it. He wanted you, but went about courting you in his own way. We used to spy on you bathing in the sea when we were young. Zephyrus was usually the instigator, claiming he could seduce you with an invisible caress … that you'd give in to his touch while you basked asleep in the sun. Leave it to one of the Winds to make such assertions. He and I had a running bet which of us you'd fall for first. The younger dragons and satyrs all made wagers on it too. But Nereus caught us and would have none of it. The man was righteously indignant that we'd be so crass."

Nyx's brows twitched and a perplexed smile tugged at her lips. "Nereus did that? I don't believe you."

"You can test me for the truth—I wouldn't put it past you to."

"Very well," she said, then waved her hand in the air. A light mist coalesced with a cool tingle over his heated skin. "Do go on, dragon. I'll know whether you lie now."

"As you wish," he said, turning and leaning one shoulder on the twisted roots of his cage and picking at a small shoot of greenery that grew from one thick segment. "After that, Nereus appointed himself as your secret guardian. We still got away with watching occasionally … I think he was just as distracted by your beauty as the rest of us—but making wagers about the flavor of your snatch were out of the question."

"He was always concerned about my virtue," Nyx said. "Such a strange quality for a satyr, don't you think?"

"Not for one as deeply in love as Nereus was with you. That was ages before you 'chose' him, as you said."

"I still don't believe you. He behaved that way with all the nymphs."

"And yet we all managed to have our fill of them when we were invited to the Haven's debauched parties. We respected him, and even back then knew he harbored deep feelings for you, so we steered clear. I never understood why he held back, though. When I see what I want, I take it … I've never seen any sense in waiting."

"You know you're unlikely to be turned down," she said, giving his body another frank assessment. "Are you telling me you never propositioned me because Nereus stood in your way? For how long?"

"Long enough for humanity to build their biggest shrines to us."

Nyx stilled, her eyes growing wide. "Your sister already reigned in Egypt … you all had established your Ascendancies … and he still waited?"

"Perhaps he took his job too seriously. Either way, he was devoted to you for longer than I can remember before you finally noticed."

With a shimmer of magic, her tall primal frame shrank, her antlers receding and her blue-green tinted skin becoming more human. She sat on the stone wall with a sigh, her shoulders sagging. "I wish I had known. We had too little time together before he was captured. Only a scant few centuries. We only had time for me to bear him two beautiful children. I would have born him dozens more—strong satyrs and lovely nymphs."

"You may yet, Nyx," Gavra said. "Let me and my brother go and we will do everything in our power to find your mate and bring him home."

A bitter grimace sharpened her features suddenly at the mention of his brother and Gavra knew he'd made a grave mistake.

"Your brother is never returning. Not after what he did."

Gavra clenched his jaw, regrouping. With effort, he refrained from lashing out in rage again. It would do him no good when he was at such a disadvantage.

"Fine, leave Aodh out of it. But I can help, if you let me."

It pained him to say the words, to disregard his brother's disappearance, but the immediate threat was sitting right in front of him. If he could get through to Nyx on his own somehow, he would find another way to get to whatever prison she had sent Aodh to.

"I wish it were that easy," she said. "But even if I did release you, it wouldn't help. Nereus is dead and my son is on a futile quest, abandoning his home and leaving it vulnerable without him. I would know if my mate still lived. Believe me, I did hold out hope for a long time. The River showed him to me when I looked, and our mating bond let me know he was alive even after he was captured. But the more satyrs and nymphs I sent to hunt for Nereus and Calder's squadron, the more men we lost, seduced somehow by that creature Meri has become. The females, at least, resisted her lure.

"We were so close. When the link finally snapped and he was gone from my mind, I knew there was no point in continuing the search. He had to be dead, and he wouldn't have wanted me to needlessly risk the lives of the nymphs who remained to find him. The satyrs were all dead by then."

"Calder lived. Did you ever test your connection to your son while he and his father were lost?"

Nyx shook her head. "I knew he was capable and could take care of himself. But you're right, I believed him dead too. It was a surprise when he returned."

"Yet you still have no hope for Nereus," Gavra said flatly.

Nyx's features pinched, her eyes flashing with hurt and anger. "Don't you think I hoped? When Calder returned, I wanted with all my heart for Nereus to follow. They'd been captured together, or so I thought. But I was wrong about that. Calder wasn't held with the others, and he lost the connection to them too. He has no more proof of their survival than you or I. All I have is this empty pit inside me where my link to Nereus used to be."

Gavra closed his eyes, wishing her aura held even the smallest glimmer of hope, but it was clear she believed with all her being that her mate had died, and she was still deeply bound by grief.

"I'm sorry," he finally said. "He was a strong satyr. A good friend. It's just difficult for me to believe he'd have let go without a fight … without at least a final word to you. When I knew him, he would talk about you. Most of us saw you as cold and cruel even then. You were a ruthless leader beside your brother. But Nereus made me believe you had a softer side."

"Enough," Nyx said, cutting off the fresh reminiscence that had been at the tip of Gavra's tongue. She stood stiffly, her shoulders tense and her fists clenched. "I've heard enough about a man I will never see again. Don't torment me with your memories."

His two Thiasoi guards returned to their mistress's side.

"Fair enough. How long until I get a taste of these lovely creatures who have sacrificed their freedom to save the Haven?"

"It will take several more days before my blood meld with them all is strong enough," she said, turning back to him. "To avoid requiring a dragon mark, they must each become vessels for my immortal spirit. As you can imagine, this is not something that's been done before … for an immortal spirit to inhabit a mortal body, even eleven of them, it has to be done a little at a time."

"This is unnecessary, Nyx. You have me here as your prisoner to do with as you wish. I've already agreed to be your stud. Why not release these women from their unnatural bond to you and we can give you an immortal child the old fashioned way? I would gladly honor your body as it is meant to be honored. I am your servant."

The words tasted bitter as they crossed his tongue. He didn't think they'd work, anyway, not after how deeply her grief for Nereus still had hold of her, but he had to try. If it got him close enough to her to give her a full dose of his magic, he might at least be able to incapacitate her long enough to allow Assana to take control. Though he didn't know how she would keep it. Without a quick way out of the Haven, or a stronger ally inside, he was at a loss as to how to neutralize Nyx indefinitely.

Surprisingly, Nyx turned and smiled at him. It was a sad smile, but her aura still brightened when her gaze slid down his body.

Gavra returned her smile and tugged the towel from around his hips, pretending to dry himself and revealing his lower half in the process.

"My offer stands," he said, and conjured an image in his mind of Assana as she'd been mid-climax earlier so his cock would show some life.

Nyx's aura brightened and she nodded. "I will keep it in mind, dragon. Thank you for the conversation."

She swept off into the misty darkness of the Haven, the fog seeming to part for her as she moved.

When she disappeared, Gavra sagged down on his bed, falling back and draping an arm across his face. He wished like hell he had a better idea than seducing his captor to try to gain control of the Haven. Even if he could fake feelings for Nyx, he highly doubted he could ever measure up to the man who had loved her so well when they were young.

He didn't even want to think about Assana's reaction when he told her his plan, though.

CHAPTER 24

MERI

Somewhere in Europe

The five satyrs floated limp inside the huge, fluid-filled tank, tubes running from their extremities, each one delivering a slow supply of their life's essence to a series of sealed blood bags dangling around the perimeter.

The constant supply was just what Doctor Saint George had required, and now that they'd found a way to connect this tank and the valuable supply of life-giving elixir to her creation, she was on the verge of happiness.

"The first male continues to break through your mental bonds, Doctor Waters," one of the scientists said.

It took Meri a moment to register that the man was addressing her. She was no longer Doctor Saint George. That body had passed away peacefully in her sleep and been mourned by her colleagues. She had a new vessel now, a strong, youthful and intelligent woman named Adele Waters. Adele had considered Doctor Saint George a mentor for the first few years of her internship at the Alexandria Institute, then later they had been lovers.

Adele had been easy to take once her mentor confessed that she was dying. Grief made the human mind weak, and Meri had taken over once she'd taken a small sample of Adele's blood.

Now she was Doctor Waters, the obvious successor to the esteemed older woman who had led the Ultiori for the last sixty years.

"Doctor Waters?" the scientist asked again.

"Show me his brain activity charts," she said. She needed to find out how the one satyr kept working his way nearly free of his mental bonds.

Staring at the jagged mountains of the chart, she cursed, wishing again that she had immortal blood with which to control the five male captives completely. All she had was her own ancient spirit and the regular infusions of blue dragon blood to keep her mental powers strong. The satyrs had fought her at every step until she'd finally broken them. She didn't need them sane, after all—just alive.

This one male, however, was proving to be a problem and she cursed herself for leaving behind the sixth satyr in that dark cell with his ursa lover. She figured they would eventually die there, starve to death with no way to free themselves. But she'd been wrong about that.

Nereus was a problem. His son probably would have been too, but the difference was that Calder hadn't been mated yet. The other four satyr's she'd managed to break were similarly unattached. Only Nereus with his perfect beauty and perfectly inaccessible heart still fought her despite every effort she made to sever that bond he had with his mate.

The thing was, there *was* no way that bond could have held true, so his continued spikes of consciousness made no sense.

"Bring him out and prepare my lab for him," she said.

The scientist frowned at her. "Without his blood we'll need to adjust the schedule again."

"So adjust it," she snapped. "I need to get into his head and figure out what the hang-up is. I can't do that from out here. It should only take an hour or two."

The huge satyr took some effort to remove from the tank, requiring one of the scientists to dive in and attach a harness to him, carefully avoiding his horns. They used a motorized winch to carefully lift him out and lower him onto a waiting stretcher.

Meri's pulse raced as he drew closer, his impressive shape glistening with the water that sluiced off him. Despite being more or less immobile for centuries, none of the five satyrs had atrophied the way a human might have under the same conditions.

Her own partially human body required more diligent care to keep it in shape, though the magic of her spirit maintained it somewhat. Over the centuries she'd lost her appetite for regular food, preferring the special cocktail of blood from the higher races that her hunters captured for her.

As Nereus was strapped down to the stretcher, she eyed the strong pulse in his throat, suddenly salivating as she imagined how he would taste straight from the vein. Most of her sustenance was taken from vials and bottles stored after the blood was collected. As long as the owner of the life-giving substance survived, the blood still carried power, so it didn't matter when she drank it. It was always more delicious directly from the source, however.

The orderlies wheeled her captive satyr down the hall to her secure lab and then obediently took up their places to guard the door while she worked. Even though Nereus was catatonic as well as strapped down, she refused to take any chances.

Once alone in the lab with him, she stood back and

simply admired his shape. With his power neutralized he'd reverted to his primal form, as had all his brothers, and barely fit on the huge examination table. His horns stretched back from his temples, brushing past the edge and pointing toward the floor. At the other end, his shining black hooves hung off the end. They tapered up into legs that were thick as tree trunks and covered with dense fur that curled into a luxurious fleece as it dried.

Meri's eyes grazed the dark mound that concealed his cock. In another time she might have tested his body's instincts and worked him until he was stiff enough to give her a sample of his essence. It wasn't his seed that interested her any longer, however.

"Let's see if we can break that stubborn mind of yours once and for all, my love," she said, picking up a scalpel from a tray of instruments and leaning over his placid face. The familiar angles of his bone structure filled her field of vision and made her pause. If she didn't know any better, she might have mistaken him for one who was sleeping peacefully. She was reminded of a time she'd come across him this way and lost herself for a moment too long as she sat and stared in wonder at his beauty.

She shook her head, grimacing when the rest of that memory rushed back. He hadn't been alone that day, and when she'd seen the nymph he'd lain with, the sense of betrayal had been so complete her blood turned to ice.

If only it had been another of her Thiasoi sisters, they might have invited her to join them. The Thiasoi often dallied with each other when they weren't on duty, but Nereus had always been neutral and distant to the others. At first, seeing him slumbering with the afterglow of a melding had given her hope. Perhaps he would give her a chance to meld with him too; then he would surely realize that she was the more worthy nymph to mate with.

The other nymph had roused and sat up, spied Meri across the expanse of Nereus's broad chest, and frowned.

"Can I help you, Meri?" Nyx had said, but Meri was too shocked, too hurt by the presence of her Dionarch lying in the arms of the man Meri desired. She stared at the woman, rage building until she forced herself to turn and run without a word.

If she could have murdered Nyx, she would have in the moments that followed. From the seclusion of the shadowed grove nearby, she saw Nereus rouse. He distracted Nyx with a tender touch and the nymphaea leader gave him a loving look. Nereus pulled Nyx close and proceeded to make love to her with such adoration on his face, Meri's heart filled with hatred.

She'd hated every second of watching the pair of them together, watching them meld each other and knowing they had chosen each other for mates. But she couldn't tear her eyes away. No male had ever looked at her the way Nereus looked at Nyx.

She didn't care about it now, and stared down at Nereus coldly as she made a small slice at the side of his throat and bent to press her mouth to the cut. There was a time when she'd have taken his essence in other ways, but his blood was the surest way to control his mind.

The powerful tang of the magic hit her tongue and her spirit thrummed. These satyrs were the most powerful creatures of all the Ultiori's prisoners, and the oldest. They'd been difficult to control when she first captured them, but she had Nikhil and his significant power to aid her quest at the time. Now that these five males were securely under her thrall, she would do anything to keep them there. If they escaped, there would be no reclaiming them.

Nereus was the weakest link, and she had to get into his head to find out why.

She made a swift cut at the tip of her finger and squeezed a drop of her own blood into his mouth. Then with her fingers pressed to his temples, she closed her eyes and delved deep, searching for any sign of activity in the deeper recesses of his mind.

She was met with shadows as she wandered through. The landscape of his desolate consciousness resembled a long-dry riverbed, the earth black with rich silt and cracked from lack of moisture. The place smelled dry and ancient, dusty and unused. With a thought she swiftly followed the winding path of the riverbed that had once been her captive's connection to his source of power and his link to his fellow soldiers.

Nothing but more dry, cracked earth met her as she traveled, though she recognized the landscape as a replica of the Haven she had once loved and called home. There was no life left here, no spark of magic. Only rocks and dirt and withered plants. This was what she hoped to find, but it didn't explain why his consciousness seemed to flicker periodically.

Standing at the edge of an empty pit that had once been filled with the waters of the Haven's Source, she felt a prickling sensation at the back of her neck. Her body stiffened with the certainty that she was being watched. She turned slowly and peered into the shadows, looking for any sign of movement.

Taking a few steps closer, she saw a shape in the darkness that stood out from the background within a stand of dead forest. The outline of a smooth, arced horn caught the scant light. Then it moved from behind a tree, and she saw a familiar profile.

"How are you still here?" she said. "I destroyed your spirit."

Nereus didn't answer, but he turned his head and she caught the glint of his whirlpool iris.

She took a step closer, gritting her teeth. "Tell me."

"Nyx. Is she well?" he asked.

"What do I care if Nyx is well? Tell me how you even *exist* in here. I destroyed your consciousness."

His brows twitched in confusion. "No … I'm definitely here. But this Haven isn't the one I remember. I keep searching for her, but can't find her. There's nothing but … this wasteland. How did you get here?"

She tilted her head, curious what this lost version of Nereus knew and secretly irritated that he didn't seem to recognize her.

"What do you remember?"

"I remember Nyx." His frown softened into a smile. "Making love to her. Melding with her. The children she bore and how I loved them more than life."

"Is that all?"

"What else is there?" he asked.

What else, indeed. If that was all that defined his life, it would be easy enough to subdue what was left of his consciousness. Meri drew on the ancient power of her spirit, built up from eons of consumption of the blood and power of her captives.

The darkness flowed from her in waves, filling the desolation left in Nereus's mind and drowning the spark of his consciousness in the process. He disappeared beneath the surface and she waited to see if he would reappear. When she saw no sign of him, she withdrew.

Staring down at the motionless body, she shook her head. "It's such a shame you had to choose her, Nereus. I suppose I should thank you for that favor, though. If I had kept pining for you, I never would have tried to seduce Aodh and convince him to blood meld with me. I never would have had a taste of what it means to truly be immortal. Someday soon I will have that again, and permanently. Nyx may have loved you, but you were never worthy of an immortal mate. The mate I finally choose will be worthy of me when I claim my immortal body."

She went to the door and called the orderlies, instructing them to return Nereus to the tank. His blood was far too valuable a resource for him to remain outside it for too long.

As the scientists reconnected Nereus's tubes and his blood began flowing again, she left them and went to the locked door of a secure vault beyond the huge tank. The myriad tubes coming from the satyrs' tank disappeared into the wall beside this door, pumping a steady supply of blood into the locked room. She pressed her still bloodied fingertip to the bio-scanner, unlocking the door, and entered, then shut the heavy vault door securely behind her. Within the room she faced a smaller tank similar in construction to the one that held the bodies of the satyrs.

The creature that floated inside the tank was nowhere near as impressive as the five huge satyrs, but it was the most wondrous thing Meri had created in all her centuries of tests and experiments. Her entire life's work was embodied in that small shape suspended in the thick, translucent fluid.

It had years to grow yet, to become strong enough to exist on its own. If she transferred her spirit prematurely, she would be too weak to harness the full potential of the power that infused the tiny immortal creature.

Meri pressed her hand to the glass, cooing softly at the cherubic shape. She was a pretty little thing, very pink and healthy from the strength of the blood that fed her vital nutrients through the amniotic fluid she lived in.

Perfect. She was perfect, right down to her ten fingers and ten toes, but especially the powerful blood that flowed in her tiny, perfect veins. The most important part was that the child was a completely empty vessel, simply waiting for Meri's spirit to fill and give it purpose.

She wondered if Nikhil even knew that he'd succeeded in

his quest to create a child. The blood of his lover and all her brothers had been the key. The female Elite's womb had been the nest where this little creature had first taken root.

Who knew that love had been the final ingredient that she'd always missed? But it hadn't been enough to keep the child away from her. Once the embryo proved viable, she'd spirited it out of Neela's womb like all the others before that hadn't survived.

When the time came, she would be invincible.

CHAPTER 25

ASSANA

*A*ssana stood beside Silas in the shadows of the damp cave, staring back into the darkness with the din of the waterfall drowning out her thoughts. She glanced at Silas, who appeared just as apprehensive as she felt. He'd volunteered to do this alone, and for that she was grateful, but she didn't envy him the experience. She squeezed his hand.

"Are you ready?" she asked.

Silas swallowed and shook his head. "If you're too scared to go in, maybe I should be too."

"You have no reason to be scared, Silas. I do. I'm the one who nearly raped her own brother after going in there. You're not me, so you'll be fine. As long as you're in your true form when you enter the Diviner's chamber, you have nothing to worry about. She gets into your head, but you have nothing to hide and no danger of losing your sanity like I do."

He took a deep breath and exhaled slowly through his nose. "Right. No secrets. No danger of going mad … Nothing for me to worry about."

He sounded like he was trying to convince himself of that fact, which made Assana wonder if he really did have something to hide. "She'll know about your power. You have the rooting under control now. You're still storing power from me, right?"

Silas shed his clothes and drew her hand to his groin, placing her palm against his balls. She gasped at the warm weight of them and the slight tingling of her skin in proximity to their power.

"My balls feel like they're filled with warm lead. Not a bad feeling, exactly … just … heavy. I keep thinking they'll bang together and make noise when I walk."

Assana raised an eyebrow and gently hefted the soft pouch, stroking a thumb over the velvety skin. "Feels good to me," she said suggestively.

Silas groaned when his cock twitched against the back of her hand, and she released him with a grin.

"Hold that thought," he said. "We've got important work to do when I'm done here. Where will you be?"

The "important work" wasn't precisely work. At breakfast that morning, Assana's mother had commented on her appearance and noted how easy it was to tell when a third melding had occurred. She'd reminded her mother that it took time to meld three times, but Nyx had called her bluff and so was expecting the pair of them to have completed their third melding by the evening meal.

"I want to go talk to Gavra before this afternoon. If we have to go through with a third melding to appease my mother before he's released, I want his blessing."

Silas frowned and cupped her cheek. "Are you sure it's a good idea to visit him without me? If your sanity is at stake, you'll need me with you."

She wrapped her fingers around his and kissed his palm. "I'll be fine with the bars of his cage between us. I don't need to get that close to explain things to him. It's just a conversation. If we were in the same room together, then I'd worry."

"All right," he said and bent to kiss her. "I suppose this is it. Wish me luck."

She gave his hand a squeeze and said, "Good luck."

His huge body shimmered and went to all fours. A moment later, a huge brown bear stood in front of her, nuzzled her hand, then turned and walked into the dark corridor.

When Silas disappeared from sight, Assana closed her eyes and took a deep breath. Her desire for Gavra hadn't subsided since his kiss the night before ... or since she'd first laid eyes on him, for that matter. Silas's attention had been a sweet diversion, the pleasure he gave her easing the pressure of want, but hadn't succeeded in quenching the deeper draw she had to the big red dragon.

She didn't have time to wait for Silas to meet with the Diviner before talking to Gavra, though. Her home and her sisters were in danger. Her mother at risk of ruining an ages old alliance that might be the only thing standing between the Haven and its oldest enemy. Gavra deserved the courtesy of knowing that their hand was being forced. She and Silas would have to complete their third melding this afternoon or her mother would become suspicious.

Assana passed through the veil of the waterfall that concealed the entrance to the Diviner's cave and lingered in the cool water a moment to brace herself for the moment of facing the more volatile of the two men she loved. The mere prospect of gazing into his eyes again, much less having an entire conversation, made her skin tingle pleasantly. Her mind tripped over itself, lost in a haze of images of every moment she'd been in Gavra's presence since the day they'd met, and the tug of Fate's thread on her soul. She let herself be pulled along now, only because her intention was to go to him, not because it was where her desire led. It was okay if she intended it instead of letting it control her ... wasn't it?

Before she could even track the scenery along the path between the waterfall and Gavra's cage, she was standing a few feet from the steps that led to the structure itself. It wasn't a short walk, yet here she was already, barely able to recall a single pace. Her heart pounded, her mind screaming at her that she needed to be more aware, more cautious, even as she felt that tug of Fate's string as insistent as the tug of the River's power when she drifted.

Only she was sure she hadn't drifted to him. She'd only walked, propelled by her need to be close to him. As she ascended the mossy stone staircase up to the platform of his cage, she saw the shadow of his huge body draw close to her, as though he too were drawn by her proximity. They didn't speak a word until they were close enough to touch.

Assana was only one more step from pressing against the bars of his cage when Gavra wrapped his fingers around them and said, "Stop, Assana."

She obeyed, though she wanted nothing more than to take that last step.

"Where is Silas?"

"He is meeting the Diviner to ask for her wisdom. If anyone knows how we can counter the blood meld thrall Mother has over the other Thiasoi, she will know."

"You shouldn't be here without him," he said. His knuckles were white from the force of his grip, his red eyes focused intently on her face.

"I can go where I wish. This is my home." Even as she said the words, she felt ridiculous making the stubborn excuse. The danger of getting too close to Gavra was real; her instincts pulled at her as though she'd been trapped in a net and was slowly being drawn in, unable to disentangle herself from his lure.

"Well, there you have me at a disadvantage, because I know better than to let you get close to me right now, yet here you are. It's fortunate there are bars between us." His throat worked as he swallowed and she watched the muscles ripple in his neck, her eyes drawn down the length until she couldn't resist letting her gaze continue a slow trek down his strong chest, tight stomach, and the loose band of the drawstring that kept his pants just barely secured to his hips.

They weren't enough to conceal the huge erection that pressed against the fabric, the outline of his cock clear through the thin weave. Her entire body tingled and a low moan escaped her throat.

"Why are you here, Assana?" Gavra said, the words a rough, grinding sound as though he had to force them out.

Why was she here? She tilted her head, the reason escaping her for a second. She reached for it, a part of her mind finally clearing enough to grasp and hold on. She jerked back, her eyes widening.

"Gavra …" she breathed. "Oh, Gaia. My mind isn't where it needs to be. I came to tell you something that couldn't wait."

"Then tell me and get back to Silas. I can see your control slipping."

She took a step backward and nodded, then drew a deep breath, struggling against the steady, throbbing need in her belly to do just the opposite and move even closer.

"Mother is insisting he and I complete a third melding. Today. Understandably, she doesn't trust him after what happened with Nicholas."

She studied him as her words sank in. First he frowned and winced, but covered up the hurt expression quickly. Finally, he nodded.

"That … that's good," he said, dropping his hands to his sides and turning away from her. "Better, in fact, than waiting for me. I believe I know how to get through to your mother. It will be easier if you're safely mated to him before I try."

His tense posture and avoidance of meeting her gaze made her skin chill.

"Try what?"

"Seducing her."

"No … You said it wouldn't work."

"I said my powers wouldn't work. That doesn't mean I can't do it the old fashioned way. Talk my way into her bed. You didn't think us Reds always had to use our powers to get laid, did you?"

The bitterness in his voice sliced into her like a blade. In a sudden rush, that hot need she'd barely managed to tamp down blazed forth again.

"No!" she yelled. "You wouldn't."

He faced her again, his face grim. "Do you think I *want* to? Your father was my friend. But even if he wasn't, it's *you* I want. If magic won't work on your mother, I have to try another way. I think she'll be … receptive … if I'm careful."

The need to be closer to him now gripped her. Without thinking, she drifted, targeting the inside of his cage as her destination. Gavra's head whipped around when she appeared behind him with a sudden pop of disrupted atmosphere.

She couldn't let him go through with this plan of his. Not without leaving her mark on him first.

"You're mine," she said. "Not hers."

"Assana, what are you doing? Sweet Mother …" He backed away from her, shaking his head, but he was hers, and there was no where he could hide. Her craving clawed at her, the primal power of it ripping her self-control to shreds. She wanted nothing more than the solid, strong body that faced her to be locked between her thighs, his virile immortal power flooding through her while they fucked.

"She can't have you," she growled.

"Baby, if you come any closer, you're going to regret it."

She advanced, the draw to him too strong to deny. "I *need* …" Her entire mind was filled with that one, crystalline detail. Her body thrummed with that craving, pushing aside everything else. She shed her human shape, shaking off the confining illusion and breathing deeply. Without the restrictive form to hold her back, she sighed and closed her eyes, settling into her true shape and relishing the primal power it gave her … the power to *be* and to *take* … to take what was hers.

"Oh, fuck," Gavra said.

"Are you scared of me?" she purred, slipping close enough to breathe the words into his ear.

He chuckled. "Never, baby. You just surprised me. You have no idea how much I've wanted to have you come to me like this, but you're playing with fire."

He rested his hands on her hips and squeezed, pulling her close enough to emphasize how hard he was. She gasped at the pressure of his rigid shaft against her belly, and her core pulsed and heated with the need to be filled by him.

"I can handle the heat."

"Baby, it isn't just heat you're going to get. I'm going to walk away in a second. You'd best pop back out of here if you intend to stay a virgin long enough to let Silas mate you. If you stay, you're mine."

The deep timbre of his voice when he said, "You're mine" sent a shiver of longing through her entire body. True to his word, he took a deliberate step to the side, then walked in several quick strides to the opposite side of his cage, near the large bed. He stopped and leaned back against the latticed wall and crossed his arms, leveling an intent gaze at her.

She took the challenge, her instincts driving her toward him again, any other sense long gone, her inhibitions shed with the human shape she usually kept herself locked in. Nothing else mattered but having him.

His gaze grew more heated, his red eyes flashing with inner light as she approached, though he didn't move a muscle.

"Then make me yours, dragon," she said, slipping close and resting her hands on his crossed forearms. She slid her hands up along the tensed muscles, reveling in the tight, hard bulges that betrayed his strength. She grazed her nails over his biceps, up his bare shoulders to his neck, where she dug her fingertips in like claws, seeking to pull him close.

Her breasts grazed his forearms, her nipples hardening through the sheer fabric of her gown. Her entire body flooded with heat.

Gavra's body only grew more rigid, his jaw clenching so hard she could hear his teeth grinding. He closed his eyes and licked his lips.

"Assana, this is your last warning," he rasped.

His tight restraint only made her want to push him harder. Now that her restrictive control over her desires was gone, she felt free for the first time to give in to her need and not even Gavra's clear hesitance would stop her.

"You want me as much as I want you. Ever since we met, I could see it in your eyes. Look at me." She slid her hands up his neck to his jaw and brushed her thumbs along the soft skin of his cheeks beneath his eyes.

Gavra cracked his lids, the red of his irises flashing with brilliant warm light. His pulse pounded in his temples, the vein visibly throbbing beneath his skin.

"I wanted to rip that infernal dress off you and mount you in the middle of the room that day," he said. "You're fucking right I wanted you then, and you weren't even … this." His gaze rose and he uncrossed his arms, lifting a hand to graze fingertips over the curved branch of her antlers.

"You wanted me wild, my love," she said. "Be wild for me too." Taking advantage of his open posture, she slid a hand down the center of his chest, into the front of his pants, and wrapped her fingers around his stiff length. His hard, pounding pulse met her touch in his shaft and she gave him a squeeze.

He didn't even give her a chance to stroke before he was on her. He crowded her back against the bed, hooked a foot behind her ankle, and toppled her backward. His huge hands tore the bodice of her dress, fingers digging into the fabric like it was made of smoke.

Assana let out a laugh and pulled him to her, sliding her feet up the outside of his hips and hooking his drawstring pants with her toes to push them down.

Hot skin slid between her thighs as he lowered himself, bracing on both arms to hover above her. He resisted for only a second, even as she crossed her ankles behind his hips to urge him closer. The thick head of his bare cock brushed along her inner thigh, but he kept himself just out of reach of her.

"I need …" she growled, her weeping pussy aching for what he could give her if only he'd finally shed that tight hold he had on his own desire.

"This is only going to make it worse, Assana."

He started to pull away and she let out an incoherent yell of protest. Her desire surged and she gripped his waist with her legs, holding on and refusing to let him go. With a tight hold on his shoulders, she pushed him over and straddled him, shoving his shoulders back against the side of his prison. Angry at his continued resistance, she reached a hand out to the tree-root bars of his living cage. The tree itself instantly responded and a long, green tendril snaked down across the pillows, twisted around Gavra's wrist and tightened.

Another vine took his other wrist and pulled, and yet another wrapped around his neck, holding his head immobile against his pillow.

"What the fuck?" Gavra stared in shock as the vines bound him to his own prison, yanking his arms above his head and holding them there.

Now that he couldn't resist her, she shifted back on his thighs and gazed down at his bound body. She shook with hunger for what he had to offer, every inch of his huge, muscled body taut beneath her, straining against the unbreakable hold the vines had on him.

He was all hers, hard and ready, and despite his cursing protests and his repeated insistence that she would regret this, she cared only for the way the massive, rigid shaft between his thighs would feel when it filled her for the first time.

She gripped him with both hands and stroked, the contact finally enough to shut him up.

Gavra arched his back, jacking his hips up into her hands, and groaned.

"Your protests sound empty, love," she said. "You keep saying no, but I don't believe you. Tell me the truth. Do you really wish for me to leave?"

He stared back at her and chuckled, finally relaxing and giving up his struggle against his bindings.

"My true desires haven't got a damn thing to do with it, and you know it. If all that mattered was mating you, I'd have fucked you weeks ago. But I can see I'm at a loss. I can't stop you, Assana. Would you please stop torturing me and fuck me?"

She slid her hand down to cup his balls while she stroked him with her other fist. His cock was so thick she could barely wrap her hand around his girth. Her pussy tightened with the renewed ache to feel that thickness stretching her, filling her, shooting his seed deep into her.

She shifted her hips closer, spreading her thighs across his and holding his cock so he pressed tight to her slick heat. Her clit throbbed in time with his pulse and she moved her hips with the same rhythm, sliding up along his length while she held him between her legs. Her folds parted and her wetness coated his shaft as she rubbed herself against him with abandon.

"Oh, fuck, I wish I could touch you," he growled. His hands flexed, opening and closing into tight fists. "Rub that pussy on me, baby. I want to see you come on my cock, I don't even care if you fuck me."

She stared down at him, enthralled by the hungry look in his eyes. She could have his tongue too, but not yet. First she needed his cock inside her. She moved higher up his torso and leaned over, letting her breasts brush over his chest while she captured his mouth with hers. He kissed her hungrily while she held his cock between her thighs, brushing the throbbing tip in slick little strokes up and down her soaked channel. While they kissed, she positioned him at her opening.

Assana held him there, pulling back to stare into his red eyes. Her dragon … her mate … or he would be soon enough. All *hers*.

She pressed down with her hips, her opening easily parting to take his massive girth. The ridged head pushed inside, his hips lifting up off the bed to meet her downward push.

Her entire body heated, pleasure rushing through her as she sank down onto him. She groaned and took his mouth again, biting down on his lip. Raw need gripped her, feeding her primal hunger as she slowly pumped her hips up and down, reveling in the tight friction.

She braced her hands on his chest and stared down at his enraptured face as she moved, speeding up her pace to increase that growing pleasure that slowly built in her core.

How could she have waited so long for this? Gaia, a man's cock was wonderful to have inside her, and she idly wondered how different Silas would feel were she to do the same thing to him. She sighed and smiled, remembering she would have to do the same to him very soon.

Gavra surged into her, his hips grinding and circling in a way that made her gasp. She dug her fingers into his chest and grazed her mouth over his jaw, groaning against his cheek at the pleasure just that simple movement gave her.

"I could give you so much more if you released me, Assana. Let me use my hands."

"Feels too good like this …" she moaned and stretched up to grip the criss-crossed bars of his cage just behind his pillows. The shift in position gave her more stability to pump her hips on his cock. Gavra let out a low growl of approval as her breasts brushed his cheeks and he opened his mouth to latch onto one nipple. He sucked her in, toying with the hard bud and grazing his teeth over the sensitive flesh.

Assana whimpered, lost to the myriad sensations that flooded her body. It was like being filled with all the power of the River at once and having it press against the dam of her resistance over and over.

She rode him harder, frantic to find that release and knowing it would be beyond her imagining once she got there. Her need consumed her, her body moving on instinct, her hips pumping madly while Gavra groaned, meeting her with wild thrusts of his own that pounded up into her with bruising force.

The loud smack of flesh on flesh filled the cage, echoing

through the small, secluded grotto. The scents of their merged essences overwhelmed her senses, obliterating the familiar wet, lush aromas of the Haven. She wanted to taste him, meld him, and she would soon. She was close, so close now, her core throbbing and heavy with the swell of power that had built up with every one of Gavra's deep thrusts into her.

She reared back, seeking more friction, deeper penetration. The change drove his cock into a different spot that made her antlers tingle all the way to their tips. She tilted back farther, leaning backward on her hands while her hips continued undulating with his cock deep into her.

"You need to come, baby. If I could touch you, I would. Touch yourself now. Come for me, Assana."

Grateful for his commanding tone, she did what he asked, pressing her palm to the top of her mound and gripping his cock where it sank into her over and over. The swift, slick stroking sensation against her fingertips was yet another tactile wonder and she stared down, marveling at how he stretched her, how his thick shaft disappeared deep into her with each of his glorious thrusts.

Her clit protruded from her folds, hard and swollen with need. She grazed her fingertip over it once and a hot zing of pleasure shot through her, making her gasp. She touched it again, pressing down on the top of it enough for the underside to come into contact with Gavra's pistoning shaft. The sliding friction went straight to her head and she cried out.

"Oh, Gaia, yes! Fuck me!"

"Assana, fuck ..." Gavra groaned and pounded into her, each stroke rubbing perfectly against her clit as she pressed it against him. She had no coordination left to do more than writhe and twist her hips, the pleasure too great.

"Give it to me, baby. Give it all to me."

Sudden, unexpected heat filled her, her core bursting

with acute pleasure. At the same time, Gavra roared and bucked under her, his cock exploding in a rush of heat. Her own climax rushed from her just as wetly, a flood of her juices coating his cock in a slick, slippery flood.

Assana threw her head back, screaming in ecstasy. It faded swiftly, though. Too swiftly. She needed more, needed his essence deeper than her womb, needed it in her soul.

The need to meld him overtook her then, but she needed his essence on her tongue. His cock was only half-hard in her pussy now, his chest heaving and his eyelids sagging shut.

"I need to taste you," she said. "Meld with you. I need to make you come again."

Gavra's eyes opened and he regarded her lazily. "For that to happen, I need to taste you too. Give me that sweet snatch of yours, baby. You're full of me right now. I can make you come again with my tongue and you can take us both from my mouth when I'm finished."

She was loath to leave his cock, but she'd experienced the thick forked length of his tongue on her nipples and had been curious what he could do with it. Reluctantly, she slipped him out of her and moved up his torso, spread her thighs over his face, and hovered there, staring down at him.

"You want to watch me eat your sweet pussy?" he asked, and his tongue shot out, trailed up between her folds, and coiled back into his mouth again. He closed his eyes and moaned, smiling and licking his lips. "Delicious," he said, his red gaze shining up at her. "Now fuck my tongue, baby. Let me taste all of you."

He lifted his head, clamped his lips onto her pussy, and sucked, then turned his head and swirled his tongue around and around her clit until her pleasure surged fresh and hot again.

Assana let out a surprised gasp and grabbed at his head, tangling her fingers in his silken hair. She ground her pussy hard against his mouth and pulled him tight against her. Gavra's deep chuckle vibrated against her folds and his tongue snaked through her channel, seeking entry. When he found her opening and pushed into her, she threw her head back and moaned, writhing her hips in time with the slow thrusts of his tongue.

It only took him a moment before he had her at his mercy, her hips bucking and her fingernails digging into his scalp in an effort to keep him locked to her core with that talented mouth pressed to her. She came in another rush, this time a more copious flood of liquid gushing from her in a splash. Gavra let out a hungry, elated moan as he swallowed what she gave him and slowly licked her pussy clean.

"Now kiss me, love," he said softly.

She moved on shaky thighs, sliding down his torso again until she collapsed on top of his solid, warm shape. She took his mouth, careless of the coating of her juices covering the entire lower half of his face and neck, as well as dripping down his chest.

When they kissed, the world disappeared. Their essences mingled, flowing across his tongue and onto hers. Instantly his mind opened and they were melded, more quickly than she'd even managed to meld Silas.

Gavra's consciousness penetrated hers with as much erotic insistence as his cock had filled her hungry pussy. He inundated her soul with his heat, ratcheting up her barely subsided cravings back to full tilt again. She tore away from the kiss with a gasp, but he was still in her head, refusing to retreat, but all the more welcome for his persistent presence.

"Let me inside you again, baby. Get me out of your system now so you can focus."

His power overwhelmed her and she could only comply. She shifted down his body just far enough to spread her legs across his hips again and push down onto his cock. His tip pierced her again, sliding easily in. He was rock hard again and moaned as she took him deep once more.

As she began to ride him, the primal need took over, magnified by the heated red presence in her mind, his acute need to fuck her every bit as wildly as she fucked him. The desire grew exponentially with each thrust until she was completely lost to this compulsion to fuck without end. This was their purpose, after all. Her body was meant to be filled by him, absorb his power and have his seed shoot deep until it took root. Nothing else mattered but fulfilling that primal need.

Nothing.

CHAPTER 26

GAVRA

Gavra was lost to the wild abandon of having his cock buried deep inside Assana for the second time. He was so lost he almost missed the moment when her psyche shifted, but with the mental link they now had, there was no mistaking that her need had become something different than he'd first seen in her aura when she'd arrived outside his prison.

At first, he'd observed her flickering aura with concern, realizing that she was on the edge of losing control. He was wary, but wanted her too much to care. Not that there was much he could have done, being locked in a cage. Silas was the only one who could control her, and he was nowhere in sight.

He'd only stepped away from her when she'd drifted into his space to give her a moment to regain control. When she didn't … Sweet Mother, when she'd *bound him to his bed*, nothing mattered after that but letting her have her way with him.

Her beautiful blue eyes were fierce, churning pools now, her hips rocking atop him with a swift rhythm. She'd climaxed twice and he'd greedily soaked up every delicious ounce of her potent energy, and now she seemed intent on giving him more.

But she was clearly after much more than a physical release, and the moments after she melded him, he realized what he was in for and knew without a doubt that it was too soon. Not that he didn't desperately want the same thing, but they simply didn't have time for it … not when Nyx's soldiers —his prison guards—could return at any moment, or even Nyx herself. He couldn't let any of them see Assana inside this cage with him, fucking him … melded with him.

His attention and worry wavered when her tight sheath gripped him, sliding up and down along his aching cock. So perfect. Sweet Mother, he could fuck her for ages, certainly long enough to give her what she desired, but in her primal state she seemed to have forgotten the crucial detail … She may have been prepared to fuck him until he impregnated her, but it would never happen until he marked her.

That singular desire was what drove her now; he could see it in the way her aura flared with her soul-deep need to become a mother. And oh, how he wanted to fulfill that desire for her, so much that it hurt him to yell for her to stop.

"Assana! You have to leave me! For fuck's sake, your mother can't find us like this. We'll never get through to her if she knows we are Fated."

She shook her antlered head, bending down and biting his throat with sharp nips as her pussy continued to grind atop his cock in maddeningly delicious strokes. He groaned as she pulled another orgasm from him, his hands fisting in their bonds while his body bucked and twisted beneath her.

This might be any dragon's wet fantasy, to be tied up and at the mercy of a cock-starved nymph. In any other universe, he'd have happily lain here forever letting her ride him, but in this universe, there was too much at stake.

When he caught his breath again, he tried to get through to her, but that wild look in her eyes didn't change and his cock for some crazy reason seemed to be on her side.

Again she rode him like a wild thing, intent on pushing him to climax. Her beautiful naked body, larger and stronger in its primal state, was slick and glistening with sweat. Again, he worried whether his own sanity might be slipping with the surge of yet another orgasm pulled from him in waves of ecstasy.

Her skin paled, but she showed no sign of stopping. Her aura flickered, growing weak, but she kept on. When his mind cleared from another haze of pleasure, he stared in alarm as she still refused to stop.

Realizing he had to do something, he began to yell, no longer caring who heard, only knowing that she was in danger if he didn't get her to stop soon.

"Silas!" he bellowed, hoping by now that the ursa would be finished and nearby. He called out several times then stopped for breath, staring up at Assana and marveling at her energy and her intense beauty with her wild hair and gleaming antlers. Sweat trickled between her breasts, her blue-green nymphaea skin glistening.

"Assana, as much as I want to fuck you forever, my seed won't take root until I mark you. You need to stop. Rest."

"Need you more," she panted. "Need your baby."

"I know," Gavra said. "I want to give it to you, but it can't happen yet and you know it. Please come to your senses. Get control ..." He cursed to himself, knowing it was a futile argument once her primal nature was in control and her pleasure drove her. Nothing would work until she had a baby in her.

But maybe something would help ...

"Silas!" he yelled at the top of his lungs again.

"Gavra!" a distant voice called back. Gavra let out a curse and a silent thank you.

Pounding footsteps approached and he craned his head in their direction.

"Help me get through to her," Gavra said when Silas stopped outside his cage and stared in shock.

Atop him, Assana moaned. "Silas, I need you," she said. "Need your seed inside me. Need you to fuck me too."

"What the actual fuck? Now?"

"No! Not fucking now. I need you to get into her head. You're melded with her, right? Get her to stop, get her *out* of here before they find her with me."

"What? I don't have a key …"

"She has to drift out, but she's completely fucking lost to her primal nature. She needs you. I'll tell you what happened after you *get her out!*"

"Right," Silas said, gripping the bars and closing his eyes.

A second later there was a third presence sharing the space of Assana's consciousness with Gavra, and it was nothing like he expected.

The feral power of Assana's soul was wrapped in the embrace of a stolid, calm figure with roots deeply embedded into the earth. Silas's consciousness exuded cool, quenching comfort from the raging need that had flooded them both, and even Gavra's potent lust subsided.

In his mind, he heard Silas croon softly to Assana.

"Settle yourself, my love. We'll make babies soon enough. Now is not the time."

Behind him, Gavra heard the creak and crack of splitting wood and pulled himself out of the internal mental drama occurring inside their shared consciousness. He looked back at the walls of his cage where Silas had ripped it open and now reached inside.

CHAPTER 27

SILAS

Silas pushed his way through the split matrix of the roots that made up the lattice of Gavra's cage, frantic to get to Assana and barely aware of the surge of power that he'd used to break into the confines of the dragon's prison.

All that mattered was calming her crazed mind, but when he reached her, the combined scents of her and Gavra's essences nearly overwhelmed him. He paused and shook his head, his body heating with desire and his cock stiffening. He was stark naked, having left his clothing behind in the Diviner's cave the moment his link to Assana through their melded minds had broadcast her frenzied state.

He'd known something was wrong and hadn't bothered to dress before tearing out of the cave and down the path, drawn in her direction by their connection. When he'd found her inside Gavra's cage astride the dragon's bound body, he hadn't known what to think until he heard Gavra's frantic shouts for help.

Now he forced himself to focus through the haze of lust

and climbed onto the bed behind Assana. He wrapped his arms around her and pressed his mouth to her ear.

"Baby, I've got you."

"Get her the fuck away from me, Silas. Now."

Assana resisted his pull, instead sliding off Gavra's cock and bending over, pressing her chest against the dragon's torso. She looked over her shoulder at Silas.

"Your turn," she said, tilting her hips higher so her sodden pussy opened for him. Her bright pink folds dripped with creamy fluid that made his mouth water from the scent. She was filled with Gavra's essence, and it was all Silas could do not to bend down and have a taste.

His brows drew together. But why shouldn't he? The surest way to ease her need was to service her through it. That was what he did best, after all.

"Silas …" Gavra warned. "You need to get her out of here."

"No … this will work," Silas said.

"The guards, her mother …"

"They're nowhere near. The Diviner told me Nyx's secrets. We have time." Not a lot of time, but enough, he hoped. Enough for him to take care of Assana, and maybe even fulfill her mother's wishes in the process.

His entire body flushed hotly with desire and the promise of the pleasure he was about to take. First, he needed to taste that delicious cream that flowed from Assana's channel. The essence of his two lovers mixed … Ambrosia.

He placed both hands on her ass and bent his head, extended his tongue, and started at the apex of the crease of her ass, then slid down. He groaned when his tongue reached the well of delicious essence that coated her velvet folds. The spice of Gavra's spunk hit his tongue first, then Assana's sweeter tang.

He lost himself, tonguing her and tasting her, devouring her sweet pussy until she panted and bucked back into him.

"Fuck me! Please, fuck me!" she begged.

His mind rejected her plea out of habit until he remembered that was precisely what he was supposed to do—what her mother had decreed they do today. The best part was that his worry about completing a third melding without Gavra no longer mattered. The dragon was right here with them.

He was going to fuck her. The awareness of that fact made his head spin even more than the taste of his lovers' essence on his tongue.

"Silas, we don't have all day."

Gavra's impatient tone made him look up to meet the other man's gaze. Assana's antlers bracketed Gavra's face, her head buried in the crook of the dragon's shoulders and her black hair tangled with Gavra's sweat-soaked red tendrils.

"I know. I just ... I've never done this before."

Gavra chuckled. "It isn't complicated, man. She needs you, but you might want to make sure you're ready to meld us both. I'm in her head now too."

"She melded you? How deep?"

"Deeper than you've gone yet. It was like she opened up and swallowed me whole when it happened. I sensed your melding when she let me in at first, but she's been at it for hours and every time we climax, we go a little deeper."

Before him, Assana groaned, her backside flexing beneath his hands, causing her tight opening to clench and release.

"Need you, Silas," she whined, her entire body quivering like she was in pain.

"Sweet Mother, will you fuck her?" Gavra said.

Silas slid his hands down her ass, his mouth going dry as he used his thumbs to tease at her folds and spread her open. Her beautiful slick pussy beckoned, clenching again as he stroked her. The bud of her clit was hard and thick and he grazed a finger over it, enjoying the soft whimper she made in response.

He gripped his cock in one hand and scooted closer, his knees nudging against the insides of Gavra's spread thighs. The dragon bent his knees to give Silas more room, but otherwise held still, and Silas realized then that Gavra's wrists were bound by thick vines extending from the walls of his cage. He should've broken those too, but now all he needed to focus on was the ripe, juicy pussy in front of him, begging to be fucked.

"She needs it hard … rough …"

"No," Silas said. "Not from me, she doesn't."

He pressed his tip to her entrance, his head buzzing with the exquisite sensation. As he slipped in, she seemed to swallow him up and he gasped at the tight, hot friction, so much more mind-blowing than he'd ever imagined it could be.

Gaia, he wanted to fuck her hard, but controlled his reflexes, resting his hands on Gavra's bent knees while he sank into Assana's pussy and stopped to get his bearings. She let out a long, sensuous moan and her muscles tightened hard around him.

"Fuck," he said, closing his eyes and struggling to acclimate to the pleasure. He slowly pulled out again and sank back in. She let out another sigh, relaxing a bit more, and the volatile charge of energy he'd felt beneath the surface of her skin flowed into him, tingling as it was transferred into his waiting well. She hadn't even orgasmed yet and already he was absorbing the built-up power.

"You have a gift for that, don't you?" Gavra said. "More than just an ursa male's talent."

"It's a little new to me," Silas said, concentrating fiercely on setting a slow, easy tempo with his hips as he began to fuck her.

"You sure you shouldn't take her out of here and get her away from me? My presence sets her off like you wouldn't believe."

"No. It couldn't wait and ..." He let out a groan as her pussy tightened around his cock. Shaking his head, he smiled at Gavra. "And the Diviner suggested she'd be better off if we kept her balanced."

"Balanced?"

"If she's going to be with us both, she needs to find equilibrium. Now that she's gone over the edge, we have to bring her back together."

Gavra nodded and looked at his bound wrists. "Can you reach these?"

Silas's cock throbbed deep inside Assana's channel. He closed his eyes and forced himself to focus, then bent over her, stretching up to reach for Gavra's bindings. The change in angle made her moan beneath him.

"Hold tight, Assana," Gavra said. "We've got you."

As Silas stretched his hands up and gripped the bindings of one wrist, he paused, suddenly acutely aware of the perfect intimacy of the situation. His face was inches from Gavra's, whose red eyes were wild with a combination of pleasure and worry. Up close, he could make out Assana's profile through the tangled veil of her hair and he gently pulled the strands away to see her. His heart pounded at her flushed beauty, her half-lidded eyes still swirling with crazed lust. One of her moss-covered antlers had raked a red line down Gavra's cheek and still rested against it, jabbing into his cheekbone hard enough to appear painful.

"No time for sweet words, Silas," Gavra warned.

Shaking himself out of his tender reverie, he swiftly tore Gavra's hands free, then yanked the additional vine from around the dragon's neck before leaning back again. Assana's naked back arched and she rose up on hands and knees to meet him as he sank deep and began fucking her once more.

His hands free now, Gavra took Assana's face in them and kissed her, the action causing her to clench around Silas again. He closed his eyes, struggling like hell to keep a steady tempo and not give into his need to ram harder into her. The slow fucking seemed to calm her, lull her, while Gavra's caresses kept her alert.

A moment later he felt the caress of a hand between his legs and Gavra's palm cupped his balls. Silas groaned as the touch pulled away. He opened his eyes to see Gavra's red gaze and his smile.

"Need to get you both there," Gavra said. "Meld with her when you come. She's already got you in her system, I take it."

"Yeah … Gaia help me, but this is good," he groaned as Assana pushed back into his hips, her own twisting with a needy rhythm. Gavra's knuckles brushed his thrusting cock as the man started teasing lightly at Assana's clit.

She let out a sharp cry, and within seconds her entire body arched, her pussy tightening and spasming around Silas.

He closed his eyes and focused, letting the sudden, glorious surge of his climax propel his consciousness into Assana's mind. She seemed to welcome him and he immediately delved deep, searching for signs of the dragon in her mind. He spiraled down deeper and deeper, past the point of their second melding the night before and the secret desires he'd discovered in Assana's deeper consciousness.

With a plummeting rush like falling off a cliff, he plunged into her psyche, crashing through the final barrier into wild, swirling power of her deepest mind.

That's where he found the pair of them entwined. Gavra's consciousness reached for him, but Assana's was only a whirlpool of energy like her eyes seemed to be whenever she looked at him. She was even more primal and powerful inside her mind than she was in bed, and he felt that power pulling at him, sucking him into the maelstrom of her insanity.

"This is what we have to calm, Silas!" Gavra yelled over the storm. "My presence alone just makes it worse."

In his body, he could feel the continued ripples of her orgasm and the well that absorbed her power filled, his limbs aching with the magic and close to erupting into the wooden roots to give that power back to the Earth … to Gaia herself. He struggled to hold onto it, to channel it all into that well where he could store it and use it. But the wild storm in her mind wouldn't be denied. He had to do something; his presence wasn't enough on its own.

Instinctively he drew on that substantial reserve of magic that had built up over the last day of melding with her. It was his power to use now, to channel to his purposes, and he held out his hands, letting loose with his mind. Inside his deep subconscious, the roots of his body extended. They whipped around in the spiraling fury of Assana's desire, giving her an anchor to hold onto.

For a moment, nothing happened. He and Gavra simply stood facing each other, battered and torn by the storm of her mind, her spirit completely unchained. Then Gavra reached out with both hands and opened his mouth at the same time. Red magic flowed from his lips and his fingertips, swirling around to meet Silas's outstretched tendrils. They merged in a circle and the dervish that was their lover whirled within, her ferocity abating as she found her bearings.

She was a beautiful thing, once she slowed enough for Silas to track her movements. Now that she was no longer a blur of motion, she still swirled in a graceful dance, circling around and around within the corral of their barrier. He'd seen signs of such grace when she moved, but had never actually seen her dance, and for the first time he understood how the nymphs so easily seduced human men with their graceful, swaying movements, akin to the hypnotic ebb and flow of the tide.

Her dancing took her in another circuit between him and Gavra and she slowed further, her more subdued gaze locking onto his as she passed, her fingertips brushing across his chest as light as feathers. Then she pirouetted into the center and gracefully dropped to her knees, bowing her head and resting her hands on the ground.

Her shoulders heaved with exhaustion, and he was about to release himself from Gavra's smoky grip when she spoke.

"This isn't enough," she said. "I can feel myself slipping even within the power of your embrace. It won't last."

"What do we need to do to make it stick?" Silas asked.

She let out a rueful, shuddering laugh. "Nothing that won't ruin our chances to stop my mother. Let me free for now so we can talk. You and I need to make sure we're far away from Gavra's cell soon."

Silas released his hold on Gavra's magic, suddenly cold and bereft after the psychic closeness to the other man. When he opened his eyes, he saw both his lovers had left the bed and he knelt there alone, his half-hard cock chilled from her drying juices.

Gavra stood on one side of the cell, Assana on the other, donning her torn dress that seemed to stitch itself together before his eyes. She looked a little shaky, but had returned to her smaller, more human shape, her magnificent antlers gone but her hair a tangled mess. She looked like she'd been fucked for days, and when she looked at him with a slightly panicked expression, he surged off the bed and went to her.

Assana clung to him, and he immediately bent and scooped her into his arms.

"Take me home," she said weakly.

Glancing over his shoulder, he eyed Gavra for a moment. When the dragon nodded at him, he turned back, then cursed when he realized what a wreck he'd made of the barrier of Gavra's cell.

"We have to do something about that," he said, then stepped through the gaping hole with Assana in his arms. He craned his head around, eyeing the ripped and broken bars of the cage.

"I'm not keen on making an escape just yet," Gavra said. "Better not let them think I tried … or that you helped. Assana, do you have the strength to fix it?"

She let out a sigh, and Silas could feel her struggling to summon her power. She reached out a hand, motioning to the side of the cage. The broken roots shifted and grew, fresh shoots breaking out from the broken ends. She flagged and drooped.

"I need your strength, Silas. Whatever you did in my mind … help me."

He set her down in front of the cage and wrapped his arms around her torso to support her against his chest, then pressed his cheek against hers and closed his eyes. It was like nothing to fall into her mind again, like he belonged there and she welcomed him in. Just as easily, his strange new power flooded through him and he pushed it outward, like a gift to bolster her strength.

Her back straightened against him, her resolve growing sturdier as she lifted her hands and the power flowed from her, commanding the roots to reform and grow back into the latticework of the barrier that held Gavra imprisoned.

When he opened his eyes, it was like he had never been there, tearing his way through that wall to get to her. Gavra wandered over and picked up the pieces of wood that were strewn around inside where Silas had broken through, tossing them into the fireplace taking up the center of the cage.

Their eyes met across the reformed barrier, and Silas felt rather than saw the other man's impatience with his situation.

The three of them were melded now, and the depth of their connection astounded him for how quickly it had occurred. He'd imagined it taking time … imagined there would be a wait and more ceremony when it happened, likely sometime after they'd dealt with their peril and had come out the other side, with the freedom to take their time and enjoy it.

He didn't think he'd change it, though, if he had a choice. They were his. They were together; even if they couldn't entirely be together yet, they were one in at least one important way.

"She was right," Gavra said in a low voice. "It isn't enough for me, either. I need to mark the two of you, and I promise if I get another chance to, I won't hesitate. Because if I'm right and I can actually get through to Nyx the way I think I can, I don't want there to be any ambiguity about where I stand with the two of you."

Assana pulled away from Silas, moving toward the cage and hooking her fingers on one of the freshly grown bars. She kept one hand firmly locked in Silas's, however, and he followed.

"You know that's why I broke down, right? I couldn't bear the thought of letting you go to mother without being melded to me at least once … I had to be in your head. I needed that link so I would know …"

"So you would know I remained faithful?"

She took a deep breath and shook her head. "So I would

know if she had any love left for my father."

"That's something I aim to discover too," Gavra said. "Your father was my friend. I wouldn't do anything to betray him, but if her love for him is anything like it used to be, I can use that to our advantage. It's better that we're linked now, but please promise me you'll stay away when I'm with her. You … distract me." His gaze moved to Silas and his lips quirked into a smile. "Both of you."

Sensing Gavra's rising lust again, and Assana's response, Silas pulled her away from the cage.

"It's time we left. We need to go report to her mother that we've completed our melding. I'll try to come back and check in with you tomorrow. The Diviner was … enlightening, but we don't have time to stay and chat about it."

In his mind, Silas heard a deep chuckle before Gavra's voice reverberated inside his skull. *"You forget we don't need to be face-to-face, now that Assana's melded us so deeply. Get her taken care of and we can talk more when you're alone. I admit I'm more interested in this new power of yours … ursa males aren't known for their reserves of magic."*

Steering Assana down the path, he responded, *"As soon as I figure it out, you'll be the first to know."*

Halfway back to Assana's quarters, it hit Silas that the delicious aura of dragon still clung to them both. Assana was coated with it, and there was no way in hell her mother would fail to notice.

"How much time do we have before we have to see your mother?" he asked in a low voice, glancing around the forest, suddenly worried about what nymphs or guards might be watching and listening.

"She'll likely call us to dinner, so we have several hours yet. Time enough to rest." She sounded weary, her footsteps dragging.

"You reek of dragon," he said.

Assana giggled and looked up at him. "So do you." Then she bent her head to her shoulder and inhaled. "Oh, wow. Yeah, he's kind of all over me."

"And inside you," Silas murmured, his cock warming at the memory of their shared flavor on his tongue.

She slid her hand up his arm and shifted close to his side. Gazing up at him, she lowered her eyelids and whispered, "Will you share a bath with me when we get back? I was a little out of my mind when you made love to me just now. I'd like to try it again with a clear head."

"Gaia, yes," Silas breathed. "Are you sure you're not too tired for it?"

"A little, but you're excellent at seeing to my needs. I trust you'll make it easy."

Silas's nostrils flared at the thought of another session of servicing this exquisite nymph who was practically his mate, at least in the eyes of her own kind. Except this time, he could have her in every way possible.

He struggled for focus as they entered her quarters. The sprawling bungalow was yet another extension of the nymphaea palace her mother lived in, with its myriad water-falls descending around the high spires and falling past the arched bridges that spanned the many almost randomly placed towers. It reminded him of a giant sandcastle built haphazardly by a child with no other tools besides his own hands to drizzle the wet sand into structures. If they ever made it out of here, he'd love to spend his life on a beach with his lovers. One of the secluded islands in the many small lakes of the ursa Sanctuary would be perfect.

But until then, he had to ensure his mate's sanity remained intact. Now that the three of them were melded, things should improve, but Assana still seemed shaky and out of sorts.

"What is it?" he asked her as he led her to her bathroom to

her tub. It was already filled with hot water that flowed in a constant stream from a small waterfall nearby. It seemed like every structure in this place had water flowing through in some fashion.

"It's him," she said. "He's inside my mind now, too ever-present to deny, even now that I've regained control."

Silas moved to her and knelt at her feet, resting his hands on her knees. "I'm here too," he said.

"We're all here," Gavra's voice resounded in his mind. *"Assana, having both of us inside you is going to take some acclimating. Let Silas help you through it. I'll stay in the background as much as I can."*

Silas stared up into her whirlpool eyes. He gave her thighs a squeeze when she let out a shaky breath.

"I like it," she said. "It's just that I want more. Now that I've had a taste of Gavra, I want more."

Silas let out a chuckle. "I'm right there with you. We've got as much of him as we can have at the moment. Let's enjoy it." He reached up and tugged at the asymmetrical laces that held her gown together. The material fell apart beneath his touch like it had a mind of its own and was just surrendering.

Assana barely moved, watching with heavy lidded eyes as he undressed her, then let him drape her arm over his shoulders as he scooped her up. He carried her over to her bath, taking a careful step down into the water and lowering her into it onto his lap as he sat. He leaned back, cradling her against him and held her as they soaked, enjoying the way she sighed and her body gradually went limp.

"She's asleep," he said to Gavra. *"We need to talk."*

"Tell me what you learned today," Gavra asked immediately.

Rather than recount the conversation he'd had with the Diviner, he broadcast the entire memory wholesale to the dragon, preferring to avoid adding any of his own biases to the mix. His own agenda wasn't relevant to their goals for the Haven. He was only tasked to ensure the Sanctuary's link to the Source was never broken again. That would happen one way or the other, but not until they'd succeeded in handling Nyx.

*H*e'd parted ways with Assana that morning in the cave that led to the Diviner's lair. As he padded down the passageway that led into her chamber, his fur brushed along the narrow walls, sending shivers through him the entire way. He was grateful for the relative protection his true form offered, particularly his claws, but he had a feeling none of that would make a difference once he was inside.

When he passed into the misty cavern, he stared in awe for a moment at the way the beams of sunlight streamed down, reflecting off the moisture above the central pool in such a way that made the mist seem as opaque as smoke. The way it swirled reminded Silas of a dragon's breath.

The slithering noise that hit his ears made him tense, and his skin prickled with eerie awareness of the presence lurking in the room somewhere beyond that vaporous haze. He peered around, but saw nothing beyond the disturbance in the surface of the water.

"I sssee you have obeyed the rulesss, Silasss," a rich, female voice said, resonating off the wet stone walls of the chamber. "You may shed your true form now and show me your human shhhape."

He obediently shifted back into his other form and took a step closer, keeping his gaze focused on the movement of the water where the ripples had quickened and were coming closer together. The smoke changed shape then, coalescing into a statuesque torso of a female with the figure of a goddess.

When the smoke cleared he saw all of her, from her striking face and her eyes more hypnotic than Assana's, to the strange tendrils of hair that looked like they were alive. Her body was a pale blue-green, and her glistening skin was covered in tiny scales that he only saw when the sunlight caught them just so. But from the hips down, she was a beast. He'd have thought "dragon" at first, save for the presence of several tails … A dozen, he guessed.

"You have found me, Miteradoro. You are Gaia's chosen, so you may ask anything of me and I will answer."

"I am Silas Rainsong, Diviner. I don't think my … status has any bearing on my questions."

"You are a Miteradoro of the ursa. Our mother's gift. You have great power that has bearing on all your questions. Ask what you came to ask."

He stared for a second, mouth open as he tried to form a question, but a bigger question was on the tip of his tongue. He was supposed to ask about Nyx and how to control her— how to undo the damage she'd done, but all he wanted to know was what his power really meant.

"It's Nyx," he finally forced himself to say. "She's destroying our alliance, risking the lives of the residents of the Sanctuary, not to mention driving her daughter mad in the process. She's done something even worse …"

"What is your question, Silas?"

"How do we reverse the blood meld?"

The Diviner's tails shifted and coiled beneath the surface and she grew even larger before him. He had to crane his head back to look at her. Her deep blue lips tightened into a hard line and her eyes swirled with a strange luminescence. The power in her eyes was reflected in a pearly shimmer that cascaded through her scales the way Gavra's Nirvana had flowed through Silas's body, making his skin glimmer with magic as it filled him.

"The blood meld is not meant to be broken, when carried out as Dion intended." She made the statement as though there were no room for argument.

"Do you have any idea what Nyx has done?" Silas asked, his eyes widening in disbelief.

The water around her churned and frothed. The spiraling colors in her eyes became pure, opaque white, her attention seeming to focus inward. Her blank gaze persisted for several moments, the violent movement beneath the water sending small waves crashing over Silas's feet. He waited as still as a tree until she finally let out a frustrated yell.

"Sister, what have you hidden from me?!" She stared blindly around as though trying to see something through the mist. Waves of power cascaded down her torso, sending ripples of color through her body that flooded outward from her with each sloshing ripple from her pool.

The energy she exuded prickled at Silas's skin like an invisible, expanding cloud. The mist sparked with it and his wet feet tingled. His testicles pulsed from the proximity— somehow he was able to absorb some of what she emitted simply by being in the room.

The power condensed into a bright, swirling ball twice the size of Silas's head. Within the orb he saw Nyx surrounded by a group of nymphaea in some sort of ritual. All the women in the vision had blood on their lips. Their eyes were blank stares, their heads thrown back and their bodies rigid while Nyx mouthed words Silas was unable to hear.

"Is this what you have seen, Miteradoro?" the Diviner asked.

"The effects of it, yes. The nymphs are only half-willing. They believe the Haven's safety requires this of them, but they're destroying our alliance in the process. The ursa can't let this continue. We will take matters into our own hands if she isn't subdued. We have to ensure our link to the Source is protected."

The swirling orb spun faster and faster, the Diviner's rage apparent in her clenched teeth and twisting tails. With a roar she flung the orb at the far wall where it hit with a loud smack and burst into a flood of water.

The Diviner's eyes returned to their former colorful whirlpools and she looked at Silas, pinning him with her stare. "She is an immortal. Any *normal* blood meld can be nullified by a creature of greater power than the ones who created it. This will be no easy task with my sister."

"Can you break it?" Silas asked.

Her shoulders sagged and the churning ceased. Gazing down at him with still eyes, he grasped the gravity of the situation from that look. She appeared almost human now—powerless and mortal without the swirl of power in her eyes or the living tendrils on her head, which now appeared as nothing more than shining silver curls.

"Even if I could leave this chamber, I am no more than her equal. There is no single creature on Earth or in any of the higher realms who can overpower her. She has made another mockery of our most sacred ritual like the nymph we cast out eons ago, yet we cannot do to Nyx what we did to Meri without utterly destroying the Haven itself. Even if we could, we dare not subject the human world to her insanity."

Silas cursed and raked his hands through his hair. "There has to be a way to undo what she's done. I thought this blood melding shit was bad, but you say it's sacred. How can something that does this be sacred?"

"It has been outlawed since the first time it was misused this way. A blood meld is not required for a nymph to breed, so the Dionarchs and I agreed that it should no longer be permitted under penalty of exile. At one time, it was the greatest expression of love between a nymph and satyr. The blood meld between a mated pair created another creature of two minds and bodies, but one soul with two aspects. Their awareness was doubled, their power grew twofold. Their love formed an infinite loop that could not easily be broken. We took for granted its power would be respected—a blood meld created without love as its anchor is ultimately corrupt. We learned this with Meri. Her melding was not easy to break, but without love, it was not hard, either."

"Because she wasn't immortal," Silas said.

The Diviner nodded. "And because it wasn't complete. Her victim gave her his blood but didn't take hers in return. She took his body and left him untethered. If not for Neph's love of Meri's victim and his own blood sacrifice, she would have kept that dragon's body as her own. The blood meld is that powerful."

"There has to be a way ... Is Neph powerful enough to break his sister's hold on the Thiasoi?"

"There is a chance he could reason with her, but they are twins. If he attempted to overpower her melding with his own blood, it would likely only strengthen the hold she has on her victims."

Silas continued to pace, his mind spinning. It didn't matter that Neph probably couldn't help—he wasn't in the Haven, anyway—yet another detail that had Assana off balance with worry.

"Well, what the fuck *can* you do from in here?" he spat. He stopped and stared at her, hands stretched out at his sides, palms facing the pool.

"If you can bring her to me, I can create a barrier in my cave that will trap her … perhaps buy you some time. The blood melding she has inflicted on the Thiasoi is corruptible without true love to bind it. It requires multiple meldings to complete, but if you fail to interrupt the process, it will be irreversible. That was what I showed you in the orb—her ritual has to be repeated daily until it's done. It erodes the minds of the nymphs more each day and will be permanent once she's broken them completely. Once that happens, there will be no returning to sanity for those nymphs. They will be her puppets. The only way to break it is to overpower her connection to them somehow."

"Is it possible for her to willingly release them?"

"Only if another takes her place. Ideally it will be a true blood meld, anchored by love, else they will be forever bound to her, their minds no longer their own."

"What are the chances we can talk her into doing that?" he asked.

The Diviner's frown deepened and her eyes grew glassy. "My sister is strong and unyielding. Once she's made a decision, she will break before she gives in. Only her mate was ever able to get her to change her mind about something, and Nereus is beyond our reach."

"But he is alive?"

"He exists. That is all I know. To say he is alive would be a generous assessment."

Silas mulled over the information, at a loss for what to do with it. He would have to take it back to Gavra and Assana to get their take on things. His earlier question returned to his mind then, along with the pulsing reminder of the energy that he carried. He only had a vague sense of how it worked, much less how to control it, but he'd at least figured out how to avoid sprouting roots every time he serviced Assana.

"I have another question … about what I am."

"That is simple. You are Gaia's chosen, one of many potential seeds in each generation of ursa males who is encouraged to sprout and reach for the sun."

"Can I use this power to subdue Nyx?"

The Diviner shook her head. "What you are is pure potential, as are all seeds. What you become will be dictated by the conditions under which you grow."

"What did others like me become?"

"Mostly old ursa. Rarely does a Miteradoro come along who is required to fulfill his potential. You may be an exception, or you may not. That is up to Gaia to decide."

A strange prickling sensation took up residence at the base of his spine, accompanied by a humming inside his skull. He shook his head to dispel it so he could focus on the conversation.

"How will I know?" he asked.

The humming in his head acquired a rhythm and a familiar light, breathy tone that made his cock swell.

"You will know by the strength of your urge to grow …"

Silas didn't hear the rest of her statement. The rising noise inside his mind became an inexorable flood of emotion and sensation so volatile he instantly turned and ran. All he knew was that something had set Assana off, and he wasn't there to calm her.

Gavra absorbed Silas's recollection of his meeting with the Diviner with interest and only a little apprehension. There were no clear answers, nor had he expected any, but he started to see hope where he'd had very little before. While he believed he could talk his way into Nyx's bed, he still didn't have much faith in his ability to gain her trust enough to change her mind. The Diviner's assessment of the Dionarch only reinforced that Nyx was every bit as rigid as he thought.

"What do you make of it all?" Silas asked.

"There must be an answer in what she shared. I need time to think. Please make sure Assana is all right."

"Of course. What about you? She didn't damage you, did she?"

Gavra chuckled. "It would take more than one wild nymph to wear me out. Her mother, on the other hand ... Nyx is actually capable of real damage to a dragon like me."

"The Diviner didn't sound like she thought you could overpower Nyx. Are you still going to try?"

"No, I know it's impossible. I'd have bedded the woman eons ago if my breath worked on her. Believe me, I did try. Then Nereus *came along with nothing more than sweet words and utter worship and I knew there was no hope for me. It was better that way. She was a challenge for me—a conquest, nothing more. Nothing like Assana."*

"Assana wants you enough to risk her sanity."

"And I love her enough to stay safely caged and away from her."

"We can't stay like this forever," Silas said. *"After today, it's clear to me that we need to be together for her sake, otherwise she'll keep swinging wildly between the two of us, never finding true north. We can't keep doing that to her. Now that we're melded, we have to find a way to get you out of there soon."*

Gavra heard footsteps and mentally shushed Silas. He sat up on the bed where he'd lain down damp after a fresh bath. Beyond the latticework barrier of his cage, several figures advanced up the sun-dappled path. Nyx walked in the center, striding with purpose while the nymph maidens around her marched with the same strange, mechanical gaits as when he'd arrived. There seemed to be a pattern to their mindlessness, as though it waned with time or distance, reinforcing Ephyra's statement that Nyx wasn't yet able to maintain complete control over them throughout the day. But how long until she broke them? How long until they couldn't function without her hands up their asses like a puppeteer controlling their every action?

He ambled toward the front of his cage, ignoring his discarded clothing and opting to conjure something more flattering to his large form. He exhaled a long breath, the wisps of smoke coiling down around his legs into snug red leathers with a faint scale pattern embossed on them. On his upper torso he conjured a sleeveless black tunic with a deep split at the throat.

By the time Nyx made it to the edge of his prison, he'd also conjured comfortable leather boots and smoothed his hair into a sleek tail at the back of his neck.

He was done looking like a prisoner. If he wanted her to treat him as an equal, he should behave like the dragon she once knew in their youth.

Nyx was in her primal form again, as regal and imposing as the goddess she once pretended to be when humans cared about such things. This was no mere act, Gavra knew. This was simply her nature, and he was reminded once again why he'd never been worthy of her when a mortal satyr had been.

It took more than a god to match a goddess. Nereus possessed more honor in his little finger than most men, and most immortal males like Gavra relied on their power more than their conscience to justify their behavior. It had taken him falling in love with Nyx's daughter to understand that. To love a woman was to be willing to sacrifice his own integrity for her sake. Even if he were half as honorable a man as Assana's father had been, it wouldn't come close to being worthy of her love. Hopefully Silas would make up the difference.

He stood inside his cage, silent and waiting patiently for her to address him first. She had an expectant glimmer in her eyes that intrigued him and gave him hope for a productive conversation. He assumed that's all it would be again tonight, at any rate.

Nyx said nothing, however, and with a wave of her hand, the roots that bound the cage together slowly writhed and parted, leaving an opening in the wall large enough for him to walk through. On the other side, the Thiasoi guards took up positions in two lines that flanked the opening. Nyx stood at the end of the path … or was it a gauntlet? He suddenly couldn't decide whether walking through would mean freedom or torture.

"Come join me for supper, Gavra. I have a need for more of your tales tonight. It seems they help me sleep."

He held back a retort that he had other ways to help her

sleep. If more stories about Nereus were what she wanted, he had many more to deliver. With any luck, he would be able to draw it out long enough to delay her plan and come up with a plan of his own to get through to her, or else to subdue her. He wasn't picky.

Without hesitating another moment, he gave her a cocky smile and stepped outside his cage.

"My lady, all you had to do was ask. Nereus is nothing if not a perfect hero worthy of all the songs."

He kept up the steady stream of narrative as they walked, regaling Nyx with a series of short anecdotes about her lost love. The entire way his skin itched with awareness of the automaton soldiers who escorted them. But the closer they came to the palace, the more his mind tuned in on Assana and Silas.

"Keep her away from the dining room tonight," Gavra said to Silas as his only warning. He couldn't be this close to Assana without worrying about her self-control.

"We are expected to dine with Nyx tonight, remember? She needs proof of our melding."

Gavra silently cursed, but didn't dare attempt another communication lest Nyx catch on that his attention was anywhere but fully on her.

"We all wanted you, you know," Gavra said, returning to the thread of his story. "Well, my brothers were perhaps the exception, but I craved your attention, as did the Winds. We were sure you would choose between the five of us. We were so certain of this that we never even considered Nereus was already working to win you over. He wasn't exactly hiding it, either. Would you believe we laughed at him when we found out? Zephyrus taunted him. He bet Nereus that he would have you on your back with your legs spread by the end of summer."

"Zephyrus has no imagination," Nyx said, her voice filled

with mirth and remembrance. "I remember how hard he tried, too. You may have been able to satisfy me then, but Zephyrus and his brothers are better off sticking to the sky. What did Nereus say to his bet?"

"He only shook his head and smiled, like he knew some secret. I found out later that he'd spent several seasons carving out a secret grotto for you that would be private, yet let in the sea and sun. I'd finally realized he had something the rest of us were missing. Once I convinced him I had no designs on you myself, he confided in me. For a man so confident, he was still uncertain he could win you over, but I knew he would once I realized the lengths he'd gone to."

"How were you so sure?" Nyx asked, leading him into the palace's dining room. She filled two heavy glass goblets with sparkling wine and motioned for him to sit at her right while she took her spot at the head of the table.

"Because he had no guarantee of your acceptance, yet he still worked his hands bloody to create something beautiful for you. That was when I knew that, though he was mortal, he would bleed for you. He would risk his own life's essence to make you happy."

He would bleed for you. Gavra pursed his lips and stared into his goblet as he sat, an idea beginning to form in his mind that he was more inclined to reject than put any stock in. Blood couldn't be the answer to their dilemma, could it?

"He did bleed for me, and I him," Nyx said in a voice so soft Gavra almost didn't hear her. When he glanced up at her with furrowed brows, her gaze was fixed into the distance, her eyes rimmed with unshed tears. She inhaled shakily and blinked several times. With a small smile, she turned to look at him.

"We were the last," she said. "It was rare for a nymph and satyr to choose the blood melding ritual when they mated. Nymphs are capricious and get bored so easily, so most partnerships remain open. It was forbidden to perform the ritual if they couldn't demonstrate true love and commitment to their mates. The connection it provides would be … confining … for a nymph who would rather flit between partners for a few centuries than commit to a single satyr. When I saw how he bled for me without asking anything in return, I knew there could be no other mate for me. No other male was worthy of fathering my children. I didn't wait after that."

A pair of petite nymphs in gauzy sunshine-colored dresses entered and began serving the first course. Gavra's shoulders were rigid after Nyx's confession, his mind on alert for the approach of his mates, who must be due any second. He could sense them somewhere nearby, but forced himself to maintain his focus on Nyx and their conversation.

"When did he first show you what he'd built?"

"He didn't," Nyx said with a shrug. "I wasn't oblivious to him, or to the rest of you, believe it or not. Finding a mate wasn't on my agenda. You could say I lived vicariously through my nymphs, and somewhat through my brother's own dalliances. His grew boring after a time, and the nymphs' tedious escapades only served to highlight how very different Nereus was. They flocked to him the way they flocked to you when you visited. Yet unlike you, he never indulged. Not once did I hear one of my nymphs bragging that she'd succeeded in bedding him. They would even band together in the hopes of seducing the elusive Nereus *en masse*, because *surely* where one failed, many would succeed."

"Strength in numbers," Gavra said with a chuckle. "It would have worked on me."

Nyx smiled. "It always worked on you. You were low-hanging fruit to them. They made more effort with your brothers, but had as little luck with them as they did with Nereus. What do you think that says about you, Gavra?"

"That I'm a giver?" he said with a wink.

That elicited a short laugh from her. "You haven't changed. It's so refreshing to find something constant in this world. Thank you for that."

"I aim to please, as always. So was it their futile efforts that made you notice Nereus finally?"

"At first, I was concerned. I asked Neph if he thought there might be something wrong with Nereus. The two of them weren't as close yet as they would become later, but Neph had more contact with the Thiasoi soldiers than I did, so he would know if one of his men were dysfunctional. The madness bleeds in sometimes where we least expect … I worried he might come to harm if he weren't well and had to fight. A sexually suppressed male is a dangerous beast on the battlefield—as dangerous to his own side as to the opponent's."

"Neph wasn't worried?"

"No. I didn't believe him. I thought my brother was too distracted with his own pointless affair at the time." A sharpness to her tone belied her bitterness where her brother's "affair" was concerned. Gavra was all too aware that Neph's distraction came in the form of a white dragon, and the reason the nymphs could never seduce Aodh was because their male leader had already succeeded in winning him wholeheartedly. His darker brother's resistance to them, however, was a different story entirely.

Letting Nyx digress onto a tangent about his brother wouldn't do him any good. Seeking to rein in the conversation, he said, "So what did you do?"

"I went looking for him. I was genuinely worried after I started hearing more rumors that he was frigid or unstable, or—Dion forbid—sterile or impotent. Satyrs aren't that difficult to seduce, as a rule."

"About as easy as a red dragon?" Gavra asked with a wry twist to his mouth, hoping to infuse a bit of humor back into the discussion. A pleasant shiver suddenly coursed over his skin when he heard a brief echo of Assana's voice drawing near. It was all he could do not to crane his head around to look for her and Silas. He had to pretend Nyx was his sole focus.

"Easier," Nyx said. "They don't even have your need to dominate. As long as a satyr is able to take pleasure in it, he doesn't care whether he's on the top or bottom."

Gavra raised an eyebrow. "Did Nereus have a preference?"

Nyx's eyes twinkled wickedly. "Wouldn't you like to know? Perhaps I'll share that secret another time. For now, allow me to indulge my maternal needs and include my daughter in the conversation." She rose from her seat with a warm smile and walked toward the entrance to the room with open arms.

Assana and Silas stood in the doorway, and Gavra finally allowed himself to turn in their direction.

His heart clenched at the sight of the pair, cleaned up and dressed in typical Haven finery—garments of moss, vines, and shimmering gauze that appeared as though they'd been grown right on the wearer's skin. When Assana accepted her mother's embrace, her gaze met Gavra's across the room. Her aura flared brightly and her eyelids fluttered as though that simple glance had conveyed his need to touch her.

He quickly averted his gaze from her, looking at Silas instead. The dark-haired ursa had a hand at Assana's waist, sticking close to her even as her mother pulled away and greeted him.

"Silas," Nyx said with a nod. "Please sit and join me and my new guest. The main course will be served shortly."

Assana eyed Gavra for a second, then shook her head. "I'm not hungry, Mother. We just wanted to stop in and show you that we completed the melding. We'd like to … well, we'd like to go back to bed, for obvious reasons."

Nyx turned back to her daughter and gripped her shoulders, holding her at arm's length. She reached down and grasped Assana and Silas's entwined hands, a shimmer of liquid power seeming to drip from her palms and trickle between their fingers.

The ancient Dionarch smiled. "My, my, you two have forged quite a deep bond today, haven't you? There is plenty of time for you to conceive my grandchild. We have a special guest tonight, and he deserves the honor of your presence as much as I do. Please sit."

Nyx urged them both toward the table again, her brusque manner allowing no more argument from either of them. Gavra braced himself, his traitorous cock already rousing at the mere sight of the pair, much less their approaching scent. Thankfully they'd succeeded in removing any trace of him from their bodies, but their own aromas combined were a heady concoction from just a table's width away. He swiftly covered his arousal by dropping his napkin in his lap and leaning over to snag the decanter of wine.

He filled the two glasses set before Silas and Assana before refilling his own and Nyx's, and merely nodded to the others in greeting. He was under no illusions that Nyx's statement had elevated him beyond the status of prisoner, so he chose to wait to speak until he was addressed directly.

Assana gracefully covered her flustered state as she sat. Her arousal blossomed this close to him in a way it never did with Silas alone. At least Silas's presence lent an excuse for it, where Nyx was concerned, but he couldn't help but smile to himself.

"You look beautiful, Assana," he whispered into her mind, which caused her to clumsily bump her glass, nearly toppling

it over if it weren't for Silas's quick reflexes. Silas glared at him and Gavra raised an eyebrow.

"You look good enough to eat, too, Silas," he said. *"In fact, I have the most delicious image of the pair of you lying back and letting me lick each of you in turn until I taste both your Nirvanas thick on my tongue."*

Assana let out a desperate little moan.

"Are you all right?" Nyx asked.

"Just realized how hungry I am, Mother," Assana said, waving a hand. "How soon until we eat?"

"No need to wait," Nyx said, snapping her fingers. The sunshine-clad nymphs appeared in an instant, laden down with dishes that they placed on the table. The rich aromas of the food just barely obscured the scents of his lovers, and Gavra finally succeeded in diverting his attention to his stomach instead of his dick.

The four of them indulged in the meal for several minutes, and Gavra was grateful for the feast, realizing how famished he was. His body's other needs tended to take a lower priority to his carnal needs when he had a particular craving for a lover.

Gradually Assana's aura calmed as she took sustenance, though it still retained a vibrant red glow. It was lucky that her mother didn't have a dragon's ability to see auras, or they'd have been found out by the way Gavra's power so strongly infused Assana's energy.

"Did you decide to release the prisoners, Mother?" Assana asked. "I'm surprised you only invited the red one to supper and not his brother too."

Assana seemed a little stronger now. Strong enough to challenge her mother, at least. Nyx's jaw clenched and she stared at her plate.

Without looking at Gavra, Assana shot a thought to him. *"Being near you gives me strength, even though I feel my resistance fading. I want you, but I ... I think I can resist while the meld is strong."*

Gavra could only give her a silent mental nod in acknowledgment. He was far more interested in Nyx's response to her daughter's question. He gave the female Dionarch a pointed look.

"Why isn't my brother joining us, Nyx?"

She lifted her antlered head and set down her fork, regarding the three of them imperiously. "You know what that *dragon* has done. He was apparently missing the same sense of honor that you have. Perhaps Nereus managed to rub off on you, but not your brother. He is safely confined to a place where the Lamia won't be tempted to seek him out. Allowing him so close to the Haven—even in the confines of the Sanctuary itself—was too great a risk."

Gavra tilted his head, perplexed by the utter lack of irrational language or emotional posturing. She sounded *reasonable* in her explanation, even if the punishment was severe. She was exceptionally good at masking her insanity, that was clear.

"What risk is Aodh to your home? How does he bring any more danger here than I do? None of my siblings or I ever threatened the Haven. Aodh would lay down his immortal soul for it, if it came to it ... for your brother, especially."

Nyx's serene exterior faltered only a tiny bit, the buried animosity blazing in her eyes for a split-second before she controlled it again. Gavra wasn't sure whether it was a testament to her self-control or merely evidence of how close to the surface her madness really was.

"His intentions have very little to do with it. Blood melds never completely die. Once an exchange is made, it sticks. It may fade over time, but once that stain sets, the mark is permanent and offers its original owner a beacon to reach the one who possesses it, across any distance, in any dimension. Your brother was *tainted* by having Meri's spirit inhabit his body. To have him within the boundary of the Sanctuary could have risked all our lives. The safety of the Haven had to be preserved at all costs. He is somewhere … some-*when* … inaccessible to the Lamia now. We will be even safer once you have helped sire an army of new satyrs to defend us."

Tainted. Some of her madness made sense now, but if what she said was true, they could use the lure of Aodh's taint to their advantage when they were ready. He forced himself to relax.

"He is comfortable, at least?"

"He is in no danger of going hungry."

"And what of your own brother? He's conspicuously absent too."

Nyx shrugged. "Neph wouldn't have allowed me to quarantine your brother the way I did. His absence is only temporary, at least until he can find a way back in. For the moment, he'll simply have to remember what it feels like to be human."

"Maybe he'll help look for Father," Assana said as she took a sip of wine.

Nyx went rigid at the comment. She stood abruptly and set down her goblet with a loud thunk on the table. Wine sloshed over the edges.

"Supper is finished," she said, her eyes a stormy churn sparking with volatile energy.

Assana's eyes widened and her already tenuous hold on her self-control wavered. Her skin rippled with evidence of her primal nature awakening within and she let out a low, long moan. Silas immediately stood and wrenched her chair around to face him.

"Assana, baby, hold on. I'm here." He gripped her hands, then cupped her face, but she only stared blankly at him. Then her head flew back and she let out a piercing wail, her entire body bucking out of the chair and nearly knocking Silas off his feet. A pair of majestic antlers as beautiful as her mother's erupted from her head. When her transformation was complete, she turned that familiar wild-eyed look to Gavra.

Too quickly to track, she lunged across the table at him, clawed fingers grasping, a look of pure hunger burning in her eyes. Silas barely managed to grab her by the ankles and haul her back, but she twisted away. She let out an incoherent shriek of protest and tried again.

Gavra ached to go to them both, to complete another melding that he knew would calm the wild beast in her, but didn't dare let on his true desires. He shoved his chair back as swift as a breath and pulled Nyx away from the table with him, as though protecting her from her daughter's insane outrage.

"Your daughter doesn't seem well," he whispered in her ear.

"And here you probably thought I was the mad one," Nyx said. "Let her mate handle her."

Nyx didn't seem inclined to leave, however, though Gavra knew without a doubt that his proximity was making things worse as long as he stayed on the sidelines. He would either have to get involved, or leave.

"She isn't settling down," he commented when Silas spun her and then bodily climbed on top of the table to pin her down. She twisted beneath him, turning crazed eyes to Gavra. Inside his mind he heard her plea.

"Need you now ..."

"She will," Nyx said, though her frown suggested she might be having doubts herself.

"Perhaps she needs to be serviced by a dragon," Gavra suggested. "See how she looks at me?"

Nyx shook her head. "She chose her mate. The only

females you'll be servicing are my Thiasoi as soon as they are fully melded by me. Come." She gripped him by the arm and turned, leading him away.

The back of his neck prickled with the dark glare Silas shot him, along with the string of mental curses the other man filled his mind with.

"Perhaps she needs to be serviced by a dragon? You fucker, that's exactly what she needs, but you know you can't do it in front of her goddamn mother or she'll see firsthand how deeply melded we are. Get the fuck away from us and stay away until you can actually be with us the way we need you."

Gavra clenched his fists in frustration, but kept his eyes focused straight ahead, only half paying attention to the path Nyx led him down along the fountain-lined corridors and waterfall-adorned staircases of the palace.

CHAPTER 30

GAVRA

After a few minutes, Gavra and Nyx came to a door with bottle-glass windows so thick he couldn't make out what was on the other side.

It wasn't until they stopped and she failed to move farther that he realized she was shaking. He looked down at her in alarm. Her body had shrunk into its human state, her black waves no longer topped by the huge antlers, only a delicate, pearl-encrusted crown.

She appeared about to collapse, but when he slid an arm around her waist to offer support, she cried out and smacked at him.

"No! I can't. You aren't him. You aren't my love, my Nereus! Get out!"

Taking a deep breath, he steeled himself for more potential madness and pulled Nyx bodily into his arms, ignoring her protests and her stinging smacks and clawing hands as he held her tight against his chest.

"Nyx, I have no interest in replacing your mate. Please let me be a friend to you if I can. Shh." He continued to hold her and murmured words of comfort while she flailed in his arms. He was alarmed by the delicate feel of her frame against his much larger body. She reminded him of his sister Belah in those anguished days after he and his brothers had resurrected her after bargaining with their own blood to reclaim hers from their enemy. Belah had rejected the idea that her true love was lost to her, at first, but once she'd resigned herself to the truth, she'd grown strong again.

As much as Nyx insisted Nereus was dead, this fragile bundle of chaos in his arms spoke differently. Her love still thrived, so the man must be out there somewhere.

He hoped Assana was right and Neph was lending his power to the search, because it broke his heart to see such a strong, fierce female brought so low as to compromise her own morals for the sake of what she believed must be done.

Once her fighting subsided and she clung limp and crying in his arms, he lifted her up and cradled her against his chest, then pushed the doors to her chamber open.

He carried her into the room, which had a wide, open veranda on the far side that overlooked the entire Haven. The view stretched all the way down to the crashing seashore of the cove where he remembered once fantasizing about making love to this very woman he held.

She'd long since belonged to another man, and her heart did still, but the time hadn't diminished how much he still cared for her. He carried her out onto the porch and sat with her on his lap, gently stroking her back while she cried.

Eventually she grew quiet and he glanced down, curious whether she slept, but she was only staring at the glorious sunset that was one of the things he had always loved about this place. It was the only time the sky seemed to hold dominion over the otherwise mist-shrouded valley. Only for a few moments at the end of the day did the air clear as far as the eye could see across a calm, mystical sea that led Mother-knew-where.

Nyx took a long breath and said, "Do you believe he lives?"

"I believe that you must, or else you wouldn't ask that question."

She nodded and closed her eyes. "I don't know how to *be* without him anymore. I managed well enough with Neph … my brother is my true balance and always has been. But without Nereus all these years, I've just been an empty buoy, tossed about in the surf with nothing to anchor me, no ballast to keep me steady."

"You were right before," Gavra said. "I believe if Nereus lives, he would find a way back to you. That he hasn't yet only means he can't, but not because he's dead. You said the two of you were blood melded …" He hesitated, uncertain whether this was a safe line of questioning, but he had to know for his own reasons as much as to illustrate to Nyx what she likely already believed.

She sighed and extracted herself from his arms, giving him a gentle squeeze on the shoulder when she rose to face him.

"Yes, and his mark on my soul is as inexorable as my own would be on his. I have no idea if the mark would disappear if he were dead. All I know is that it hasn't. I was able to bide my time for ages, because even in his absence we were still connected by the River. That mental link kept hope alive. But that went away several months ago, and all I have left now is the blood mark."

"Not enough to give you balance," Gavra said, looking up at her.

"Not even close," she confirmed, stepping into her room.

Gavra stood, aware that their conversation was far from over, but uncertain what she might ask of him next. Even if he wanted to, seduction was likely the exact wrong course of action, at least tonight. Besides, he couldn't get the image of wild and wanton Assana being pinned down to the dinner table under Silas.

He stepped off the balcony into her room and bowed his head. "If you'd like to call your guards to escort me back to my cell, I will say good night."

"Nonsense." Nyx glanced up from the tipped decanter she was emptying into a pair of glasses. "You've proved yourself a loyal friend tonight, Gavra. You'll remain in the palace as my guest for the rest of your stay in the Haven, but please accept my invitation to join me for a little while longer and talk."

"I would like that," he said, accepting the overfull wine-glass and realizing as he brought it to his lips that it wasn't wine—she'd apparently graduated to stronger spirits and was intent on getting drunk. Taking a sip, he girded himself against the potential disintegration of her sanity.

She took a long swallow from her own drink and the subsequent warmth that infused her aura seemed to steady her. She straightened her back and looked at him.

"I would mate you, if it made any sense. Perhaps in time it will, if Nereus is truly dead. I remember how well you admired me, and what a good friend you were to Nereus. You favored me over my brother, at any rate. I know I shouldn't appreciate that so much, but I do."

"You still hold Neph partly responsible for the Lamia, even though it was my brother who made the mistake of falling into her trap."

"I've always forgiven Neph his poor decisions. Save for that one. He tied himself to your brother to save him. Without Neph's blood, your brother would have been lost. I think that's what kept him from mating all these years."

Gavra held his tongue. It sounded like Nyx was oblivious to the fact that their brothers had been carrying on a love affair for ages before the incident that redefined their world.

She drained her glass and refilled it where she stood, then moved past him, heading back to the balcony.

Outside, the sounds of waterfalls harmonized with the faint rush of crashing waves that grew louder the darker it became. The distant sunset was a deep, blood red, the orb of light sinking past the glassy horizon.

Nyx paused at the railing, taking a sip from her glass and staring off into the distance. She had a haunted expression that cut deep into Gavra's heart. She'd been waiting too long for her love to return, hesitant to take action, because Nereus was always the one who fixed things for her. Nereus or Neph or her son, Calder.

Now that she had finally chosen to act, it wasn't based on logic—only the utter pain of abandonment and loss, and fear of being unable to hold onto the little she had left.

He stood beside her, leaning against the balcony railing and nursing the strong spirits she'd poured for him.

"This beauty is worth protecting by itself," Gavra said. "But I worry that you're compromising too much for it. There are other ways … the dragons will help, if my siblings and I command it. You can trust us."

Nyx's entire body shuddered like a strong wind had blown through, chilling her. She cocked her head to the side and in a strangely throaty voice said, "No. We must breed more immortals. The Haven will be at risk no matter what. We must be ready to fight back."

She seemed in the grip of a trance, which deeply alarmed him. He'd seen her Thiasoi in their blood meld thrall, and he'd encountered countless mind-controlled Ultiori hunters, as well as the Elites, before he and his siblings went into hiding to protect their own sacred home. Her stare wasn't quite the same blank, unseeing gaze, but it wasn't far off.

He reached out and gripped her arm, shaking her. "Nyx,

what's wrong? Sweet Mother, please tell me you're not under some spell like you put on your own guards."

She blinked and shook her head, letting out a bubbling, drunken laugh. "Oh Gaia, no. You thought I was mind controlled, didn't you?" She giggled and sat down. "The River trance is … involuntary when I get enough spirits in me. My mind wanders and *pop*, I'm in the flow of it. What did I say?"

He scowled and sat in the chaise across from her. "That we need to breed more immortals."

"Ah, yes. That's where you come in, my handsome, virile beast." She leaned over and gave his chest a flirtatious tickle. "You'll fill all my maidens with your seed and watch the little satyrs grow, immortal every one." She sat back with a dreamy hum, turned a wobbly head to look at him, and smiled.

"I think you're missing something in your plan. Your Thiasoi maidens aren't immortal, and if I mark them—which I have to do to get them pregnant in the first place—their babies will be more dragon than nymph. Possibly *all* dragon. And not immortal ones."

Nyx raised a finger and shook it at him. "That is where my genius plan comes in. Did you think I would blood meld my girls without a good reason? Oh, no … Once the melding is done, I will inhabit their bodies with my spirit. Our immortal spirits … yours and mine … can bond without a mark of any kind. Why have just one perfect little immortal satyr-dragon baby when we can have a dozen?"

"Perhaps because your nymphs would rather choose who breeds them?"

"They *did* choose. Never once have I coersh … corersh … *forced* them to do this. They are Thiasoi every bit as honorable as Nereus's men. They would lay down their lives to protect the Haven. Like he did. Oh, Nereus."

Her slurred speech and wildly fluctuating aura would have been amusing, if not for the revelation of what she intended. She would take them that deep into the blood meld that they lost their minds. Did she even realize how her actions would likely break the poor women she controlled?

There was no more reasoning with her now. At the thought of Nereus, she'd fallen into a blubbering mess again, sobbing into her hands. Once again, Gavra scooped her into his arms and carried her inside to her bed. She clung to him desperately.

"Please tell me you understand. Tell me Nereus would understand, would know that I had no choice. I had to protect the Haven. It has to be this way. Our time is too short to wait any longer. My husband is gone, my brother and my son have betrayed me. I am the only one left who can make this decision."

"Assana is still here, Nyx. Let her come into her own, find her power. She can help you defend the Haven without compromising the integrity of your soldiers. She is stronger than you think."

"My daughter is a fool. She could have had you along with the other Thiasoi but she chose that ursa instead."

Gavra frowned. "You would have blood melded your daughter, too?"

"I gave her the choice because she is my daughter. She doesn't realize when the stakes are this high that sacrifices must be made. It only proves how very *weak* she is, and I have no hope that the male she chose will be enough to tame her primal nature. You saw how crazed she was. Perhaps she's having second thoughts? Maybe I will ask her again. There is still time, if she hasn't become pregnant yet. An immortal grandchild would be lovely …"

She let out an almost happy hum and her eyelids fluttered closed. Within a few seconds, she was snoring softly.

Gavra stared at her, no longer suppressing the worry from his expression. She *was* mad, but she'd rationalized her actions so well she convinced herself they were the only sane options. She was willing to sacrifice the minds of her own soldiers—her daughter included—to build an immortal army, sired by him. As if there weren't enough ursa and nymphs who would stand in defense of the Haven. All the higher races would defend this place if she would just ask.

Something about her trance earlier had struck him, though. He didn't know much about how the nymphaea's sacred River worked, only that it gave the ones connected to it a kind of second sight. It had been as though her words were plucked from the current itself, not decided on by her. A mystical decree beyond anyone's control. But why? Why weren't the immortals that existed already enough? There weren't many of them, true, but they were strong, and at the moment were all still on the same side— against the Ultiori—and he saw no reason why that should change.

Did her statement suggest some of them may betray the rest? That seemed highly unlikely. None of the immortals had solitary agendas. They were all focused on protecting their sacred homes and their people. None quite as rabidly as Nyx, but they weren't evil.

Gavra continued to ponder what he'd learned as he stood and covered the sleeping woman with a blanket. When he faced the door, however, all thought came to a halt.

He threw the door open and was at a near run toward Assana's quarters when sense kicked in again and he slowed, then stopped. Taking a deep breath, he sent Silas a silent message.

"How is she?"

Silas didn't answer, but through their reopened link, he experienced a rush of desperate lust and short, panting breaths. Assana's mind was a cyclone of need yet again, and he would go to her soon, but needed to do this right if he were going to preserve their secret long enough for the plan he was forming to work.

"I am free. I am coming to you soon," he shot to Silas before turning back the other direction and running down the huge staircase to the grand hall.

Finally, he found what he was looking for. Half a dozen Thiasoi all sat around an open fire pit looking utterly exhausted as they passed a heavy bottle between them. When he approached, Clio jumped up.

"Is she sending you back already? We were sure she intended to keep you all night."

"She doesn't want me for sex. But she does want me to stay in the palace now. I have something I need to do, but before I do, can you tell me where I should sleep? She'll want me near her quarters."

"Doesn't want *you* for sex?" Clio asked. All the women stared at him with wide eyes, their gazes drifting over his leather-clad body with interest.

"You didn't *actually* believe your mistress was sane, did you?" he asked, smirking at them.

"No, but that gives crazy a whole new meaning," Clio said. "She must really be saving you for all of us." She gave him a smug look, but was otherwise unenthusiastic about the revelation.

"Try to contain your excitement," he deadpanned. "Can you show me where to sleep, or not?"

Ephyra rose to her feet. "Come on. The fact that she's not in our heads now must mean you got through to her, at least for a little while." She led him back through the door that led across a well-appointed barracks and into the palace proper.

"She got herself drunk, is what happened. Being with me brought back old memories, I guess."

They walked for a few more minutes, half his mind tightly attuned to the direction of his mates and their states of mind. Nothing but the same wild maelstrom he'd sensed before existed where they were.

Finally, Ephyra stopped in front of a door, shoved it open, then leaned against the jamb. She stared up at him with wide, anxious eyes.

"Please tell me you know how to stop her. My sisters and I have only agreed to do this because we truly see no other way. Tell me you have another way." She tugged at the laces of her gown and the gauzy mesh fell open, baring her breasts. "We will all be yours eventually, one way or the other. You can have us whole with clear minds, or broken by her spell. We all agree."

Gavra gazed down at the offering almost distractedly. If he'd had this offer any other time, he'd have jumped at it. The value of almost a dozen nymphs offering themselves to be his mates was immense. A grand enough gesture that it would be worth every effort to give them what they asked for. Any dragon worth his horns would take it, but Gavra couldn't.

He took a step closer to her and gently tugged her garment closed, then cupped her cheek.

"Lovely Ephyra, you are not mine. There will be a mate for you, but it will be someone you don't have to compromise to win. I'm going to find a way to release you all from Nyx's spell before she ruins you completely, but I need to do it right. Do me a favor, though … Please don't guard this door tonight. If she is in your head, I need your last memory of me to be watching me go inside."

He bent then, pressing his lips gently to Ephyra's forehead. She let out a shaky breath and nodded.

"I want to ask what you plan, but I know better. It's hard enough to hold onto my own thoughts when she's inside my head."

"My plan right now is to simply go to bed. Please make sure your mistress is not alone when she wakes up, though.

As strong as she is, she still needs your friendship, despite the things she's done."

"Nyx *is* the Haven, now that Neph has disappeared. We would die for her."

"If it's in my power, I won't let it come to that," he said and closed the door behind him.

CHAPTER 31

SILAS

Silas didn't have room for thought, his instincts having kicked in the second Gavra and Nyx left the dining room and he was forced to take matters into his own hands. Old habits died hard, however, and despite knowing what Assana needed, it still took him a second to overcome that ingrained ursa male need to be told what to do to satisfy her.

Her mental cry drove him to action. Her distress was even more dire than any of the ursa females he'd serviced through estrous.

Assana's antlers gouged grooves into the wooden surface of the table, her supple body writhing beneath him as he pinned her to the hard surface. He shifted to grip both her wrists in one hand while she bucked beneath him, her pelvis hitting his thigh and grinding against him while she moaned his name.

His vision went hazy with the wet heat of her rubbing on his skin. With his free hand, he rucked up her sheer gown and slipped his fingers between her legs. Her hot, throbbing clit was a swollen protrusion beneath his touch and Assana let out a sharp gasp when he rubbed it, her entire body going rigid from the pleasure.

"That's right, baby. I'm going to take care of you. Make you feel better."

"Fuck me!" she growled through clenched teeth, her eyes swirling with wild energy before rolling back in her head when he pushed three fingers deep into her flooded channel.

His cock ached and twitched in anticipation. He pulled his fingers from her and tore at his trousers, heedless of the wet, sloppy mess she'd made of his hand. Gaia, he wanted to taste her as much as he wanted to fuck her, but he couldn't do both at once, and it was his cock she was begging for.

The scent of her need surrounded him, filling his lungs until he was drowning in it, almost shaking with his own near-crazed lust. He freed his cock and had to press his entire body down on top of hers to hold her still. It felt wrong in so many ways to be taking her like this—for her to be no more coherent than a wild animal whose only clear communication was, "Fuck me." At least there was no ambiguity in that message.

Another tilt of her hips pressed her entrance right where he needed her, and with a grunt he slid home, piercing her in one violent, fluid thrust. Assana's head flew back, the sharp points of her antlers kicking splinters of wood off the surface of the table when they hit. She wrapped her legs around him, barely allowing him the freedom to move.

With a frustrated snarl, he released her wrists and reached behind him to pull her ankles away from his ass. He pushed her legs toward her shoulders and spread them wide, holding her behind the knees as he pulled out and slammed back in, staring down at the glorious merging of their bodies while he entered her.

"Hold on, Assana," he said. She stared up at him with a

gaze of wonder and gratitude, and reached back to grasp the edge of the table above her head with both hands.

She surrendered to him then, her body rippling with power while he fucked her. The small bundle between her thighs beckoned and he pressed a thumb to it and rubbed. In the depths of his being, he readied his reservoir for what she would give, his balls already tingling in anticipation. She arched her back off the table, and within seconds, she was crying out his name as she spasmed from her release.

Silas let go of her thighs and braced himself over her as he continued to pump several more times. The delicious, clenching spasms her sheath inflicted him with were too good not to enjoy for just a couple more seconds. Gaia, if he could fuck her forever, he would. When he felt the familiar tension in his balls grow intolerable, he finally let go, letting out a harsh groan as he spilled his semen deep inside her.

Raw power continued to flow off her in waves, like a fever that had yet to break. He knew he wasn't close to done sating her yet, but she was subdued for the moment. He slipped out of her and lifted her in his arms, hurrying to carry her out of the palace as far away from Gavra's energy as they could get.

He sensed the dragon, testing their distance and the influence of power for several minutes as he jogged with her held tight against him. Assana's quarters on the far side of the palace were a small pocket of serenity with the sounds of waterfalls outside and the comfortable bed within. When they entered the sunset-gilded rooms, she twisted in his arms, the slight clench and release of her buttocks under his arm signaling she was in need again and he didn't have time to waste.

He didn't even make it all the way to the bed before she roused and gripped him by the shoulders. The shift in her weight threw him off balance and he fell back against the wall while her mouth crashed down onto his. She wrapped her legs around his waist and he held her, eagerly responding to the kiss and the slick press of her pussy against his navel. He slid his hands to cup her ass, moving one farther down and aiming his erect cock at her core once again. His tip brushed against her sodden folds, still dripping with his essence. The slight caress caused a shiver of pleasure to course through her and she moaned into his mouth. Bracing her arms around his shoulders, she let her body slip down his torso just enough that his cock slid into her again.

Silas braced his feet wide on the floor, knees half-bent while he held her hips tightly in both hands and guided her down onto his shaft. Summoning some of the immense power he had at his disposal now, he lifted her as though she were feather-light and slammed her back down again. Assana let out a cry that was half pleasure, half delight.

"Oh, yes! Fuck me like that. Give it to me, Silas."

For several strokes, he did the same thing, hammering her down repeatedly onto his cock. Each time, his entire body seemed to burst with the pleasure of his shaft sinking so deep into her he lost himself. He shifted positions, spinning them and pushing her back against the wall. This way was just as good, having her pinned beneath him so he could pound into her with merciless thrusts of his hips.

Sweat coated their bodies and his thighs strained from the effort. There were other ways he could fuck her, he knew, and he intended to try them all.

Gavra's awareness flooded into his mind a little later while they were in still in the midst of their wild tangle. The dragon's mental presence was like a door being opened onto the dark room of Silas's mind, light from the other side flooding in. Gavra only called out, but Silas was too busy to respond. He was concentrating on the beautiful twist of Assana's torso now lying on her bed before him. One of her legs was hooked over his shoulder as he pierced her pussy from the edge. He had one of her luscious breasts clutched in his hand, two fingers buried in her ass while he bent over to take her nipple, eager to hear the rising orgasm explode from her in a torrent of filthy curses punctuated by his name.

He had no room to entertain dragons who couldn't do their duty to their mates.

When Assana's sweet orgasm filled the air again with melodic cries and fingers clutching at air, he hauled her up and spun them both around, falling back into a chair beside the bed. She lowered herself onto his cock again without instruction or urging, the first small sign that her delirium might finally be subsiding.

They orgasmed together, limbs entwined and mouths hungrily lapping at each other. His constant watchfulness on her conscious mind told him she wasn't completely back to sanity yet, and her persisting shape—the more voluptuous, muscular form with heavy antlers and luminescent skin marked with vine-like designs—signaled she still wasn't completely sated yet.

In a rough, scratchy voice, he said, "Gaia, what does it take to bring you down from this? I'll fuck you all night if I have to, but I have a feeling it won't be enough."

His skin prickled as though the air pressure had changed. Within his mind, that open door produced a figure who walked through and leaned against the wall just inside his consciousness. He turned away from Assana's undulating torso to look over his shoulder. Gavra was there, in the flesh, looking far more put together than he had any right to look after the evening Silas had endured.

"She's a handful, isn't she?" Gavra asked coolly.

The sound of his voice elicited a sudden clench of Assana's muscles around Silas's cock that made his eyes widen, and Silas grunted. She jerked her head up from where her cheek had been resting against his shoulder while she slowly rocked on top of him. One of her antlers banked hard against his temple and searing pain shot through his head.

"Fuck!" He pressed a hand to the wound and pulled it away. Blood coated his fingertips.

"Those are wicked. Need help getting her back in the box, brother?"

"I got this," Silas said with a scowl. He gripped her by the hips and struggled to stand, falling back into the chair with a huff. "Maybe just … spell me for a few?"

"You know it's easier when we work together." Gavra strolled toward him, his body loose and languid, but his eyes glinted with need.

When he reached them, he bent and met Assana's upturned mouth, a low rumble sounding in his chest as they kissed.

"How long until the guards catch you and haul you back to your cage?" Silas asked.

Gavra's attention was fully on Assana when he answered. He cupped her cheeks, fingers brushing sweat-soaked strands of hair from her forehead. He seemed to be inspecting her for damage, and Silas sensed the opening of the dragon's mind and an invitation to join him deep within that secret place the three shared.

"I've got all night, and if everything works out, I'll never set foot in that prison again."

CHAPTER 32

GAVRA

The pair were in Gavra's head again, though not as deep as they'd been earlier that day when they'd first completed the meld. The forced separation wasn't ideal. This time, he'd make sure to take the time to do it right and add his own magic to the mix.

He clutched Silas by the back of the head, fingers digging in hard. The ursa moaned and his eyelids fell shut with his surrender. Inside his mind, Silas's presence grew more potent while the glow of his aura brightened with fresh desire.

His hunger for this man surged to the surface in a torrent and he captured his mouth with a growl, plunging his tongue in deep. Silas reached up and cupped the back of Gavra's head, pushed his fingers into the tightly bound hair at his nape, and pulled the thong free. Red curtains cascaded around Gavra's face, framing the dark brows and mahogany skin before him.

"Sweet Mother, I missed you," Gavra said when he released Silas's mouth. His gaze flitted over the ursa's face, committing the strong angles and curves to memory. He frowned when he saw the deep gouge in Silas's forehead that still trickled red.

Blood. Their blood was the key, but a tricky argument to make. He lifted a hand and brushed his thumb beneath the cut, drawing away a smear of red and staring down at it. How much? Would it only take a drop from each of them for the meld to take?

"Gavra …" Silas said with desperate urgency.

Right. It was too soon to make the suggestion. Assana needed him too much now. He wiped the blood on his shirt and exhaled a short breath of red smoke. Wispy tendrils coiled from his lips, settled on Silas's brow, and the wound knitted together within seconds.

"Come to the bed," he commanded as he wrapped his arms around Assana and lifted her off Silas's lap. The ursa's cock slid free of her, slick and shining with her sweet juices. The aroma made Gavra's mouth water.

He lay Assana on her bed, fending off her roaming hands that pawed at his clothes and her hungry mouth licking and sucking at any bit of exposed skin she could find.

"Need your cock. Please!" she cried over and over.

"I think what you need is my tongue. Lie back, baby. Let me take care of you." He glanced over his shoulder to see Silas still sitting in the chair with a dazed expression. He jerked his head to the other side of the bed. "Get over here if you want to get fucked for a change. We'll give that cock of yours a break for a little while, but your ass is mine."

Silas's head fell back and he sighed. "Thank fuck," he said, every ounce of tension falling from his sweat-drenched body. "You can do whatever the fuck you want to me as long as I don't have to decide … or move."

He rose slowly and made it to the bed before collapsing beside Assana. Rolling toward her, he bent to suck one of her nipples as though he couldn't resist one more taste of her.

The muscular curve of his ass cheek beckoned to Gavra as strongly as the juicy petals between Assana's spread thighs.

Standing back for a second, he took them both in. They embraced languidly, kissed, their hands roaming over each other with lazy desire. It was far past his turn to give to them.

With a breath, his conjured garments dissolved and he climbed onto the bed at their feet. As he crawled toward them, he pushed Assana's legs wider, sliding one hand up the inside of her thigh.

His other hand took a similar path, gripping Silas by the back of one strong thigh and turning him onto his belly. The ursa complied, shifting closer so that his leg draped over hers. The pair remained half-entwined, kissing and touching while Gavra slowly moved in, hovering over them.

He teased one hand higher up Assana's thigh, sliding along skin slick with her essence. She let out a soft moan into Silas's mouth and bent her knee to spread herself wider. The movement pushed Silas's leg higher. On his other side, Gavra cupped Silas's ass, teased fingers along the tight opening and farther, caressing the underside of his balls and then along the length of his cock.

The slight contact made Silas twist even more, bending his leg and draping his thigh fully across Assana's belly so his ass lifted and parted, his tight rosette bared for Gavra's eyes.

Sweet Mother, they were both so perfect and needy right now. Beyond any experience he'd had with past mates long dead. The females he'd claimed in the ancient past had been no more than vessels—human breeding stock whose minds barely withstood his mark before he lost them completely. He'd lost the taste for mating after only a couple centuries of it, resorting to simple trysts for the sake of replenishing his energy and no longer marking any partner to breed.

With the pair of them deep within his mind, there was no

question about their mental strength. Assana may have seemed fragile the way her sanity vacillated, but imbalance was the nature of her kind, and she only needed attention from the right partners and an infusion of fertile seed strong enough to let her conceive a child. She would be so powerful, so glorious once she found that balance.

Holding them both in his mind like the treasures they were, he spread Assana's folds and dipped his fingers into her. The slick walls of her pussy gripped him, pulling him in. He bent down over her mound, inhaling the rich scent of her sex mixed with Silas's evergreen aroma.

Lashing out with his tongue, Gavra drew a pattern into the flesh above her cleft, the intricate mark appearing in glowing red almost before he had a chance to deliberate over whether it was right to give her now. It had to be right— there was no other moment better than this to mark her. She let out a soft yelp of surprise that turned to a sigh of ecstasy when he finished and sank his tongue deep into her, letting it fill her as full as it could.

He parted her folds wider, pulling back to admire the beauty of the blossom between her legs. The flesh was darker than the rest of her, the folds a deeper blue in her primal form where they were pink when she was in her human shape. He loved them either way, and especially loved the throbbing little pearl of pleasure nestled at the apex.

He took her clit into his mouth and sucked, swirling his tongue around and around, then flicking with determined rhythm until Assana arched into Silas's embrace and cried to be filled again. The orgasm would tide her over for now, but he had an ursa to make love to first.

Gathering more of her copious fluids on his tongue, he shifted focus. He gripped Silas by the ass with both hands and spread him wide, then bent and slicked his fluid-coated tongue around the tight ring of muscle.

Silas squirmed, hips pushing back against Gavra's mouth. He rose up on hands and knees and Gavra followed, tonguing him from behind while Silas repositioned himself between Assana's thighs.

"Mark me first," Silas said. "Then fuck me."

Gavra pulled back, eyeing the slick, puckered opening in front of him. So tempting to put his mark right there. He idly rubbed a thumb around and around, pushed it in and enjoyed the way Silas moaned and his body shivered.

No, he decided he wanted to mark the ursa in a place where he could see it anytime he liked—not just when he was about to bury his cock in him.

The way Silas relaxed and opened for him told him the man was ready now, and he didn't hesitate.

"I'll mark you while I fuck you," he said as he rose up and pressed the tip of his stiff, aching shaft to Silas's ass.

With one shove, his cock slid deep like he belonged there. Silas grunted and let out a curse as he buried his face against Assana's breasts. Gavra paused long enough to enjoy the tight heat of his lover, closed his eyes, and savored the tangled sensation of their minds. As he began to move, their mental connection deepened, the three of them descending once again into the shared depths that belonged to only them ... the part of their souls reserved for each other ... the part that only existed when they were bound this tightly by Assana's nymphaea magic.

He was only peripherally aware of the movements of their bodies, inasmuch as the pleasure filled him while he fucked Silas with instinctive, rhythmic thrusts. Beneath him, he felt Silas pull Assana's hips up and slide his cock into her yet again. Assana moved beneath them both, hips rising to take Silas into her.

In their minds they merged. Their souls became one. The fresh mark he'd made on Assana's body had pierced through to these depths and shone like a beacon between him and Silas, drawing them both tightly to her.

Gavra sank his cock into Silas over and over, the friction pushing him closer to Nirvana and filling him with the potent magic that he always drew in when aroused, as easily as he drew breath. Focusing that power, he bent over Silas's back, extended his tongue, and lashed it out across the expanse of Silas's shoulders, down the middle of his back, and around until easily half of the dark skin was etched with the glowing red mark that signaled who this ursa belonged to.

When the power of the mark took hold, they broke through another mental barrier, falling even deeper into each other to the point that Gavra lost track of where he ended and they began. The pleasure grew threefold, and for the first time, he had a taste of what it would mean to meld them so deeply they not only shared a mind, but also a body and a soul that were inextricably bound.

Their combined power would be more than enough to prevail in their quest, and with their unending love to build on, the three of them would be invincible, but this simple melding wasn't enough to reach that level of power.

The chorus of their voices merged in the night as they climaxed again and again. It didn't matter who was inside whom when their minds were so connected. They were all three inside the other more deeply than their bodies were capable of achieving.

To imagine how much deeper their connection would become once they were blood melded ... every definition of home he'd ever imagined shattered. *This* was the thing worth dying for, worth living for, worth *bleeding* for. He didn't shed his own blood lightly, had only done so once for family, but for this ... for these two people, he would gladly tear out his heart to have what a melding such as that promised.

CHAPTER 33

ASSANA

Assana came back to herself in the warmth of a bath and couldn't help but wonder if the last few hours had been a dream. She remembered feeling Silas inside her during her primal, lust-crazed attack on Gavra inside his cage. She remembered Silas carrying her back to her quarters and bathing her, then making love to her again with his slow, gentle, and oh so deliberate care. He'd brought her back down to earth, anchoring her with his tender touch, rooting her to her sanity once again.

Perhaps they were still there and she'd fallen asleep again. Perhaps she'd only dreamed losing her mind for a second time so that Silas was forced to pin her down and fuck her right on top of her mother's dinner table.

Her mind objected to the idea that any of it could have been imagined. Her very sane, rational mind reminded her that every moment had indeed occurred the way she remembered it. Her body flushed with humiliation and she turned her head and pressed it into the strong shoulder she rested against.

"Please tell me I dreamed it," she said, hoping that a

second opinion might be enough to prove she was wrong, despite her own mind insisting she wasn't. She still wasn't quite used to trusting her awareness of events after the last few days of losing control when she least expected.

A warm rumble vibrated the chest beneath her and a soft brush of lips against her ear carried a low chuckle.

"Much of it happened inside your head, true, but every second was real, baby. Just look down and you'll see."

The voice was the first bit of evidence that her memory and senses weren't betraying her. She was not in Silas's arms, but in the arms of the man she had despaired of ever truly being sane enough to touch again.

She bit her lip and her heartbeat sped at the thrill. The humiliation meant nothing if he were truly here now, naked with her cradled in his arms. She wondered where Silas was.

The best part was that she felt completely fucking *sane*. There was no crazy, uncontrollable urge to devour his entire body with her snatch. Though the thought of having him inside that part of her did incite a pleasant tingle in her nether regions. She glanced down as he instructed and let out a soft gasp, then lifted her face to look at him.

"You beautiful fucking dragon, you did it. You marked me!"

"And not a second too soon. You were running us both ragged with that appetite of yours."

"Did you mark Silas too? Where is he?" She looked toward the other side of the large, sunken tub but saw no sign of her sweeter, gentler lover, though if recent memories were accurate, he'd come to her rescue and fucked the ever-loving shit out of her for several hours earlier.

"He learned he doesn't quite have the stamina for an ancient nymph in rut. Not even an ursa female in full estrous is as much of a challenge as you are."

Gavra tilted his chin toward her bed and she craned her

head around to see a massive, slumbering beast lying on his side. A mark as intricately beautiful as hers covered the entire expanse of dark skin on Silas's back, pulsing with the rise and fall of his breathing.

"Poor thing," she said, sighing and sinking back into Gavra's arms.

"How do you feel?" Gavra asked.

She took a quick assessment of her body's aches, noting a fading soreness between her thighs and fatigue in her muscles. She cataloged all these things quickly and clearly, with no encroaching haze of need like a looming thunderhead on the horizon. Her mind was nothing but clear, blue skies over calm water. What a relief.

She let out a deep breath and said, "I've never felt better. Thank you."

"Good. Because there's something we need to talk about."

The tightness in his voice made her look into his eyes. He regarded her with slightly creased brows, his crimson irises aglow with determination, yet the connection she still had to his mind betrayed the slightest hesitance. What was he so afraid to tell her?

Her stomach lurched when the images from the evening came back.

He'd been having dinner with her mother, cleaned and dressed up in a manner befitting an honored guest of the Haven's Dionarchs. She remembered the pang of jealousy she'd suffered when she and Silas walked into the room and she saw the pair smiling and leaning toward each other as though engaged in intimate conversation.

That split-second had been the beginning of another swift descent into primal need for her. Need to claim him before her mother could touch him, though she'd told herself she could resist.

No. She calmed herself with a deep breath. He'd come to her tonight. Marked her. And he had stayed.

"You … didn't seduce my mother." She stated it as though it were fact, hoping like hell that she was right.

Gavra shook his head. "It was wrong of me to think I could … that I *should*. There's no way I'd be able to get through to her, anyway, not as decisive as she is … as determined. I think there's only one person in existence who could make her change her mind, and he isn't here."

"My father … You mean him, don't you?"

"Yes. Which brings me to the difficult thing I have to say. After hearing what Silas learned from the Diviner today, I think there's only one way to save your Thiasoi sisters from Nyx's thrall, and I think we can get through to Nyx at the same time. The three of us together can make it work, but we all have to agree to this."

His heartbeat pounded even harder in his chest beneath her hand, and the muscles of his jaw twitched when he paused, as though he didn't relish the idea one bit.

"What is it?" she asked with a worried frown.

"Shit. Silas should be awake … Silas!" he called across the room. The sleeping ursa didn't move or even twitch. "Silas!" Gavra called again, this time pushing a mental message through their minds to their other lover.

The huge man groaned a protest, stretched, and rolled over. He blinked blearily at them and scowled, but his expression cleared when he saw Assana. He smiled.

He sat up and scrubbed a hand over his face and through his hair.

"You look much better." He stood and ambled over to them, naked and huge and beautiful, his dark cock already thickening with arousal as he approached.

He clambered into the tub with an ungraceful step, dropping down onto the submerged bench with another groan and making water slosh over the edge. An involuntary sigh escaped his throat and he sank farther into the water, sliding under completely and then rising up again to slick hands over his sleek, black head.

When he opened his eyes again, he grinned, then grew serious at their expressions.

"Time for business, I take it. So … what next?"

Assana looked at Gavra expectantly. His expression hadn't softened, and she chewed on the inside of her lip, apprehensive about what decision he'd come to.

"There's a way to break the blood meld on the other nymphs, but we can't do it without making sure Nyx is neutralized at the same time. She'll fight us if we try … may hurt one of them, if we aren't careful. But if we work together, we can do it."

"That's good," Assana said. "What's the catch? It can't be that easy." She looked at Silas. "What did the Diviner tell you?"

Silas frowned at Gavra like he was trying to figure the other man out. Finally, he shrugged. "She was cryptic about it, and I haven't exactly had time to process the information. All I know is that the blood meld can't be broken except by overriding it with a stronger creature's blood."

"Are you strong enough?" Assana asked, giving Gavra a confused look. "I thought you said your power wasn't enough to subdue her. Why would your blood override hers?"

"I'm not strong enough on my own. No *single* creature is strong enough to break her blood meld. That's what the Diviner said. But the three of us together, with our powers melded, can succeed."

Assana shook her head and gave him an incredulous look. "That isn't how melding works. We just get into each other's heads when we meld. We only share consciousness …

thoughts, feelings, and the like. You know this. Our powers aren't magnified."

"I shared my power with you earlier today," Silas said. "To help you mend Gavra's cage. Maybe that's what he means."

"No," Gavra said. "You were just transferring energy. That's innate for you. You probably could have done it even if you weren't melded with Assana."

"Then how?" Assana asked. "Melding isn't enough by itself."

"It is if we're blood melded."

Assana's heart dropped into her stomach and that helpless vertigo she'd thought gone returned with a vengeance. Goosebumps covered her skin.

"No." She shook her head, sliding off Gavra's lap and moving away to put as much space as possible between herself and those awful words. "You don't mean that."

"I wish there were another way, trust me."

"Silas, please tell him there's a better solution. Your magic … you can do amazing things with it. Surely that's the answer."

Silas stared back in shock, his gaze darting between her and Gavra. The two males looked at each other and Silas's expression hardened.

"We should find another way," Silas said. "Maybe there's something I haven't tried yet that will work. Something that will let us share power. This power I have is still new to me."

"Thank you," she said with relief and went to him, slipping beneath his arm and onto his lap in the water.

"You don't think I *want* that to be the only way, do you?" Gavra asked. "Sweet Mother, shedding blood is the last thing I want. But I've been over and over it in my head. Your mother won't relinquish her thrall over the Thiasoi as long as she believes it's the only way to protect the Haven. If you want to free them, this is how it has to happen. They trust you. If we can make you strong enough—merge our powers with a blood meld—your blood will take precedence."

"But then I'm no better than her! Or …" Gaia forbid, was he going to make her spell it out? "Or that awful bitch who melded your brother and destroyed everything when we punished her for it. I won't be like them. Blood melding is an abomination to our kind. It's disgusting. Vile. The only nymphs who do it are either evil or insane. Yes, my mother is fucking insane. We need to fix her. How is this going to do that?"

"Tell me," Gavra said, his jaw clenched and the muscles spasming, "was your father also insane when he blood melded your mother?"

Assana's mouth fell open and she shook her head. "How dare you! They did no such thing! They wouldn't! And we won't, either!"

Silas held her when she turned her head away and buried her face in his shoulder, unwilling to look at Gavra again. That he would even suggest such a thing hurt her heart. Of all the worst things he could have offered as a solution, why? Why did it have to be that?

The sound of rippling water reached her from the other side of the pool, and the level in the tub dropped a couple inches. She was so closely attuned to Gavra's presence that she felt the distance grow between them like an elastic band stretching taut.

Tears streamed down her cheeks and she wrapped her arms tighter around Silas's shoulders. She hated this feeling, this fear that the distance might grow too vast, that the connection they had that kept her sane would reach its limit and snap. And where would she be after that? Tethered to one of the men she loved when she knew it took them both to make her feel whole?

But he was asking far too much.

She kept her eyes firmly shut, but was acutely aware of Gavra's movements. The dripping trickle of water as it slid from his skin, the soft rustle of fabric as he dried himself off, and the exhalation of breath as he clothed himself again. When he grew still, she could sense his gaze on her. Silas tensed, his embrace tightening protectively, and she was grateful for his loyalty, even if their divided state felt every bit as wrong as the idea of carrying out the act Gavra had suggested.

From the edge of the tub, she heard Gavra let out a long breath. Leather creaked, and she cracked her eyelids to see him crouching down so he was closer to eye level with them. He looked as pristine and perfect as he had at dinner the night before, his conjured clothing fitting his well-muscled body like a glove. But he was troubled, his furrowed brow betraying his unhappiness as he regarded them.

"I have to go so your mother doesn't suspect anything. Just know that this is not a suggestion I would have made if I thought there were any other way. I haven't shed my own blood in thousands of years—I vowed I never would again, unless I found a love worth making that sacrifice for. The two of you are that love. Nothing else could make me do this, not in a million years."

"You don't want to do it for our love, though," Assana said. "You just see it as the easiest answer."

"It isn't easy for me. And believe me, I've considered the other possibilities. The ideal solution would be for your father to return and restore your mother to full sanity. But if there were even a remote possibility of that happening, Nyx would know. She'd wait for him. I fear she's given up hope, even though she doesn't have proof that he's dead."

The reminder of her father's absence sent a piercing pain through her chest. He'd been gone so long, sometimes she forgot what he looked like.

"She still loves him?" she asked in a small voice.

"With all her heart."

"Calder believes he's alive … If we can wait long enough, maybe my brother will find him?" She clung to that small glimmer of hope even though her very connection to the River was enough for her to know it wouldn't be that easy. Calder was out there looking now, but their enemy was devious, and her mother's corruption of the Thiasoi was happening too quickly to be able to stall long enough for a miracle.

Gavra's throat worked as he tried to reply. She could tell he didn't want to lie to her, but he didn't want to hurt her, either. Finally, he said, "I will try to stall her as long as I can. It's my seed she wants, after all. Maybe I can figure out a way to dictate when this breeding actually happens. Never would be too soon, but maybe I can buy us a month or two … give your brother time to find your father."

That would have to work. She nodded. "Stall her until the equinox. At least that might give my uncle time to find his way home too, even if my father is still lost."

Anything would be preferable to the solution Gavra had offered. She'd rather spend the rest of her life lost to the insane lust that controlled her primal state.

He gave her another solemn nod and stood, turning to leave. The farther he got, the more the fear of losing him grew with the distance stretching between them. Her panic overtook her and she lurched across the tub, scrambling wet and naked over the edge.

"Wait!"

Gavra paused just before her door and turned to her. She launched herself into his arms and he grunted at the force, but held her in a tight embrace.

"I love you, Assana. This is all for us, even though it might not seem like it. We'll figure it out, I promise."

"When will you come back?" she asked, hating how desperate she was to hold onto him, but she couldn't shake the fear that their disagreement had strained their connection to a dangerous degree.

"Tonight, after dusk."

He squeezed her tighter, his heat warming her even as the water that coated her body seeped in through his clothing. He didn't seem to care, and when his hands slid down over her sides, thumbs grazing the full curves of her breasts, her body became so hot that the water might have instantly evaporated. Her breath hitched and her pelvis involuntarily tilted closer, the ridge of his erection pressing against her belly. Gavra cupped her naked backside, pressed her tight against him for a moment before he let out a low growl.

"Sweet Mother, but you are perfect. A perfectly tempting distraction. I have to let you go now before I lose myself and we all forget why we're here. I *will* be back, and when I am, this ass is mine."

With that, he gave her wet ass cheek a hard, stinging smack, then gripped her by the hips and pushed her away. He offered a final nod and wicked smile to Silas, who had moved up behind her.

"Yours is too, in case you forget."

Silas chuckled. "My ass was always yours. See you tonight."

CHAPTER 34

GAVRA

Gavra spent the bulk of the day feeling like a stranger in his own skin, but it had nothing to do with the deepened melding with his mates. They were dragon marked now, and their bond might be the only thing that felt *right* about this entire situation.

His love for his mates was worth *every* sacrifice, his blood was the least of it, and he was certain it was the solution to their dilemma. Despite what he'd told Assana, he knew it would be foolish to wait. If the Ultiori had her father and he was still alive after all this time, there was no way they would be foolish enough to let him escape. Yet Gavra would try to stall Nyx, anyway.

He stealthily made his way back to the room Ephyra had shown him and paced for several hours as the sun rose, its mist-veiled light illuminating the palace with a surreal, greenish glow. He missed the sky with a vengeance, but were he to fly here he would get nowhere. The skies beyond the cove at the far end of the Haven were no more than illusion. If Nyx hadn't closed off every avenue of exit from this place, he could have just flown out. But the Source was the only exit now, and he wasn't about to leave without ensuring Assana's home was safe and her sisters no longer under the thrall of a mentally unstable leader.

Even his huge, luxurious bedchamber felt confining. If only he could shift … stretch his wings for a moment … not to fly, just to get out of his head, out of his body for five minutes. The only other thing that let him feel like himself was making love with Silas and Assana. Sweet Mother, even being forcibly bound by her had been liberating. He'd live inside a cage forever if he got to have her that way on a daily basis—wild and unchained, riding him like the world was about to end.

A soft laugh caused him to stop in his tracks and he turned, cutting short his circuit across the room. Nyx stood in the shadows of the entry to his room, the closed door behind her.

"How long have you been there?" he asked, disconcerted that he'd failed to notice her.

"Long enough to figure out you've got something serious on your mind. At least, you did until a moment ago." She cast a pointed glance at his crotch, where his erection strained at the front of his pants. "If you're in need of energy, my nymphs are at your service."

If only it were that simple, but his life hadn't been simple for a very long time.

"I have more than enough energy to last until your ritual. How soon until your nymphs are ready for me?"

"Eager, are we?" Nyx asked.

"You have to know my siblings and I cloistered ourselves for millennia. This is a long overdue adventure for me, so of course I'm eager. I can't help but worry that we're doing your goals a disservice by rushing things, though, which is why I ask."

"The babes won't be born full-grown, you know," Nyx

said. "So the sooner we begin, the better. The Thiasoi will be fully melded by the end of the week and ready for you."

"You and I both know that simply wanting to conceive is not enough of a guarantee. It never has been. I think that's why the divine ones made sex so damn enjoyable for us."

"It will work," Nyx said, though her brows twitched with uncertainty. "Come, I'll show you how powerful the melding already is."

She held out her hand and he took it. A split second later, the air rushed from his lungs and his eardrums popped. Cool mists settled on his skin as he opened his eyes and found himself standing at the base of the Source's massive falls, staring down into the dark water of a huge pool. Around him, the air was displaced several more times with soft popping sounds as the eleven Thiasoi appeared.

"This is the core of the Haven's power, as you know," Nyx said. "The Source provides the life force that sustains our realm, the ursa Sanctuary, and to a lesser degree, your Glade and the turul Enclaves. We are at the core of all the higher realms, closest to the origin of power. This is why I bring my maidens here to conduct the melding. Simply being near the Source increases the power of it."

She made a circular motion with her hand and the eleven nymphs gathered around the pool. Their motions seemed natural today, not jerky and mechanical the way they did when they were clearly under her thrall. He glanced around at them, meeting Ephyra's gaze for a second. She swiftly shifted her eyes away, looking at her mistress in anticipation.

"Only four more sessions and they'll be ready for you. Three more after this one. Watch and you'll see."

With another gesture, the water in the pool between them began to spin and swirl, the surface bubbled and then seemed to swell into uniform shapes around the edges. Small crests rose up before each of the nymphs and then gradually transformed into small, bowl-like shapes held up on thin pedestals of twisting water.

Nyx produced a blade and made a circuit around the circle. Each nymph obediently lifted her wrist over her bowl and allowed Nyx to make a small slice in it, the blood welling and spilling into the vessel.

Gavra clenched his teeth, old memories surging back at the sight of the brilliant red of their blood flowing from them. The color of their blood was something all the races had in common. As a Red dragon the substance seemed somehow sacred to him … something it was his responsibility to safeguard. He shook his head at the ridiculous notion, but deep in his soul, he believed his instincts couldn't be that far from the truth.

When all eleven nymphs had completed their offering, Nyx made a motion and the eleven small basins merged together into the center of the pool, the large, single vessel floating to the edge where Nyx carefully lifted it and brought it to her lips. She drained the blood within, then set it back onto its liquid pedestal and held her own wrist up over the rim.

She lifted an odd, hook-like blade that shimmered with pearlescent light and made a swift cut into her own wrist. Her life's blood flowed into the bowl for several seconds. When the flow stopped, she reversed the process; the basin spun and split into eleven smaller bowls, which were distributed before each of the nymphs.

As the nymphs drank, Nyx explained, "It must be an equal exchange. Their minds become open to me, but more than that, so do their bodies. This is why the blood is required. My spirit cannot inhabit them without their blood inside me."

"Do their spirits go into you?" Gavra asked.

"I have a section of my mind reserved for their safekeeping, yes. They aren't strong enough to control my physical form."

"Why would anyone wish to complete a blood meld if it's so restrictive?" he asked.

"This is a necessity—it isn't meant to give them control of me. We aren't sharing power. They are surrendering their bodies for the sake of breeding, and that's all. I can use them as extensions of myself in other ways, if needed."

The last part had the edge of a threat, but Gavra couldn't help but push.

"Was that how it was with Nereus? Was he only an extension of you when you blood melded him?"

Nyx's gaze shot to him, her eyes wide and her lips pressed together. "It was *not* like this with Nereus. We loved each other. A mating meld is meant to share love and is all the more powerful for it. It made us one in *every* way because we surrendered to each other completely in that moment. Losing him has been like losing half of my very soul, so don't you dare make light of it."

He gave her a pained look. "Are you not denying these maidens a chance at a bond like that by forcing them to breed with me? They deserve a love like you shared with him. We all do."

"Sacrifices must be made. You ought to know. How much have you given up for the sake of your sacred home, for the safety of your kind? How many thousands of years did you give up the very thing that defines you? Dragons are designed to breed. To fuck, to give pleasure and take it. How often did *love* cross your mind before you went into hiding before, Gavra? Your life meant nothing until you and your siblings made that sacrifice."

He blanched at the truth of her words, even though she still had no idea the extent of the actual sacrifice he had made. They'd hidden to protect their children. Not only were the dragons in danger of overbreeding to the point of a population explosion that would rival humanity's, they were becoming far too plentiful and easy to capture by their enemy, giving the Ultiori increasing advantages over the higher races.

Their population needed to be controlled, but the bigger sacrifice was the one he and his brothers had made to restore their sister to life. Without Belah, they weren't whole. Love of family had guided their decision to trade their blood for hers. Nyx didn't know that part of the story, and he would never tell her, but she was right when it came to the sacrifices he had made—and love had never crossed his mind then, because he'd never had a love worth making a sacrifice for until now.

He closed his eyes and took a deep breath, willing himself to calm and stick to his plan.

"You are right, and I will do everything in my power to make sure Nereus's love for his home is not wasted. Seven days seems too soon, if we're going to do this right. Have these nymphs proven their fertility? Will they conceive easily?"

"They are Thiasoi maidens. Virgins make for far more powerful soldiers because their primal nature has never been sated. They're hungry enough for a conquest that they make dangerous opponents. But you're right, their wombs are untried. Do you doubt your own virility so much?"

Gavra laughed. "Not one bit. I've sired hundreds of dragons, unlike my siblings. Still, it's been ages, and I want every advantage we can get now. We should wait at least until the equinox."

Nyx tilted her head and frowned. "The equinox? That's more than a month away. I don't know ..."

"Are you so worried about defending this place that you can't wait a few more weeks when you're already stuck waiting years for these children to come of age? My kind is awake now and ready to be on the offensive, where the Ultiori are concerned. My siblings and I have helped the ursa fortify their barrier so that nothing unwanted can pass through—trust me, I've tested it. The turul are still your allies, and if need be, can be called on to defend the Haven in the interim too. We can wait, especially if it means ensuring my seed takes and all eleven of these maidens are given the gift of motherhood. Or should I say you are given the gift eleven times? They will be the children of your spirit, after all ... Of our spirits."

He lowered his voice and held her gaze, hoping to impart some sense of longing—to remind her of the desire he'd once possessed for her all those eons ago and imply that he might still want her. She may still pine for her lost mate, but it never hurt to remind a woman how desirable she was.

Nyx's eyelids fluttered and she swiftly glanced away. Lifting a hand to her throat, she swallowed several times, then wiped at her eyes.

"Nereus used to talk like that. So intense. We were inseparable when I first discovered his desire for me, but it was on the Spring Equinox when he made his first promise to be mine forever and asked that I share the most sacred melding with him. He said he longed for our union to bear fruit and wanted there to be no question as to the depths of his feelings for me and our unborn children. When we melded, I knew. We were one mind, one body, one soul, and I knew. And when we made love, I could feel his seed moving through me, and my womb opened like a flower and took him in."

"You conceived the first time?"

"Oh, not the first by any means, but the first time we blood melded. Gaia's light shone on us that night. I don't know if it was the timing or our melding, but that was when

Calder was conceived. I … I think you're right. I want my Thiasoi to have every advantage. We will slow down the process. This will give their minds more time to acclimate to my spirit, too. Thank you for your patience, Gavra. You are a good friend."

"Will you allow them a break for the evening? I'd love to have you to myself. I missed this place—it used to be my favorite destination when I wished to avoid the responsibilities of my rank."

"If I recall, you had a habit of wearing out your human pets and had to visit the Haven to burn off your excess energy. Your stamina rivaled the most virile satyrs in the Haven."

"I had a running bet with most of them to see who could last the longest. They rarely won."

"That was always a sight to behold. Your orgies were spectacular events."

He gave her a sly grin. "I knew you were watching. I'm disappointed you never participated."

"I didn't want to steal your thunder. Here, come with me." She reached a hand out again and he took it, bracing himself for another drift.

When he caught his balance again, he found himself at the edge of a familiar pool surrounded by moss-covered rocks that looked like luxuriously carpeted cushions. Bodies covered his old favorite spot now. About a dozen ursa males tangled with twice as many nymphs. The nymphs all looked very well-attended, and the sounds they made attested to the males' skills.

He remembered being that free and full of energy, happily fucking female after female, urging each one to her peak and relishing the flood of her energy before hungrily moving on to the next. He'd enjoyed males on occasion too, but had never craved them so much until he'd set eyes on

Silas. The strong, woody scent of these males reached his nose and made him hard with the memory of how Silas had felt beneath him. But he loved nothing more than the combined aroma of both his mates—their mingled scents and flavors were ambrosia to his senses.

"Have any of the nymphs conceived yet?" he asked, hoping to distract himself from the ache to return to Assana's quarter and spend the next day in bed with his own nymph and ursa mates.

"A few have. They went into this exchange with open minds, deciding that they would meld as many males as they could to ensure more chances of conception. So the ones you see here are likely all fully melded, but they will pair off when one conceives. She'll know the father by the energy of the embryo. Have you ever made love to a pregnant nymph?" She hurriedly waved a hand. "You wouldn't have, of course. They only crave the touch of their baby's father during the pregnancy. But the closer the bond the parents share, the stronger the babe will be when it's born, and the more rewarding the experience whenever they make love. Nereus and I have two exceptionally strong children."

"I am aware," Gavra said, giving her a sidelong look. "Dragons are like you in that way. This means you will need me to stay until the children are born, of course."

Nyx stiffened beside him, the first sign that she was anything but eager to proceed with the ritual she had planned. She turned and walked away without a word. Gavra followed her down a pebbled path through the misty forest. Her aura was a mess, flickering with uncertainty and desire that seemed contrary to her decisiveness earlier.

Eventually she climbed a steeper path, and they came out onto a clifftop that overlooked the cove, the entrance of which was almost completely hidden by fog. He could hear the crash of waves on the beach below, but couldn't see the water at this time of day. It was as though they stood on a remote little island of stone in the center of nothingness—alone and isolated from the universe.

Nyx turned to look at him, a deep worry etched on her face.

"I need these children to exist for the sake of the Haven. I can feel the shape of power in the world changing—shifting away from our kind to something darker. We immortals are the ones who will keep the power whole, but there aren't enough of us. I feel it slipping away each day … the River's flow recedes like there's a drought somewhere, sucking the life right out of the world."

"Then we need to gather the others. My siblings and I already knew we had to act. Finding mates was our goal when we left the Glade. The other immortals must feel the urgency as well. There are more than a dozen of us. We can double our numbers within a year, if we're all working toward that goal. Find yourself a new mate, Nyx. Love will only strengthen the power of the children you conceive. You and I aren't in love. I will help you with this, but let me go on record now and tell you I don't believe this is the solution. Our spirits aren't fated to bond within a child. We need to find the mates Fate intends for us. If Nereus truly is still out there, let him return to you and give you another child. Or find someone new to love."

She gave him a sad smile and lifted a hand to his cheek. "You have changed so much. I never knew you to be so senti-mental. But it's not so easy, once you've lost your only love. Believing in love again seems impossible. This isn't easy for me … I don't love you, and the idea of melding with you even through one of my nymphs feels like I'm betraying my love for Nereus, but my love for the Haven must take precedence. It must be protected, at all costs."

She stared so intently into his eyes he almost felt hypnotized by her whirlpool gaze. Her eyes narrowed, and for a second he started to worry that she was seeing too much of what he held closely guarded inside. He let out his breath when she finally gave him a small smile.

"What are you smiling about?" he asked.

"Perhaps if all goes well and I can be sure the Haven is secure and well-guarded … after that, I may revisit your suggestion. And perhaps you will still hold some fondness for me then. Do you think a deeper love is possible between two old friends who probably know each other far too well?"

Gavra chuckled. "Stranger things have happened."

But as they gazed out over the blankets of mist that protected the Haven, he knew the likelihood of her considering him a friend at the end of this was slim.

CHAPTER 35

ASSANA

The heavy chains of sheer exhaustion weighed Assana down for much of the day. She and Silas slept, tangled together like a pair of saplings who'd taken root too close and grew with their branches entwined. Every few hours, they'd rouse halfway to consciousness, only aware of a fresh hunger that needed sating, and they'd give in to pure instinct to fulfill that need. Most of the time it involved the press of bodies against each other, the slide of lips across skin, tongues in the hollows of the landscape of flesh that shared the bed. She wasn't quite aware of whose body moved above or beneath whose, only that she loved the feel of him against her, inside her, around her.

When his mouth brushed down her belly, trailing a hot line from her breasts, he paused over her mound, teasing the shining mark until it brightened and pulsed with the rhythm of her need. Even in that intimate moment, Gavra was there with them, his pervasive power a constant presence inside their minds—aware, if not actively engaged.

Gavra's desire for them seemed to flood through their minds at every turn, as though he needed a place to divert it so he could focus on whatever task he sought to accomplish away from them. And they greedily accepted it, like a blanket of love granted to bodies chilled from loneliness. While the pair of them had no problems finding new reasons to make love, Gavra was the fire that drove them to push their limits.

Eventually, true hunger took precedence and they stole a few moments to recharge with the food Assana's maids left. Then they would bathe and fall back into bed and resume the decadent routine of sleeping and making love.

It was full dark when the naked body beside Assana roused, its warmth gravitating toward her and his solid, hard length pressing to her back. She sighed and pressed her backside into him. With one hand, Silas cupped her naked breast, thumbing her nipple and sending a warm shiver down her belly to pool between her thighs. The heat burned even hotter when a different hand cupped her cheek from the front and Gavra's lips found hers as he slid close and nudged a knee between her legs.

She sighed into Gavra's kiss, simultaneously sinking back into Silas's attentive arms while pulling her beloved dragon close. They spoke no words as they caressed each other, hands roaming across bodies and sensation crossing all the barriers of their minds.

She opened for them both, her body aching to be filled yet again, and they answered her silent plea, merging together and sliding deep into the ocean of desire between her thighs. Together they plunged down, down, down into that secret, sacred place they shared in their melded minds where their bodies were simultaneously the entire universe and only a single pearl.

When they were one like this, nothing was too daunting to overcome. Everything was possible. Assana's entire world existed only in this bed with the men she loved.

~

THE MAGICAL, silvery pre-dawn light filtered in through the windows surrounding Assana's quarters when she woke to an empty bed. Silas's and Gavra's scents still surrounded her as evident as the soft depressions they'd left in the bed on either side of her, and the warmth from their bodies still pervaded the mattress and the pillows. The sound of a rough moan reached her from across the room, and a shiver of sensation rushed through her that was both familiar and alien. It was not her own body that experienced the pleasure, but Silas's, and she sat up and peered through the wide archway into her bath where her two lovers were half-immersed and making love.

She climbed off the bed and padded silently to them, mesmerized by the synchronicity of their movements. Silas was bent over the edge of the bathing pool, his hips and ass just above the water, while Gavra speared him from behind, his torso bent over and pressed to Silas's back.

Their massive bodies flexed and gave, pushing into each other in fluid, hypnotic rhythm that didn't cease when she drew near. If anything, their tempo increased with her proximity until Silas clawed at the stone floor, his body shaking with pleasure and his impending climax. Gavra clutched at his hip with one hand and threaded the fingers of his other into the hair at the back of Silas's head. He leaned back and yanked at the root, pulling Silas onto his slick shaft over and over, forcing him to arch his back into a bow.

Assana watched in wonder, kneeling down beside them and reaching out to slide a hand down Silas's curved spine. He let out a low groan and his entire body quivered under her touch. His dark beauty had her enthralled, and she threaded her fingers through the wet, ebony tangles of his hair and pulled gently. Silas turned his head, giving her a sidelong look and a wicked laugh. Assana took advantage of his immobilized state and leaned down, taking his mouth and plunging her tongue in deep.

Silas lifted a hand and grasped the back of her head, holding her and hungrily returning her kiss until he pulled away with a sharp exhalation incited by Gavra's swift, urgent thrusts. She let her hand trail down over the curve of his throat, fingernails grazing the rough stubble that had grown in over the last few days since they'd met, wondering at how swiftly she'd come to adore this beautiful, strong, yet gentle ursa.

She let her hands roam farther, one sliding over his chest, the other his back, enjoying the way his huge dragon mark shimmered under her touch. He was trapped within their dragon's spell, pleasured to within an inch of his life by Gavra's steady fucking, and she indulged herself with the feel of his hot skin beneath her palms, moving both hands lower until she let the fingertips of one rest atop Gavra's shaft where it disappeared into Silas over and over. Her own tight backside clenched and released in sympathy, half the pleasure Silas felt echoed in her own body through their melding. She explored beneath his hips with her other hand, sought out and found his glorious, steel-hard shaft, and gripped it in her fist.

"Oh, Gaia, yes!" Silas said, half groaning, half yelling the words. As she stroked him, Gavra's thrusts crescendoed to a punishing pace, his hips smacking harder and harder against Silas's ass. He released Silas's hair and reached for Assana, pulled her roughly to him, and found her mouth just as their shared climax hit.

She drank in the rough cry Gavra exhaled into her mouth, aware of the gust of powerful breath that accompanied it. Breathing him in, she sank against his side, one hand still tightly gripping Silas's pulsing cock, sliding her semen-covered fingers up and down his shaft while his orgasm continued to erupt.

The two men slowly relaxed and Gavra slid his mouth off hers, but still held her tightly. His mouth rested at her ear, his breathing heavy. After a second, he took a deep breath and slowly eased out of Silas, collapsing back into the bath.

Silas sank down into the water too, disappeared beneath the surface for a second, then rose again and looked at her.

"Sorry we didn't wake you," he said. "You seemed like you needed the rest."

She had been exhausted, but now her body felt alive with want. The mark on her pelvis tingled, only heightening her awareness of the swollen need between her thighs.

"I'm awake now," she said.

"That you are." Silas prowled toward her and settled on his knees in the water between her legs. He pushed her thighs apart and pulled her closer until her backside was just at the lip of the tub.

She let out a soft gasp when his fingertips brushed over the hypersensitive flesh of her mound, right over her mark.

"It's sensitive, isn't it?" he asked, looking up at her as he drew a delicate line around the pattern. "Does yours hurt?"

"No … it feels good," she said.

"Mine, too, at least when either of you touch it."

Behind him, Gavra moved closer. He had one hand between his thighs with a cloth, cleaning his shaft with almost idle movements. He reached out his other hand and gently placed it at the center of Silas's back, then drew a wide circle around the circumference of the mark with several fingertips.

Silas's eyes fluttered closed and he moaned. "Yeah, like that. I'm already hard again."

Gavra chuckled. "I think it's her turn."

Silas's roaming fingers teased lower down her bare

mound, his thumbs sliding into her cleft and parting her. He pushed the hood of her clit back, exposing her tight, pulsing nub to his gaze, then dipped his head and gently teased his tongue along the underside.

Assana's core flooded with heat and she rested a hand on his head, her fingers clawing into the wet tendrils of hair. She lifted her legs, placing her heels on the edge of the tub and letting her knees splay wide to open for his mouth.

Silas let out a murmur of appreciation and leaned back, eyes fixed on her.

"You're soaked and you weren't even in the water."

Gavra loomed closer, tossing the cloth away from his cock that now glistened clean and wet and still hard. He gripped Silas by the shoulder, moving him to the side.

"I need a taste of her before I go. Just one more …"

Silas gave him a worried frown. "It's almost sunrise. You need to get out of here before someone sees you."

But Gavra was already kneeling between her thighs, clutching the backs of her legs with both hands and covering her aching snatch with his mouth. He tongued her clit, then delved that tongue she loved so much deep into her channel, teasing back and forth along the sensitive nerves just inside.

Assana's breathing quickened and she leaned back on her elbows, dizzy from the pleasure. Silas stood back and watched, waiting his turn for another taste of her. Her ecstasy built higher and higher, but Gavra seemed to sense when she was at the edge because he stopped abruptly and pulled back with a growl.

"I need to be inside you so fucking bad," he said. He bent to kiss her, wrapping his arms around her. He hauled her close, scooping her against his chest and sliding beneath her in one fluid motion. She rested sideways on his lap at first, her hip tight against his thick, jutting shaft as their tongues tangled.

He took her breath away with his kiss, his touch, his free hand deftly toying with her nipples before drifting lower to delve between her thighs and push them apart again so he could reach her juicy core. She eagerly parted for him, her hips tilting up into his touch.

"Spread your legs and let me in," Gavra murmured into her ear. She did as he asked, bracing a hand on his shoulder and shifting her backside so that she straddled his lap with her back to his chest. She propped her feet on the edge of the pool again and lifted up into a low squat until the tip of his cock brushed against her opening.

The pleasure of his thick length sliding in was unbearably good, and she let out a long moan as he filled her. She leaned back, reaching up behind her with both hands to grasp at his shoulders for leverage as she began to fuck him, pushing up and down with her feet flat on the wet stone.

Silas moved back in, slipping between Gavra's thighs and lowering himself. He tongued the dragon's balls, his gaze fixed on her moving pussy. Gavra wrapped an arm around her midsection and tightened his hold when she was on an upswing, eager to slam back down and feel the tight push of his cockhead against her insides.

"Slow down, Assana. Let Silas have a taste of you. I've got you. Let me do the moving for a few."

She held on, starving for more of them both, but trusting them to give her what she needed. Gavra continued to hold her against his chest with one arm while he braced himself with his other and shoved his cock hard up into her. As she remained poised there, open and ready for his penetrating thrusts, Silas bent again and teased his tongue along the soaked folds, starting where the dragon's thick shaft was buried inside her.

He licked and sucked and teased her mercilessly, working

her into a frenzy with his talented tongue, while Gavra buried himself in her as deep as he could go.

She was nearly outside herself with pleasure, able to experience every angle through her connections with their minds, but much preferring her own exquisite experience of the pleasure they gave her. Her mark flashed neon with her wish to have the dragon's seed shoot into her and take root. Below her, Silas's own huge mark lit the entire room with a red glow that rivaled the encroaching sunrise.

"No holding back, baby," Gavra said. "Come for me. Come when I do. Let me hear you scream."

Her voice was already hoarse from her cries of pleasure, but it rose at his command and she yelled his name when Silas's tongue and the delicious stretching push of Gavra's cock sent her over the edge. Gavra let out a roar of bliss that shook the entire room, and then his molten semen filled her. He kept thrusting into her for several moments, the flood of his orgasm continuing and her own climax still shuddering through her in wave after wave.

Finally, Gavra's hold eased and Assana's legs gave out. She sank onto his lap with his cock still solidly buried inside her and simply let him hold her. Between her thighs, Silas shifted and pushed his big arms around them both, then rested his cheek against her thigh with a shaky, satisfied sigh.

Assana stroked Silas's head while her own rested back on Gavra's shoulder. The dawn-lit interior of her bath glowed warmly with the pulsing magic of their marks. She'd never been so fully content and happy in her life than she was in that moment, with one mate deep inside her and the other on his knees before her, rumbling in utter satisfaction while she petted him.

"I love you both so much," she whispered, and they responded each with a gentle kiss on the closest bit of her skin they could reach—Gavra's lips on her shoulder and Silas's to her inner thigh.

Her serenity was interrupted by a loud crash and an expletive in an all too familiar, angry voice.

"How could you!"

The yell pierced their comfortable afterglow with the force of a cyclone. Assana's head shot up and she was suddenly aware of the churning of the water in her tub and the shaking rumble of the earth beneath her. Both men looked toward the doorway, Silas craning his head around to see.

Her mother advanced on them, her primal form even larger than Assana remembered. Her huge, antlered head grazed the ceiling and her eyes were a maelstrom of rage. She carried a pair of objects that Assana vaguely recognized, but didn't have time to fully register what they were before her mother dropped them and raised her hands. She made a swift waving motion and Silas was lifted bodily out of the water and tossed to the side like a bag of wet sand.

"Mother, no! He's done nothing wrong!"

Her mother didn't seem to see her, though, and only raised her hands again. Assana felt her own body being lifted as though a strong current had captured her, and a second later she was tossed to the other wall, hitting hard and smacking her head with a crack that left her dazed and struggling to find her bearings.

"I should have known you and your siblings were all alike. You are thieves! You come into my home and do nothing but steal everything of value. You are no different than the other dragons, and for that you will pay!"

Assana struggled to sit, raising a hand to her mother to try to reason, but the room spun and vertigo forced her to clench her eyes shut with only a faintly muttered plea falling from her lips. Gavra stood at the edge of the bath, imposing at his full height and seeming to grow larger before her eyes.

"Your daughter was promised to me by Fate centuries ago, as was Silas. There was never anything you could do to stop our mating, Nyx. Give it up."

Huge, crimson horns grazed the ceiling above his head and ruby scales shone all over his wet skin. Assana could only watch in awe as he grew even larger. She'd seen his sister in full dragon form, but had yet to see Gavra take that shape.

Nyx howled at him in fury. "You made me a promise, dragon! How easily you betray those who trust you. How long until you do the same to Assana? Does she know how much your kind *lie* to get what you want? You are here for only one reason, and I will *not* let you renege on your promise!"

She lifted her hands again and rotated them around each other, fingers swirling in the air. The water in the bath churned higher and higher, twisting into a writhing column that split and shot out, coils of it wrapping around Gavra's ankles and yanking. His massive body slid an inch toward the edge of the pool, but he grew even larger and his horns dug into the ceiling above him, halting Nyx's efforts to pull him off balance.

"I was a fool to trust you, but never again!" she yelled, redoubling her efforts. Vines shot down from the ceiling above, wrapping themselves around Gavra's horns and extending, coiling tight around his neck and shoulders.

Gavra let out an enraged snarl and grew larger still. Huge red wings erupted from his back, the sharp talons at the tips spiking into the floor and digging in. The rest of his body morphed, his horned head doubling, then tripling in size as it elongated. He reared back and his horns pierced through the wooden slats of the ceiling, splintering the wood and vines until light shone through.

"You have interfered with the balance of our alliance long enough, Nyx!" he bellowed. "I won't allow you to continue with this fool plan of yours."

"There is no power strong enough to stop me, dragon!"

Gavra roared and clawed at the air in front of him, advancing on Nyx until his entire huge body spanned the width of the bathing pool and his tail snapped out behind him, shattering the wall of glass that enclosed Assana's quarters. The rush of the nearby waterfalls filled the now destroyed space, but it was nothing compared to the ruckus of conflict before her.

Silas regained his footing on the opposite side and stood back, watching the fight unfold. His fists opened and closed and Assana could sense his need to act, to do something, but she knew there was nothing either of them could do to subdue her mother.

Gavra inhaled and let out another loud roar, staring her mother down with wild red eyes. He opened his jaw and a stream of glittering opaque red streamed out, coiling around Nyx like a snake. Some of it flooded into her nose and mouth while she struggled in its grasp, coughing and writhing.

Was that going to be enough? Assana sat up, holding a palm to her temple and watching—hoping—that Gavra's power would be able to neutralize her mother's rage.

Nyx's eyes flashed wide with panic for a second before her struggling arms broke free of the smoke and she clapped her hands together.

With a series of loud pops, several new figures appeared in the wreckage of the room. A dozen pairs of hands now waved in the air and vines erupted from high and low, tangling around Gavra's winged shape. He turned his head, snapping his huge jaws at the Thiasoi maidens. Watery barriers shimmered around them, blocking his attacks.

He inhaled sharply and breathed flames at them, but the shields held. The vines tightened, constricting around his body.

"No! Mother, you're hurting him!" Assana jumped up and threw her own power into the mix, sending a collection of vines up from the floor to push the binding ones away from Gavra's chest, but she wasn't strong enough to break them. Before her eyes, the vines she'd summoned only added to the tightening mass that twisted around Gavra's huge, scaled body.

Silas ran to her and stood behind her, twined his fingers in hers and said, "Take my power, try again."

He gave his energy to her through the center of his palms but as much as she tried, she couldn't increase the power of her own magic enough to tear the vines away. They only constricted more and more, tightening around Gavra's neck until he let out a hoarse, strangled sound.

Gavra finally relented, his contorted wings drew in, disappeared, and his body shrank again. When he was just the shape of a large man bound in vines and kneeling at Nyx's feet, he choked out, "You will never have me. I do not belong to you."

Keening in rage, Nyx snapped her arm to the side and the vines flung Gavra across the room, flattened him to the bed, and tightened in several criss-crossing bands to hold him down. Several pairs of hands grabbed at Assana and Silas, tearing them apart.

Assana yelled a protest, but could only watch in despair as her Thiasoi sisters proceeded to lash Silas to a bare post on the opposite side of her ruined quarters while the others did the same to her.

Try as she might, she couldn't break free, nor would her magic affect the bindings that held her in place.

Gavra strained as hard at his own bonds. Nyx stood at the foot of the bed, staring down at him while her mindless thralls stood at her back.

"You will serve your purpose tonight, dragon. As soon as I complete the blood melding with my maidens, they will have their way with you." Then she turned to Silas. "As for your precious Sanctuary, you can say goodbye to it. None of you are *ever* leaving the Haven again. The Source is being severed from the outside world. I cannot trust anyone who doesn't owe their lives to the Haven."

"No!" Silas yelled, his muscles straining ineffectually at his bindings. He rocked his entire huge body, nearly succeeding in cracking the post he was tied to, but a flick of Nyx's wrist had him so thoroughly bound in even more vines, he could no longer twitch more than enough to draw breath.

Within another blink, Nyx and her soldiers drifted out, leaving nothing but a cloud of dust in their wake.

CHAPTER 36

GAVRA

Gavra bucked against the net of vegetation holding him down, but no amount of fire, breath, or sheer force of will worked. He attempted to shift again, but the vines just cut deep into his flesh without any give. He gave up with a snarl, throwing his head back against Assana's pillows.

Earth magic. Fucking earth magic was what had trapped him to begin with, the nymphs having just as solid mastery of it as the ursa did. His fire was no match for the power Nyx had unleashed with the blood melded aid of her soldiers.

But Assana and Silas might be able to break it ... They'd been able to penetrate the barrier of his cell in the Sanctuary, at any rate.

"Silas! Can you get free? We have to get out and stop her before she cuts off the Source for good!"

A muffled roar reached his ears from the east side of the room, but he couldn't turn his head far enough to see what state Silas was in. It sounded like the ursa was buried in rubble.

He closed his eyes, focused his mind, and let his

consciousness sink down into the depths of their shared space.

"*Show me how you're bound,*" he said.

"*Fucking all over,*" Silas said. "*Can't move a goddamn muscle over here.*"

"*Assana?*" Gavra asked. "*Can you unravel the vines?*"

"*No,*" she huffed. "*Mother's magic is too strong for me too. We have to get out. She's going to destroy my sisters' minds if she continues. Did you see their eyes before? They were bloodshot.*"

"*It won't matter if she manages to follow through. We'll all be trapped here,*" Silas said.

"*Think!*" Gavra commanded. "*There has to be a way out of this.*"

Assana's figure shimmered in his mind, her shape no more than an apparition made up of her glowing energy. It was like looking at an aura with the perfect outline of the woman he loved, right down to the anxious look on her face.

She stared back at them both, one at a time, her sequence of thoughts and emotions tripping over each other like her rapid heartbeats. Slowly her aura changed, along with her expression. Within those moments, Gavra witnessed her power blossom, growing and unfurling with each decisive conclusion she made.

With their minds melded, they had the deepest under-standing of each other's potential—the extent of his power was as naked to them as theirs was to him, and Assana must have been able to see everything as clearly as he did. More clearly, judging by the way her gaze grew laser-focused on Silas. Gavra directed his attention to the ursa's presence in his mind and saw what Assana did. Silas's deep green energy had tendrils of power that extended from his hands and feet, and a steady flow of magic coursed through from some outside source.

Assana spoke in a clear, strong voice that echoed through the room around them as well as inside their minds.

"Silas, you have the power to break us free if you just focus. Gaia's magic is what binds us now. I've seen how you siphon that energy from me when we make love—I feel how it travels through me. I think ... no, I know you can absorb the magic in the vines that bind you, if you try."

Silas's image pulsed with recognition inside Gavra's mind, but hesitated. *"I don't know if I can hold more than I have already."*

"Give back to her if you have to," Assana said. *"You can redirect it, can't you? Like you did that first time you helped me."*

Silas closed his eyes, his brows drawing together in concentration. His body pulsed with ever-growing power as Gavra watched. Slowly the ursa's feet grew thicker, the tendrils that flowed from him hardening then sinking into the ground like roots.

The magic that bound him was slowly absorbed the way the growing rings of a tree in the forest will absorb any object bound too close. Bit by bit, the constricting vines dissolved into his body until they disappeared completely.

Gavra still wasn't able to turn his head to see what was happening, but the creaking sounds that filled the room from the direction Silas had been held were evidence that it had worked.

"I've got you," Silas said, his voice now coming from the side Assana was on. Then the pair of them hovered over Gavra's face, Assana pressing a kiss to his lips while Silas gripped the vines that held him and they disappeared.

As soon as his upper body was free, Gavra sat up and watched in wonder as Silas gripped the rest of the vines and they seemed to flow into Silas's limbs as though they'd always belonged there.

Assana flung herself into Gavra's arms.

"I'm so sorry! I was wrong. I know what we need to do, and we need to do it now before it's too late."

"What's that, baby?" Gavra asked. "I still don't think we're strong enough even with Silas's grasp on his skills."

"Mother had the power of the Thiasoi on her side, thanks to her blood meld with them. She wouldn't have been able to bind you otherwise, would she?"

Gavra blinked at her, surprised at her swift understanding of the situation, though perhaps he shouldn't have been. This was her home, and the blood meld was part of her heritage, even if it had been outlawed since she was a child.

He shook his head. "Without their blood meld, we'd have had a stalemate at the very least, or would still be fighting each other now."

"We have to do it too. If we do, we can merge our powers. We'll be three times as strong."

Silas shook his head. "There are a dozen of them. They'll still have an advantage, especially with Nyx in control."

"They're missing the one thing we have," Assana said. "She's never properly melded them the way lovers do. The way we have already done. We have a much deeper connection to each other, thanks to that bond. I feel it even when we're apart."

She hopped off the bed and dug through the rubble, searching for something. When she came back, Gavra saw a sharp, jagged piece of glass held in her hand. Understanding dawned and he swiftly grabbed the shard.

Assana stared at him. "We have to do this. It was your idea! You were right, I realize that now."

"Not like this," he growled. "If we blood meld, we do it right, with a proper mark that honors our union." He looked at Silas. "It's your turn, brother. You're the only one who hasn't left his mark on us."

Silas opened his mouth, then shut it again. He blinked

several times and shook his head. "I don't know what you've heard of ursa matings, but it's the female who marks the males."

"Not always," Gavra said. "Male ursa's marks have power too, as will yours because of what we'll do after. Assana, are you still wet with our seed?"

She dipped her hand between her thighs and drew back fingers slick with aromatic juices. "As wet as I've ever been."

Gavra grabbed Silas by the hand and pressed their palms together.

"Manifest your claws," he said.

Silas complied, his expression still bewildered. His hand transformed into a massive paw, giant claws jutting out from the tips of what were once his fingers.

"Brace yourself. This is going to burn," Gavra said. He inhaled and breathed a steady fountain of flame at Silas's claws, careful to avoid hitting flesh, but singeing some of the fur off nonetheless.

Silas winced and his arm tensed, but he held still until Gavra was finished. When all five claws glowed red, Gavra turned his chest toward Silas.

"Mark me. Your claws should break my skin, now that they've been tempered in my fire. Then do Assana and yourself."

Silas gritted his teeth and pressed his claws to Gavra's chest. White-hot pain shot through Gavra's body and he inhaled sharply, holding his breath as Silas sank his claws into flesh and tore a series of deep gouges down in a diagonal pattern above Gavra's left nipple.

Gavra clenched his eyes shut, gasping for breath. His world had turned red, but he told himself over and over that red *was* his world and this was right. His blood was meant to flow for these two people. He would bleed for them and only them.

His head still buzzed with pain and his chest was a burning coal when he felt the gentle, cool caress that calmed the raging agony. Slowly he opened his eyes to see two heads bent to his chest, and two tongues licking at his wounds.

His mates pulled back a second later, lips stained crimson with his blood.

"We've done each other," Assana said. "It's your turn to do us."

"Then she'll seal our wounds," Silas said.

In a daze, Gavra could only nod. The pain throbbed in the background now, his blood inside them already forming a bond. His body was increasingly aware of the deepening senses of two others as though they were extensions of his own consciousness—his own being.

He bent to Silas's bloodied chest and licked, tasting the earthy tang of iron. Then he bent to Assana's breast and did the same, marveling at her blood's honeyed flavor.

In an instant, his senses exploded into a kaleidoscope of colors and images. He gasped out loud, and heard his mates' voices echoing his own.

"Oh, Gaia, this is wonderful!" Assana exclaimed. She gazed around at the other two, her eyes meeting Gavra's, and he clearly saw himself the way she saw him—larger than life and more strikingly red than he'd ever imagined. Her gaze slid down his body and he raised his eyebrows at her open admiration.

"You want me now," he said, giving her a cocky grin.

She rolled her eyes and said, "I always wanted you. That's no secret." She dipped her hand between her thighs and smeared a layer of fertile liquid over his wound. The claw marks stitched together, leaving a series of pink scars behind.

When all their wounds were sealed, Assana stood and found her gown, then dug through the detritus of her room some more.

"We should get moving," Silas said, hovering at what used to be the door.

"There's something we need first," Assana said. "I could swear I saw them when Mother showed up. If she was carrying what I thought she was, they'll help."

She kicked over an upturned vase and knelt. "Yes!"

Gavra went to her, kneeling down and reaching out for the pair of items she held in her hands.

"What is it?" he asked, worried by the fresh tears that streaked her cheeks.

In one hand she held a long staff-like object made of polished aqua stone. It had a bulbous head at one end and lush green vines coiled tightly around its handle. In her other hand was a goblet crafted of the same iridescent stone with more vines wrapped around its base.

"These are the ceremonial marriage talismans, the bride's chalice and the groom's scepter. Every nymphaea family has a set that's passed down. This pair belonged to my parents and were meant to go to my brother when he took a mate. She must have intended to give them to me and Silas. Oh, Mother, why couldn't you have seen reason?"

Gavra took the scepter from her. The length of polished stone immediately glowed a bright blue and the vines wrapped around it writhed into motion. He cursed as they coiled up his arm and he tried to drop the object, but the vines held it firmly to his hand.

Assana laughed. "They won't hurt you. Look." She held the chalice up to show him the vines traveling down her own arm. They seemed to sink into her skin, leaving behind a deep blue tattoo that covered her arm from wrist to shoulder. Slowly the mark faded until only the subtlest glow remained.

"It's just another way to signify the bond between mates. It knows we are bound together. Silas, if you grip the staff, I think it will mark you too, now that we're blood melded."

Silas reached out hesitantly at first, then with a sure grip he held the lower end of the scepter beneath Gavra's fist. Vines coiled up his arm as well, made their marks and disappeared beneath his skin.

"How will this help us?" Silas asked.

Gavra met Assana's gaze, their minds attuned well enough that they need not speak what they both knew he would need to do. A moment later, Silas nodded as he grasped the plan.

"If you think you can pull it off, I wish you luck," he said to Gavra.

"Shall we go save the Haven?" Gavra asked, standing and looking down at them both.

"I'm ready, but you need a little work first," Assana said.

"Right. Mother forgive me for this." Gavra hated himself for the trick he was about to attempt, but all the higher realms depended on his success.

Reaching deep into his memory, he focused on the image he required. His old friend's face was one he would never forget, and as he transformed his body into the new shape, he silently asked forgiveness from the man himself.

"Nereus, if you are out there anywhere, please forgive me for what I am about to do to the woman you love. It is necessary, and with luck, you will soon return to undo the damage."

He took a deep breath and opened his eyes.

"Well?" he asked, holding his arms wide and looking down at Assana.

She grimaced at him.

"Not right? What needs changing?" he asked casting his gaze down his transformed body. He'd gotten the lower half right, at least, from the cloven hooves all the way to the fur-covered legs, but he couldn't see the rest without a looking glass.

"Oh, no, you are absolutely perfect. I'm just completely creeped out by the idea that I just fucked a guy who now looks identical to my father."

CHAPTER 37

ASSANA

For the first time since she'd come of age, Assana didn't fear her primal form. As she stood amid the rubble of her ruined quarters, her blood sang with the flow of power that linked her to her two mates. Gavra's command of fire and blood warmed her lungs and flooded her heart. Silas's command of the living earth steadied her limbs and strengthened her bones. When she called on the wild, fluid grace of Dionysus that gave her kind their power, both men responded, their bodies shining with the dewy sheen of desire and swaying toward her like they were about to begin a mating dance.

The fact that Gavra now resembled the giant, fertile satyr whose image filled her earliest memories only bothered her a little. It was merely a mask he wore. The flesh and bone beneath that image was hers as much as her own body was, and she knew the shape of what lay beneath the illusion as intimately as she knew her own heart and soul.

They moved as one, their minds melded more closely than ever, their souls superimposed on each other until their magic flowed together, the energy amplified exponentially as they synchronized.

No words were needed now. They were in perfect harmony—one being in all but their physical forms.

Assana's own purpose was clear—release her sisters from the blood bond to her mother while Gavra distracted Nyx with his disguise. Silas would use his power to protect the Source at all costs and preserve the flow of sacred water to the Sanctuary. Through his power, he could channel what was needed to the two of them.

No doubts troubled their minds; there was only the driving need to act and to prevail.

As one, they drifted to the Source, each one landing equidistant outside the circle of Thiasoi who were now bound in the blood melding ritual her mother had coerced them into. Only this time was different than the first one Assana had witnessed. Her mother hovered in the center of the circle over the swirling waters of the Source. Her arms were outstretched and blood flowed from open veins in her wrists. Her magic controlled a constant arc of red fluid into the mouths of the Thiasoi and their upraised wrists were a mirror to hers, the crimson liquid merging to land on Nyx's tongue.

Their eyes were closed, all twelve women completely unaware of the appearance of their visitors. Assana's mother was overconfident that there was no way she could lose.

Assana would have to take her mother's place in that circle, but they needed to get the attention of the Thiasoi, first.

"We are one, Assana, remember," Gavra said. *"I dare not destroy my illusion by using my true powers. You must do it for me."*

She knew what she must do. Taking a deep breath, she filled her lungs and exhaled. The air felt heavy and rich as it left her lungs, the same way the water magic felt when she controlled the flow of it from her fingertips. Instinctively she knew she could control this smoke as well. She silently commanded the red tendrils of dragon magic to part, and they split into a dozen wispy strands, coiling above the circle of nymphs and sinking down around their heads.

Though they were water shifters, even nymphs had to breathe, unless they were prepared. The smoke easily flowed into the nostrils of all the women and their bodies convulsed. The flow of blood ceased as the eleven Thiasoi went rigid, their backs arching as though they were all overcome with pleasure. They let out soft moans and sighs as the red magic took effect, flooding them all with desire.

Nyx's eyes flew open and fixed on Assana. Fresh rage blossomed in her cerulean depths. She bared her teeth, coated red with the blood of her soldiers, and raised her blood-streaked arms, calling forth the power of the Source she levitated above.

"Don't be a fool, daughter. You cannot win this battle."

Assana held her back straight and her head high. The thrumming power of the dragon smoke was still tightly bound to her mind, connecting her to the deep desires of her Thiasoi sisters. With the smallest tug on that connection, they easily responded, the circle parting as Clio and Ephyra stood aside, leaving a gap for Assana to approach.

She spared only the briefest glance to the other nymphs, but it was enough to see the struggle for control they all had and the hope that blazed in their eyes.

"I was not as strong as you before, Mother, but I found something that you seem to have lost when you began this misguided quest."

Again, she mentally tugged at the threads of smoke that now filled her sisters' minds. Across the wide pool of the Source, the circle parted again. Assana motioned to that side.

"Look who I have found. Would you disagree that your power is nothing compared to what it was when your love for Father was strong and true?"

Nyx gave her a baffled look and turned. When her gaze landed on the figure on the other side, she stiffened and then began to slowly shake her head.

"It cannot be. I don't believe it!"

"Give her more, Assana. Now!" Gavra silently commanded.

Assana exhaled another lungful of red power, directing the full force of it to her mother this time.

Nyx's antlered head still shook in denial, but she took a small step closer to the figure who resembled her lost mate. Assana took advantage of the slip and redoubled her mental command of the seductive smoke her mother had inhaled, instinctively knowing to fill it with the influence of her own strong desire for love from the essence of the man who wore the disguise her mother responded to.

Gavra stood unmoving on the other side of the pool, staring back at Nyx with Nereus's deep blue eyes. He was so convincing, Assana's heart hurt at the look of betrayal in his eyes, and had the urge to beg forgiveness from her father for not honoring his memory more often over the years.

His black brows drew together and his mouth turned down in a disappointed frown. His eyes were filled with hurt and heartbreak.

"My love, what have you done to these nymphs? What could be so important that you forgot your own sacred promise to your people?"

"Is … is it really you?" Nyx asked, her voice cracking as she took another step toward Gavra.

Gavra held his stern expression, his brows tightening slightly. "Who else would ever have the balls to call you on your foolishness? This is not the woman I fell in love with. That Nyx was kind and passionate. Unwavering in her loyalty to her people and always fair. What have you become while I was gone?"

Nyx clenched her hands into fists. "You don't understand how hard it's been. The enemy has all but destroyed us. The dragons have stolen our children. We have no more friends among the higher races. I was forced to take action to protect the Haven—*our home*—at all costs. It would have been a dishonor to your memory for me to do anything less."

"But I am here now. I will keep the Haven safe."

Assana took another step closer, reaching the edge of the pool and the sides of her sisters. She gave both Clio and Ephyra a gentle squeeze of their hands, but didn't dare let her concentration falter until Gavra had succeeded in convincing Nyx to go.

Nyx still hesitated, shaking her head. "No, you must be a trick of my mind. Have I gone mad and conjured you from memory?"

"I am here, Nyx. In the flesh. I have returned to you for good. Leave this place and let your nymphs have their freedom again. With my love and blood combined with your power, the two of us can ensure the Haven is safe. Come with me and let me help you redeem yourself."

He held his arms out wide, as though inviting her into his embrace. In one hand he held the scepter, which glowed from the fresh bond he'd made with her and Silas. Before Assana's eyes, the vine tattoo flared beneath his skin, snaking its inky pattern up his bare arm again.

With a gasp, Nyx ran to him and launched herself into his arms. "Nereus! You really are here!"

Assana's skin prickled with a chill as she watched him press his lips to her mother's. The image looked just the way she remembered the two of them, but despite how convincing it was, she knew it was only an illusion, and it made her sick to see her lover kissing another woman.

"This is all it will be, Assana," Gavra reassured her. He exhaled a long breath while his lips were fixed to Nyx's, filling her lungs with an even more potent cloud of his smoke than Assana had been able to conjure. Nyx let out a moan against his mouth and pressed her body to his.

"Take me and make love to me, Nereus. It has been so long."

He wrapped both arms tightly around her, and gave Assana and Silas each a nod. Gavra's figure with Nyx in his embrace grew translucent like a shimmering fog. The pair seemed to flow together, and then they disappeared into the drift.

Silas and Assana both burst into motion.

"Hurry!" Silas said, rushing to the edge of the pool.

Assana turned to Clio. "Does she have your mind still, sister?"

The tall, athletic nymph slowly shook her head. "The connection is still there. Stronger than before, but she is gone. We're beyond the point of breaking the bond now, though. We can feel our minds fading. She could return at any moment. How … how did you find Nereus?"

"I didn't," Assana said. "And you're probably going to hate me for what I have to do, but it's the only way to break her hold on you. Give me your dagger."

Clio handed the shining blade to Assana and she grasped it tightly in her hand, steeling her will for the distasteful thing she had to do in the name of restoring order to her home. She lifted a foot and moved as though to step into the water of the pool, summoned the power within her, and stepped forward.

The surface of the water held her easily, her command of it far stronger than she'd imagined. From the other side, Silas did the same, though slightly more uncertain in his movements. But the power belonged to all three of them now, and he traversed the distance to her as though they were walking across solid ground and not the liquid surface of the most sacred substance in their entire world.

Second-most sacred, she amended to herself, as she raised her wrist and made a slice into her vein, then repeated the process with the other hand.

"Are you ready?" Silas asked, coming up behind her and resting his big hands on her upper arms. The tingling pull of Gaia's power infused her through his touch, reminding her how closely connected her kind was with the Earth, even though they were water creatures.

"Sisters, what my mother has done is a terrible betrayal of your trust, but to undo it, you must trust me with the same precious gift. You must give me your blood and accept mine in return. This is only an exchange driven by loyalty and love for our home—which I know was the argument my mother used—but I only ask just enough to break her hold on you."

Ephyra's voice rose in challenge. "How will we be able to break the bond to you, then? We love you, Assana, but we are not your slaves any more than we were hers."

"Promise that you will stay to protect the Haven and I will help you all break the bond. You just need what I have found already." She turned her head and gave Silas a reverent look. "True love and a blood bond with your mate … or mates. Nothing can break that bond once you find it, and I will do everything in my power to ensure you all are given that chance, even if I have to hunt down Fate to do it."

The eleven nymphs looked around at each other in a silent exchange. Finally, Clio nodded.

"We accept your promise, sister. But you are not the Dionarch. You don't have command of the Source and she was using it to magnify her power."

"Perhaps not, but what I do have is Gaia's blessing."

Behind her, Silas slipped his hands down her arms and

held her gently by the wrists. He lifted her arms up high and she focused her power on the life's blood pumping through her veins. It didn't respond at first, still simply flowing down her arms and dripping into the pool at her feet to leave swirling clouds of red in the clear, calm water.

"It's my turn now," Silas murmured in her ear.

She heard the now familiar creaking sound of his power manifesting itself, and glanced down to see his strong legs thicken and grow mossy bark around the calves. His feet erupted into long roots that plunged down into the water of the Source, splitting into hundreds of pale green tendrils as they went deeper and deeper.

As the power of the source was absorbed into his roots, she felt the cool flood of it seeping into her body, and once again she focused her mind on her blood, and on her sisters'.

With her eyes closed, the flow of their life-sustaining fluid became a bright, vibrant presence, and she called to it the way she called to the River when she sought its power. They all answered, raising their arms and surrendering to her. She opened her mouth to accept their gifts and let her own blood flow in return, sending it arcing out in eleven different directions to their waiting tongues.

CHAPTER 38

GAVRA

Gavra had only experienced drifting on a handful of occasions, and having the power to do it himself for the first time didn't exactly make it second nature. But when Nyx fell into his arms, he knew he couldn't simply lead her away by the hand. The illusion had to be complete, and this was a part of it. Luckily, he'd paid attention to the inner workings of Assana's mind when she'd drifted them all to the Source earlier, so he attempted to repeat exactly what she had done. He called on the power of their sacred River and aimed his consciousness at his destination the way a sailor steers the rudder of his boat.

He'd intended to take them both to her chamber in the palace, but at the last second changed his mind. When they emerged from the drift, his skin felt wet and cool as though he'd just taken a swim. Nyx clung to him, and he was reminded of a time when he would have relished having this beautiful, powerful nymph want him the way she did now.

Except it wasn't him she wanted, but what he represented to her in his disguise. All this love that filled her now—this desperate need to hold onto what she'd lost at all costs—was for a man he could never hold a candle to where love and honor were concerned.

No. He rejected that thought immediately. If he didn't love Assana so much, he wouldn't even be here now, and his success in carrying out this plan depended on that love and his honor of his bond with her and Silas, not to mention his desire to maintain peace between all the higher races.

He tightened his arms around Nyx for a second, drawing on that love for her daughter. He could have destroyed this woman completely—ruined her mind with his power, cursing her with a never-ending craving for sex and nothing else, then bound her in this place and left her insane. He had the power to do just that now, and more. Silas had succeeded in making his connection to the Source—the divine nexus of power that fed the Haven and the Sanctuary and provided the magic that made the nymphaea and the ursa who they were. Gavra had that power now, along with the immortal power of air and fire he had always been attuned to. All the elements were at his disposal.

But was what he planned any better than leaving Nyx a mindless sex fiend locked in a cave? Sure, he could give her a few moments of true happiness before he locked her in, but it would all be a lie.

Again, he silently asked for Nereus's forgiveness before he gripped Nyx by the arms and turned her.

The secret grotto Nereus had built his mate was even more detailed than Gavra remembered it, though it hadn't been complete when Nereus showed it to him all those eons ago. The cave walls had been polished smooth so that the pale veins of quartz that shot through the dark granite glowed.

The center of the grotto was filled with a clear pool fed by a lazy cascade of heated water flowing down the back wall. More glowing stones lit the pool from beneath. A dry alcove occupied one side of the grotto, and above it, a wide opening cut into the stone ceiling let in the filtered sunlight. Particles of mist floated in the air, catching the light and reflecting it to Gavra's eyes, making the entire room seem like it was filled with golden dust.

This was the place where Nereus had first seduced his bride and proved his love to her through the sheer effort it had taken to create such a beautiful, secret retreat.

"Come, my love," he said, leading her to the silk covered bed in the alcove. The light that came in was enough to sustain cascades of flower-covered vines that grew from planters carved into the wall itself.

She kept looking up at him, her eyes wide with wonder, but also apprehension.

"I never took another lover after you," she said as though that might be the worst thing she could do.

"What we might have done while parted is no matter now," Gavra said. "I would forgive you all of that, because our bond is so strong I know your heart will always be mine. Come and tell me what is truly troubling you, Nyx. What you have done to the nymphs who guard the Haven is out of character for you. Please help me understand."

She turned when they reached the bed and wrapped her arms around his neck, pulling him close and kissing him again and again. "Please, let's make love before we talk about all that. You are back now ... We must make another baby, the Haven needs more satyrs, so there is no time to waste."

Gavra tolerated the kisses. It was in his nature to revel in female attention, and this would be no different, if not for the dire circumstances.

"Nyx," he admonished, holding her back at arm's length. "You're avoiding my questions. Tell me what you're hiding. You were always open with your thoughts before, even when it came to your opinion of your brother's choices."

She let out a huff of frustration and scrunched up her face. "I need you! Don't you realize you still have the same effect on me you always did? Don't you want me just as much?"

The wanting would be the tricky part, and as Gavra allowed her to grab his hand and put it between her thighs, he summoned his desire for Assana to help him maintain the illusion. His cock hardened and he leaned down and kissed her hard, putting all his pent up passion for Assana into the act.

"Gaia, yes, I want you. You are all I've thought of all these years. And yes, I want nothing more than to fill you with my seed again and make as many sons as you desire, but there is still something you must explain to me. Why have you been holding a dragon captive? Our daughter tells me you intended to breed with him … to force your nymphs to carry babies made from some unholy union between your spirit and his and gestated inside their wombs. Do you have no respect for their sacred right to choose their own mates? And with a dragon, no less. They're great for a romp, but to *breed* with? What were you thinking?"

Nyx scowled and shook her head, her eyes flashing with that same unhinged anger that rose to the surface whenever she was challenged. It swiftly disappeared and her mask fell in place again, her sweet smile with it.

"My love, I had to. The Haven is in danger; you should know this after being our enemy's prisoner for so long. Surely you understand how important it is that I do whatever I can to protect our home. The Haven's balance of fertile power is at stake—there are too many females and not enough males—we can't sustain this level of imbalance much longer, unless Dion himself sees fit to visit all my nymphs and grant them the gift of his own seed. You know the divine ones no longer answer our prayers the way they once did."

Gavra gripped her arms and shook her, genuinely frustrated. "That does not give you the right to blood meld them like a fiend, Nyx! This is not who you are!"

"How do you know who I am now?" she shot back. "You've been gone! You have no idea how difficult it's been without you! Please, Nereus, why can't we just make love? Why do you have to be so damned honorable now, of all times? I need you! Dammit, I needed you all along and you were gone. It took all my strength to hold it together. I had to do something!"

"You think fucking that dragon was going to help?"

"I wasn't ..." she objected, but her brows twitched together, betraying her half-lie. Immediately she realized her mistake and backpedaled. "No, Nereus, I wasn't! I would have let the nymphs have him how they saw fit. It would just be my spirit inside them to mix with his, to give them immortal children. We need powerful sons to help protect the Haven!"

"How can I believe you, Nyx? I saw him bound to Assana's bed. Were you going to make her participate in that abomination of a plan? Force your own daughter to be no more than breeding stock? I would rather see the Haven rot."

"No!" Nyx yelled, shaking her head wildly and grabbing at his arms even as he turned away. He paced back toward the pool and stopped, Nyx chasing him the whole way.

"Please, Nereus I can't do this without you, I know that now. I won't go through with it if you promise me you'll stay. I'm sorry for what I've done, please believe me. Let me fix it!"

"I don't know if I can trust you anymore, my love," he said, giving her a heartbroken stare and backing away like he hated being near her now.

"Please! Don't go. I'll do anything you ask, just please forgive me, please stay!"

"Anything I ask?" Gavra latched onto the offer like a lifeline.

"Yes!"

"There is something you can do for me."

"What is it?"

He stared down at her, setting his mouth in a grim line. This would be the key. Closing his eyes as though he hated the thought of what he had to ask of her, he let out a long sigh.

"If you want to prove yourself, do this. Confine yourself to this grotto I built for you, remind yourself everyday why you loved me to begin with and why I loved you. Remind yourself how we each earned that love. Because you are not entitled to my love, Nyx. Not without earning it the way you did when we were young. Stay in here and prove to me that you have earned my love by remembering how to be the honorable woman you once were. When I return, if I believe you are that woman again, I will stay and we can be together."

As he spoke, he began to back away from her toward the entrance to the grotto. Nyx eagerly hung on every word, so clearly anxious to prove herself again to Nereus that Gavra knew his tactic was working. He hated himself for it, but Sweet Mother, it was working and he had to see it through.

When his heels hit the steps leading up and out of the grotto, he ascended them slowly, raising his hands and seeking out the power he needed to complete his task. Silas's channeling of the power of the Source gave him the deepest well of energy he could ever imagine and he took advantage of it, letting it flood from his palms. He mixed his own magic with it as he created a barrier that would hold this powerful, beautiful woman who had fallen from grace. He extended the barrier out from the entrance, creating an unbroken shell of magic that encompassed the entire grotto so she would have no way of escaping, though from the earnest look of love and longing in her eyes, he doubted she would risk losing Nereus again.

She rushed toward him as he completed the prison, tears streaming down her cheeks. Gavra's heart lurched as she collapsed to her knees, crying out her husband's name and begging his forgiveness. The words echoed hauntingly in his ears as he turned and walked away.

CHAPTER 39

SILAS

Silas's limited understanding of what his power could do had in no way prepared him for the overwhelming flood of it that coursed through him now. Every single one of his senses were fully engaged. His vision filled with the mesmerizing pattern of the trails of blood that criss-crossed between the nymphs as they made their exchange with Assana. Her fertile, delicious scent filled his nostrils, mixed with the coppery fragrance of the blood. Her warm body was a welcome weight against his chest and he slid his hands down to rest at her hips, not wishing to interfere with her melding of her sisters, though his palms ached to touch her in a more intimate way.

The sounds that reached his ears seemed to come from all sides, and even from beyond the waterfall-bordered clearing where the other pools of the Source were. He could hear Nyx's pleas as she fell victim to Gavra's trick. Their plan was working, but he wasn't yet prepared to rejoice; he had yet more to do.

The flow of the Source to the Sanctuary had been interrupted when Nyx began this new ritual, and it was time for him to reconnect the flow and keep his promise to Sathmika.

The flow of Gaia's energy seemed to instantly grasp his desires, and he surrendered to the need to fulfill that last duty to his home, to fulfill his potential as a Miteradoro.

Closing his eyes, he reached even deeper with his senses, down into the farthest reaches of the Source until he hit the core of power. Gaia's magic shot into him with the force of a lightning bolt.

In his mind he heard a rich, female voice echo. He knew the voice, yet she was somehow still foreign to him, like his ears had only just attuned themselves to the language she spoke.

"There is no return from this path once you commit to it, Silas. Be certain this is what you want before you allow it to happen."

But he had made his oath long ago when he was a young ursa joining the ranks of Sanctuary guardians. He would do what was required to see his home kept safe, and this was one thing that must be done. He must ensure the Sanctuary's link to the Source could never be broken again.

"I am sure. I made a promise, and I intend to keep it."

"As you wish. Grow, Miteradoro."

The pure, vibrant power of all life filled him, pushing deep through the extended tendrils of his body and up into his limbs. His back arched and he gasped. He released Assana and lifted his hands, staring at them as they transformed, becoming the verdant, woody green of new saplings and then hardening and leafing out. They longed for the sun and he reached his arms up high, knowing instinctively that this transformation required the light above to work. As he stared upward, his arms grew and his torso elongated, pushing higher and higher toward the sunlight.

"Silas, what's happening?" Assana yelled, staring up at him.

He couldn't tilt his head down to look at her, but his consciousness was still tightly bound to hers in their sacred blood meld bond. She had completed her own task, as had Gavra, and they both stood at the edge of the wide pool of the Source now, staring up at him in worried awe.

"This is what I must do … It's my task to complete. Please understand. I love you both, but *my* home was at risk too."

"Of course we understand, Silas, but what the hell are you doing?" Assana asked.

"Couldn't risk the chance of the connection being broken again. This will make it permanent. It has to be done."

"Sweet Mother, not like this!" Gavra yelled. "There has to be another way."

"What's wrong, you don't like how hard I get when I'm doing the right thing? My dick's bigger than yours now, isn't it? I can't see it, but it feels huge."

Gavra uttered an expletive that was half laughter. "Just tell me you can come back to us like you were once it's done, brother."

Silas's growth picked up momentum from the power flooding into him and seeking out the nourishing light from above. He tried to focus on Gavra's request, but everything was moving too fast. All he could do was give in to his swift upward climb, the branches his arms had become splitting and growing into numerous limbs that continued their steady expansion into the sky.

When he was sure he could go no farther, his upper leaves reached the top and he knew this was the foundation of his home—the Sanctuary lay beyond that magical wall, and he had to carry the power of the Source beyond it. He pushed and felt the barrier give like a soft membrane. It bounced back and he pushed again, the energy flowing through him still nourishing his upward growth and his climb. Eventually the membrane gave way and he was through, the parted shield of magic snapping back into place around him, sealing shut as though he hadn't just ruptured it. His huge trunk still penetrated between, connecting the Source with the realm beyond.

His realm. His home.

Silas's awareness blossomed as his body loomed above the familiar waters of Gaia's Lake in the crater atop the highest mountain in the Sanctuary. It had been emptied again, yet now gradually filled with clear water. Within moments, the rush of Gaia's Falls cascaded over the edge in a roaring flood.

From his vantage high in the atmosphere, he saw the ursa arriving, first one at a time, venturing up the mountain, and then more and more until the entire mountaintop that surrounded the lake was covered with ursa.

They cheered. Every last man, woman, and child on that mountaintop cheered him on. When his highest leaves brushed the Sanctuary's magic barrier, the raging flood of power from the Source subsided slightly, remaining a steady, constant flow. He could feel it pushing outward now instead of up, feeding all the living creatures in the Sanctuary with its power as his massive, leafy canopy fanned out to shelter the entire mountaintop.

Amid the din of cheering ursa, he still sensed his mates, and was finally able to shift his focus away from his task to seek them out.

But what he found was not the rejoicing cheers of the two people he loved most. They stood at his base inside the Haven, hands pressed against his trunk, and called to him emphatically as though they'd been trying to catch his attention for hours and were hoarse from the efforts. Gavra banged his fists on Silas's thick bark.

"Brother, don't make me set you on fire to get you to come out of there. Come back to us!"

"Silas, please!" Assana cried. "You didn't have to do this. We could have found another way! Come back!"

He tried to speak, but his words only came as a creak of branches and a rustle of leaves in the wind. He tried to lean down to embrace them, but his trunk could only sway so far before the tension bounced him back. Their worry and fear for him was as clear to Silas as his own elation at his accomplishment. This was something amazing, yet he began to panic within his new shape because he couldn't figure out how to undo it, or if he even should.

At a loss for any true action, he pulled his focus inward, sinking deep into that secret place he shared with them. Their images were more distinct than he remembered, Assana more vibrant and beautiful, Gavra more powerful and potently seductive. The dragon's eyes blazed blood-red —his anger clear.

"What the fuck did you do?" Gavra asked.

"Only what needed to be done to protect the Sanctuary."

"Oh, Silas. Hasn't this shit with my mother taught you anything?" Assana asked.

He held steadfast to his convictions. "It had nothing to do with your mother. I haven't harmed anyone. This will remove any possibility of our alliance failing again. The Haven and the Sanctuary are forever tied together now—one is no longer dependent on the other for its wellbeing. If anything, this will make our bond stronger, the way my bond with the two of you was strengthened when we shared our blood. It had to be this way."

Assana's eyes were wet with tears and Gavra's jaw clenched tight.

"But we've as good as lost you, don't you see that? You're a *tree*, Silas! As glorious and beautiful as you are, I can't make love to a tree. What happens if I need you to help calm my primal power? I'll go crazy without you!"

"You don't need me for that anymore. Look at you, Assana—you're *in* your primal form and have been for hours. Gavra's right here, and what are the two of you doing? Talking to me. Not banging each other's brains out like that first time."

Assana let out a frustrated wail and covered her face with her hands. Gavra smacked his fist against Silas's trunk hard enough for the force to shake him all the way up to his highest branches.

"We still need you, you bastard," Gavra growled.

"I need you too," Silas said softly. "But I don't know how to undo it, and even if I did, I don't think I would, because these two realms *need* me to do this. If I undo it, then we'll all be weaker for it."

"I won't give up," Assana said. "We have so much power between the three of us now. I'll find a way for you to come back and still hold this connection open permanently. We *have* to, Silas. I want you to be here to hold our baby in your arms when it's born."

Oh, Gaia, no. Had she really just said that?

His entire monolithic form shook with emotion at the revelation, but he could only hold her in spirit, not in the flesh. He did just that, drawing Assana's mental image into his arms and burying his face in her ethereal hair. She felt so real within the circle of his embrace, but this wasn't her true body, nor was it his.

"Will you come back to us if we find a way?" Assana asked.

"I will always come back to you if there is a way."

CHAPTER 40

ASSANA

"When did you know?" Gavra asked, clutching Assana's hand as they walked into the Haven's palace and made their way to the great hall.

"This morning," she said, remembering the moment vividly, though it had all felt like a dream at the time. "When you came to us last night and you and Silas made love to me, it felt so amazing to have you both in me as one. Do you remember how our souls connected in that moment?"

He nodded, tugging at her hand and turning her to face him. "It was like our bond had produced its own source of power. There was this light in the center of the three of us that hadn't existed before, right where all of our auras merged."

She frowned. "I couldn't see our auras then, but yes, it was like that … a tiny little universe came into being where we were joined." She pressed her hands to her abdomen and smiled. "Right here. And it clarified everything. When Mother showed up, that's why I knew you'd been right to want the blood meld. That used to be the way we completed the mating bond, at least when we did it properly with mates we truly love. It made no sense *not* to do it then."

He smiled at her, and her entire body flooded with warmth at his look. Thankfully it was Gavra she was actually looking at now, with his blood-red eyes and clean, strong features, instead of the mirage of her father. Despite how put-together he appeared, she could sense his deep weariness. The day had taken a lot out of them, and a part of her ached over Silas's absence.

Gavra slid a hand to the back of her neck and pulled her into a kiss, then drifted his lips over her cheek and nuzzled at her hair. "Sweet Mother, it feels so good just to touch you without fear of driving you mad, but I admit I'm going to miss that wild nymph who tied me to the bed."

Assana pulled him tighter and manifested her antlers, then completed the full shift into her primal form.

"This wild nymph?" she asked, giving him a sly grin. She flicked her wrist in a circle and vines shot out from the throne that rested on the dais behind her lover. As they yanked him backward and he tumbled onto the huge, pearlescent seat, she summoned the new power she'd discovered and blew a gust of red smoke at him that immediately dissolved every stitch of his conjured clothing.

Gavra's eyes flashed with lust, and though he pulled at the vines that held his wrists and ankles tight to the arms and legs of the throne, he didn't struggle much. His cock roused, proud and thick and stiff, the sight of its weeping tip making her core drench with need to feel him buried in her.

She shed her gown and advanced on him, climbing up the steps to the throne. He stared up at her, licking his lips like a hungry beast, but she had to remind him that she was the hungry one here to eat him alive. She tangled her fingers in his hair, yanking it free from its tidy binding.

"I like it when you look wild too, you know," she said,

then pulled his head back and covered his mouth with hers, kissing him with every ounce of strength left in her, every desperate shred of hope, sadness, love, and despair. When she climbed onto the throne and straddled him, she sank down, taking him deep, and the delicious stretch of him filling her made her feel invincible.

Despite his absence, Silas remained fully present in their minds, and when they climaxed, Assana sensed the flow of power including him as though he'd been right there with them, touching them, the entire time.

"I love you both so much," Assana whispered.

"I have the biggest woody right now, you guys. Like so big, I bet you can see it from space."

"Silas, that joke isn't funny anymore," Assana said.

"It's fucking hilarious," Gavra said, chuckling at first, then laughing loudly when Assana punched him in the shoulder. "Let him enjoy it. When we get him back, he knows he won't be able to measure up against me."

MAKING love with Gavra on her mother's throne was one thing—a wild, rebellious act that many an unruly child might have done when lashing out at her parents—but actually claiming the throne as her own proved far more challenging for Assana to process.

When she and Gavra cleaned up after their spontaneous interlude, she stood back and stared at the looming seat.

"It's yours now, at least temporarily," Gavra said. "You know you can handle it."

"It still feels wrong ... like I broke the rules somehow. Maybe it's just that uncle Neph's seat isn't there." She glanced around and found one of the many maids that kept the palace running. Within moments, they'd located her uncle's throne and had it repositioned in its rightful spot, yet she still couldn't sit.

She was staring at the thing uncertainly when several new figures entered the great hall and gathered around her.

"We will follow you, sister," Clio said. "And not just because of the blood bond we have. Will the dragon be sharing the dais with you?"

Assana shot a look to Gavra, realizing that the thought had never occurred to her. They shared a silent exchange and then both shook their heads.

"It wouldn't be my place," Gavra said. "The thrones belong to Nyx and Neph. They are the Dionarchs and always will be. Assana is your de facto leader, by all rights. She should sit until the Dionarchs return."

He placed a warm hand at the small of her back. The touch urged her forward without quite pushing. She took a deep breath and glanced around at the Thiasoi, who were all staring at her expectantly. They depended on her to make the decisions now, and while the idea of commanding them was not that alien to her, she still hesitated to take on that level of authority.

Clio stepped forward and put a hand on her shoulder. "Trust us, sister. Know that we trust you as much. Let us take advantage of our blood bond while we can. Let us serve you and the Haven."

Despite her concerted efforts not to make use of the blood meld between her and the Thiasoi, she couldn't help but sense the unanimous agreement among all eleven of them. Surprised by their thoughts all clamoring in her mind, she turned and faced the group.

"You don't have to do anything for me. The Haven owes you for the sacrifices you were willing to make. I have a lot to make up to you all."

One by one, her fellow Thiasoi maidens dropped to one knee and bowed their heads.

Dumbfounded, she barely registered Gavra's whisper and his gentle nudge. "It's time for you to sit, baby," he said softly into her ear.

Swallowing the huge lump in her throat, she nodded and stepped to the throne. As though seeking to encourage her, Gavra sent a deliciously naughty image into her head of the pair of them tangled in ecstasy atop that very seat only moments earlier.

"Anytime you wish me to take your place for a moment, I will, but only if you are astride me when I do. The burden of leadership sometimes needs a cushion."

Before her, the eleven maidens began to smile, and a few of them let out soft titters. Realizing they'd also had a peek into her mind, she scowled.

"I know we can't help the link we have to each other now, but I would appreciate it if you all didn't eavesdrop."

"As you wish, mistress," Clio said, lifting her head and grinning widely at Assana, then at Gavra. "But if you would do us a favor, some of us would love to know if there are more dragons like him who are seeking mates. If you want us out of your head, we should get on with making a proper blood bond to a chosen mate."

"Meetings can certainly be arranged," Gavra said. "That is, if your mistress is willing to allow my kind to visit."

"Gaia, yes! Of course, there is the matter of no one being able to pass through the Sanctuary's barrier besides ursa, but in time I'm sure we will be able to open the Haven to the other higher races. Turul as well, if they like. I will do everything in my power to ensure our alliances remain strong, but Mother was right about one thing—the safety of the Source is paramount, and now that it's permanently linked to the

Sanctuary, too, we have to tread with caution when granting access from the outside. Our enemy is still out there."

The mention of that permanent link with the Sanctuary caused emotion to surge and she found herself at a momentary loss for words, filled with longing for Silas. Within her mind, she sensed his comforting caress, but it did little to ease her ache to see him in the flesh.

The Thiasoi all shared concerned glances and Assana forced herself to take a deep breath and focus on them again.

"You all have liberty to visit the Sanctuary and seek out mates there, of course. With Silas bridging our realms, I'd like five of you to serve as advance guard and work with the Sanctuary guardians in whatever manner the Queen requires. You may leave as soon as you are ready. Four of you will need to visit all the grottos in the Haven and make sure our current ursa guests are well and that order persists, now that my Mother is no longer in charge. Clio and Ephyra … will you two remain as my personal guard? If you'd rather not …"

"We would be honored, mistress," both nymphs replied in unison.

"Thank you," Assana said, finally feeling some of the weight of worry lift from her shoulders. "You may proceed with your tasks now."

The maidens all stood and broke into their required parties before departing. When they were gone, Clio and Ephyra remained, both with apprehensive looks. They hadn't moved to their assigned places where her mother's personal guard usually stood.

"What is it, sisters? Does something else trouble you?"

"Not a trouble so much as a request," Clio said. Ephyra nodded and shifted closer to her fellow Thiasoi. Their hands gravitated to each other as though they were magnetized.

"We'd like your blessing, mistress," Ephyra said. "Clio and

I have been deeply melded for ages, but we realize now that bond alone is not enough for us."

Assana raised her eyebrows. "It's never been a secret. Why would you need my blessing?"

Clio glanced at her lover and set her jaw. "We'd like to blood meld, but didn't want to overstep … We didn't want it to seem like we were too eager to shed our bond to you."

Quickly, Ephyra jumped in. "We still wish to do our duty to the Haven and breed with a male … to give the Haven sons to defend it. We just don't want to wait any longer to make our own bond permanent."

A surge of love propelled Assana from her throne. She descended the dais and stood in front of the two women who'd been her closest friends for thousands of years.

"You don't need to give the Haven sons if that isn't what you wish. Be together, if your love is true you have my blessing for a blood meld. And if you ever meet a male who suits you both, you have my blessing for that too—sons or no sons, I just want you to be happy."

She pulled them both into a fierce hug. Clio murmured into her ear, "We want you to be happy too, Assana. Of all of us, you deserve it most."

"I am happy, I promise," she said, but knew deep down that it was partly a lie.

"You succeeded, Assana. We all did," Silas said, his deep, rich voice filling her mind with pride and love. She clenched her fists wishing like hell that she could touch him, but it wasn't possible to embrace a thought or a voice. Returning to her throne, she reached for Gavra's hand where he stood at her left and gripped it tight. She would never let him go as long as she lived.

"If I ever get you back, you are never allowed to leave me again, you got that?" Assana shot to Silas's mental image in her mind.

"You promise you'll tie me to the bed and I'll stay," he said.

Assana let out a frustrated growl. Her need for them both was so strong she almost wished she could blame it on insanity, but no. There were no such excuses for this new burden of love she bore. Her mind was as clear as the bright blue sky, her wild impulses tamed and controlled until she chose to unleash them. Her eyes were wide open and her heart so full it nearly burst.

"You will come back to me, Silas. And I promise when you do, I am tying you both *to my bed and never letting you go again."*

CHAPTER 41

VRISHTI

*V*rishti stared up at the glorious, huge canopy of the tree, awed but also terrified what it might mean. Her mother was tight-lipped ever since the Queen had arrived and ordered an emergency council to take place at Gaia's Falls. The scene of the crime, so to speak.

Most of the ursa in the Sanctuary were here, all of them rejoicing at the immense power that had flooded the place when the tree erupted from the lake bed more than a week ago. They hadn't left since, but the arrival of a handful of leather-clad nymphs with dark tattoos and bows had made it obvious that something big was happening.

The nymphs were in the meeting with the clan leaders and the queen now, and Vrishti stole close to the secluded copse at the top of the falls, hoping to catch some bit of information, but the noise of the waterfall drowned out any voices.

All she wanted to know was whether the dragons had been freed or if they were still held captive inside the Haven. Would Aodh return to her or … or what? Was she going to have to go after him? Word had gotten out that the Haven would welcome any ursa visitors, though the nymphs didn't seem as keen on traveling the other direction. Aside from the five warrior-like females who had arrived, there had been no other visitors.

She shifted uncomfortably on the warm rock she'd staked out to give her a good vantage of the meeting taking place. The Queen stood higher than the others wearing a distinctly angry expression that Vrishti was sure was directed at her mother. The nymphs kept pointing at the tree. Then her mother spoke up, gesturing emphatically. The Queen yelled … Vrishti was sure she was yelling because she actually heard a syllable or two rise up over the din of the waterfall, though she couldn't make out full words.

Her mother looked pissed, then apologetic.

Fuck, she wished she could just *hear* them. Were they talking about Aodh at all? Did the dragons even matter, or was this amazing tree that had burst up through the lake last week the only thing they cared about?

She pressed her hands hard against the stone, fingernails clawed in frustration. Beneath her hands, the earth seemed to quiver and a familiar warmth swelled in her belly. She'd learned to recognize the core of her power. The kernel of Gaia's magic that lived inside every female ursa was the first thing her mother had taught her about when she'd arrived, and since that day, she'd worked hard to nurture it, though she'd been told that until she hit her first estrous, the bulk of her powers would remain dormant.

The power swelled in her like the rising tide of an orgasm, but she knew better this time. It could be harnessed to perform magic if she wished, or to shift into her bear form. She still wasn't quite sure how to deliberately summon it, so she had learned to take advantage of it when it appeared.

She did so now, pressing her palms harder against the

stone and pushing the power downward. Closing her eyes, she directed the power to move farther, the living energy obeying her command. It traveled under the grassy expanse between her and the group of females having their pow-wow and silently emerged, no more obvious than a blade of grass in the center of their group.

In her mind's eye, a tiny flower bloomed, and instantly she could hear every word being spoken. She was shocked to hear that one word was her own name.

"Vrishti has the power, but she isn't ready to use it yet. She won't be until she assumes the mantle of Summer, and you know the ritual can't happen until the equinox at the earliest."

Her mother had explained as much to her on repeated occasions, but why would that be important now?

"Then you must guide her," the Queen said. "It's a Rainsong who made the sacrifice at *your* command, Sathmnika. It has to be Rainsong power that undoes it."

Several voices rose up in protest and a foot stomped down on the flower, blocking out all the voices. Vrishti cursed and shifted her focus, pushing another tiny flower up through the earth in a different spot.

"Let the nymphs speak!" the Windsong clan leader yelled, her voice carrying high enough above the roaring water that Vrishti clearly heard the words from where she sat. Everyone quieted and one of the nymphs stepped forward, her feet barely missing Vrishti's new flower.

"We have no wish to cut off the connection made. Our mistress merely wishes for her mate to be returned to her. Can we all agree to find a way to form a new bridge between the Source and the Sanctuary?"

A bridge ... Vrishti stared up at the tree.

"So that's what you are," she said. "You're a bridge. Can I climb down your trunk and find my love?"

The leaves of the canopy above her rustled, though there was no breeze at the moment.

"… remove him from the tree and it destroys the bridge," her mother was saying. Suddenly Vrishti understood what all the fuss was about.

"Is that you in there, Silas?" she asked. The leaves shifted again, branches creaking. Her belly warmed and she drew back the power she'd sent to the lakeside, deciding she needed to focus her efforts elsewhere now.

With her face tilted toward the upper branches of the tree, she pulled the power to her own ears this time, listening closely to the seemingly random sounds the tree made. Gradually she discovered she could make out words, and the more she listened, the clearer they became.

"Figured out how strong you are, have you, Vrishti?"

"Silas, is that you?"

"In the flesh ... or should I say, in the wood? I think Assana's tired of all my tree jokes, but I can't let her get wise to the fact that I'm fucking terrified and really wish I'd known this would happen before I agreed to do it."

"So you want out?"

"I want to be there when Assana has our baby. What's she going to do? Climb up and put a newborn in my branches? But I can't ... there's no way out. I am the fucking tree."

"And if you let go, you're afraid the Sanctuary will lose its connection to the Source. I think it's just a physics problem. Can you send the power back the other direction in a loop?"

The leaves chattered together, creating their own air current that rippled across the surface of the lake. As she waited for a response, Vrishti studied the monolithic tree, pondering the pale green leaves with the tiny buds of white flowers. The tree looked like it had just broken into bloom with spring, though in reality, the Sanctuary was nearing the end of summer and on the verge of autumn. Yet the spring equinox was only a few weeks away, the seasons inside being the reverse of those outside, at least in Earth's northern hemisphere.

"I can't figure out how to reverse the power ... and believe me, I've tried."

"Not reverse it. Send it forward, but in a cycle, looping back on itself. You've created a siphon that pulls the power up from the Haven, replacing the old link with one that can't be broken. Like a pipe where there used to be a shutoff valve being replaced by one with no barrier. Can you extend the flow beyond that, push it back to where it starts and create a constant cycle? Perhaps the flow will sustain itself once it gets moving."

"Let me try ..."

The breeze picked up, blowing through his branches but despite that new noise, Vrishti could still hear the hum of power that flooded through the giant tree. The thick wood of his branches groaned, and she saw one flower lose its petals, leaving behind a small green object. Then more of the flowers followed suit, petals falling everywhere and coating the surface of the lake with a carpet of brilliant white.

"Something's happening. Silas, did you do that?"

"I ... I'm trying to force the flow forward, but it's getting away from me. It's starting to move faster now. I don't know if this is good. What's happening?"

"You're making fruit," Vrishti said, marveling at the speed with which the tiny buds grew into larger fruit that turned red and began to fall as they ripened. Excited ursa began to dive into the water to retrieve the apples and gather them up.

Within moments, however, the fruit was gone and the leaves faded, grew yellow, then gold, then orange, and the first few fluttered off the branches.

"Fuck," Silas said. *"I think I did something bad ..."*

"No! I think it's working. Keep going!"

"The flow is too much for me. I can't control it."

Words of alarm rose up from the crowds on the shores of the lake. Vrishti looked over and saw several people pointing down the mountain to the vista of the Sanctuary and all the hillsides beyond.

"Oh, shit," Vrishti said. "The whole place is changing seasons now. Silas, can you get it under control?"

"I'm trying, believe me, but all I understand is summer. I'm a Rainsong. None of the other seasons feel like home to me, so I aimed for summer, and I think that's where we're headed."

"That's where we *were*, but we're definitely looking like winter out here."

Near the waterfall's crest, the group of clan leaders and nymphs had stopped talking and were now staring up at the tree in shock.

"Vrishti, tell me what to do. You're Sathmika's daughter—you ... you're smarter than me."

"I think ..." She paused and frowned, trying to give him some advice based on her ursa studies, but having no good ideas. Around her the mountainside cooled, the leaves of all the trees transforming along with Silas's branches now until they browned and fell. Within moments, the entire Sanctuary was gray with winter light, the trees all bare of leaves.

"I think you need to just let it flow until you can get your bearings."

"Help me."

Suddenly a pair of hands were on her shoulders and someone was shaking her. She tore her focus away from the tree and saw the ursa Queen, Emma, standing in front of her with a worried expression.

"Vrishti, what's happening? Was that you? We all saw you speaking a spell. Did you do this?"

The other clan leaders stood nearby, along with the nymphs. Occasionally they glanced up at the tree, their awe growing when the bare branches began to sprout with pale green shoots of fresh growth that unfurled into new leaves.

"It isn't me. Silas is pulling the power through, trying to create a loop. I think … if he can get enough momentum in the cycle, it will sustain itself so he can leave the tree."

"Fuck. Is that really what I'm trying to do here? It's moving too fast still. Little help, maybe?"

"What is he saying to you?" Emma asked.

Vrishti shook her head, surprised the others couldn't hear him.

"Just listen," she said, and tapped at Emma's temple.

The Queen frowned, but closed her eyes and focused, then let out a laugh. "He's got a colorful mouth on him, doesn't he?"

"Are you going to fucking help me with this or just fucking stand around chatting?" Silas said, sounding like he was in a near panic.

Emma rushed back to the other clan leaders and motioned for them to gather. The four women clasped hands in a circle and began to chant while slowly rotating in a clockwise direction.

"Silas, I think they're trying to help you now. Let them, all right?"

"I can hear them. Thank you."

Vrishti closed her eyes, listening to the steady chants of the four clan leaders and mentally translating the song from its ancient tongue to her own language. It was a song about the seasons, the cycles of nature, of life, and the universe. Of death and rebirth, night and day. After a few moments, Vrishti heard Silas start to chant along, and the tree above seemed to move and sway in the same rhythm.

She watched into the night, and slowly the speeding seasons began to regulate, to lengthen, until there were hours between instead of minutes.

"Something's happening," Silas said as the sun was rising above the crest of his canopy. *"I feel the power moving around me now, instead of through me, like it's taken on a life of its own."*

"That's good, right? Is it sustaining itself now?"

"I... Oh, shit ..."

"Silas? Silas! What happened?" Vrishti stared up at the tree, calling to him, frantic for a response, but the leaves no longer spoke beyond conveying their need for sun and water and nourishment from Gaia's power. They were back to their pre-spring buds now, and when she stared around at the rest of the Sanctuary it looked the same as the tree ... with fresh new growth and pale green leaves signifying the emerging rebirth of life after a long, cold winter.

"Silas!" Vrishti called again. "Please answer me. Tell me what happened! Are you there?"

"I'm right here," said a deep voice behind her. Vrishti spun around, her heart pounding into her throat. The man himself stood there, in the flesh ... in the very *naked* flesh.

Vrishti flushed and immediately stared up at the sky. "What a relief!"

Silas chuckled. "You need to get over the naked thing, sister. You're an ursa."

She forced herself to lower her gaze, but pointedly kept her chin up and her eyes locked to his. She let out a sudden breath of pure relief.

"You did it," she said, grinning at him.

"I had help. Thank you for that."

"It just made sense."

The Queen came forward and patted Silas on the shoulder. The other clan leaders fell in around them, Vrishti's mother coming forward with a chagrined look.

"Silas, please forgive me. It seems my daughter is far brighter than I gave her credit for. If I'd discussed my plan with her to begin with, we could have avoided letting you be trapped like that for so long."

Silas gave the woman a long look and nodded. "I would do anything for my home, but the people in the Sanctuary are just as important as the Sanctuary itself. We'd be nothing without them. Now, if it's all the same to you guys, and forgive the lack of honorifics here, but I'd *really* like to get back to the Haven now."

"Please take me with you!" Vrishti blurted out, rushing toward him and grabbing his arm. She released him, suddenly feeling odd about that particular statement. She'd been here once before, but then it had been a different ursa male along with a collection of dragons who she'd begged to let her tag along.

Silas raised his eyebrows. "Yeah? Why? There aren't any males in there who aren't taken."

"There is one … well, he's taken too, but he's mine. Or I mean, he *will* be taken once I claim him. I have to find him now and let him know … something important."

She winced inwardly, realizing that she had an audience that included the Queen as well as her own mother, who she hadn't bothered to confess to that she'd found her mate.

Silas stiffened and frowned at her. Softly, he said, "You mean Aodh, don't you? Gavra's brother."

His shift in demeanor from open to cautious alarmed her. "Yes. He's all right, isn't he?"

Silas put his hands on his hips and exhaled, shaking his head. "We don't know, honestly. Nyx hid him away somewhere… 'safe,' she said, but we have no idea how to get him out of wherever it is. I'll take you to the Haven if you want to talk to Assana about it, but that's all I can offer."

She hazarded a hesitant glance at her mother.

"Daughter, no," Sathmika said, stepping forward to stand between them. "You aren't ready for this yet. If your estrous comes while you're away, you may not have a way to balance it. You need to stay at least until it happens."

"Mother, I have to go. I made Aodh a promise. If he's trapped, I have to try to help him."

Behind her mother, Silas gave her an impatient look, then turned and started walking toward the lake and the route she knew would take them into the Haven. In the brightening dawn, she saw what made him so eager to go. The entire wide expanse of his back was covered with a huge, glowing tattoo. A dragon mark, she knew from her studies. It was red and pierced the morning as splendidly as the sunrise, signaling his purpose.

He had to get back to his mates. And Vrishti had to go save her own.

CHAPTER 42

ASSANA

*A*ssana paced the floor in front of the dais where her throne sat. It was all she could do not to drift and go to Silas now that she knew he was back in the Haven, finally, miraculously released from his prison inside the monolithic tree that now joined her home permanently with the ursa Sanctuary.

"He can drift now that we're blood melded. Why isn't he coming straight here?" she asked out loud, even though she knew the answer already. Silas wasn't as comfortable with the mode of travel that came second nature to her, especially not with a passenger in tow.

"Baby, sit. They'll be here soon," Gavra said, looking far too relaxed.

They. She groaned in apprehension at the reminder that he was bringing a visitor. What the hell was she going to say to Vrishti? An apology didn't seem appropriate, but what else was there? "Sorry my crazy mother banished your lover into a time bubble"? "Wish I could help, but bummer, I can't because I'm not a fucking immortal"? Even with the power she'd gained from her lovers, Assana still didn't possess the ability to time travel. Only Nyx and Neph could control the River to that degree.

She took another circuit across the floor and ran straight into Gavra on the way back, too distracted to look where she was going. He slid his arms around her and held her still. She remained rigid and frustrated for a second before letting out a long sigh and relaxing, allowing him to wrap her in is embrace.

"It's been more than a week! I know we've had him with us … in our minds, in our souls … but I miss the feel of him so much."

"I know," Gavra said, brushing his lips over the top of her head. "I miss him too." The gruffness of his tone made her realize how tightly bound Gavra's control was over his emotions.

She tilted her head back to look at him. Studying his tense features for a moment, she reached up and touched his smooth, square jaw.

"You really do, don't you?"

One corner of his mouth twitched, and his brows relaxed. "I love you both more than life. Of course I miss him. Not having him here with us is like missing a fucking limb."

"Don't fucking talk to me about missing limbs. I'm glad to be back to the four I started with."

Assana twisted around with a yelp, her heart surging into her throat.

"Silas!" She leaped from Gavra's arms at the naked, towering ursa who had somehow snuck up behind her. He opened his arms and welcomed her, letting out a satisfied growl when she bounded up, wrapping both arms and legs around his torso as he enveloped her in a fierce hug.

Holding his cheeks in both hands, she showered his face with kisses, then slowed when she reached his mouth. Her lips merged with his in a hungry, urgent tangle. Silas's arms tightened around her, his hands slipping down beneath her backside and squeezing.

Remembering her responsibilities, she reluctantly released him and looked into his eyes, then around the room behind him.

With a frown, she said, "Where's Vrishti? I thought you were bringing her here."

"Clio and Ephyra met us when we arrived. They insisted on giving her a tour and debriefing her on everything … which they said might take a few hours. Those two are my heroes, by the way. They told me not to waste time getting to you. Drifting's not so bad when I know you're at the end of it."

Gavra's red shape swooped in from behind her. Silas barely had time to turn his head before he was attacked. Both of Gavra's hands bracketed his face while the dragon devoured his mouth. Assana caught a flash of teeth as Gavra bit the ursa's lip then swept his tongue in deeper. Silas's already stiff cock pulsed between them.

"Don't you ever fucking do that again," Gavra growled, still holding tight to Silas's head, their foreheads pressed together.

"I learned my lesson," Silas said. "But after all this time as a bystander with you two, you both fucking owe me."

He slipped a hand to Gavra's neck, his other arm tightening around Assana. Before she could catch a glimmer of his intentions from their shared consciousness, the air condensed around them, the telltale wetness of the drift tickling her skin.

Her ears popped and she found herself in a familiar, though unexpected space.

Gavra let out a gruff laugh. "My fucking cage? Why here, of all places?"

"Assana's quarters are still a wreck, and this was the only

other place I've been in the Haven that I knew had a bed. You want a different one, you're welcome to take us there … later. Right now, I need you both too damn much."

He rolled her over, pinning her to the bed beneath him. His stiff erection pressed between her thighs and he ground his hips into her with a low rumble. Pushing himself up with both arms, he gazed down at her.

"You all right with this?" he asked.

Breathless, she nodded at him, but frowned when he hesitated with one hand poised over the laces of her gown.

"What is it?" she asked.

Silas turned a hooded gaze to Gavra and licked his lips. Fixing his attention back on her, he said, "Ah, this is going to sound crazy, but … will you top me the way you did him the first time?"

Assana's brows shot up and she looked at Gavra, who was standing by the bed, grinning at them both. "Brother, you're a brave, brave man."

"What? She's got control of herself now."

Assana laughed. "Just because I can control it doesn't mean my appetite's diminished any, but I did promise to tie you to the bed when you returned." She took a deep breath and pulled him down to her, taking his mouth yet again and kissing him deeply. While their tongues tangled, she released her hold on her civilized human shape, releasing the primal power and letting it have free rein.

The delicious impulses sparked through her body, her skin tingling with energy. Her gentle ursa lover was back, and he wanted her wild like her dragon. Who was she to deny him his heart's desire?

She tightened her thighs around his hips as her body swelled with the heat of her unleashed lust. Her antlers emerged from her head, the stiff protrusions alive with wild energy.

With a smooth twist and push, she flipped them both. Silas let out a soft "oof" of surprise, his eyes widening when he was beneath her. His cock kicked against his belly between them and she purred in pleasure at the heat of it, sliding her bare, slick folds up along the length.

The bed dipped behind her and Gavra rested his large hands on her shoulders, slid them down her chest, and hooked the bodice of her dress with his fingers. She inhaled sharply when he grasped the fabric and wrenched it apart, tearing the garment cleanly all the way to her crotch. He cupped her breasts and pressed his mouth to her neck.

"Take him the way you took me, baby. That's what he wants. Give it to him."

Silas slid his hands up her thighs, pausing at the tops, and brushed his thumbs over the parted flesh, pulling her farther apart so that her stiff clit was visible. She kept her gaze fixed to his face, enjoying the rapt attention he had on her core. He licked his lips just as his thumb came into contact with her clit, sliding her juices over it and rubbing in a slow, delicious circle.

Gaia, that was good, but Gavra was right. Silas had asked for something, and she intended to give it to him.

Grasping his wrists in both hands she pushed his arms above his head and held them there. Silas arched beneath her, letting out a hum of approval when her breasts brushed his cheeks. She paused in that position, taking her time summoning the vines to bind his hands and enjoying the hungry sucking of his mouth as he devoured each of her nipples in turn.

Behind her, Gavra made a similar noise of affirmation and she felt the rear panel of her dress grow taut as he ripped it from hem to back. The two halves fell off her shoulders and hung destroyed around her elbows. He grazed his palms down her arched back, over her bare ass, and teased one thumb between the cheeks around the tightness of her opening.

"Baby, I've wanted this since Fate sent you to my dreams years ago. I'm going to have this ass tonight while Silas fucks that hot little cunt of yours."

Assana tightened her grip on Silas's bound wrists, her eyelids fluttering closed. Neither of them had made any overtures toward taking her like that, though both men had eagerly played with her ass multiple times. She'd begun to wonder if it was only Silas's more ready rear that Gavra desired. Now she knew better.

Gavra held her cheeks spread and she lost herself when his hot breath ghosted against her sensitive opening, followed by a soft press of his lips there. It was only a kiss, then a gentle lick of his forked tongue that toyed around and around before sliding down between her legs and tickling between her parted flesh.

Silas continued sucking her nipples, his mouth making regular circuits back and forth while his swollen cockhead brushed against her lower abdomen. He stopped suddenly and let out a harsh grunt, his head falling back against the pillow.

Assana opened her eyes and looked down between them to see Gavra's big hand wrapped around Silas's shaft, his tongue coiled around the head as he licked and sucked until Silas's hips pushed up into him.

"Fuck," Silas groaned when Gavra stopped. "You fucking tease. I need more!"

"You need to get into this tight pussy, don't you?" Gavra asked, then pressed Silas's tip to Assana's opening and slid him up along the length of her slit, then back, swirling his head around and around her stiff, throbbing clit.

Assana moaned, realizing that despite her primal need to fuck, she was as much Gavra's toy as Silas was, and she loved it. She dug her nails into the pillows on either side of Silas's head, and when Gavra finally positioned Silas at her soaked opening, she pressed her mouth to Silas's lips. They moaned into each other, tongues thrusting and sliding as Silas lifted his hips, eagerly pushing his cock deep into her aching pussy.

Gavra's hand remained between them, thumb and forefinger bracketing Silas's root until he was fully seated into her. He kept his hand against her folds as Silas slid out, fingers toying gently with her clit. Then his mouth was between her cheeks again, tongue darting out and swirling around and around her rear opening, wetting it with his saliva.

With one hand still steadily teasing her clit, he pressed two fingers of his other to her sensitive rosette. She groaned into Silas's kiss, her senses reeling from the sudden simultaneous thrust of the cock into her pussy and the fingers into her ass. Pleasure jolted through her at the combination of sensations, and she didn't dare release Silas from the kiss lest she lose herself completely.

Gavra added another finger to the pair in her backside, twisted his hand, and flared them, stretching her opening more. At the same time, Silas changed his tempo, began fucking into her harder, faster, the thick head of his cock rubbing exquisitely at the sensitive bundle of nerves inside her channel. Her clit remained the sole focus of Gavra's other hand and her pleasure climbed ever higher.

"Sweet Mother, your ass was made for my cock as much as his was, I think," Gavra said. He pushed his fingers deeper and his thighs brushed the backs of hers as he positioned himself. Then his fingers were gone and the smooth, hot thickness of his cock pressed at her opening. She bore down, readying herself for him. The deliberate loosening of her muscles opened her pussy at the same time, allowing Silas to plunge in even deeper at the same second Gavra slid home, his cock slamming into her in one swift thrust.

Reflexively, Assana bit down on Silas's lip and she grunted harshly. Tears came to her eyes at the sudden, overwhelming blast of pleasure that tore through her.

Silas let out a grunt of his own, then laughed and stared up at her, tongue testing at his bloodied lip. His gaze was feverish when it met hers, his cock fat and hard as he plunged it deep. It was all she could do to hang onto sanity, but then she remembered that she was allowed to let go. Wild was how they wanted her.

She released a near howl in response to the currents of ecstasy that tore through her body. She pushed back against their cocks, twisting her hips in time with their thrusts, urging them both deeper, harder.

"Fuck yeah," Silas said, grinning up at her, his eyes bright with excitement and lust. His bound hands opened and closed, his thick arms flexing, using his bindings to leverage himself to fuck her deeper. "Let me have your mouth again, baby. I want a taste of you."

Delirious with pleasure, she obliged, lips crashing against his and growling when his teeth sank in enough to draw blood from her this time. The sharp tang of his blood hit her lips too, and she took his lip into her mouth and sucked. The power of their exchange plunged into her soul, sending her flying over the edge in a bucking, writhing torrent. She reared back, the movement pushing her harder onto both their cocks.

Gavra was there, his mouth at her throat, his hands cupping her breasts as he held her against his chest, hips smacking over and over against her ass as he continued to fuck her harder than he'd ever fucked her before.

"That's right, baby. Take our cocks deep. Feel us in you all the way. Need to get deeper … feel you both together inside like before. Oh fuck, there … there you are."

His cock swelled, his snarl in her ear rising in pitch and volume until it was a roar. Silas bucked beneath her, his voice joining hers and Gavra's as they hit their shared climax.

And together their consciousnesses merged, becoming a twisting kaleidoscope of power, light, and love, all surrounding that new entity that they'd created together the first time she'd had both men fill her womb with their seed at the same time.

They were four, in that moment. Three souls together, with a fourth held cradled between them. Their blood, their power, and their love made whole in the brilliant new life of their child.

Assana remained poised there, savoring the way their souls merged more deeply than their bodies. Slowly, she came back to her physical self and its myriad aftershocks. She'd fallen onto Silas's chest and his lips brushed the side of her cheek, hot breath gusting against her skin while his cock still softly pulsed within her. Gavra's arm was wrapped around her, his hand softly clutching her breast and his mouth pressed to the center of her back.

She sighed as her dragon slowly eased out of her, hating his departure, but comforted by the way his essence remained locked with hers in their minds. When Gavra slipped to the side, she rolled off Silas. As an afterthought, she banished the vines that bound him and his arms immediately wrapped around her, turning her so that his chest was to her back.

Silas rumbled his contentment against her shoulder. "I needed that. Thank you."

Gavra turned to his side to face her and shifted closer, his legs brushing against hers. She reflexively slung one thigh over his, and Silas braided his legs with theirs. They lay in a tangle of limbs and afterglow, her world complete between her two mates.

Silas slipped a hand down her stomach to rest against her womb. Inside her, the tiny bundle of power pulsed in response.

"If it's a girl, we should name her Vrishti," he said. "I wouldn't have made it back here without her help."

Assana murmured softly in agreement. She definitely owed the ursa her gratitude. "And if it's a boy?" she asked.

"If it's a boy, we call him Woody," Silas said.

Gavra let out a sudden snort of laughter.

"In your dreams, bear," Assana said, but couldn't suppress a grin.

"Doctor Waters, specimen number five is spiking again. He's off the charts this time."

Meri cursed, her scalp prickling with agitation and the sense that everything was about to go wrong. She'd managed to subdue Nereus for a few days, but it hadn't lasted. As she watched, his fingers began to twitch. If she had to, she would permanently neutralize him, but hoped that wouldn't be necessary. It would be a major setback to her progress with the vessel. She needed Nereus's blood if she was going to stay on schedule.

"Delay his flow for twenty-four hours and dose him with the drugs. I'm needed at the Johannesburg facility, so report the results to me there."

The white-coated technician nodded and adjusted the meters on the digital monitors in front of him. The troublesome twitching in Nereus's fingers stopped and the jagged readout of his cerebral activity evened out. How long it would stay that way, she didn't know, but she couldn't stay and watch.

The Alexandria Institute's facilities had been experiencing periodic interruptions in their network connectivity that troubled her. Their technology was the most advanced possible and was constantly being updated, their security protocols changed daily. Yet something—or someone—had managed to breach several of their local networks within the last few days. No data had been compromised, but if they didn't nail down where the breaches originated from, it would only be a matter of time.

After losing control of the three Elites shortly after she'd lost Nikhil, she'd tightened security, effectively creating islands of each of the Institute's several dozen facilities. The organization wasn't entirely off the grid, and relied on their wide area network to function. She didn't have the brain power to control all the thousands of Ultiori who worked for her now. The vessel was a much higher priority.

Luckily the facility the vessel was in was completely isolated from the others, hidden away in a remote location at the farthest reaches of civilization. No one knew its precise location but her. Not even the technicians who lived there full-time knew where they were.

But the Ultiori's resources depended on maintaining the security of the other sites, so she had to leave to ensure none of them had truly been compromised.

Returning to her office, she closed and locked the door, then pulled a small bottle from the top drawer of her desk. Removing the dropper, she opened her mouth and deposited a single drop of the crimson liquid onto her tongue.

Within seconds, the power of the River flooded her and she drifted, targeting her destination with the ease of thousands of years of practice.

She arrived seconds later to another room, not much different from the one she'd left. The office she kept in the Johannesburg facility had windows, however, and a brilliant sunset cast a pink glow over the dim interior.

Unlocking her door, she exited and swiftly made her way to the security wing of the facility.

"What do you have?" she demanded. The security commander nodded and stood, moving to the heavy door that led to the holding area where they kept new captives before they were processed and assigned their own cells.

"Quite a lucky break, actually. I think you'll be pleased," he said, keying in his code and leaning in for the retinal scan to capture the image of his eye. She followed him through the doorway and stopped in front of the windowed cell door several yards down the hall.

"This one escaped the Canadian facility's breach, but we managed to catch up with him in Madagascar the other day. There's no way he's getting free again."

Meri's eyes widened as she met the familiar gaze of the man on the other side.

"You missed me, I can tell," Calder said. "But I have all the time in the world to catch up. You might want to pull up a chair.

Thank you for reading "Dragon Rebel"! If you loved it, please visit the retailer and leave a review!

But wait, there's more!
The Immortal Dragons' quests for mates continues. Read about the White brother Aodh's quest for his mates by picking up "Dragon Guardian" today, or keep reading for a preview.

And don't forget, subscribing to the Dragon Beasties mailing list gets you **two free sexy dragon shifter stories** not available for sale anywhere.

DRAGON GUARDIAN

TIME IS OF THE ESSENCE. But is it friend, or foe?

For Aodh, the answer is clear. Trapped in a magical prison on an island thousands of years in the past, time has become his enemy. The only person who can save him is Neph, an old lover he didn't exactly part on good terms with who is also one of the twin leaders of the nymphaea.

Neph, however, has a different view of time. Time is what allows him to court Vrishti, Aodh's fated mate and a powerful ursa princess. But as long as she remains a virgin, her true power will remain trapped inside her. It's practically Neph's duty to help her unleash it.

They'll need her power for the coming war. Their mortal enemy looms ever closer. Every strategy is fair game now, not just on the battlefield—but in love as well.

For the first time in Neph's and Aodh's storied history, sharing a third might just be the charm.

Read on for an excerpt, or buy now.

~

Chapter One

The Island of Ceylon, Inside a Temporal Bubble

FORGET FATE—TIME had just moved to the top of Aodh's shit list.

As an immortal, he'd taken time for granted. It was as plentiful as the air he breathed. But being trapped in a prison on an island in the river of time meant little expectation of enjoying more of his infinite life with his mates.

His life was no less infinite in this place—it was literally an island, and one he'd visited many times. Or *would* visit, he supposed. He didn't quite have the same broad perspective of time that the nymphaea had. But there was no mistaking that Nyx had locked him in a time bubble that day she'd sent him away from the Haven. He had no way to escape, and no expectation of being found anytime soon.

Because thanks to fucking Time, he now had even more than he wanted. The future he'd come from was more than three thousand years away, by his estimation of where ... or *when* he'd wound up. Even if Nyx came to her senses or, Mother forbid, Neph found out and came looking for him, it could happen at any time within that vast window of his past that now, paradoxically, stretched ahead of him like some well-trodden road he'd just as soon not walk down again.

Once was enough. He was ready to get on with his life, but the getting on part started where he'd left off, not ... *now*. Whenever now was.

His time might be infinite, but the space he had on this island wasn't. Shortly after arriving, he'd tested the boundaries, shifting and flying as far as he could until he hit the edge. The magical barrier surrounding the island hadn't provided any resistance, and for a moment he'd believed he could just fly past the shore and into the world beyond, but within seconds he found himself turned around and aimed back the way he'd come without so much as a tilt of his wing.

He'd tested every direction, and finally determining that there was no escape within his power, he'd decided to get the lay of the land and spent a few hours flying a circuit around the borders. He recognized the place within only a few miles of winging above the island's moonlit shores. Ceylon wasn't vastly different from the last time he'd seen it, though parts of it looked distinctly less worn down, and it was missing the odor he recalled from when the dragons had first instituted their hibernations and retreated to the ancient temple on this very island.

Nyx had wanted him clear of Meri's influence, and she had certainly succeeded in her goal, because everything about this place suggested he was a few centuries too early for the nymph to even exist. She'd only been a few decades old when he'd fallen into her trap like some hapless fool. At the time, Meri had been one of the newest additions to the powerful squadron of the Haven's Thiasoi soldiers, hand-picked by Nereus himself. That meant she was in the circle of trust, one of the rare positions of honor granted only to those dozen assigned protectors of order within the Haven. Her lack of attachment to one of the Thiasoi satyrs had meant she was perfect for their needs. A little too perfect, it turned out, once Aodh learned how she'd orchestrated the entire relationship to suit her own purposes.

He landed in a secluded cove that reminded him of the once-accessible entrance to the Haven. He dug his talons into the sand and shifted, staring out at the starlit water, still trying to process this turn his life had taken. As wild and open as this island was, it was still as much a prison as the room he'd been trapped in at the Stonetree Lodge no more than a day or so ago.

He stared up at the stars blindly for several moments. When he focused on the bright pinpoints in the black velvet, he had the perfect clock right there in the heavens, but what he saw didn't improve his mood. The arrangement of the constellations and the tilt of the Earth's axis only confirmed what he dreaded—Nyx had sent him far enough into the past that his presence would be meaningless to the enemy his blood might serve to lure. In fact, if his interpretation of the stars was correct, he was a good four centuries before Meri had even been born.

He clenched his fists impatiently, wishing for some outlet for the rage that bubbled forth. More than three thousand years—all the mistakes he had made stretched before him now, yet he could take no steps to change them as long as he was trapped here. And for how long. he had no clue, but given the vindictive Dionarch's command of time, he wouldn't put it past the Nyx to leave him to rot for centuries —he could very well be trapped here until he caught up to his own present, one plodding century at a time.

The island was familiar to him, at least, though the last time he'd visited, it was at least five centuries older. The vegetation was still lush, but the landscape now was harsher, having not been softened by age.

Ceylon was significant to his race, though it had been all but forgotten over the ages. His mind turned over the ancient memories. They hadn't cared about the place in some time, having far greater things to worry about than their ancient hibernation grounds. Dragons endeavored not to dwell on the past as a rule, and he and his siblings were no different. But something itched at the back of his mind. Some lost nugget of history that might be meaningful if he could just grasp it.

The hibernations ... they'd begun not long after he and his brothers made their ancient pact to resurrect their sister. Their enemy had grown too strong, too ruthless for them not to take serious precautions. There had been six hibernations since the first. Six temples within which their children slept to protect each generation until they grew powerful enough to protect themselves.

The most recent was the temple in Sumatra, built by the Guardians of the last generation. Their ancient tradition had begun with the very first temple. Except they hadn't built the first one. Only five of the six temples had been built by the Guardians for the younger generation. The first temple had already existed, though they had no explanation for its presence or its design. The legend was that Fate and the Mother Dragon had created it for them in their time of need, and that the immense power infusing its many rooms, and even its very walls, was a divine gift intended to protect their young while they weathered the storm of attacks from their enemy.

That temple was on this island.

AODH STARED down at the slab of unmarred stone, struggling to reconcile his memories of the temple with what lay before him. The first dragon temple had been the only one with a visible above-ground structure, which had been painstakingly carved out of a granite mountain. *This* mountain that Aodh stood atop now. Yet here he was in the spot where a temple should have existed, and there was nothing but solid rock.

He shifted and took to the air for yet another circuit around the huge formation. There had to be a clue somewhere ... a doorway perhaps. A magical cloak that had hidden the structure from his kind until they'd required it for their first hibernation. That event was still several centuries in the future from the time he'd been trapped in, and the temple had most certainly existed then.

He could recall every smooth, polished surface of the floors and walls, the carved stone columns that lined the corridors and supported the barrel vaulted ceilings. The intricate designs adorning the massive doors to each of the chambers intended for the first generation of newly designated Court dragons to hibernate within.

He and his siblings had found the temple when they decided to protect the future generations of dragons from their enemy's relentless hunting and capturing. Older generations were strong enough to stand against the Ultiori hunters Meri had corrupted and controlled, and the army of mind-controlled soldiers that she used Nikhil's vast military skills to command.

This island had drawn them in, not only due to its location being closely guarded by one of the ursa clans, but by its relative remoteness even from the other races. It had seemed ideally suited to dragons in much the same way the monastery's island had when they'd built that mountaintop refuge. In fact, the residents were some of the most receptive humans they'd ever met, once they arrived. It was as though they'd already recognized Aodh and his siblings as gods, tripping over themselves in order to serve.

The temple had shocked them with its ideal location, size, and magically protected barriers that opened only for them. The power infusing the place was so familiar it had to have been built by a dragon, but if it hadn't been any of them, their only conclusion was that the Mother Dragon had prepared it for them, with Fate as her guide.

So where was the fucking thing?

He wore himself out hunting the rugged mountain for

something—*anything*—to indicate that the temple existed in this spot. He could envision it in his mind's eye, yet not even a hint of dragon magic existed where the temple should have been. Only stone and dirt and trees.

Landing at the peak of the mountain, he let out a frustrated bellow that echoed around the entire island prison. He dug his claws into the stony ground beneath him, kicking up boulders and flinging them into the air. He paced around what should have been the domed cupola roof, but was only dirt-covered rock.

As he paced, his tail swung from side to side in angry sweeps, tossing aside every loose object in his way. The not knowing ate at him. He had no way out of this place and no indication he'd be released at all. As far as Nyx was concerned, he was better off dead, only he couldn't die. She likely intended to leave him here permanently.

His mind churned over the implications of that thought. If he remained here, eventually his time would overlap with events he recalled. Except he remembered the day he'd entered the nonexistent temple with his siblings, and he hadn't been here. Only the perfect temple had stood in this spot, completely empty and waiting for the youngest generation of dragons to begin their hibernation within.

His talons hit something too hard to break and he realized he'd been unconsciously clawing into the earth beneath him in his rage. He angled his head to the side to peer with one big eye down at the ground. Something gleamed through the dirt, and he expelled a blast of hot wind from his nostrils to blow the dirt away.

His pulse picked up at the sight of the vein of crystalline quartz that shot through the stone. He remembered the shape of this stone and the way it let light filter into the temple below. Drawing back a fisted talon, he smashed it against the mountaintop with all his might, but only met unyielding stone with no hint of an echo to indicate what he stood on might be hollow.

With renewed energy, he worked to dig away the dirt and rocks from the area. After several hours of work, he'd clawed and swept several square dragon-lengths of the mountaintop clean so that the solid stone beneath was visible.

Taking a deep breath, he summoned as much power as he dared, then launched himself in the air a few hundred feet and angled his head down while he hovered, his massive wings holding him aloft. A gust of blue-white fire blasted from his mouth and hit the center of the stone beneath him with an impact that sent dirt and stone flying out in a massive cloud.

The entire mountain trembled, pieces of it crumbling away from the monolithic slab of stone. When Aodh ceased his blazing inferno, he landed with a heavy thud, gaze fixed in the center of the stone where his fire had been focused, his breathing shallow with utter disbelief.

An unmistakable starburst pattern adorned the stone where his fire had hit, a result of the quartz cracking and a vein of solid gold beneath it instantly melting and flooding into the cracks. It gleamed bright yellow, dimming to orange as it cooled, but the pattern was as familiar to Aodh as the scales on his own tail.

That starburst was the apex of the roof of the temple—a structure they believed had existed forever. Except if he'd been the one to create that pattern, that could only mean one thing.

He was the architect. Not the Mother or Fate, though Fate was most certainly the engineer behind this predicament he found himself in. Aodh himself had just put his mark on this island as the first dragon to set foot here, and though the paradox twisted his mind into uncomfortable knots, he knew better than to fight Fate. Just as attempting to fly through the barrier of his prison would only send him back in from the other side, running away from Fate's plan would only send him full circle, straight back into the trap he sought to avoid.

With a deep growl of resignation, he set to work. Most temples took an army of skilled Guardians several decades to complete. As the sole architect and artisan, he estimated this particular temple would take centuries.

At least he knew he'd have something to do for the next four hundred years.

Want to read the rest? Buy now.

ABOUT OPHELIA BELL

Ophelia Bell loves a good bad-boy and especially strong women in her stories. Women who aren't apologetic about enjoying sex and bad boys who don't mind being with a woman who's in charge, at least on the surface, because pretty much anything goes in the bedroom.

Ophelia grew up on a rural farm in North Carolina and now lives in Los Angeles with her own tattooed bad-boy husband and six attention-whoring cats.

Subscribe to Ophelia's newsletter to get updates directly in your inbox. If newsletters aren't your thing, you can find her on social media.

http://opheliabell.com/subscribe

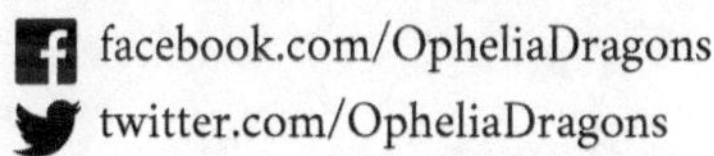

facebook.com/OpheliaDragons
twitter.com/OpheliaDragons

Immortal Dragons Series

Dragon Betrayed

Dragon Blues

Dragon Void

Dragon Splendor

Dragon Rebel

Dragon Guardian

Dragon Blessed

Dragon Equinox

Dragon Avenged

Immortal Dragons Box Sets:

Immortal Dragons: Books 1, 2, & 3 + Prequel

Immortal Dragons: Books 4-6 + Epilogue

Black Mountain Bears

Clawed

Bitten

Nailed

Stonetree Trilogy

Fate's Fools Series

Fate's Fools

Fool's Folly

Fool's Paradise

Fool's Errand

Nobody's Fool

Eye of the Hurricane

Fool's Bargain

April's Fools

Thieves of Fate

Aurora Champions Series

(Set in Milly Taiden's "Paranormal Dating Agency" world)

The Way to a Bear's Heart

Hot Wings

Triple Talons

Midnight Star

Once in a Dragon Moon

Second Skin Series (Romantic Suspense)

Mad Dog

Mile High

Valentine's Day

The Devil's Daughter

Marked Man

Rebel Lust Taboo

Casey's Secrets

Blackmailing Benjamin

Burying His Desires

Doubling Down

~

Standalone Erotic Tales

After You

Out of the Cold